Gregory Maguire is the bestselling author of *Mirror Mirror, Lost, Confessions of an Ugly Stepsister, Wicked: The Life and Times of the Wicked Witch of the West, Son of a Witch* and *A Lion Among Men*, which have earned him rave reviews and a dedicated following. He received his doctorate in English Literature from Tufts University, and has taught at Simmons College and other Boston area colleges. He has also served as an artist-in-residence at the Blue Mountain Center, the Isabella Stewart Gardner Museum and the Hambidge Center. Gregory has lived in Dublin and London, but now makes his home near Boston, Massachusetts, with his partner, their two sons and daughter.

Praise for Gregory Maguire:

'As moving and tragic as it is refreshing and scurrilous... [an] outstanding novel' *Independent*

'A vision that fantasy writers will find hard to resist' *Publishers Weekly*

'Highly absorbing... Maguire's precise, slightly archaic language... sweeps the readers through this mysterious and fascinating story' *Booklist*

'An outstanding work of imagination' *USA Today*

'A magical telling of the land of Oz before and up to the arrival of Dorothy and company... A captivating, funny, and perceptive look at destiny, personal responsibility, and the not-always-clashing beliefs of faith and magic. Save a place on the shelf between *Alice* and *The Hobbit* – that spot is well deserved' *Kirkus Reviews*

'A staggering feat of wordcraft... [Maguire] has created... one of the great heroines in fantasy literature' *Los Angeles Times*

'Captivating and beautifully written... a rich canvas of colorful characters and fantastic events rendered by an artist attentive to every surface and texture' *Book Magazine*

LOST

By Gregory Maguire

Novels in the Wicked Years
Wicked: The Life and Times of the Wicked Witch of the West
Son of a Witch
A Lion Among Men

Mirror Mirror
Lost
Confessions of an Ugly Stepsister

LOST

Gregory Maguire

R
headline
review

First published in 2001 by Regan Books,
an imprint of HarperCollins Publishers

First published in Great Britain in 2009
by HEADLINE REVIEW
An imprint of HEADLINE PUBLISHING GROUP

1

Cataloguing in Publication Data is available from the British Library

ISBN 978 0 7553 4173 3 (Hardback)
ISBN 978 0 7553 4174 0 (Trade paperback)

Typeset in Columbus by Avon DataSet Ltd,
Bidford-on-Avon, Warwickshire

Printed and bound in Great Britain by
Clays Ltd, St Ives plc

Headline's policy is to use papers that are natural, renewable and recyclable products
and made from wood grown in sustainable forests. The logging
and manufacturing processes are expected to conform to the environmental
regulations of the country of origin.

HEADLINE PUBLISHING GROUP
An Hachette UK Company
338 Euston Road
London NW1 3BH

www.headline.co.uk
www.hachette.co.uk

For Maggie and Dan Terris, with love

The division of one day from the next must be one of the most profound peculiarities of life on this planet. It is, on the whole, a merciful arrangement. We are not condemned to sustained flights of being, but are constantly refreshed by little holidays from ourselves. We are intermittent creatures, always falling to little ends and rising to little new beginnings. Our soon-tired consciousness is meted out in chapters, and that the world will look quite different tomorrow is, for both our comfort and our discomfort, usually true. How marvelously too night matches sleep, sweet image of it, so neatly apportioned to our need. Angels must wonder at these beings who fall so regularly out of awareness into a fantasm-invested dark. How our frail identities survive these chasms no philosopher has ever been able to explain.

— Iris Murdoch, *The Black Prince*

Scrooge The name of the miserly old man in Charles Dickens's *A Christmas Carol* (1843) appears to be based on *scrounge*, though this word, of dialect origin, was not in general use until after the First World War, when it was popularized by servicemen. Dickens may have had in mind, at least subconsciously, an original dialect word such as *scringe* or *scrunge*, both meaning 'to steal.'
— *Cassell Dictionary of Proper Names,* 1992

Saints Gervaise & Protase (June 19) SS. Gervaise and Protase, who were brothers, suffered martyrdom together at Milan ... St. Ambrose ... had them exhumed. Many striking miracles were manifested ... Thus did these holy martyrs achieve a fresh triumph.
— *Pictorial Half Hours with the Saints*
Abbé Lecanu, 1865

Saints ... were 'very special dead people,' [rather than] apparitions of the ordinary dead, of everyday ghosts.
— *Ghosts in the Middle Ages: The Living and the Dead in Medieval Society*
Jean-Claude Schmitt, 1994

Contents

Stave One:
Somebody Else in the Vehicle 1

Stave Two:
At the Flat in Weatherall Walk 37

Stave Three:
From the Chimney Inside the Chimney 117

Stave Four:
As Dante in the *Purgatorio* 189

Stave Five:
For the Time Being 299

Acknowledgments 332

Stave One

Somebody Else in the Vehicle

said the attorney-type into his cell phone. He wiped the wet from his face. 'There must be. It's in the carpool lane.' He listened, squinting, and motioned to Winnie: *Stop. Don't open the car door yet.* Already, other drivers were slowing down to rubberneck. 'Where are we, Braintree, Quincy? On 93 north, anyway, a half mile beyond the junction with 128. Yes, I know enough not to move anyone, but I'm telling you, you'll have a hell of a time getting an ambulance through, what with rush hour – there'll be a backup a mile long before you know it.'

He listened again. Then, 'Right. I'll look. Two or more, maybe.'

Returning from a few quiet days on Cape Cod, Winifred Rudge had missed her turnoff west and gotten stuck on the JFK toward Boston. Woolgathering, nail biting, something. Focus was a problem. Late for her appointment, she'd considered the odds: in this weather, what were her chances of being ticketed for violating the diamond lane's two-riders-or-more rule? Limited. She'd risked it. So she'd been at the right place on the downgrade to see the whole thing, despite the poor visibility. She'd watched the top third of a white pine snap in the high winds. Even from a half mile away, she'd noticed how the wood flesh had sprung out in diagonal striations, like nougat against rain-blackened bark. The crown of the tree twisted, then tilted. The wind had caught under the tree's parasol limbs and carried it across three lanes of slow-moving traffic, flinging it onto the hood and the roof of a northbound Subaru in the carpool lane. The driver of the Subaru, four cars ahead of Winnie, had braked too hard and hydroplaned left against the Jersey barriers. The evasive action hadn't helped.

Winnie had managed to tamp her brakes and avoid adding to the collection of crumpled fenders and popped hoods. She had been the first out in the rain, the first to start poking through dark rafts of pine needles. Mr Useful Cell Phone was next, having emerged from some vehicle behind her. He carried a ridiculous out-blown umbrella, and when he got off the phone with the 911 operator he hooked the umbrella handle around a good-size tree limb and tried to yank it away.

'They said don't touch the passengers,' he yelled through the rain.

Afraid her voice would betray her panic, she didn't even like to answer, but to reassure him she managed to say, 'I know that much.' The smell of pine boughs, sap on her hands, water on her face. What was she scared of finding in that dark vehicle? But the prime virtue of weather is immediacy, and the wind tore away the spicy Christmas scent. In its place, a vegetable stink of cheap spilled gasoline. 'We may *have* to get them out, do you smell that?' she shouted, and redoubled her efforts. They could use help; where were the other commuters? Just sitting in their cars, listening to hear themselves mentioned on the WGBH traffic report?

'Cars don't blow up like in the movies,' he said, motioning her to take a position farther along the tree trunk. 'Put your back against it and push; I'll pull. One. Two. Three.' Thanks mostly to gravity they managed to dislodge the thing a foot or so, enough to reveal the windshield. It was still holding, though crazed into opacity with the impact. The driver, a fiftyish sack of a woman, was slanted against a net bag of volleyballs in the passenger seat. She didn't look lucky. The car had slammed up against the concrete barrier so tightly that both doors on the driver's side were blocked.

'Isn't there someone else?' said Winnie. 'Didn't you say?'

'You know, I think that *is* gasoline. Maybe we better stand off.'

Winnie made her way along the passenger side of the car,

through branches double-jointed with rubbery muscle. The rear door was locked and the front door was locked. She peered through pine needles, around sports equipment. 'There's a booster seat in the back,' she yelled. 'Break the window, can you?'

The umbrella handle wasn't strong enough. Winnie had nothing useful in her purse or her overnight bag. The cold rain made gluey boils on the windows. It was impossible to see in. 'No car could catch on fire in a storm like this,' she said. 'Is that smoke, or just burned rubber from the brake pads?' But then another driver appeared, carrying a crowbar. 'Smash the window,' she told him.

'Hurry,' said Cell Phone Man. 'Do they automatically send fire engines, do you think?'

'Do it,' she said. The newcomer, an older man in a Red Sox cap faded to pink, obliged. The window shattered, spraying glassy baby teeth. As she clawed for the recessed lock in the rear door, Winnie heard the mother begin to whimper. The door creaked open and more metal scraped. Winnie lurched and sloped herself in. The child strapped into the booster seat was too large for it. Her legs were thrown up in ungainly angles. 'Maybe we can unlatch the whole contraption and drag it out,' said Winnie, mostly to herself; she knew her voice wouldn't carry in the wind. She leaned over the child in the car's dark interior, into a hollow against which pine branches bunched on three sides. She fumbled for the buckle of the seat belt beneath the molded plastic frame of the booster. Then she gave up and pulled out, and slammed the door.

'I'll get it,' said Red Sox Fan, massing up.

'They said leave everybody where they were,' said Cell Phone, 'you could snap a spine and do permanent damage.'

'No spine in her,' said Winnie. 'It's a life-size Raggedy Ann doll, a decoy.'

The emergency services arrived, and Winnie, valuing her privacy, shrank back. The fumes of the spilled gasoline followed her

back to her car. She sat and bit a fingernail till she tore a cuticle, unwilling to talk to the police. To her surprise, the traffic began crawling again within fifteen minutes. The police never noticed that she was another illegal driver doing a solo run in the carpool lane.

And then, despite her missed exit, the snarl-up, the downpour, the rush hour, she wasn't late after all. Damn.

'Someone's been here before us,' observed the older woman in the mulberry windcheater, pocketing the keys. She flopped her hand against the inside wall to knock a light switch. The air was stale, almost stiff. A few translucent panels overhead blinked, and then steadied. Winnie noted: It's your standard-issue meeting room. It proves the agency's fiscal prudence and general probity. A few tables with wood laminate, sticky with coffee rings. Fitted carpets of muddy rose, muddier in the high-traffic zones. Folding chairs pushed out of their congregational oval. As if whatever group that met here last night had cleared out with rude speed.

'Someone's been here, but not the cleaning crew,' said the woman. 'They don't pay me for housekeeping. Oh, well, come in, and we'll set ourselves up by ourselves.' A veteran in the social work world, wearing one of those grandmotherly rain hats like a pleated plastic freezer bag. She wriggled out of her jacket, which was a bit snug, and she smiled sourly. Her nylon sleeves hissed as they slithered.

Other rectangles of light kicked on. Outside, obscured by the reflections flaring in the broad plate glass, a few more couples emerged from cars. Women huddling under the arms of their husbands, the human forms smudged into anonymity by the rain. The observable sky seethed in slow motion over Wellesley, Needham, and this patch of Newton.

Winnie, on edge because of the accident, because of the

challenge of the day, hung back in the doorway for as long as she could. She pictured the Weather Channel's computer-graphic impression of the storm. Moisture trawled in from the Atlantic, unseasonable icebox Arctic air sucked down over the Great Lakes, a continental thumbprint of weather, fully a thousand miles broad. A thumbprint slowly twisting, as if to make the undermuscle of the world ache.

She harvested the details; that was what she was good at. That was all she was good at. Anyway, that was what she was there for, and no apologies. She noticed that, as more fluorescent tubes kicked on, everything became more manufactured, more present, the shadows cowed and blurred by multiple light sources. This Styrofoam coffee cup fallen on the carpet. This chair turned on its side, *FF* scrawled in Magic Marker on its seat.

By the moment the leader grew more cheery and despotic. She brisked about. Winnie and the other supplicants hung back: this wasn't their terrain, not yet. Over their chairs they hung their London Fog knockoffs, their L. L. Bean Polartec parkas, and, in one instance, a retro fox fur suffering from cross-eye. 'A little bit of leftover Hurricane Gretl, they tell us,' said the leader. She addressed the spatter against the windows. 'You. Stop that. It's supposed to be too late in the season for you. So long. Scram.'

Thunder blurted, a distant throat-clearing of one of the more cautious gods.

The leader was undaunted. She made her way past the bulletin boards shingled with curling color photographs. Hands on hips as she surveyed the detritus of discarded handouts, crumpled napkins, spilled sugar. 'Look at this mess. A group of Forever Families having their quarterly meeting, I bet.' In one corner, toddler-size furniture squatted on its thick limbs. The leader swooped, collecting things. She stepped on a stuffed monkey, and it complained with a microchip melody playing, inevitably, 'It's a Small World, After All.'

Winnie turned away, busying herself with a small notebook and a pen.

'If you help yourself to that old coffee, be it on your own head,' said the leader. 'I'm telling you. Nobody even bothered to put the milk away overnight. Do they pay me to be the mother to the world? They do not. But I'll do a fresh pot in a minute. You, you can't listen to me? You can't wait? Go ahead. Be my guest.'

The balding young man with his hand on the lever of the thermos said in an apologetic murmur, 'Sorry. I'm groggy. I didn't sleep all night.'

'Caffeine addiction. Let me take a note.' This was only pretend terrorism, since the leader followed up with a pretzel of a smile. 'Name tags, name tags?' she went on. 'People, please, as I get the brew going, find your name tags, people. We're starting late, but that's okay: the rain, the traffic, we're not all here. *I'm* not all here. Name tags, people. Here's mine, I'm Mabel Quackenbush, or I was last time I checked.'

Winnie frowned. Surely she'd been incognito in her application? She'd meant to be Dotty O'Malley, a favorite alter ego she adopted on bowling nights. But there was her badge, staring out at her amidst the Murrays, the Pellegrinos, the Spencer-Moscous:

W. Rudge

Obediently W. Rudge slapped the gummy-backed label to her Tufts sweatshirt, but she arranged her drenched scarf to conceal her name. Then she took a place in the circle of chairs as near the back as she could. When they were all settled, the leader said, 'I'm the Forever Families coordinator for today. Mabel Quackenbush, from the Providence office. We had twenty-three registrants. I don't know where everyone else *is*. If I could get here, anyone could. Believe me, I-95 was no treat thanks to Hurricane Whosie. I left at *seven* and we *crawled*.' Mabel Quackenbush embroidered the uninteresting story of her journey. A warm-up and a stalling tactic, as new arrivals tiptoed in, shook the wet off their coats, and settled in their chairs.

The room became close. A mothball fug aspirated off damp woolens. Winnie wanted to see who the rest of the registrants were, but she looked at their reflections instead, at the streaked imprecise flatnesses in the windows.

> Out of the many-colored earth
> That eats the light and drinks the rain
> Come beauty, wisdom, mercy, mirth,
> That conquer reason, greed, and pain.

John Masefield, if she remembered correctly, who linked reason with greed and pain. Or was it de la Mare? There was that habit again – some people did it with pop songs – of giving one's life a soundtrack. In her case, snippets and sound bites of doggerel.

Don't diagnose reason, greed, or pain, she corrected herself: simply observe the symptoms.

Mabel Quackenbush turned her head this way and that, ducklike. She knew her job. She drew folks in. The skin on her chin was loose, an unbaked cinnamon roll. Behind her half-lenses her eyes blinked, as if with slow washes of albumen. She was beginning to look earnest. Please God, no opening sermons concerning children with humps and fins for limbs, who nonetheless, immortal souls all, deserve life, liberty, and the pursuit of Happy Meals.

She tried to nip that crankiness in the bud. Winnie, she said to herself, go easy on these folks. Be fair. You haven't been here ten minutes yet. Don't you cut them into pieces. Let them do it to themselves, if they're going to.

'Nine-fifteen, and we're still missing, let's see, five couples,'

said Mabel, counting. 'Well. Latecomers will have to fend for themselves. Now. *So.*' She had fanned piles of photocopies at her feet. She peered down at them dubiously, and then said, 'First things first. The name thing, the round-the-room thing, a word or two: who you are, where you've come from this morning, anything personal you want to share about why you're here. No pressure.'

Winnie shrank into her sweatshirt. In Lewis Carroll's Wonderland, Alice could smallify herself by sipping from a tube of something that said DRINK ME, but in real life you only shrunk inside.

'Chat,' ordered Mabel Quackenbush.

The couple hunched in their folding chairs at Mabel Quackenbush's left was required to start. Joe and Cathi Pellegrino. (Durham, New Hampshire.) Joe talked, Cathi saturated a Kleenex until shreds of it clung to her cheeks. Four stillbirths. *Four.*

Next, Cookie and Leonard Schimel. (Braintree, Massachusetts.) Leonard had the limp, Cookie had the fox fur. Leonard a legal practice, Cookie the ache that derives from a hysterectomy. They both had money, but only Leonard had style.

Then came the Spencer-Moscous. (Brookline with summers in Provincetown.) A gay couple. Geoff was a recording technician for Channel Five and Adrian taught fourth grade. The Pellegrinos, the Boudreaus, the Murrays, and the Schimels glanced warmly at the Boys.

The Fogartys didn't smile. Winnie practiced summing them up in a remark: they look as if they spend their highway hours inventing biographies of anthropomorphized meadow animals who all end up as roadkill.

'W. Rudge,' said Maisie Quackenbush.

'Here,' said Winnie.

'W? Wanda? Wilma?'

'W.' Oh, all right. 'Winifred.'

'And you hail from?' said Mabel, as if Winnie were a slow contestant on a talk show who somehow had slipped through the screening process and needed prodding.

'Came up from the Cape this morning, but I live in Jamaica Plain,' said Winnie. 'Unmarried.'

Mabel, waiting for more, glanced at some papers. When the silence lengthened, she said, 'Well, glad to meet you, Wini-*fred*.' She put the stress on the last syllable, which seemed unnecessarily hostile.

The wives inched nearer to their husbands, grateful for them. To her right, the Boys grinned at Winnie with a solidarity she didn't feel. She tried not to notice, and turned inquiringly to the next pair.

Murray, George and LouBeth. (Billerica, Massachusetts.) Infertility of a private nature.

The Boudreaus. (Weston, Massachusetts.) Their two young children had died of smoke inhalation when a Guatemalan au pair forgot to check the lint trap. Hank Boudreau had insisted on trying again, but Diane was too far into the Change.

The room got quiet. Someone cleared her throat. Someone crossed and uncrossed his legs. Despite her best intentions, Winnie found herself thinking that Diane Boudreau had sacrificed any claim to pity by being such a shameless bottle blonde.

Finally, the Fogartys. Malachy Fogarty, previously of Dublin. (Currently Marblehead.) Mary Lenahan Fogarty was unsettlingly petite, a clutch of narrow limbs in a wraparound skirt and three sweaters. 'Postanorexic,' she confessed, 'with all that that entails.'

'And so, the theme of the day,' said Mabel in a quieter voice, taking off her glasses and tasting the tip of the earpiece before putting them on again, 'is loss. We all suffer from loss, or we wouldn't have come today. Simple as that. But no matter which loss has brought us here, what Forever Families does is *recovery*.

Recovery of the possibilities of life. Knit the wounds and heal the scars and do something for someone else. And maybe, accidentally, for ourselves. Now: here's the commercial.'

Every business has its lingo. Wounds, scars, recoveries. The lanolin blather of the compassion industry. But Winnie allowed that though Mabel Quackenbush looked as if she'd take no prisoners, at least she was up-front about the sales pitch.

At first Winnie scribbled some notes. Mabel had the spiel down cold. Mission statement, Commonwealth accreditation status, history. Forever Families operated in nine states as well as the District of Columbia. It had been profiled in *Boston* magazine three years ago. Copies coming around.

But then Winnie's mind wandered. She watched the ripples of rain sliding down the smoked glass. Curtaining the reflections of the eager and frightened faces. She found herself capable of being easier on her fellow applicants when studying them in glass.

The vacant-wombed wives. The husbands. Winnie supposed that the Brookline Boys, technically not really husbands, were mid- to late thirties, but the other fellows in the room were midforties at least, and Malachy Fogarty older still. Each husband was bigger than his wife, each husband sat back in his chair as his wife leaned forward, each husband looked prosperous and wary. Each wife looked nuts.

Sunk low in the guts of the building, a furnace began to hum louder, as if trying to drown out Mabel's pitch for Forever Families over other local agencies. The infomercial won. Mabel blinked at them with mercy in her eyes, mercy overlaid by a proper respect for the cash of clients shopping in the baby market.

Winding down, she intoned, 'For most of you, there *is* a Precious One in your life. Maybe already born. Out there. Waiting. You've already taken the first step. Congratulations on brooking our hurricane, which Forever Families scheduled to winnow out the sheep from the goats. Now let's have our coffee, shall we? Fifteen minutes, people. When we come back, I'll give you the skinny on the legal angles of international adoptions, we'll review issues of health and welfare, we'll do some other fun and games. Then after our lunch break, we'll have our visit by a Forever Family, the Stankos from Pepperell. They have three Precious Ones from Moldova.'

Suddenly Mabel Quackenbush looked exhausted, as if she'd rather be home tucking into a Sara Lee coffeecake than sorting papers with the tips of her shoes. 'Stretch, now. Scatter and chatter. Look at the displays.'

Winnie wasn't much of a coffee drinker, but as the only solo registrant she was a natural target for a social worker on the prowl. So Winnie hid in a herd of other bleary registrants and lined up for a cup of lukewarm water flavored with coffee stains. When she'd dumped enough sugar in it to make it tolerable, she headed for the hall, hoping to stand outside in the covered walkway and light a cigarette. But one of the Boys ambushed her by the coatrack.

'Are you a Scrooge or a Cratchit?' he said.

She flinched and laughed, blushing. She didn't want to talk to anyone. Was this Geoff or Adrian? They both reeked of the benignity that middle-class professional gay men seemed to prize these days. 'I'm a humbug, if that's what you mean,' she went on, trying to be honest, though it wasn't her strong suit.

Unforgivably forward, he reached out and opened her scarf so it spread across the bosom of her sweatshirt. Within the latticework of the intertwined sprigs of red-berried holly was stamped the image of Mr and Mrs Fezziwig dancing with Christmas cheer. Eight, ten, a dozen pairs of Fezziwigs, cavorting in perfect synchronization.

'It's the famous illustration, I recognized it,' he said. 'I read *A Christmas Carol* to my fourth-graders every December. I know the Fezziwigs when I see them.'

This silly Bond Street scarf, a Christmas present from John Comestor some years back. 'I can't remember if you're Geoff or the other one,' she said, to change the subject. 'You put your sweater on over your name tag.'

'Adrian. Adrian Moscou.'

'Of the Spencer-Moscous.'

'Oh, that. Boy, you sound appalled. Not that I blame you. That's Geoff's thing. He's the one in the family way. But Geoff and I didn't sign up as a hinged name, not today. Too risky, considering what's at stake. Our *Precious One*. I suppose the Forever Families staff ran our Social Security numbers through a computer check, because Spencer-Moscou is how the phone company lists us.'

'Creepy,' said Winnie. That must be how Forever Families got her real name. W. Rudge. She had signed up as Dotty O'Malley, hadn't she? These days her memory wasn't reliable.

'It *is* creepy,' said Adrian Moscou cheerfully. 'Well, it's a creepy day. Hurricane Gretl – whoever heard of a hurricane this late in the year? More proof of global warming, I guess. Now, are you going through this process on your own or is there a partner waiting in the parking lot?' Meaning, probably, was she a dyke.

'Which one of you is going to be the mommy?' she countered.

'Well, neither of us wants to be the daddy,' he said, without taking offense. He shrugged. 'I guess we'll just be like the virgin governesses from Victorian novels, and spend our lives in the service of a Precious One who never bothers to learn our names.'

'Innocent and heartless,' said Winnie.

'I beg your pardon?' he said.

'What James Barrie said children were like. In *Peter Pan*. Innocent and heartless.' The actual sentence had been *gay and innocent and heartless*, but Winnie wasn't up to uncorking that line of camp.

The Pellegrinos drifted over. So did Malachy Fogarty,

munching antacids. Now for the capsule histories. These folks, free on a workday morning? – they didn't need to adopt children. They needed to share. To get in touch with their inner childlessness. They were the reason Talk Radio wasn't called Listen Radio. Winnie treaded the oily waters with a blank expression, preparing caustic observations to serve John Comestor tomorrow when she got there. He'd love all this. But when the Pellegrinos regrouped to mutter with the Boudreaus, and Malachy Fogarty bolted off, hunting for the men's room, Adrian Moscou said, 'I know, you must be the reformed Scrooge, and you're here to adopt Tiny Tim.'

She couldn't bear to be thought of as being sentimental as everyone else here. Tiny Tim indeed. The coincidence of Adrian's lighting on the Scrooge reference was shocking and even upsetting, but really, she thought: Tiny Tim? Anything *but*. Out of nerves, or pride, she admitted, 'I'm not here to adopt a child. Only to observe the process. I've got a novel in progress, and I'm researching. Every little bit helps. You know.'

'Neat,' he said. 'Cool. We're the raw material?'

'Well, you have to admit, it's ripe stuff. Baring our souls like this.'

'Embarrassing. But you do what you gotta do. At least it's all in the service of something other than ourselves.'

'That's what we say, anyway,' she said. 'Some of us lie to ourselves better than others.' He raised an eyebrow, not sure what she meant. She found she was glad that Mabel Quackenbush was ready to reconvene. She excused herself from Adrian Moscou. When Mabel Quackenbush started the next portion of the program by asking if there were any questions so far, Adrian raised his hand.

'Ms Rudge here is a writer,' he said. 'She's doing research on a book. That makes me wonder about who gets to see our applications? How secure is the private material in our files?'

'Oh, a writer,' said Mabel Quackenbush. 'I didn't know, Winifred. How nice.' She had seen everything before and knew how to handle this one. 'Would you like to tell us more?'

Winnie wouldn't really. But her cover was blown. She looked everywhere except at Adrian Moscou.

She tried to think of what to say. Through the pause, the sound of a truck in the lot, its backing-up beepers punctuating the sound of wind: delivering more babies to the loading dock?

'I'm sure you're not here to plunder other people's stories,' said Mabel Quackenbush. 'This is serious business. I hope I don't have to ask you to leave.'

Winnie said, 'No, you don't. I'm legit. I filled out all the forms. I'm just doing a book about adoption. A novel, that is. The smallest bit of real detail makes the biggest difference. My character is off to Central Europe to adopt a child. I take notes' – she brandished her spiral-bound notebook in a jaunty manner – 'I'm a compulsive note taker. Everything hits home eventually. I could do some good for the industry, you know.'

'Have you published anything?' asked Mabel doubtfully, in the same voice with which she had asked the couples if there were other children at home.

'Sadly, nothing you'd have heard of,' said Winnie. W. Rudge's children's chapter books came out with pleasant regularity but little fanfare. Her only adult publication, *The Dark Side of the Zodiac*, was a trashy self-help succès de scandale, brought out under the name of Ophelia Marley. It was her cash cow, to the extent she had one, though its udders were going dry.

Mabel Quackenbush stood up. 'The head staff must be in by now, unless the storm has kept them home. I'll run upstairs and have a quick powwow. In the meantime, let's get going on a role-playing assignment. You too,' she said blithely to Winnie. 'Might as well soak it up before we get the security guard to come break all the bones in your typing fingers. Now, people, count off, one two three.'

They did. Winnie was a one. She joined a smaller circle with Adrian Moscou, Leonard Schimel, Diane Boudreau, and Malachy Fogarty. Group one was told to act out this scenario: You've got a Precious One in the kitchen and an Original Mother shows up with documents proving the prior relationship. What do you do, dear?

'I'd be a mess. I admit it. I'd just weep,' said Adrian Moscou. 'Then call FF for advice, probably. Weep some more.'

'You litigate,' said Leonard Schimel. 'Nothing like it. You litigate fast you litigate hard you don't let up. Take out a restraining order. I have connections.'

'What's the problem?' said Diane Boudreau. 'I'd invite an Original Mother in. Put on a pot of coffee. The more open the better. I intend to let our child know the full scoop, soon as he or she can understand English. You can't keep this stuff under the rug.'

'Are you mad?' said Malachy Fogarty. 'An Original Mother? I'd turf the bitch out. She gave up the child, didn't she? I'd get a gun.' They would have laughed had he not sounded as if he meant it.

Attention turned to Winnie, who hadn't spoken. She shrugged, and said, 'Since I'm not here to adopt, I don't need to play this game, no matter what Mabel says.'

'But this scenario, it's like story writing,' said Adrian. 'Isn't this your job? You should be good at inventing what to do.'

'I should be very good at it, shouldn't I?' she said. 'But I can't open that door, I can't see that scene. I can only write the scenes I can see.'

'You have to play,' said Diane Boudreau. 'Or we'll trade you to another group.'

'I'll record our observations. I'll report to everyone else. I'm good at that.'

Mabel Quackenbush was taking her time upstairs. They sat in

a stalemate for a few moments, listening to the laughter and then the more careful discussion from the other two groups. Then to the rain beating yet more heavily across the parking lot, against the glass.

'Good thing they're not doing Hallowe'en tonight,' said Diane after a while. 'Think of those little kids walking out in this weather! So dangerous.'

'Little plastic skeleton masks dripping with rain,' said Adrian. 'I like it. Adds verisimilitude, wouldn't you say, Winifred? Corpses liquefy, you know. That's why they plant so many trees in cemeteries. Soak up the juices.'

'Cheery,' said Diane.

'Geoff and I are going to a party tonight,' he said. 'The job is to come as the person you'd most like to be haunted by. Geoff has the easy costume, he's doing Bruce Springsteen from *Born to Run*. White T-shirt, jeans, cap. Helps that he has the body for it too,' he added, smugly proud. 'Who wouldn't like to be haunted by the Boss?'

Nobody asked Adrian what thrill he was going as.

'Isn't the idea of haunting that you don't get to choose who does it to you?' said Diane.

'We're haunted by the IRS, bloody ghouls,' said Malachy. 'Half the reason I want to hire a kid is to get the adoption tax credit and the dependent child credit.'

They tittered unconvincingly. Adrian turned to Winnie. 'So who would you choose to be haunted by, in your wildest fantasies?'

'I'm a writer, I spend too much time with literary fantasies as it is,' she demurred. But she admitted to herself, she was taken with that image of kids trick-or-treating in their costumes, an early snow coating them. Not bad. Troubling and calming at once. The snow making ghosts of every pint-size witch and hobo and ballerina. She scratched a few words on her pad.

When Mabel Quackenbush got back, she looked terse, the last Soviet apparatchik. 'You. Sorry. They ran you through the computer. They said you have to leave. No discussion.'

The group bristled slightly, though was it on Winnie's behalf or not?

'Bummer,' said Adrian, daring to show his hand, anyway, bless him. 'What gives?'

'It doesn't matter,' said Winnie, 'never mind. I'll clear out.'

'You can check in at the front office if you want the reasons,' said Mabel. 'Awfully sorry, dear.' She looked ready for a fight.

She walked Winnie to the door, a kind of senior citizen bouncer. In a lower voice she said, 'They know who you are. They left me a note in my box, but I didn't see it because I was late, what with the rain and all. You applied under a pseudonym? Why? You should have guessed they don't allow that.'

'I'm sure there's been some mistake,' said Winnie, blathering slightly, 'but it doesn't matter. I'm going abroad tomorrow anyway. I can use the time to pack. And the roads are only going to get worse.' She picked up her things and tried not to move too hastily. She didn't look at Mabel as she left.

Winifred W. Rudge, out at her car a half hour before lunch, thinking: how small, how touchy everyone in there is. How could that be? Does being unlucky in the egg and sperm department erase all personal dignity? Who needs to write fiction anymore?

But it wasn't them; this she knew. It was her own eyes, seeing things crabbed and phony; it was her own ears, set to discriminate in favor of the ludicrous and not the humane. This was part of her problem. It was what had given her the bleak vision to create *The Dark Side of the Zodiac*, it was what made acid-edged gossip with John Comestor so much fun. When, really, what was so terrible about Mabel Quackenbush pitching daddy-woo and mommy-lust

19

at childless people, if small kids got connected with families? Beware becoming superior, she said to herself. Or desiccated. Or dead.

She fumbled with her car keys, hoping that no one inside the Forever Families stronghold was watching her exile. She began to be aloof, seeing herself as if from five feet away. Not with a cinematographer's eye, framing everything, calibrating the apertures, roasting the scene with lamplight – but seeing herself as a middle-aged writer, struggling with money, frightened about the future. What does the working novelist look like, when she gets in a car on a rain-snowy afternoon in a Boston suburb? A writer handicapped in her profession by a limited capacity for sympathy?

The wind tore the door out of her hand; the hinges creaked. The storm moved on. Her hair seethed. Suddenly she undid her ridiculous scarf and let it blow away, a surrender flag of latticed green and red, the dancing Fezziwigs sent winging out over the concrete retaining wall, flagging down the traffic crawling on a snow-choked Route 128.

Beaky, she said of herself; a nose like an iron doorstop. Firm flat cheeks. A small bluish dot on one nostril that looked like ink, but was some residue of imploded capillary, the result of a magnificent nosebleed when she was twelve. Not tall, not dumpy, neither slender nor stout. A serviceable body shape, shy of glamour, though not yet quite fallen.

'Why *did* you blurt out about being a writer?' she said aloud. Her words in a string following the scarf. 'Did you guess Adrian would squeal on you? Did you hope so? Were you *trying* to get kicked out?'

Safely in the car, patting rain off her forehead with a handkerchief, she added, 'And since when are you talking to yourself?'

But you're a writer. That's what you do. You just usually don't do it aloud.

She hunched over the wheel, hating herself for being such a mess. Peering as the rain turned to snow and back again, she went skidding and sliding east on Route 9, and she watched the sky skid and slide above. The gray towers of Huntington Avenue and South Huntington loomed out of the laid-paper texture of the day's damp atmosphere.

The car was down to a crawl by the time she got to Huxtable Street, and she scraped a neighbor's fencepost as she slalomed into her parking space. But her mood had lifted, revived by the promise of seeing her cousin tomorrow. She'd tell him about the gay teacher picking up on the scarf; John would appreciate that. What would she say if John asked her why she'd liberated the scarf? Well, she wouldn't tell him she had done so. Let Scrooge and all that — that *pastness* of life — let it go, let it blow off.

She made her way cautiously up the wooden steps of the semidetached house. Shabby, shabby, unornamented, unconsoling. Home. And then as she fit her key into her lock, she paused, even though the cold rain flecked against her face — remembering the opening lines of *A Christmas Carol*. Scrooge's first intimation of his dark epiphanies:

Marley was dead: to begin with.

Scrooge, having scorned relatives and employees and the filthy poor alike, headed home full of sour stomach, and twisted his key in his lock, and saw the door knocker turn into Marley's face with — she knew it well — *a dismal light about it, like a bad lobster in a dark cellar . . .*

There was no knocker on her door. But she sensed a jolt of presence, or imagined she did. Maybe nothing more than a field mouse who had come into the house due to the unseasonable snow. She bent over and peered through the flap of the mail slot. Like many who make their living exploiting the public's appetite for

magic, she was a stone-hearted rationalist. She didn't expect to peer into a void of any sort – no trap of stars and galaxies – no wispy haunted otherworld. Rather she worried about surprising some neighborhood felon out to relieve her of stereo and computer components. But there was nothing, just the cold heavy air of an unoccupied house. A light was on in the kitchen, bronzing the wall on which she had stenciled blurry and unconvincing pineapples. The pineapples winked out and returned. Power surge in the storm? The dishcloth lay crumpled on the braided rug where, several days earlier, late and hurrying, she'd dropped it.

She twisted the key in the dead bolt, then in the lower lock, and pushed open the door. Readying herself for the melodic ding that would ring for thirty seconds until she had punched in the code. She was knocked against the doorjamb, but not by an intruder, just by surprise. The wrong amplified alarm was kicking on. The other one. The 'This is not a test' siren.

The noise was so huge that she had to force herself down the hall to the closet where the control unit was mounted. Her four-digit code didn't kill the racket. She punched it in several times, then thumped the keypad until she accidentally hit the right circuit-breaking button. And the next thing that would happen, if the system worked, was that someone from the central office in Nebraska would call and ask her for her code word. If all was well she was to utter the secret signal, at which the Nebraska folk would cancel the request for Boston's finest to send a car. But in the event that a gun was pressed to her back, she was to say some other word instead, and the cops would be there in five minutes.

The phone rang, and she was on it in a flash. She picked up the receiver and snapped, '*Marley, Marley, Marley*, it's all right; there must have been a short. We're having a storm here. I tripped it myself. No need to send a squad car.'

No sound on the other end.

'Is that Ironcorp? Ironcorp Security? Are you on speaker-phone? Pick up the handset, damn it.'

Silence, then the connection broke. Unmusically a dial tone sawed.

She held the phone in her hand an instant longer, but away from her. Then the shrill triad and the condescending message: 'If you'd like to make a call . . .'

'I'd like you to shut up and get out of my life,' she said to the recorded voice, and replaced the receiver with a bang.

Almost immediately the phone rang again. She looked left and right – what if an intruder had been breaking into the house through the basement just as she was letting herself in the front door? What if she wasn't alone in here?

She picked up the receiver and held it out, waiting to hear a voice. No one spoke, but there was a hiss again.

'John?' she said. 'Is that you?'

Another pause, then a voice. 'Could that be Winifred Rudge?'

'Well, is this Ironcorp Security or not?'

'It's Adrian Spencer-Moscou, Adrian Moscou, on lunch break at Forever Families. Feeling guilty about blowing the whistle on you. Look, I'm really sorry and I hate myself and for punishment I'm—'

'Everything is fine. Did you just call and hang up? You're tying up my line and the police will show up at my door if I don't hang up immediately.' This she did.

Then she waited for the call from Ironcorp Security, or for the Boston police to swing by and check out the suspected breach of her household defenses. Neither of which, in half an hour, had happened. Storm or no storm, someone should at least *call*, thought Winnie. What am I paying thirty-eight bucks a month for if the system doesn't work? I could be facedown in a thickening glue of my own blood by now, and who would care?

But it took her some time – a noisy cup of tea, slammed cabinet doors, egregious and theatrical cursing – to get up the nerve to go upstairs. In fact, who *would* care if she got herself murdered or maimed?

To avoid answering that question, she kept on packing. She ordered the taxi for the early morning trip to Logan Airport. Dragged a basket of laundry into the musty basement and put on an underwear load with a little bleach. It looked to be a long afternoon.

She couldn't get it out of her mind that something was there in the house with her, though each room seemed to be filled only with her empty life.

Who would you choose to be haunted by, if you could choose?

Of course there's someone else in this house, she said to herself: it's that pesky Wendy Pritzke again. Wendy and her story. Would it become another exercise in Gothic excess, born of the grimier side of Winnie's sensibility? She could do milk-chocolate children's books on the one hand, arsenic-laced bourbon foreboding on the other. How easily Neverland is corrupted into the deserted island of *Lord of the Flies.* How quickly Tinkerbell regresses to being one of the flies pestering the gouged eye sockets of the pig that the lost boys butcher.

Who was Wendy Pritzke? Winnie couldn't quite tell until the book had begun itself. She had details and conundrums, but no amount of random detail could add up to a convincing life. Rather, she believed that it took a convincing life to confer meaning and significance to random details. And she didn't know much about Wendy's life, at this point.

But Winnie doubted that Wendy Pritzke was going to linger in England; Wendy Pritzke was probably lighting out to *Mitteleuropa,* London being only a pit stop on her trip. Wendy Pritzke heading for somewhere darker than anyplace accessible to the Circle Line.

Wendy Pritzke's departure for Romania from Heathrow Terminal Two. Her bad flight over the Channel, the coastal flats of France, the sharp shadowed pockets of Alpine valleys . . .

Don't spend your time on Wendy today, Winnie lectured herself. You're not ready yet, you haven't even left Boston. But a new book took hold as it would and in its own time, and little governing it. When Winnie went down to move over the wash, she carried the portable phone with her in case Ironcorp Security ever got around to responding to the alarm. She also brought a note-book to catch a few sentences or twists of plot, or brief revelations of character if they occurred to her while she fiddled with the lint trap. All she could scrawl, over and over, was *Wendy, Wendy:* Peter Pan's unromantic friend, his stand-in mother, as if there were something to learn from that.

Since her taxi was ordered for 5 A.M., she got ready for bed early, flumping a hot-water bottle under the coverlet and appreciating the jelly glass with its half inch of McClelland's single malt. She knew that John, expecting an update of her travel plans, would have turned off his ringer and switched on his machine, so she dialed his number without fear of waking him at four in the morning.

But the phone only jangled and jangled, the familiar double ring of British Telecom. The machine didn't pick up.

Heaving herself into bed at last, she turned to set the alarm on the digital clock radio. The gelid blue numerals pulsed

00:00
00:00
00:00

They were spelling *OOOO, OOOO* at her, she thought. Odd. So there *had* been a power cut with the storm; that was probably why the alarm had gone off. But even if the clock lost track of the hour, it usually began to count the minutes again from the moment the power was restored.

00:00

00:00

She fiddled with the back of the clock. She couldn't get it to work. Its innards must have been fried. She had to get up and hunt for a travel alarm. She found one, and checked its battery to make sure the thing wasn't dead. She had no neighbors with whom she was chummy enough to ask for help, no friends left to call even at the respectable hour of 9 P.M. So she was glad that the small plastic clock still ticked its time and pipped its alarm responsibly.

But she settled against the pillow knowing that a bad night's sleep was ahead. She was unsettled by everything today, from the accident on the JFK Expressway to the broken alarm. That storm had swept in bad cess. A power outage is a simple thing, but thinking about the emasculation of time:

00:00

00:00

Well, it gave her a clammy feeling in her throat.

Throughout the night, the house shuddered, the furnace gasping emphysematously, the windows bucking in their casings. A shade flapped up suddenly in the study under the eaves. Peter Pan breaking in? She turned away from the noise, not alarmed. Who says he stayed sweet and nonviolent? After all, his mother had closed the window against him. Why wouldn't he come back and slay her? He never grew up, he was lost and still unclaimed, so by these modern days he'd have learned something about kids and guns, in schoolyards and high school cafeterias and railroad tracks. He'd know how to do it.

But she surprised herself by sleeping soundly, only waking a few minutes before the alarm at 4:15 A.M. She felt unperturbed and not even very tired. Already mentally shifting over to Greenwich mean time, she hoped.

She finished packing and brought her suitcases to the door. A scrap of paper she must have missed in clearing up the mail on the floor yesterday, a circular. She picked it up and glanced at it before dumping it in the wastebasket. She'd seen its sort a dozen times: a flimsy white card printed in blue ink, posted to 'Resident' at 4 Huxtable Street. Mailbox Values asks: Have You Seen Us? Two photos printed beneath, one of a Hawaiian girl with eyes set close and outturned, another of a blond toothy woman in her fifties. Have you seen us? 'Over ninety-five children featured have been safely recovered.' Call 1-800-THE-LOST.

She crumpled it up before throwing it out. Then she stood in the window bay so the taxi driver wouldn't honk at that hour. The rain looked snowish again, the street a black hollow, the precipitation white and silver against it. Well-lit city streets at night, especially when empty, look like movie sets. Down Huxtable Street she imagined a small tribe of costumed children, trick-or-treating in the eternal dark. A patient, voiceless throng of ghosts, suited up with rubber masks of Frankenstein and Ronald Reagan, plastic faces of aliens and witches, hobo char. They waited before her house. They did not ring the bell. In their midst the taxi pulled up and stood there, its bumblebee yellow realer than they. She set the burglar alarm. She locked up her house. She didn't know when she'd see the Huxtable Street house again, but she hoped when she came back the story of Wendy Pritzke would be far enough along on paper that it would no longer be haunting her.

She was hunting for a story that was but wasn't the story of Wendy Pritzke.

It was the first time she'd flown to England on a day flight. The flight attendants looked casual, as if this were a busman's holiday for them, and the departure lounge was nearly empty. Winnie half expected to be waved down the jetway without having her ticket or passport checked. The woman who checked her in, a tall lippy red-head whose badge said FRETTA, was yawning even as she made announcements over the PA system.

'This is close to upsetting,' said Winnie. 'Why is no one flying today? Is the weather worse than I thought?'

'It's a new route. People are still getting used to it,' said Fretta.

'I fly to England all the time. I've never seen a departure lounge so tomblike. Do you find passengers freaking out when it gets like this?'

'Oh, someone's always freaking out. We're not very busy today, but there are a few more people to check in behind you. Have a nice flight.'

'If the flight is so empty, may I be upgraded without cost to business class?'

'So sorry.' Fretta scanned the lounge for another passenger to check in, and cracked her knuckles.

Winnie found her seat – 31K – and, feeling chastised, post-poned searching for a better spot. There was hardly anyone in this section of the cabin. Not a squawling baby, not a pair of retirees chattering, no businessmen tap-tapping on their personal computers. Fretta didn't even bother with a tray when she brought Winnie a plastic glass of orange juice. 'Here,' she said, as if handing a sippie cup to a toddler.

Winnie shucked her shoes and donned the complimentary sanitary socks. She tortured herself into her assigned seat, feeling crowded even while alone. The rain on the runway made slices of colored light out of Charlestown or Winthrop or whatever town that was across the finger of black harbor. A pretty sight, but distant, and Winnie had scarcely nudged a Robert Louis Stevenson into her mind

> The rain is raining all around,
> It falls on field and tree,
> It rains on the umbrellas here,
> And on the ships at sea

when plain rain had shifted once again to slow unnerving snow.

She'd forgotten to order a minicab to meet her at Heathrow. Damn. She might flag down Fretta and find out if the international phone was available, but the hostess was off somewhere, probably yakking with one of her girlfriends or offering the pilots No Doz. Winnie slumped her head against the window, half asleep, aware of how the folded blanket was liable to slip off.

Her first and most important destination was Rudge House in Weatherall Walk, that quiet cul-de-sac on Holly Bush Hill at the very crown of Hampstead. The Rudge family home was recent by English standards, its original rooms dating to the early nineteenth century. Yesterday, really. But in the 1930s the house had been partitioned, and by the time her generation came along to inherit something, the only part left in family hands was the top-floor flat. It might have been Winnie's flat, had her father not died so young, had her father's sister not married a widower with a child, John Comestor. Winnie loved the house and wished her stepcousin John could afford to buy the whole thing back, piece by piece, but he couldn't, and it would be senseless of her to get involved. Nice enough that she had a place to stay, that he put up with his peripatetic faux relative. Especially since the house should have been hers.

From her frequent visits and occasional short-term residencies, Winnie possessed a mental map of modern London. It revolved around Rudge House, just ten minutes from the drafty Heath. Her personal London included libraries, theaters, museums, parks, and a few homes whose memory she treasured for having been the setting of bedroom adventures.

She also had her own more immutable London, an older city of the mind, the one that she had been forming from the age of eight. As for so many Americans it was a literary London. But she didn't care for overheated Bloomsbury. She'd never signposted her internal London for Dickensian inns, nor for the salons of Pope and Boswell. Even the universal allure of Shakespearian England and the Puritan London of Pepys and Milton had not stuck all that much. Winnie's firmest London was a template of childhood reading.

She could see it in her mind. It seethed with that vitality particular to stories. The swallow in her bird's-eye view circled about in haphazard fashion, admiring her ur-London. It included Primrose Hill, where the Twilight Barking of *One Hundred and One Dalmatians* started. Here was a street in Chelsea called Cherry Tree Lane, along whose sidewalks the perennial English nanny-goddess Mary Poppins hustled her charges. Here was Paddington Station, in whose airy concourse a bear called Paddington had been lost, then found. Here was Kensington Gardens, Rackham's bleak version, with sprites and root goblins just out of sight, and Peter Pan, the original lost and abandoned child, a baby dressed in oak leaves, still crouching there even when thousands of mourners were depositing floral bouquets at the death of Princess Diana.

London was a trove of the magic of childhood, for anyone who had read as obsessively as Winnie had done before the age of twelve. Pull back just a bit, and more of England became implicated: a bit of river out toward Oxford, on which a rat and a mole were busy messing about in a boat. Peter Rabbit stealing under some stile in the Lake District. Somewhere on this island, was it in Kent, the Hundred Aker Wood, with those figures who have yet to learn that sawdusty toys die deaths as certainly as children do. The irrepressible Camelot, always bursting forth out of some hummock or other. Robin Hood in his green jerkin, Kipling's Puck of Pook's Hill, and just underneath it all, places only slightly less England, the dreary improbabilities of Alice's Wonderland, the bosky dells of the theocracy of Narnia, the wind-tortured screes and wastes of Middle-earth.

The memory of the power of this early reading was part of what had prompted her to write for children. The person who would become a lifelong reader should stumble upon very rich stuff first, early, and often. It lived within, a most agreeable kind of haunting.

And magic England was endlessly reinvented, modern masters like Philip Pullman and Sylvia Waugh and J. K. Rowling piling it on with their daemons and their Mennyms and their Muggles. All those books with side-by-side worlds, forever springing leaks into one another.

The only Dickens that had ever really appealed to Winnie Rudge was *A Christmas Carol*. Partly the family legend, to be sure, but also it was the Dickens story most like a children's book. The door knocker as Marley's face! What did Scrooge deserve, if he hadn't shaped up? To be left out of life, beyond the locked windows of the nursery like Peter Pan, or worse—

00:00

00:00

She startled herself awake. The security alarm going off again? No. It was the airplane window; it was streaked with sudsy blood.

She wrenched her neck, catapulting away, across the aisle. Or perhaps she had screamed. Fretta the flight attendant poked her head from the galley. 'Everything all right, I hope?' she said brightly.

Winnie pointed to the window.

'Oh, that. Ground crew de-icing the plane. A warm substance called glycol or something.'

Pink, medical, watery. Winnie stood up and said, 'I hope the restrooms are usable?'

'Oh, yes. We're not cleared for takeoff in this weather, so make yourself comfy.'

She stumbled to the toilet. She wanted the anonymity of takeoff. She wanted another London for a template, not one in which the promises of childhood lived on so adroitly to mock. She sat on the plastic seat and thought about it. Kenneth Grahame wrote about the idylls of childhood in *Dream Days* and *The Wind in the Willows*, and his son Alistair's death on a railroad track was probably suicide. One of the original Lost Boys for whom James Barrie had invented *Peter Pan* had also killed himself. Christopher Milne, the Christopher Robin of his father's tales, whinged in print up until his death. The curse of childhood fancy.

She pushed the lever. Power flush. The two neat ends of the toilet rolls, side by side, flapped their white paper hands at her in the powerful disruption of air, as if waving her back to her seat. This airplane is jinxed, she thought. 'The Haunted Loo.' Just my luck.

She dozed fitfully again during takeoff, and only woke when a lukewarm breakfast thing was slung at her by Fretta, who seemed now to resent that the plane was required to carry any passengers at all. Winnie tore at the shrink-wrapped breakfast cheese and managed to spill the indifferent coffee. Later, walking about the cabin to wake herself up and shake the bad feelings down, she stopped to peer out a window in one of the emergency doors. Perhaps the flight was already halfway there, accelerated by Hurricane Gretl. Nothing to see but the anonymity of clouds.

Nothing to see but blue. No islands or boats, no smaller aircraft veering away beneath them. Just three or four thin layers of cloud, unraveling like freshly laundered shrouds between her triple-socked feet and the seamless blue floor of the sea.

Standing still at 550 miles an hour.

Her London would be a way stop, and so she didn't bother to map it in the mind. There were a few friends to see, some last-minute purchases to make. She had Jack the Ripper on her mind, and wanted to look about Whitechapel and Aldgate, in the event there was a book in it for her. With her tendency to cheery morbidity she had fastened on a lane to the north of Whitechapel High Street, a loop of passage called Thrawl Street. None of the nine murdered women had been found there, but it was a central point around which several of the murders could be arrayed. Emma Smith, Martha Tabram, Annie Chapman, and Mary Kelly. Anyway, the words *Thrawl Street* appealed to her.

She went back to her seat. While she was gone, a woman had moved into the empty seat across the aisle. A teenage mother in a sequined cowboy blouse, coddling a fussy lump of infant wrapped in butter mint blankets. Where had this mountain mama gotten the cash to fly? She was a one-woman crisis, ringing the call bell every three or four minutes. *The bottle, could you warm it? The bottle, it's too warm now, could you try another? Don't you have no apple juice?* The mother had a dirty face and wore her exhaustion proudly. Her baby was her license to be demanding. Perhaps no one had ever listened to her whining before.

You had to feel sorry for the sprout, though, and didn't blame it for fussing. How its mother brayed! *How big of a deal could it be to crank up the heat in this frigging place? It's, like, freezing.*

Thank God for the airline magazine, she thought, diving into it with phony enthusiasm.

It was mild monsters like these that made Jack the Ripper go after young women, she decided: who could tolerate yielding the world to someone who behaved as if she had given birth to the very world herself?

She woke with a crick in her neck, for the moment thinking, perversely, of Mabel Quackenbush. Mabel giving her the bum's rush out of Forever Families! The indignity. But in her sleepy mind Winnie also thought of another Mabel, the dull friend of little Alice in Wonderland. Alice, frightened at the monstrousness of Wonderland, wondered if she'd been changed in the night, turned into someone different – maybe Mabel, who knew such a very little.

How do you know, waking out of your nepenthean pardon, that you have returned back to the prison sentence of your own individuality, and not someone else's?

The flight came in over Windsor Castle almost a full hour early. Winnie watched with the usual anxiety. Now the landscape was still seen from the air, for one more instant, and now the bare thorny trees around Heathrow were springing up like pop-up figures against the horizon, snapping the third dimension back into the world. It made her feel nauseated and safe at the same time.

She stumbled up the jetway and was herded into the correct immigration line by a stout unsmiling Asian woman buttoned too tightly into a uniform. The immigration officer glanced through her passport, unimpressed by its stamps and seals and page-broad visas, and he said simply, crisply, 'Reason for your visit?'

She must not be awake; for a moment she couldn't understand the question.

'Business or holiday?' he continued as if she were drunk, or slow.

'Just passing through.'

He didn't even bother to ask her final destination, but that was fine with her as, in so many ways, she didn't know it.

Since the Piccadilly Line originated at Heathrow she easily found herself a seat. Now there was nothing to do but sit back and wait to see John, and plan out more of the weeks to come, to cram them full of artifice and nonsense, as if the more detail, the more significant. She worked up some jovial remarks so she could enter with a flourish. *And the choice of airplane movies! Keeping the sound off, I watched something done by the Muppets – a version of* Madame Bovary, *near as I could tell.*

She changed at Leicester Square and then alighted the Tube at Hampstead Station. She pushed with the evening commuters into the lift that heaved them up, away from the smell of Northern Line burning rubber brake pads, to disgorge them onto Hampstead High Street. From there it was a short slog up the hill at Heath Street and left into Holly Bush Steps, the steep stairs cut into Holly Mount. Winnie's suitcase and leather catchall and computer slowed her down, like physical manifestations of jet lag. Then, around the corner and out of sight of the neighborhood: the house in its secluded half-square, part gracious courtyard and part car park.

Brown brick like old puddings, a somewhat squashed-looking fanlight over the door, small bleak flush-framed windows, flecked with the impurities in the glass, and double-flecked with the speckling rain.

> O Western wind, when wilt thou blow,
> That the small rain down can rain?
> Christ, that my love were in my arms
> And I in my bed again!

Well, there was the western wind, bringing the first bad breath of Hurricane Gretl, and the small rain too, but nothing would bring that lover back.

She rang the buzzer first, to alert him, and slid her key into the lock. She stepped over a mound of mail on the floor. The stairwell smelled of prawns and Dettol. She paused, fixed her hair, and arranged a less-tired look on her face, and went on up. At the top, a few plastic drop cloths were folded on the carpet by the bristly hedgehog shoe scraper. She pushed open the door with one hand, calling, 'Brace yourself; sadly, it's only me.' He was not there at once to help with the luggage; strange. The foyer looked curiously dark and chilly. Struggling with her bags on the threshold, she saw no note on the hall table. Yet the place seemed full of something anticipating her, the way her own house on Huxtable Street had seemed, was it just yesterday? 'John?' she said, and went in.

Stave Two

At the flat in Weatherall Walk

there was no milk in the fridge, no ice in the tiny freezer unit, little to plan a meal around but tinned pears and a jar of Tesco's mild curry. The better furniture was hung over with drop cloths, the leather-bound books evacuated from their shelves. The museum-quality nineteenth-century prints of bugs and wild boars and roses leaned against one another in a corner of the parlor. The kitchen was being torn up, and plaster dust had settled uniformly in any room without a door. Unconnected wiring threaded from walls, and a smell of lazy drains, something rotting, unfurled from the sewer all the way up to this flat. Winnie wrenched open a window. But no sign of John? How come?

She swept up empty lager cans and the remains of the triangular packaging of ready-made sandwiches – tuna and sweet corn, chicken tikka, egg mayonnaise – proof of workers on-site, as recently as today, probably.

The answerphone was unplugged, she saw. But John had known she was coming, he'd known for weeks.

She flipped through piles of mail hunting for a note. Nothing. The postmarks went back eight, ten days. Could he have been called away with such urgency that there was no time for a note? John Comestor was in shipping insurance, specializing in the approval of policies to the aging merchant fleets that served the Baltic. He assessed the dredging of harbors, the temperament of the labor market, any pending legislation that bore on trade. He converted into cost analyses and risk thresholds the slim anecdotal information he could glean over glasses of vodka in dockside shacks. He hated working up the final reports, but he liked the

vodka in dockside shacks, liked the smell of diesel, fish, and intrigue.

He avoided the main office in the City whenever possible. If he had to be home in England, he booked himself comatose with Latin American film festivals or lecture series at the ICA. Sometimes when Winnie was expected they'd schedule a motoring trip on the Continent, conducting haphazard investigations of the remains of Cistercian abbeys, or the Bavarian follies of mad King Ludwig, or, one wonderful time, vineyards in the Loire. John would read the guidebooks aloud while Winnie drove.

They made a comfortably unromantic team, their tempers strained only by Winnie's preference for settling on a daily destination every morning and booking rooms ahead. Winnie knew that John enjoyed romantic enthusiasms elsewhere, and by long custom the discussion of it was avoided. It didn't impinge. Winnie's relationship with John wasn't a relationship. It was cousinhood, and stepcousinhood at that.

It was a relief to see that John's clocks weren't going *00:00 00:00* at her. But the hour was late, too late for Winnie to hope to get Gillian, John's office staffer, on the line. Unless, of course, there was a crisis in the Baltic, in which case Gill might be working late. But the phone there just rang its double pulse, over and over, unanswered.

John had friends, and Winnie knew them, but generally she preferred to keep her distance. How much easier for stepcousins to maintain a quiet truce about the nature of things, keeping everything informal and vague. How much easier not having to negotiate debts and favors, lies and silences, the rates of emotional exchange that would occur at the consolidation of two social systems into one.

A gentleman, John honored her feelings about this by forgoing invitations to soirées and drinks parties when she touched down.

Obliquely, Winnie knew about Allegra Lowe, the lead so-called girlfriend, who did arts therapy of some sort, and about various university roommates now in places like Barnes and Wimbledon and Motspur Park. Their numbers were written in pencil in the back of John's directory. But she liked standing apart from all that. So, for her own comfort tonight, she decided to forgo approaching anyone in her age bracket and instead to phone John's friend and financial adviser, a divorced man nearing retirement. Malcolm Rice lived in St. John's Wood, enjoying the chilly splendor of a big semidetached stucco house that sported too many French windows for the central heating to cope with.

She recognized the voice that answered the phone as that of Rice himself, since he spoke the digits of the phone number she had dialed, a phone habit probably dating from the days when local operators connected every call. She found herself slipping into a complementary formality whether she wanted to or not. 'Mr Rice, please.'

'Malcolm Rice speaking.'

'Good evening – Malcolm. It's John Comestor's friend Winifred here.' A latent Englishness – she heard it – came up in her voice, unbidden. It was an involuntary echo of her grandfather Rudge's speech, not the American party game of attempting the superior spoken English of the English. 'Sorry to bother you at home, Malcolm. I hope you're well. I've just arrived this evening on a day flight from Boston, and I'd thought that John was expecting me, but he seems to be away and the place is torn up by the builders.'

'I see,' said Malcolm Rice, as if sniffing a request to crash at his place. Stalling, preparing a line of defense. 'I see.'

She added, 'I'm perfectly comfortable here, but I'm surprised that John changed his plans without telling me. Do you know where he is, or when he'll be back?'

'I couldn't say. Do you need to come round for a drink?'

'No, no, I'm fine. But I'll hope to see you sometime.' She hoped not to see him at all, and she hung up. As she unpacked her toiletries, she thought: Was Malcolm Rice's *I couldn't say* intended to mean that he didn't know where John was, or that he wasn't about to reveal it? Could John actually be off on a love adventure in Majorca or Tunis? Or had Winnie underestimated him, and had he and the deadly Allegra Lowe decided finally to elope?

Uninterested in Tesco's mild curry over pears, she took herself out to the street to hunt down what supper she could. She checked out various bistros in the steep glary center of Hampstead. She settled on the only restaurant with a couple of free tables and went in. Filled with chattery diners trying to be heard above the mood music, the place reeked of cigarette smoke and a fennely *saucisson*.

Winnie was tired and unsettled about John's absence. But she was here to work, and work she would. She tried to think not of herself but of Wendy Pritzke, and of how London might seem to a Wendy just passing through on her way to the haunted Carpathians. She didn't yet know who Wendy Pritzke would turn out to be, but whoever she was, she was agreeably lustier than Winnie. Wendy Pritzke would have lavishly thick, spiritually profound hair, not Winnie's lackluster fringe. What would Wendy order? Everything bloody and garlicky, that foul sausage in its ditchwater juices. A beer. Whereas Winnie told the Italian waiter with the drooping eyelids to bring her a salad and a wine. The salad arrived, frills of green doused with vinaigrette and arranged around a single withered olive, accompanied by a sad little Chardonnay. It seemed ridiculous and fitting, and she wolfed it down, wishing she'd brought a book to read, or a newspaper.

Over the years Winnie had earned a name for writing short novels about kids with limited access to magic. Her books were

early chapter books, designed to help third-graders develop confidence in reading. The circumscription of children's lives had suited her. She could avoid the dreadful and the absurd, she could be funny, she could poke a moral at her readers when they weren't looking. Problems could be solved in sixty-four pages. Pushing herself – maybe prematurely, she realized – she wanted to find in the character of Wendy Pritzke some more tension. Give her a task more Herculean than domestic, and see how she'd make out. Winnie also wanted to see, of herself, how she'd fare at starting a book whose end she couldn't predict.

What was Wendy Pritzke doing in London, with her vague, sentimental morbidity? She was a novelist obsessed with the story of Jack the Ripper. Winnie didn't know if Jack the Ripper would end up being a character or a red herring in some domestic trial of Wendy's. The chronic fun of writing, the distraction of it, was not knowing.

'Looking bleary. You're ready for another glass of wine.'

Britt, what was his name, Chervis or Chendon or Chimms, something out of Noël Coward. Another pal of John's, from the same staircase at Oxford or the same club or posting.

'No, I'm ready for the check,' she said, striving to be civil. 'Sit down for a minute, though, if you want.'

'I thought I'd ask you to join my party.'

Winnie didn't glance over – did his party include Allegra Lowe? – as not to know somehow preserved her own American right to occupy this worn red plush English chair. 'Just arrived, and the time differences,' she said inconclusively, then brightly, 'but, Britt, I haven't seen John yet.'

'No more have I. Is he expected?'

'He's always expected. That's part of his public relations profile, isn't it?'

'Ah,' said Britt, 'you have me there. At the end of the day, though, what's the difference between public relations and private identity?'

She had no idea of the answer in general, let alone what he meant about John. She rose to leave so as not to appear to have been stood up. She kept her shoulder turned against the corner of the room from which Britt had emerged. Insincerely she promised to phone him, and made her way out with a deliberate lack of speed, feeling bovine. La Pritzke under the same circumstance would have bounced, she decided. But too bad.

She went up and down Hampstead High Street, stained a savage yellow by the street lamps. In English winds no brisker than usual for the season, Winnie dallied before the windows of the shops. Though it was only the day after Hallowe'en – only November first, for the love of God! – the candle shop was pushing beeswax candles striped to resemble candy canes.

She bought a Wispa before she could talk herself out of it and ate it with an air of defiance. When she got back to Rudge House and climbed the two flights of steps to John's place, which occupied the whole top floor, she threw the wrapper in the pile of rubbish the contractors had left. Then she felt abusive of John's hospitality, especially since something was, if not wrong, certainly out of the ordinary, so she hustled all the trash into a white plastic garbage bag. A bin liner, that is. A pipe began to knock, someone in a flat downstairs using a protesting shower, and she was startled moment-arily. The phone rang once, but stopped before she could get it. Not yet 11 P.M. here, which meant her body was remembering it was not yet six in Boston. Far too early for bed.

In his bedroom John kept a small television set, which with grave propriety they always shifted to the sitting room while she was visiting. She opened the door to his room, suddenly thinking she might find his corpse swinging from a beam, naked but for black net stockings, one of those accidental hangings resulting from

a mismanaged exercise in autoeroticism. No corpse was there. No
TV either. The room was orderly, no sign of panic or haste. Well,
John was the type who would stop to straighten the bedclothes
before leaping out of a burning building.

She remembered the other morning arriving at Forever
Families, and the wreck of furniture in the community room there.
As if something had flown up at the darkened windows, terrifying
the families away.

She turned to leave his bedroom. This room had never meant
anything to her, of course, but in general the bedrooms of single
men had a certain seedy danger even when kept orderly, and
appointed with good eighteenth-century furniture. Her eye was
caught by the mid-Victorian portrait of a gentleman in his declining
years. She knew the piece well; John liked to display it above his
chest of drawers. The plate screwed into the oak frame, which was
overwrought with gilded acanthus leaves and pears, read SCROOGE.
But she knew from being shown it by John that someone had once
scribbled on the painting's back *NOT Scrooge but O.R.* Meaning
Ozias Rudge.

Being familiar with the painting, she rarely gave it notice,
but tonight she was jumpy and obeyed her instincts to focus on
what came to mind. So she looked at it again, its occluded figure
hardly more than silhouetted against patches of icy blues and pale
browns.

The man stood in a curiously modern pose, anticipating the
drama of Pre-Raphaelite compositions. Or perhaps this painting
did date from the era of Holman Hunt, and the features of the
figure had been cribbed from some older, more conventional
portrait. The effect was more illustrative than biographic. Seen from
below, the figure faced the viewer at a looming slant, one hand out
to steady himself on the doorsill of the threshold he was crossing.
In the room behind him, an unseen fire in a grate cast up a dramatic

blue backlight. On the right, a scrape the color of bone seemed to imply a bed-curtain, but it was torn from its rings in two places and the fabric had the gloomy effect of an apparition raising its arms over a headless neck. The piece had no special merit except in its sensationalism. If this was indeed Scrooge, those must be the bed-curtains that the Ghost of Christmas Yet to Come said would be stolen from around his sorry corpse. Or were they a mediocre painter's failed attempt at the limning of a ghost? Whatever. The old man staggered toward the viewer, but his eyes were unfocused and his knees about to unhinge. A lovely tortured Scrooge, if such it really was; if, improbably, it really was the portrait of a relative, it was an insult. Most likely the annotation on the back had been done by some wag disappointed to have inherited so little from the old miser. Scrooge, or Rudge? It didn't matter. Whoever it was, he didn't know where John Comestor was, either. Or if he had seen anything, he wasn't telling; his eyes were trained inward, at some abomination in his own mental universe.

Enough of this. She was working herself up into a good case of the jitters. She located the TV eventually in the kitchen, underneath a drop cloth. The workers had been keeping an eye on something while they worked, or ate their sandwiches. She dragged it into the lounge and propped it on the massive Iberian credenza that probably had housed the salvers and spoons of some order of nuns now extinct. But before she could find the remote, she dialed her number at home to check her messages, in case John had called while she was in the air.

The voice of the recording told Winnie that she had seven new messages. The first five were hang-ups, worrying in their own right, as most callers who didn't want to leave a message slammed down the receiver quickly once they realized it was a recording. Not to do so was in itself a message: This is a hang-up: I know you're not there, and you know I know, but you don't know who I am.

Maybe computerized telemarketing calls, she asked herself, or Ironcorp, responding at last?

The sixth call was from Winnie's agent, asking how long was she going to be away, and when could they expect the new manuscript; her editor would love to begin to breathe word of a second Ophelia Marley book in the pipeline even if it was a year upstream yet. 'This is the novel?' said the agent with dubious enthusiasm, having pressed for a *Dark Side of the Zodiac II* in one form or another. 'Your Romanian book, isn't it?' He sounded defeated already. A month in Romania is hardly *A Year in Provence*, he meant. Winnie deleted the message. Whether it would be a second book by Ophelia Marley or a first-ever Winifred Rudge adult novel, she wasn't sure. She still couldn't know if she would be able to write the story of Wendy Pritzke. Nor if there was any story there to be written.

The seventh voice was familiar but newly so, and she couldn't place it at first. Male. 'You mentioned you've suffered a breach of security; what is *that* all about? Are you cowering behind a potted palm with nothing to defend yourself but a plastic spatula from Williams-Sonoma? If so, come out, come out, wherever you are. We're going to have a meal at Legal Seafoods over near M.I.T., and we'd love you to join us. We'll tell you what you missed during the second half of the indoctrination session. And by the way, I'm cute but I'm *real* dumb. Only in my fourth-grade classroom this morning did I put you together with the W. Rudge who wrote *Crazy Hassan's End-of-Season Flying Carpet Sale*. My students die over that one.' He left a number. It was that Adrian Moscou of the Forever Families meeting. He was feeling guilty over having blown her cover. And well he might. Still, it was decent of him to call.

The juddery pipe slammed again, deep in the walls, so loud that it startled her. She dialed the Massachusetts number, her finger readying to break the connection if one of them answered in person. Mercifully a machine picked up. 'Winnie Rudge returning your call. I'm away for a while, in Europe. Back, oh – whenever. But do keep in touch. And beware going ahead with that adoption group, they're all charlatans and hucksters.' She stuttered the sentence to a stop, and then added, 'I don't mean that, of course, I'm trying to be witty and it doesn't work at this distance. Here's my number, but don't call me.' She left John's number. The shallow good wishes of an Adrian Moscou were probably the more welcome, since John Comestor seemed to have abandoned her without a moment's thought.

The TV was unusually banal for Britain. Channel Four seemed to be importing more and more American sitcoms and the standard was dropping. She turned it off. The room known as 'her' room, a half-bedroom forced into a space created because the staircase didn't continue to the roof, was dingily comfortable, warm at least, and she pawed through some paperbacks on the windowsill. Edmund Crispin, Hilary Mantel, several Ishiguros. Then an old Iris Murdoch, its orange Penguin spine bleached citron by sunlight. She settled under the duvet and opened the book at random, and read.

'The division of one day from the next must be one of the most profound peculiarities of life on this planet. It is, on the whole, a merciful arrangement. We are not condemned to sustained flights of being, but are constantly refreshed by little holidays from ourselves . . .'

She put the book down. The pipes in the back of the house continued to bang, intermittently, well into the first stages of sleep, when her body could only remember flying, pitching through nothingness at all those hundreds of miles an hour, and then she was sleeping faster than the speed of sound, so the clanging pipes were left behind.

*

She lay in bed. Through the gauze she could see the sun, an imprecise disk in a sky the color of weak tea. The bells of St. John-at-Hampstead tolled the hour of nine, and a few minutes later she was in the bathroom when she heard a key in the lock. She called out, 'Hi, you!' in case he'd be alarmed, though she knew if he was coming home from an escapade he'd be as embarrassed as startled by her presence.

She finished her teeth and came out. It wasn't John, but a couple of workers in sweatshirts and jeans.

'Well,' she said. 'Good morning. I'm the house guest.'

She could sense them holding back from glancing at each other. An uneasiness to it. 'Come in, come in, I'm presentable, aren't I?' Her terry-cloth robe was snugly wrapped up to her clavicle. 'I won't be in your way, will I?'

'Sorry, we weren't expecting you,' said the slighter one, an Irish slip of a kid, barely in his twenties. 'Or not exactly you.' The older man shrugged off his wet jacket and just looked over the top of his glasses at her. Winnie took a step back and decided not to speak again until she was dressed.

She emerged fifteen minutes later. The guys had set themselves up in the kitchen. The fellows moved with a feminine deliberateness, laying out tools precisely, like nurses arranging the sterilized implements for a surgery. 'I'm Winnie, a friend of John's,' she said, with relish smashing around an old percolator as she prepared her coffee.

'I'm Jenkins,' said the older man, 'and this is Mac.' Mac grinned in a snaggle-toothed way, looking both innocent and weaselly.

'Didn't John tell you I was coming? Do you know where he is or when he'll be back?'

'We were hoping you'd be able to tell *us* where Mr C is,' said Jenkins.

'I thought he'd be here, but he's been cleared out a little while

now, to judge by the mail,' said Winnie. 'When did you last see him?'

'Monday,' said the older man. 'Mr C called us here and gave us our instructions. Some kitchen reconstruction. He drew out his plans for us well enough, and gave us a key, but he led us to believe he'd be in and out all week. And he's just vanished.'

'How much work have you managed to get done since Monday?' asked Winnie, trying not to sound schoolmarmish. It didn't look like much.

'We've been here eight hours a day, nearly, for four days,' said Jenkins, looking at Winnie in the eye, which seemed to suggest defensiveness.

Mac sunk his hands into the pockets of his loose workman's trousers and rubbed his upper thighs in a slow motion. His voice went ominous even despite the late-adolescent squeak of it. 'A bad job, this, but we've *been* at *work*.' Winnie felt a chill – she didn't know these guys from Adam. And where *was* John? She looked up from the sack of ground coffee. 'I'm not sure there's milk,' she said as casually as she could, beginning to sidle away from them.

'Oh, there's milk,' said Mac, 'milk there is. We brought a carton.'

'I take two percent. I'll just run out—' Was the security chain attached and the bolt drawn, or had they just let the door close behind them? 'Why don't you fellows find the plans and let me see them when I get back? Anything else you want while I'm out?' She held up the percolator and tried not to break into nervous giggles: hers was an interrogative gesture that could be read two ways: *Coffee, anyone?* or *Would you care to be scalded into first-degree burns?*

They didn't answer, which froze her in her pose for an extra few seconds, and then she was interrupted in her campaign to flee by the sound of knocking. It originated behind the pantry wall, much like the rap of human knuckles on wood. Three, four, five times.

'Well, hello, SOS in the baseboards,' she said, and to conceal her unfounded sense of vulnerability, 'so what have you done with John? Walled him up?'

'No, ma'am, we didn't do it,' said young Mac, tensing and relaxing in an epileptic movement, a sort of shimmy.

'Ah, but it's not her from in there, then,' said Jenkins, reaching out to touch Mac. 'Steady, lad. She's not the one.'

'What have you done with John?' she said. She couldn't look toward the pantry as the raps began again, a sequence of five hollow ominous penetrating thumps.

'Oh, not a thing,' said Jenkins.

Mac blew out through his nostrils, a colt shying. 'Give us a turn, will you? Showing up without notice? We thought it was *you* done that knocking. Coulda been so. But there it goes again.'

'You're mad,' said Winnie in a voice she hoped sounded reasonable and disarming. There was some hesitant light in the greasy sky, some wind kicking grit and desultory rain against windows. It was London in November, neither more nor less. 'How long has this been going on?'

'The week.'

'What are you talking about?' A knocking pipe, surely. A stone rolling in the backwash from a flushed toilet, echoing from the drain below. A bad board up on the roof, something telegraphing its Morse code into this space. 'Tell me what John assigned you to do.' She was exasperated suddenly; why couldn't her stepcousin oversee his own redecoration?

From an inside pocket, Jenkins took a sketch drawn in John's meticulous hand. Winnie could read it easily. The elimination of the pantry door, the crowbarring of the doorframe. The removal of the pantry shelves, the removal of the plaster from the back and side

pantry walls. All to gain fourteen inches. By exposing the brick of the fireplace stack, some turnaround room would be freed up. For what? 'Oh, I see,' she said, 'roof access here. A staircase more ladder than anything else, and the roof garden he's been dreaming about ever since he inherited this place.'

She looked up. She hadn't looked closely before. The old pantry doorframe had indeed been crowbarred out and the pantry shelves removed, and a few spot lamps shone brightly on the wall beyond. Half the plaster was already gone, revealing behind it not bricks but dingy white boards, vertically laid. On the plaster that remained she could see some faint dried brown streaks that suggested roofing problems. 'So it's not such a huge job, is it? It took you four days to get this far? What's kept you? Bad weather for punching through to the roof?'

'It's that thumping,' said Mac. 'It's dangerous news.'

'Well, you're out of your minds,' said Winnie, but less unkindly. 'Have you gone downstairs to talk to the other residents in the building?'

'The flat below is for sale, represented by Bromley Channing,' said Jenkins. 'I don't think it's occupied. Nor did we go to the pensioner on the ground floor. Mr Comestor didn't want us to let anyone know we were interfering with the original structure. There are regulations about this kind of job. He's doing this without planning permission from Camden Council.'

'I know the downstairs lodger. Well, I've met her anyway, in the vestibule,' said Winnie. 'I'll go see if she's having secret renovations of her own done. That's the eerie noise, no doubt. You're held up all week long by the sound of rapping?' She began to laugh. They looked affronted, and she didn't blame them, but she couldn't help it.

'Don't be daft,' said Mac. 'It's not just that.'

Jenkins put his hand out. 'Let her investigate, and if we get thrown out, it's a job we're well rid of. You'd choose to take it on your own shoulders, miss, we shouldn't say no to you.'

They stood there momentarily. The rapping was silent now. As if something inside the wall were holding its breath, waiting to see what she would do. 'Boggarts?' she said. 'Goblins? Nice.'

'Nothing so mild,' said Mac. His eyes slid away, his lower lip tightened.

She was amazed she'd been alarmed at them, even for a moment. They were out of a pantomime, Good Gaffer Jenkins and his grandson, Dull Jack. Still she mustn't laugh at them. 'Rudge House backs up on a property over on that other street, what is it, something Gardens. Rowancroft Gardens? Rudge House shares a party wall with one of those late-nineteenth-century redbrick homes around the way.' She pointed at the step down into the two-room nook he used as an office and a library space. 'John's flat walks through right there, and borrows some space from that newer building. Anyone in that house could be buttering toast and you'd know it up here.'

She went and slapped on some makeup to take care of the bags under her eyes, and thudded down the stairs with a will. Still stinging with the unexpected absence of her host, she felt brighter of spirit, at having something to do.

The tenant on the ground floor of Rudge House was home. She opened the door timorously and peered through the crack. Winnie revved her volume up in respect for old-age deafness. 'I'm Winifred, a friend of John Comestor from upstairs. May I come in?'

'I'm hardly respectable on a Friday morning,' said the woman, 'but enter at your own risk.' Winnie was let into a small, cramped front parlor with impressive molding and a fruity smell of flowers left in greening water. The tenant was a Mrs Maddingly, and she behaved as if she were scared her name might come true. The front room was shingled with Post-it notes lecturing on household

management. CLEAN THE LINT TRAP said the TV. IS THERE POST TODAY? asked the bookcase, which sported a shelf of Hummel figurines with their faces turned to the wall. MESSY! suggested a doorpost, apparently referring to a pile of newspapers on the floor. PILLS AT MIDDAY PILLS PILLS said a sheet of paper taped to a sofa cushion, and several other items of home decoration chimed in PILLS, PILLS. 'How may I help you?' said Mrs Maddingly, interrupting the published opinions of her furniture.

Winnie perched on an ottoman without being asked, and said, 'Forgive me for barging in like this. I'm staying upstairs while John is away, and I'm curious about the noises in the building.'

'Oh, do you hear them too?' said Mrs Maddingly. She was a tiny woman, and when she lifted one hand to steady herself on the mantelpiece she gave the impression of a commuter hanging on to a strap on the Tube. 'I can't understand the language of it, can you?'

'We hear a rapping noise upstairs, in the pantry wall I think, something that backs into the chimney stack,' said Winnie. 'We thought you might be having some renovations done here.'

'Nonsense, stuff and nonsense,' said Mrs Maddingly. 'I haven't lit a fire since the last time. I don't care for nosy neighbors, I'll tell you that, and how they alert the emergency services at a moment's notice. All their questions. Don't be forward, I told him.'

'Are you alone here?' said Winnie. 'Have workers been in?'

'Well, there's the little ones,' said Mrs Maddingly, 'but I'd hardly call them workers. Slackers, more, skiving off whenever I'm not looking.'

Winnie raised an eyebrow, feeling as if she hadn't actually woken up yet. This seemed a half-dream corrupted by jet-lag weariness. 'Workers? On the premises?'

Mrs Maddingly nodded to the figurines but put her finger to her lips, as if she didn't want to say anything that would cause them to turn around.

'Oh,' said Winnie. 'But has anyone else been in your flat this week?'

'Chutney sunlight, chamomile nightshade,' said Mrs Maddingly. Winnie was prepared to write the old woman off as being, as the English so mercilessly say, completely gaga, when a straw-colored cat passed a doorway. Mrs Maddingly remarked, 'There's Chamomile now.' So the figurines were pressed against the wall to keep the cats from knocking them off the shelves, probably.

'Mrs Maddingly,' Winnie tried again, 'there's a funny noise upstairs and I don't know what it is, and John isn't around to tell us. When did you last see him?'

'Who?'

'John Comestor.'

The woman gave a wry smile that seemed to be detachable, like a Cheshire Cat smile, and said, 'Days ago, or weeks, or was he down the stairs this morning?' She looked at a sign on the mantelpiece. 'I must remember not to forget my pills, you know.'

'What language do you think it was?' said Winnie.

'I'm not following you,' said Mrs Maddingly. 'The young are so imprecise in their speech. It's not their fault, but there you are.'

'You said you'd heard noises and didn't know the language.'

'Oh, I can't hear a thing except the cats,' said Mrs Maddingly. 'If you hadn't come to call they'd be yowling up a storm. Now as a rule I'm deafer than a stone wall. But all week they've been speaking very urgently indeed, as if they have something to tell me, only of course, who can speak the language of cats? Chutney is quite impossible, doesn't enunciate for one thing, and what vocabulary he has ever had is sorely dwindled to a few well-chosen syllables. The word for *ghost* is lost, for instance. But the cats are going on about something, although who can tell what it is?'

Oh, John, thought Winnie, why aren't you sitting next to me

to hear this? 'You've been here a while, haven't you?' said Winnie, trying another approach.

'Indeed I have,' said Mrs Maddingly. 'My husband and I moved in after the war. We once had two floors, don't you know, and we'd have liked to buy the whole house, but then I'm not talented at climbing stairs any longer, so maybe it's for the best. Anyway, poor Alan is dead, and that's fine, that's all right. We don't need the space now, and a good thing too. At today's prices, too dear by half. I couldn't afford to purchase an envelope anymore, so it's good all my friends are dead and not expecting the annual letter.'

'You remember the upstairs. You lived there once,' deduced Winnie.

'Oh, I did. Rooms, you know, rooms and rooms.' She waved her hand vaguely, as if there might once have been half a city block's worth of spare bedrooms and salons annexed to the house. 'They've all been invaded by others.'

'Do you know how old the house is?'

'Absolute ages. These front rooms are the showpieces you know, late Georgian. Not a very prepossessing Georgian, one might add, a bin-end variety. Hardly more than a cottage, really. But the rooms are low and cozy, and I have walnut coping about my boudoir. It's gone wormy they tell me but so will I before long, so I don't mind. The back bit goes into the new building; I have some steps to a useless box room that I can't get to. The floors don't agree with each other and the steps don't agree with my knees. Do you want to see?'

'No.' Winnie studied Mrs Maddingly. Despite herself Winnie was looking at life as if for her book. She was double-living through a day with genuine concerns because the needs of her fictions were as strong as those of her life, or stronger. Domestically, while John Comestor was AWOL, there was a conundrum rapping its fingers on his walls, but narratively it was also knocking on her forehead, pretending to be a ghost or a specter of some sort, and she couldn't concentrate.

Winnie sensed herself looking at this house not as John Comestor's house, but as a place where brash capable Wendy Pritzke could come across the ghost of Jack the Ripper. Winnie was channeling Wendy Pritzke, dialing her up. She couldn't help it.

Jack the Ripper was late 1800s. So this house would have been standing when he disappeared without a trace, to leave the most famous unsolved murder mystery of his day, and ours.

What if Jack the Ripper had gotten boarded up behind a reconstructed wall? What if that was why he had never been found? What if he had followed some toothsome filly home to her Georgian house in the village of Hampstead, only to meet a filthy end there at the hands of some vengeful husband or father or brother, and had his body bricked into a chimney stack?

Only to be exhumed more than a century later?

It was a worrisome habit she had, of vacating the premises mentally and transposing herself into the same premises, organized otherwise, fictionally. Like Alice and the mirror over the mantel, where the world looks the same but different: not just backward, but uncannily precise, and precisely strange. Or as Lewis Carroll had otherwise put it:

> He thought he saw a Banker's Clerk
>   Descending from the bus:
> He looked again, and found it was
>   A hippopotamus.

'I must have my pills,' said Mrs Maddingly, as if Winnie had been lobbying for their removal.

'It's not noon, and your signs say MIDDAY,' said Winnie.

'If I don't have them now I might forget. I should take them

while I remember.' She teetered toward a sideboard and with a crash she let the drop front of an antique desk fall open. Within were three small crystal glasses on a shelf lined with old newspaper, a grimy decanter of amber liquid, and an empty bottle of prescription drugs.

'What are you doing?' said Winnie as Mrs Maddingly poured herself a healthy portion of whatever it was.

'I am afraid of dropping the damn things and having them roll under the hearth rug, so I dissolve them in sherry and drink my obligations down. So sorry I can't offer you any.'

'It's not even ten o'clock in the morning,' said Winnie, not so much scandalized as disbelieving. 'I wouldn't touch sherry at this hour if you paid me.'

'It's terrible to be old and sick,' said the woman agreeably, smacking her lips. 'In praise of modern medicine, though, which keeps us alive enough to criticize ourselves and others.' She lifted her glass in a toast, and downed the contents. 'Now then, where's Chutney? It's time for his little tot too.'

Winnie left the cats, the flat, the dotty old dame, and the clutches of the Wendy Pritzke story, or at least as much of it as she could.

Maybe Chutney was trapped behind some baseboard, and scratching, and Mrs Maddingly just hadn't noticed.

Oh, but it could be anything, anything but what it seemed to be: a figure trying to communicate through the wall at them, trying to say something, something. What was it? Beware your childhood reading, Winnie said to herself: There is no Narnia in the wardrobe, there is no monkey's paw with a third and damning wish to grant. You live in a world with starving Eritrean refugees and escaping smallpox viruses and third-world trade imbalances and the escalating of urban violence into an art form. You don't need the magic world to be really real; that would be a distraction.

And the world – she stood in the hall outside John's doorway, afraid for a moment to go in – the world was already upside down or inside out; it was already Alice's mad Wonderland. That was the secret of Alice, Winnie remembered, she'd spoken about it once at a conference of fantasy writers. Even if Tenniel had drawn her with an encephalitic head, little Alice in the stories had been the correct junior citizen, sober and sane. It was the world around Alice, the Wonderland, that had gone mad. From the authority of the podium Winnie had theorized about it jocularly. Back in Winnie's great-great-grandfather's day, England had been soldered together with trust in the eternal verities of God's divine plan as worked out in Crown, Empire, the class system, and the family. And then mild unlikely insurrectionist Lewis Carroll had written the first Alice in the late 1860s, 1871 for *Looking-Glass*. Absurdity, sedition, planted at almost the very epicenter of the Victorian epoch.

A reading child back in those early days, corseted, even strait-jacketed by Victorian certainties, could delight in a story stuffed with nonsense. Time was malleable during a mad tea party in which there could be jam yesterday and jam tomorrow, but never jam today. Creatures could shift shapes, a sheep into an old lady, a baby into a pig. Fury could win out over reason. In the nineteenth century, reading Alice was refreshing because it was an escape from strict convictions about reality.

But now? Now? Children in the twentieth and this early twenty-first century hated the Alice books, couldn't read them, and why should they? Their world had strayed into madness long ago. Look at the planet. Rain is acid, poisonous. Sun causes cancer. Sex = death. Children murder each other. Parents lie, leaders lie, the churches have less moral credibility than Benetton ads.

And faces of missing children staring out from milk cartons – imagine all those poor Lost Boys, and Lost Girls, not in Neverland but lost here, lost now. No wonder Wonderland isn't funny to read anymore: We live there full-time. We need a break from it.

'You,' said Winnie to the boot scraper hedgehog, 'might as well make a statement. I'm standing here lecturing myself because I don't want to go in there and find I've wandered into a madhouse. Life is mad enough already. For one thing, John is gone. Where is he?'

The hedgehog neither answered nor waddled away in search of greater privacy.

'Well, that's proof of nothing,' said Winnie. 'I like to keep my own counsel too.' She threw back her shoulders to appear proprietary, and entered John's flat with what she hoped was convincing briskness. '*That's* a stink you've raised, then,' she called out. 'Ooh, Lordy. Something die in here?' She picked up the morning post and riffled through it to make sure there was no letter from John for her, then fanned the air away from her nose and went into the kitchen.

Mac and Jenkins had managed to remove most of the plaster. 'Aha, progress,' she said. 'Is this halitosis common to old houses?'

'It's the stink of the devil,' said Mac.

'The devil is going to have a hard time getting a date, then.'

Mac poked out his lips at her; was it a grin or a sneer? 'I have a bad worry, there's things with dark wings hovering over this whole place. I don't give a toss what she found out, Jenkins. We should get ourselves out of here and take the sacrament of absolution.'

'You're as spooked as an old bog woman,' said Jenkins. 'If you can be no help, at least keep your shite to yourself.' He was perspiring around the ears and forehead, and the collar of his sweatshirt was damp.

'What's the matter?' said Winnie. She didn't like the look of Jenkins, clammy as a cold boiled ham. 'What are you yammering about?'

Jenkins picked up a hammer. He reached out his arm and held the hammer toward the newly exposed wall boards at the back of the pantry. When he was still two feet away, the hollow banging sound began. It was rhythmic and steady. As Jenkins moved the hammer nearer, the banging picked up in speed and volume.

'Well, that's clever.' Winnie kept her voice flat, even steely. 'A sound-and-light show without the light. Now do you mind telling me where John is? I'm beginning to be tired of this.'

'I make no representation, for how do I know?' said Jenkins.

'He's in there; he's dead,' said Mac. 'We didn't do it, but what could be the reason for the thumping of the bohrain? It's a death drum, and his body is hammering to get out.'

'And so that's the smell of his corpse, I suppose,' she said. 'Well, he always was a man of tidy personal habits. He'd be mortified to know he was so aromatic.' She wrenched open a window and let some remnant of Hurricane Gretl, making its English landfall, sweep cold rainy air in across them.

'Look, look,' she said, and hustled for some paper, partly to turn her back on the pantry boards, to show them she wasn't scared of noise or smells. 'I had no luck with the downstairs neighbor, a sweet old thing named Mrs Maddingly, who's half loony herself. Probably her cat has gotten caught in some crawl space and, by the smell of it, has spectacularly died.'

'So it's a dead cat, is it, striking its claws against the back of these bricks?' said Jenkins, but gently and mockingly, for Mac's benefit, to tease him and console him both. Mac spit.

'Not a dead cat. Dead cats have no sense of rhythm. Listen to me. I told you how this old Georgian house sits next to a place on Rowancroft Gardens. For one thing, the houses share these party walls – like any abutting houses. But for another, when the Victorian house behind us went up, the developers put some back rooms onto this existing house, to enlarge it. Look.' She sketched a

map of John's flat, the older three front Georgian rooms in a lumpy
square and a newer extension behind, running only half the width
of the original house. John's two workrooms took a chunk out of
the footprint of the adjacent building. 'You see, the equivalent
flat in the Rowancroft Gardens building must be roughly a mirror
shape to this one, only longer and with larger rooms. Its puzzle
piece probably fills in over here, on the other side of our noisy
chimney stack, assuming that these pantry boards do back onto
a chimney stack.'

'That's something Mr C never mentioned,' said Jenkins.

'So maybe I should go over to that building. I know someone
who lives there I can ask.'

'You'll not go alone. Yourself'd never know where a sound
might be coming from,' said Mac, as if eager not to be left in the
flat anymore, even with Jenkins to protect him. 'I'll join ye.'

'No, sir,' said Winnie. 'I'll get further on my own.'

She went to the bathroom and changed her blouse and
freshened her face. The someone she knew who lived there was,
damn it, Allegra Lowe. Through such mere proximity had Allegra
Lowe and John Comestor originally met. They fought briefly over
a coven of pigeons living under the eaves of her building and
fouling the windowsills of his. They'd solved the problem with wire
meshing, and good fences had made them better neighbors, and
more than that. Winnie had not been to Allegra's flat before, nor
did she want to go now. But, face it, if John was holed up in
connubial bliss there, well, better that she should know it.

She looked at herself in the mirror. 'You ready to face the
Queen of Hearts?' she asked herself. 'Hello in there.' Her reflection
did not reply. She saw the crow's-feet, the jet lag drawing down the
corners of her eyelids. The pursed mouth of mirror-Winnie
displayed a clumsy application of lipstick. She did a touch-up.

Back in the kitchen to show herself off, she said, 'Mind the fort, I'll be back.' Jenkins shrugged, a noncommittal blur of gesture. Mac didn't turn to look at her, busy thumping open a painted window frame, to create more of a draft. 'Air out this stink,' he said. Winnie chose not to think he was referring to her cologne. (Had she overdone it again?) A draft swept through, and the paper on which she'd sketched the floor plans of the adjoining buildings skittered across the windowsill and disappeared outside.

He followed her down the stairwell, with the aim, he said, of finding the paper. She didn't want his company but said to herself, *Age, experience, confidence.* Well, two out of three. At the front door, as Winnie worked the bolt, Mac murmured, 'What do you think it is, really?'

'I really do think it's something embarrassingly ordinary,' she said, in a regretful tone.

'It's penance time for him, that's what it is,' he said, jerking his chin upward. 'It means fuck-all to me, though, and I ought to be released from this contract.'

'Here you go, then,' she said, flinging open the door, and then with dignity and fake nonchalance she fled.

She tried to compose her thoughts as she made her way around to Rowancroft Gardens. Though the houses shared a wall, the invasion of nineteenth-century villa architecture into Hampstead's close-shouldered eighteenth-century village housing stock meant that she had a good five- or six-minute walk, including a desolate stretch of some few yards on a muddy public right-of-way. Over a weathered fence the branches of a hedge disturbed her mousy but carefully brushed hair. She tugged at her collar and felt like a cow in an alley, skidding in the mud, mooing curses. Emerging into Rowancroft Gardens, she saw that the rain had been replaced by an aeration of fog, the kind you get in the country during a winter thaw. The street ran down the Frognal side of Holly Bush Hill, disappearing

around a curve in the mist, its redbrick Queen Anne-eries receding into nothing but pink Conté crayon suggestions, nearly rubbed out by a cloudy editorial thumb.

Rowancroft Gardens was lower down the slope of Holly Bush Hill than Weatherall Walk, but, laid out in a more prosperous era, the semidetached middle-class homes boasted higher ceilings. Consequently the roofs lined up with those shorter Georgian houses higher on the hill behind them. Number sixty-two was just about central in the stand of ten or a dozen structures apparently put up by the same developer. She knew where it was. She'd walked past it before, looking and not looking.

John had told Winnie that Allegra Lowe lived on dividends from investments. Winnie assumed that was how Allegra could afford two whole floors of number sixty-two: the garden flat with its muslined windows and winter pansies in window pots, and the first floor with the building's best plastered ceilings and tallest windows. And – Winnie knew to expect it – the kitchen, below street level, was lit. Midmorning, and Allegra Lowe was at home.

'Oh, hullo,' she said, to Winnie's knock. Without the curse of an accompanying cough, Allegra had the sort of deep smoker's alto through which you could really hear *hullo* instead of *hello*, like someone horsey and capable, straight out of Enid Blyton or Jilly Cooper, maybe. She was drying her hands on a tea towel and looking immediate and blowsy. Winnie framed a remark intended to be admiring – 'I couldn't manage a look like that without a support group and a month's advance notice' – but suppressed it and smiled in what she hoped was an irritatingly direct American way.

'I was sure you were my client,' said Allegra tersely.

'Do you remember me – Winifred Rudge,' she said. What a clunky name she had. Winifred Rudge. *Allegra Lowe*. Winnie. *Allegra*.

'Of course I remember you, but I was hardly expecting you. Do come in.'

She didn't move aside, exactly. Winnie didn't exactly push by, either. But she gained the threshold. 'I won't be a minute, or I can come back later after your appointment.'

Allegra flapped the towel. 'They're late, they're always late, they think a miracle is going to happen and a parking space will appear automatically. Then they come in annoyed as if it's my fault. I keep my car in Chipping Norton like any sensible soul and use a minicab when in London. Daft otherwise. You may as well dry off – still raining, is it?'

'No, just bushes being wet.' She followed Allegra into a grand front hall, its lower walls sheathed in golden oak and its floor tiled in a pattern that looked copied from a kaleidoscope, trapezoids of chalky vermilion, peacock, sand, white. The imposing staircase rose up to other flats, and Allegra ushered Winnie through a pair of tall doors into her private space. In the gloom of a deeper hallway, Winnie saw other doors, slightly ajar, revealing high rectangles of Sargent-like interiors slicing through the gloom, tantalizing bits of museum-quality furniture, glints of ormolu. But Allegra led her down a set of stairs to the capacious Victorian kitchen. 'No, thank you, no tea, I'm not staying,' Winnie said.

'Tea for me, then. I get cold down here, but this is where I work.'

On the far wall the kitchen boasted the usual appliances, looking expensive, unused. Le Creuset cookware from a wrought-iron chandelier, Henckels knives gleaming on their magnetized rack. Not a single crumb of bread or smear of butter. But the center of the room was the site of some sort of activity having to do with modeling clay or plaster of Paris. A table crammed with spatulas crusted with pink gunk, bits of molding clamped and weighted down. An adjacent tea trolley was jammed with bottles of turpentine and plastic tubs of paint, and brushes standing up in a chipped earthenware jar.

Allegra said, 'I'll die of poison from whatever carcinogen they discover in my supplies. The tea gets dusty but there you have it, occupational hazard. Sure I can't tempt you?' It was something of a joke, acknowledging and trying to defuse the tension between them, and Winnie was caught between being grateful and being affronted at the gesture.

'I'm here on an investigative errand,' said Winnie, 'with apologies for not calling you ahead to ask. I arrived from Boston last night and John doesn't seem to be in residence. Do you know where he is?'

With her back to Winnie, Allegra studied the kettle. She held her hands over the beginning steam and rubbed them, warming herself, before answering, 'Well, no, Winnie, I don't know where he is.'

'It's not like him to take off just like that,' said Winnie.

'Is it not?' said Allegra. 'I wouldn't know.'

'Well, I don't think so. Not when he knew I was coming.' Winnie didn't want to focus attention on her own relationship with John, but it couldn't be avoided entirely. 'I'm here doing some research for a book; of course I coordinated my flights and my schedule to accommodate his. If he'd been called away suddenly he'd have phoned me, or left a note.'

'I suppose,' said Allegra.

'When did you last see him?'

'This is a theatrical inquisition; are you writing a scene like this?' She busied herself with a cup and saucer and spoon, moving with lazy deliberation. 'I'm not at all alarmed at John's comings and goings and they are no concern of mine. I don't make notes in my daybook. I haven't seen him recently, though. We had a meal earlier in the month, and we bumped into each other at the Hampstead Food Hall I should think, or in the road. Beyond that, Winnie, I have nothing to add.' A well-calibrated performance, remarks that led nowhere, said nothing, and therefore seemed full of portent. Winnie, admiring verbal dexterity, tried not to take umbrage.

'It's rude of me to barge in like this, and I didn't even ring up,' she said, hearing *ring up* slide into place and eclipse the *call* or *phone* she'd have said in Boston. By the smallest of substitutions could you change yourself from a *you* to a *one*. It was safer, in this big chilly shiny room, to be a *one,* especially with blush-cheeked Allegra getting prettier as her pale pomegranate hair began to curl in the rising steam. Why couldn't she and her befouling pigeons have bought a flat in some conveniently more distant place, like Highgate or Golders Green?

Winnie felt as if she had a learning disability. She sat down on a painted wicker settee and said, 'I'm jet-lagged and cross, but to be honest, I'm concerned as well. Otherwise I wouldn't have come round here, Allegra. I'm not a glutton for punishment, whatever John says.'

'I'm sure John doesn't mention you at all,' said Allegra, balancing that knife of a remark on the tip of her tongue, daring it to fall.

'There's construction work going on in John's flat. Two fellows showed up this morning with a key and some supplies. They're redoing the kitchen and the place is draped in drop cloths.'

'It's green tea. Do have a cup.'

'No, thank you. Did John mention he was having renovations done?'

'I know he has designs on an illegal roof garden, if that's what you mean. I knew he was going to have builders in. But I do try to look the other way. The less he says to me about it the better, so I won't have to tell bold lies to the other freeholders in this building.' Her expression was priceless. 'I make a good effort never to lie, Winnie.'

'I don't really like the workers. They're shady in some way, I

don't get it. They're dallying, and there's a problem with pipes that they're not addressing.'

'I shall be sure never to hire them.' Tea made and left to steep, Allegra went back to her workstation and began to measure out some dry compound in a mixing bowl. She took some pigment, a bright puce color like some garish Indian spice, and spooned it in.

'I'm here also about the pipes, Allegra. There's a strange knocking in the walls, and it's freaking the workers out. It even has me jumpy, John being absent and all. I believe John told me once that your building and ours shares a party wall—' But she hadn't meant to say *ours*, that would be perceived as a gauntlet dashed down. 'I mean the old place, Rudge House. You know what I mean.'

'Yes, of course,' said Allegra, flexing her largesse. 'The estate agents told me all about it when I bought this place. Apparently the existence of the party wall dates from the 1810s or so, a device of economy. We share a more intimate domestic arrangement than most adjoining houses of different periods.'

'And when does this house date to?'

'Built in 1889. It's not the high Arts and Crafts. The pocket-book for this street wouldn't allow it. But these houses derive from standard pattern books of the period.'

'Do you have problems with your plumbing? Any knocking sounds lately?'

'Only at the door when the doorbell is out. Because I'm on the higher end of the slope, I have little trouble with drains or with rising damp on this level, unlike a lot of garden flats in Hampstead. I don't recall John mentioning any problem such as that, but as I say—' This time she left it unsaid.

'Perhaps there's something going on in one of the flats upstairs from you? Some reconstruction? Whatever it is, it's spooking the workers.'

'Irish lads?'

'Well, yes, though "lads" is a bit of a stretch. The foreman's quite grandfatherly.'

> Me mither and father are Irish,
> We live upon Irish stew,
> We bought a fiddle fer ninepence,
> And that was Irish, too . . .

'No building work in this place, that I know of,' said Allegra, cutting through Winnie's unspoken rehearsal of the nursery rhyme. 'But if it's causing you worry, please walk upstairs and ask the tenants yourself. Not that you'll find anyone at the very top. That's a flat owned by a business in the City – MaxxiNet computer payroll systems – for the putting up of Japanese and Korean colleagues when they come for training. But the company's in receivership and no one has been in residence for months. I know because MaxxiNet requires that temporary residents stop and introduce themselves to me, and the obedient Japanese and Koreans do everything they're told. For several months I haven't heard anyone in the hall other than the family that lives immediately above me.'

'Who are they?'

'A widow, Rasia McIntyre, and her three urchins. She might be there now, though she does her big weekly Sainsbury's shopping on Friday mornings. You want to hurry upstairs and catch her before she goes. I can tell you very little more, Winnie.' She finished mixing the dusty porridge and poured out her thin green tea. 'You're welcome to something hot, but I don't know about renovations nor the whereabouts of your cousin, and. So.' She shrugged and grimaced. Then she looked down at her work and pinched a bit of the mixture between her fingers and frowned.

'What are you making up?'

'Dental compound.'

'What for?'

'I do hands, impressions of hands,' said Allegra. 'Child hands mostly, presents for grandparents, that sort of thing.' She walked to a broad table in the corner and flung off a gummy blanket. The surface of the table was tiled with pink squares and rectangles, some framed, some loose, some inscribed with names, some not. Each tile showed the imprint of one or two little hands, like instant fossils, blunt starfish impressions. 'It started out being therapy for learning-handicapped adults and developed into a lucrative little cottage industry for me. Of course, a piece in the Sunday *Times* color supplement several years ago didn't hurt my business.'

Winnie found it grotesque, but didn't say so. 'What's the strangest impression you ever made?' she said.

'I went to a Hallowe'en theme party last week. It was Vicars and Whores, and I went as a Vicar. Maybe that wasn't so strange, though, as most of the men went in drag as Whores.'

'I mean,' said Winnie, 'the handprints; what's the oddest experience—'

But Allegra said, 'Look, I was joking, right? Anyway, there's the knock. I've got my morning client at last. I'll see you out as I go to let them in. If you don't mind? There's nothing else?'

'Nothing else, there's nothing at all,' said Winnie. Vicars and Whores. The sight of adults in costume, unless it was on the stage, always unnerved her. Even the thought of it. She hustled herself up the stairs in front of Allegra, trying to focus. 'What did you say the neighbor's name was? Rose, Rosie? McIntosh?'

'Rasia. It's a Muslim name. Rasia McIntyre. She married a Glaswegian who fell into an unexpected coma and just, just *died*, no fanfare or fare-thee-well. You'll like her. Tell her I would make the introductions if I could, but duty calls.'

She flung open the door and scowled at a frantic-looking mother restraining a squirming bundle of toddler. 'I want you to submerge his whole body in the cast and keep it there,' the mother rattled at Allegra, 'and when he's dead and rotted we'll crack open the mold and make a better-behaved plaster version that *does. Not. Squirm. So.*' Winnie nodded her thanks to Allegra and headed up the stairs.

She could hear the fuss of Rasia McIntyre's household spilling down the stairwell. The sound of quarter-tone sitar music accompanying midmorning toddler meltdown almost stopped her in her tracks. But the more time she took up, the likelier that before she got back, Mac and Jenkins might have cleared out, and anything else objectionable too. So she rapped on the door.

'Yes, who is it,' said the Rasia woman, throwing open the door and continuing to yak into the portable phone, two tiny children clinging to her trouser legs. To Winnie: 'I'm absolutely strapped, can't manage a quid.' To the phone: 'Look, there's a do-gooder at the door, will you be in? I'll ring back when they go down for naps. Very good very good, ciao.' She slapped the phone on a hall surface and said, 'I couldn't get her off the phone so I'm glad you knocked, but I don't give to those who knock at the door, and you ought not to have been let in.'

'I'm not collecting for charities,' said Winnie, 'I'm a friend of one of your neighbors next door. I'm here to ask about some strange noises in the building—'

'Navida, I'm telling you, no more sweeties until teatime, you'll just have to cry,' said Rasia, detaching Navida's arm from her thigh. 'Yes, I tap the kids on their bottoms sometimes, but they're my kids and I do what I want. They don't cry more than other children their age. You can't be from the Council. Not with your accent.'

'I'd hit them too,' said Winnie, looking at them, 'and I'll take turns with you if you like. They're very noisy.' She didn't mean it but it worked. Rasia laughed.

'They're high-spirited and they miss their daddums, and I can't blame them. Is this a formal complaint?'

'No,' said Winnie. 'May I come in just for a moment?'

'If you must.' She looked more pleased than she sounded. 'Though I've more than enough to do without preparing the house for unexpected callers.'

Rasia McIntyre had a full face with strong bones and high brow. It was like looking at one of the Picassos and seeing front and profile simultaneously. Rasia had hips and shoulders, she had depth and round breadth, nothing whittled away through a diet of mere lettuce. Winnie felt bleached and parched next to the Asian woman's vigor, but she didn't mind. Rasia was realer than a missing stepcousin or a confounding knock in the walls.

The room into which Rasia led her was a kerfuffle of scarves and candles, throw pillows and expensive Turkish carpets. The floor was covered over with children's games in ten thousand pieces. On a workstation in the corner teetered several television sets, two computer screens, a stack, a printer, and a VCR. Winnie half expected the abundance of Post-it notes to read PILLS PILLS. 'I'm trying to get back into film editing, but I'm not sure I can upgrade my skills,' said Rasia. 'Everything's computerized now and I have so little patience for the manipulation of tiny bits of information.'

Nor for the tiny bits of Lego and Duplo and dollhouse furniture that crunched and splintered underfoot. 'Shit. You *guys*. Are you going to collect any of this or do you want me to ruin all your playthings?' she said. 'Navida. Tariq. We have to go out and do our errands, and this looks like the Rubble of Dresden.'

The children disappeared, shrieking down the hallway. 'If you wake the baby I'll boil all your bones,' called Rasia, but without conviction. To Winnie, 'Sorry. This place is such a tip. If you're not here to complain about the noise of the children, then what?' She sat down in her workchair and began to lace her boots, looking up at Winnie from beneath a curly abundance of anthracite hair.

'No. I don't care about the noise kids make. I'm only visiting next door anyway.' Winnie took a breath and described the layout of the intersecting houses. Then she told Rasia about the sound of knocking from the chimney stack. 'Your downstairs neighbor, Allegra Lowe, said she thought you might have some ideas, or maybe you were doing some building yourself in here.'

'Would that I were,' said Rasia. 'The children thump and play, and sometimes the baby hits her head against the wall when she wants uppies and I'm in the loo, but not this morning. I wouldn't think it loud enough to be heard in another building, anyway. We can look if you like. Excuse the housekeeping. I have a Brazilian girl named Zuli who disappeared a few weeks ago and hasn't rung to tell me when she's coming back. Did you ask everyone in your building?'

'There are only three flats in Rudge House, and the middle one is on the market.'

'Well, that'll be it, then, don't you think? The owner of that flat must be tarting up the kitchen to get a better sale price. Have you gone round to ask at the estate agent's?'

Winnie hadn't thought of that, and indeed, it was the most logical conclusion. Though wouldn't she have seen sign of other workers moving in and out in the stairwell of Rudge House?

The children had settled themselves in front of a television in a side room, and were shooting suction-rubber-tipped darts at Trevor McDonald doing a newsbreak. 'Baby,' said Rasia, 'nappy time. I can smell it three rooms away.'

At the rear of the flat, in a corner of the main bedroom, the baby lay in a crib with pink plastic bars. She was breathing heavily, but not crying. Rasia stood and looked at her. Winnie didn't; she studied the proportions of the room, the molding. 'Could I be really pushy and peer in your closet? Put my ear to the wall? I think the chimney stack from Rudge House might be on the other side of your closet wall, and the sound would be muffled by your clothes; maybe that's why you haven't heard it here.'

'But it's a mess, I haven't cleaned out a thing,' said Rasia irritably. 'I can't, you see, I can't.'

'Oh, that won't bother me, I'm a slob too.' She laid her hand on the cupboard door. 'I mean—'

'What *do* you mean? And why are you here?'

Winnie turned at the changed tone. Rasia's eyes had become plums, and she covered them with the heels of her fists. The baby stopped breathing as if she felt responsible for her mother's tears, and then started up again, ever more shallowly, tentatively. 'It's Quent's clothes in there, how can you walk in here and go straight to his clothes?'

'I never,' said Winnie, horrified, 'I never meant, how could I know? I'll just go. I'm very sorry. Stupid of me. Please. You'll scare the baby. Please.' Rasia was bawling now. 'Please, you don't have to do this. I'll go. I'll let myself out. Are you all right? Let me get you a tissue.'

They had tea for an hour. Winnie felt hijacked, but she deserved it. She pretended an interest in seeing pictures of Quentin McIntyre and Rasia Kamedaly at their wedding, on vacation in Madagascar, or visiting the old Kamedaly family home in Kampala following the repatriation of Asian properties seized during Idi Amin's reign. Quentin looked like a well-used shaving brush, his blond hair bristling in all directions. Quentin at home in Loch Dunwoodie. Quentin at Keble College. Quentin and Rasia with the kids. In the end, Fiona whimpering on her shoulder, Rasia led Winnie to the bedroom again and drew back the heavy drapes. 'Open the wardrobe, pull out his things,' she said, 'it's been nine months now, I've got to think about Oxfam sooner or later.'

Winnie was beyond resisting. She'd unlocked this Pandora's box and clearly there was no stuffing the vermin back within. She pulled out suits and sports coats, tailored trousers and boxes of laundered shirts. When she opened the topmost drawer she saw a

heap of men's briefs, white, blue, and tiger skin. She closed the drawer on all that.

'Here's the wall, then,' she said, reclaiming some briskness at last, and she put her ear to it. 'Look, it is plastered unevenly; this probably is the early-nineteenth-century chimney stack, just as I guessed. Might this have been a fireplace once, boarded over when central heating came in?'

Rasia, playing with Fiona, didn't answer.

Winnie leaned into the shadows vacated by Quentin's clothes.

There was a sound in the stone, or so she thought, but it could just be the sound of a vacuum, like the seashell magnifying back to the ear the sound of the ear's own echo chamber. In one ear Winnie heard the aeons creak, the sound of stone speaking its lone word; she heard it translated, today, as the moment-by-moment evaporation of the McIntyre-Kamedaly marriage, only a ghost of itself and dissolving by a few more molecules every hour or so.

Then she pulled herself together, stood up, said, Stuff and nonsense, but to herself, and aloud, 'I can hear nothing, really. I feel a fool to have barged in like this,' and helped Rasia McIntyre carry the heaps of old clothes out to the landing.

But Rasia seemed better, and Fiona was gurgling at her sippie, and the older children began to grin at Winnie and flirt with her despite her ignoring them. As the women pummeled clothes into Marks and Spencer shopping bags for carrying to one of the charity shops, Rasia said, 'Your friend Allegra holds a duplicate key to the upstairs flat. For emergencies. Didn't she tell you?'

'She didn't. But never mind. She must know nobody's there, so it didn't occur to her.'

'If you want to be thorough, ask her for it.'

'I'm not such good friends with her—'

'You're not such good friends with me, and you've helped me clear out Quent's clothes,' said Rasia, 'something my sisters have

been begging me to do for months. They offer to come up from Poole every weekend and I have said No, no, I'm not ready. Then you barge in and rip the place to shreds without a flinch of shame. Surely you can go ask your friend for the key.'

'Oh, I could if I wanted,' said Winnie, 'but really.'

'Really what?' It was Rasia's turn to be nosy, and Winnie had no intention of satisfying her curiosity, no matter what Rasia was owed.

Pulling on her jacket, Winnie said, 'Do you know my cousin? A friend of Allegra's? John Comestor?'

'She has plenty of people come and go and I don't make it my business to supervise,' said Rasia with an attempt at primness that she spoiled by continuing, 'but I see what I see. What does he look like?'

'Average height. Trim. My age, a bit younger. Cocoa brown hair, I guess, longer than is the convention for men his age, but kept trimmed in back. Dresses casually, jackets and jeans mostly. Boyish, you'd say. A John Cusack type.'

'Sounds like most men in Hampstead. American?'

'English.'

'I'll keep the curtains twitching.'

'Oh,' said Winnie, 'it's nothing to me whether they're seeing each other or not. I know they're an item. Out of respect for my feelings they both play it down, but I don't care. He's gone missing, or anyway he's out of town without notifying me. That's all, and that's the end of it.'

'Well, he's not staying upstairs, hiding out from you,' said Rasia, 'though since Allegra has the key to the flat upstairs he could easily do it. But I'd hear the coming and going on the stairs, and the shower running and the loo flushing. There's been none of that.'

'Can I repay you by hauling one of these sacks down to one of the charity shops on West End Lane?'

'Thank you, no.' Rasia McIntyre crossed her arms around Fiona and kissed the scraps of baby fuzz on her scalp. 'You can help me by coming back to see me sometime, if you want. You know something of what it's like to miss your man, I can tell.'

'How very kind,' said Winnie. She saw Rasia flinch at the sudden formality. But Winnie couldn't help it. She descended the stairs with no attempt at grace or silence.

She chose not to go back to Rudge House through the muddy right-of-way. Then, as she headed around toward the cross street, she changed her mind entirely. John had just abandoned her to his mess of redecorating problems and North London neighbors. Why was she taking this campaign on her own shoulders? Why get involved in it at all? She'd go find a bite of lunch first.

She looked at the pedestrians on the high street quickly, with interest, as if they might, coincidentally, be John. They weren't.

She stopped – a pain in her side, a twinge, a premonition, something – and steadied herself, one hand on a blue lighted Metropolitan Police display case. Or maybe she'd been drawn to the posters? Two pages, side by side. The first, printed both in English and in some exotic fringed script, appeared to publish the news of the disappearance of a soft-faced Southeast Asian boy whose photo showed him with streaked blond hair. The text said he had gone missing from the Imperial Karaoke Club in New Road, Dagenham. The second page, fully in English, pleaded for information about a man murdered at the August Notting Hill Carnival. He'd been attacked and killed at Westbourne Park Road. 'Did you see the attack? Have you heard anything about the attack? Do you know those involved?' Both announcements printed an 0800 number for any leads. Anything at all.

And all these people on their way to lunch, walking by.

She found one of her usual haunts and used the facilities and

ordered a beaker of cabernet. The place was filling up. She took a sip and thought of John, his theatrical exits and entrances. Despite herself – her condition and her therapy the same – her mind sidestepped toward the story of Wendy Pritzke. Would anyone like John be making an appearance in her story? Should he?

She took out the stenographer's notebook and flipped it open. There were the pages of scrawl from the Forever Families debacle. It seemed weeks ago already. She turned to the next white page and picked up her pen. She sat there and did not write.

There was wind, and more of it than she'd expected. Hilly North London, its thoroughfares made canyonlike by the facades of mansion blocks, was a maze of wind tunnels. Embattled, she headed back up the slippery paving stones to look at the redbrick house again. There was something about the mix of English rain and the effluvium of English petrol that made London pavements more slippery than any others she'd pounded. Or maybe it was her American rubber soles refusing to travel well. She reached out to steady herself. 'Oh, I'm a bundle of nerves; that's being in the presence of a good idea, it does it to me,' she said. He didn't answer nor complain.

The house – it was always about houses – was as far from grungily redeveloped Whitechapel as you could get.

If you savored Dickens for the muck of it all, you were disappointed in the contemporary environs of Aldgate and Whitechapel and Spitalfields. Most of Dickens-land had been destroyed in the Blitz.

You could buy booklets, and she had, of Jack the Ripper walks. Anyone could hunt down those few remaining sites that Jack the Ripper would have known: the White Hart Pub on the corner of Gunthorpe Street, the Artillery Passage, Ten Bells Pub, which the prostitutes who became his victims must have frequented to drum up trade. Turn left and sample Tubby Isaacs's East End cuisine of eels. Straight ahead, Durward Street, murder site of Mary Ann Nichols.

It was as if all that could never be known about the identity or the fate of Jack the Ripper was compensated for by loving devotion to whatever was left.

And, if you were interested, there was so much of the rest of London standing today that had stood in the winds of the late nineteenth century. It just wasn't in the City.

Could Jack the Ripper have fled Whitechapel eventually and disappeared into another neighborhood? Even, why not, to this street in bourgeois leafy Hampstead?

He (the great unknown he), the murderer of prostitutes, named the Ripper for his tendency to claw out their throats and prevent them from screaming, he could have struggled up this street as she was now doing. In his day it would have been sluiced with carriage ruts, a mess in this weather; filthy; horse manure softening and liquefying and running downhill in this rain as loads of red brick were trundled up from the kiln. The rise of a pink coral reef in the fog of coal-burning London . . . Had the exteriors of the buildings already been finished by the time Jack the Ripper appeared in the street? Were the final details of interior lath work, plasterwork, woodwork, the plumbing for gas lighting still being fussed over, when Jack the Ripper reached the house that would later be number sixty-two, and could, or would, go no farther?

'You're stuck on this,' he said, 'I can see it on your face; you're drunk on it. The shame of it all! Can't you write something dim and domestic like Anita Brookner, some damp-browed seamstress too educated for her world? You'd like to wield bloody knives, but I tell you, you're not constitutionally suited for it.'

'Don't tell me what my constitution suits me for,' she said. 'We all succumb to our contagion of choice. The question is, what if Jack the Ripper came to his senses and fled the scene of his crimes? What if he tried to set himself up as a laborer in outlying Hampstead Village? Or, of course, he could have taken a position as a butcher's assistant. Only he falls prey to the spell of some gamine young Hampstead woman? Perhaps an Irish maid, recently engaged to swell the staff of the new household? Maybe he makes a delivery here and catches sight of a pretty red-headed maid down there in that kitchen. Look how public the windows are! You can see three-quarters of the room, more if you stoop down and look. Maybe, having evacuated himself from the nightmare zone of Whitechapel, scene of his frenzies, maybe he doesn't even *remember* himself as Jack the Ripper. Maybe he reads about it in the used newspapers that he wraps meat in and he doesn't recognize himself. Split-personality type. But there's something about the pretty chin, the glimpse of stockinged ankle as a kitchen maid teeters to collect a basin from a high shelf. He slides the choice cut of lamb from side to side, and its blood gums through the paper and smears his apron.'

'We'll have some supper and we can rent *Dressed to Kill* or *Psycho* if you like,' he said. 'I can tell you're way beyond reruns of *Upstairs, Downstairs* by now.'

She laughed. 'Well, you know how much has been made out of the mystery of his disappearance. You know better than I. At one point they proposed that he was a syphilitic member of the royal family. He was a Mason, a surgeon, an insurrectionist. All this excites the fancy, as they say.'

'I can see your fancy is excited.'

'Don't go on yet. I want to look in that kitchen window and imagine what he might have seen.'

'You're looking for some leggy copper-tressed maid for a serial murderer to sink his meat cleaver into?'

She murmured, 'Why, if a prostitute were unable to defend herself, would a kitchen maid in a middle-class house do better?'

'You've said the prostitutes were mostly drunk,' he answered. 'Besides, kitchen maids work

with cooks, and cooks know cleavers pretty well themselves. But I like your plot better when the man in the household comes home and finds some thug messing with his child bride or his nubile teenage daughter or his parlor maid. The good paterfamilias kills him and bricks his body up in the chimney still under construction. Up there in the maid's quarters. Pater hides the evidence of the murder, to avoid the scandal and shame. The delicate ladies, after all! What do you think? And that's why no one could ever find Jack the Ripper to arrest him. The son of a bitch was done in himself.'

'The story would go better, John,' she said, 'if the intended victim could do the murder.'

'Too politically correct. Though your American readers would lap it up, no doubt.'

'Her father or beau could still dispose of the body to protect her honor and to shield her from prison.'

'You are incorrigible,' he said.

'I'm entirely corrigible,' she answered. 'I think. Does that mean corruptible?'

'I know you're corruptible. Corrigible means *correctable*. Shall we get out of this vile weather and find a scotch and soda somewhere?'

They moved past the house, laughing, Gothic fancy serving as a rather hearty appetizer.

She felt herself in the muzzy grip of too much wine at lunch. As she approached the front door of Rudge House with her key in her hand, the door opened of its own accord. Or rather, she saw, of the accord of Mrs Maddingly, who stood there dressed in a shapeless coat the color of beef gravy. 'Ooh, a gale,' said the old woman appreciatively. 'I'm off to the post office to get my pension. You haven't seen Nightshade I take it?'

'A cat? One of your cats? I have not.'

'She'll turn up, or he will; I forget which it is, not that it matters to me, I'm not a cat,' said Mrs Maddingly. 'In fact, it didn't matter to me as a human, either, except when dear Alan was interested, and he was the only one who ever was. You haven't seen him either?'

'Your dead husband?'

'The same.'

With some irritation Winnie said, 'Was I expected to?'

'No, no,' said Mrs Maddingly, passing her in disgust. 'I meant to say did you *ever* see him? I can't remember if you and I were friends back then. How do you expect me to remember trivial matters like that?'

'I'm sorry,' said Winnie. 'I'm just— no, I never had the pleasure.'

'And you never will now,' said Mrs Maddingly in a smart tone. She glided past and hopped off the front step, and pattered down the pavement on unsure feet. Maybe she was drunk, thought Winnie; maybe that was what gave her the courage to venture out. She watched the old woman test the pavement, as if expecting it to give way. Her flyaway hair was a corona of white; she had the look of an old ewe too long unshorn.

Winnie pocketed the keys and went on up, pausing only to remove her muddy shoes and leave them on the drop cloths the fellows had laid out to collect their own boots and umbrellas. 'Well?' she asked the hedgehog. 'Any word from Interpol or Scotland Yard while I've been gone?' The hedgehog squatted on the plastic and again refused to comment. 'Hello, hello,' said Winnie, entering the flat, willing John to have mercy and show up. 'John?' she said in a voice of hopeful irritation.

Except that the smell had abated, the place was no different, unless it could be said that a stalemate can grow staler. She could feel rather than hear the presence of skeptical Jenkins and slight-minded Mac there, not working. She wasn't surprised to find them more or less as they'd been several hours earlier. 'Good going, fellows. You've made no progress at all?' Her words came out tarter than she meant them.

'We were kept—' said Mac, and stopped.

'We're dying to learn what you've turned up in your walkabout,' said Jenkins. He made a gesture, as if to touch the brim of an imaginary cap. His deference was mocking. She regretted her temper, its small stings and seizures, and she amended herself in that room: drew a breath, crossed her hands on her waistline like a figure from an older generation. She tried to smile.

'You've been considering the matter still,' she said.

'The noise is louder,' said Mac, and crossed himself. 'Mother of Christ.'

'The wind is picking up too,' said Winnie. 'Maybe there's a break in the flue above, a chink in the plaster somewhere.' Bizarre, that it should be left to her to be the rationalist in the room. She who for several years had drawn sound five-figure royalty checks for *The Dark Side of the Zodiac.* John would have enjoyed that irony, were he around. 'Have you considered that?' she said. 'The chimney as a kind of huge pipe organ, coughing?'

'You've a daycent portion of comment,' said Mac, 'for someone who just walks in without warning—'

'Don't, Mac, just stow it,' said the older man, 'it does no good.' Something passed between them, but Winnie couldn't tell what it was. Dread, superstition, suspicion of some sort. Of her?

'A message come in on the answerphone,' said Jenkins, jerking a finger toward it.

'John,' she said with relief, 'well, it's about time.'

'A man,' said Jenkins. 'We heard the voice, but it wasn't for us.'

'We listened by to hear if it was you ringing us,' said Mac, as if put out that she hadn't called in with her findings.

She went to the machine and pressed Play.

She thought at first that it was John. No. Adrian Moscou again.

'. . . you said don't call but you left your number so I thought I would. London's a long way to go to avoid our dinner invitation. But you've got a rain check. So give a call when you get back. I'm still wearing hairshirts for blowing the whistle about your being a writer – I may have to kill myself if I don't hear from you. Besides, Geoff wants to push ahead in our application, but I'm more Capricorn and skeptical, so we wanted to hear your impressions of the child merchants of Forever Families. We feel somewhat – uh – marginalized in that crowd. Anyway, we like your books, or my students do anyway, so there might be—' The tape cut off.

She was tired of not getting where she wanted, of not being able to flee what she'd rejected. 'Give me the damn crowbar, the adze, whatever it is,' she said, pacing into the kitchen. 'If you won't do the job John hired you for, I will.' She picked up an L-shaped lever with a wedged tip. She approached the boards of the newly exposed wall and ran one hand over them. The fellows must have been working this already; she could easily nudge the pronged edge around the nailhead she'd found. 'Is this the idea?' she said, and put her weight on the implement.

The nail allowed itself to be worked out to a distance of two inches or so. 'Hard work,' she said icily. She couldn't loosen it farther so she replaced her tool around a lower nail, in line, and did the same. Again it stopped at a certain distance. 'These nails have clawed points or phalanges back there?' she asked. 'Or bolted tips, somehow? Well, we ought to be able to work this board away with our fingers, if we all put our backs into it, and then yank it off, shouldn't we? Come on, something, anything.'

'She'd charm the Y-fronts off Jaysus himself,' said Mac. 'The noise is stopped. What's she done?'

It was true, the pounding was gone, but the silence itself was eerie, like the running down of a clock timing something urgent.

'I probably just let a little air into the space,' she said, getting to work on the third nailhead. 'Now that I've started, are you going to take over? I've got some business in the City . . .'

But when Jenkins came forward to take the crowbar, the rapping began again. Fiercely, less mechanically, more like the scrabbling of a trapped beast. Mac said, 'Bloody hell!' and Jenkins flinched and retreated.

'Ah, the blood pressure,' said Jenkins, 'and me just run through the last of the tablets.'

They all backed up and Winnie laid the crowbar on the floor. She said, 'From there to here, from here to there, funny things are everywhere.'

'What the fuck?' said Mac.

'Dr Seuss,' she answered.

'We'll be needing some doctor or other,' said Mac. 'Dr Freud. Or maybe Dr Kevorkian.'

Winnie's voice was softer than she'd have liked. 'It's just annoying. How can we be spooked by redecorating? The kitchen that rejected new fixtures? What does it want?'

'Holy shite,' said Mac.

The nails, one by one, began to retract into the walls, like a cat sheathing its claws.

It was like trick photography, like watching a video in rewind. Cool and constant. Time in reverse, time broken. Winnie felt her grasp of things shudder, her thoughts wheel out, seeking for a scrabblehold elsewhere, in a world more obedient than the aberrations on display at this hobbled moment. Somewhere else, children on playgrounds were quietly ganging up on the unpopular isolate. Junior varsity teams were suiting up for a scrimmage. Middle-management types were plotting office putsches over the water-cooler. Some bored child was tossing a book of Winnie's on the floor. Some mother frantic for a cup of Tension Tamer tea was hacking through the cellophane wrapping with a meat cleaver. Everywhere else, furnaces were firing up, trucks were backing up, computers were booting up, things were going forward, except here, where the nails were retreating.

In a moment there was no sign of Winnie's efforts, and the flat had gone silent again.

'A whole *week* of this?' she said.

'No,' said Jenkins, 'we haven't been able to get as close as you just did. Nerves.'

She put her weight on her heels, her back against the kitchen cabinets. 'You'd better tell me everything,' she said. 'You'd better just start at the top. Where are you guys from? Have you done work for John before? What's the first thing you noticed that was strange?'

They didn't speak. 'Why would you not trust me?' she said. 'You just better,' she added.

'I'm from Raheny, in Dublin,' said Mac after a minute. 'And here four years and some, staying with mates in Kilburn, off Mill Lane. Been at this sort of thing since weekend jobs with my da. Five, six years now. Never seen the likes of this.'

'Have you got a real name, Mac?'

'Mac's good enough for you if it's good enough for me,' he said. He had the look of a ferret with mumps, his narrow elegant nose blooming out of a face raw with the last of adolescent acne. 'I've been with himself the past two years.' He nodded sullenly to his partner.

'Colum Jenkins,' said the older man, his hand on his left

shoulder, rubbing it. 'Building's been my trade the past dozen years, working now for myself, previously on a maintenance staff in a clinic in Birmingham. And I think my domestic arrangements are none of your concern. I did some work for a friend of Mr Comestor's and was recommended; Mr C rang me a month ago or so. I came out to look at the job, deliver an estimate, collect my deposit. The usual. Mr C was a pleasant enough chap, a bit distracted, you might say—'

'Distracted? How?'

'Oh, Monday morning we arrived, lots of to-ing and fro-ing on the phone. Some buyers interested in the flat below came pounding on his door to ask him some questions about the neighborhood. That sort of thing, don't you know. He didn't look like a man who stayed in one place with a newspaper for very long, did he, Mac? So when we arrived back on Tuesday and he wasn't here, we weren't so very surprised. We thought he'd be back in a moment, or maybe I'd just misunderstood. That was the day the nasty weather began. I left a note asking his permission to do the bathroom first. I didn't care to risk breaking through to a chimney stack whose shaft could well have shifted over time, allowing in the rain, leaving us dealing with the elements. But Mr C left no written reply on Wednesday morning to answer my proposal. He just disappeared. So we spread out the dust sheets, put our wet things to dry, and got to work, or thought we would.'

'So it's been rainy weather all week?'

'Had to set out the oilcloth in the hall the first morning he was gone, Tuesday, it was, to drop our wellies on. We've not had to pick it up yet. Very English weather.'

They were all skirting the imponderable: that some thing or other had pulled the nails back into the wood so efficiently that the nailheads were once again flush. It was too strange, like biting into an apple and tasting a mouthful of cauliflower.

'Why didn't you just say, 'Oh, the hell with this,' and take off?' she asked.

Mac looked as if he'd made that very remark to Jenkins repeatedly over the past four days. 'It's bad doings, and worse to come,' said Mac.

Jenkins sighed. 'Mac is spooked if a mouse runs across his path, thinking it is the devil's agent. But though I don't fathom it and I don't like it, I'm ashamed to be scared of it. And I don't want to leave it till Mr C comes home. I've a reputation, and a good one, the which I worked hard enough to get. And we don't know where Mr C is.'

'There must be a missing persons bureau at the police station,' said Winnie. 'Why not call?'

'*You* ring, give *your* name, and tell some authority that you're scared of your assignment?' said Jenkins. 'Go ahead, try it.'

'You're not telling it all,' said Mac. 'He isn't,' he said to Winnie.

'What's he leaving out?'

'You mind your tongue,' began Jenkins, but Mac said stoutly, nearly in a shout, 'This is a fecking waste of time. And there's naught to it anyway, so just belt up.' He turned to Winnie and continued. 'Wednesday we just stood around some, joking about it, trying to show we weren't pissing ourselves with fright. Then yesterday even in the rain we thought we'd get up on the roof and look down, try to find a hole from above and block it. If it was a suction thing, a dark wind howling down the bones of this house, well, we'd clog its arteries and give it a stroke. Give the whole house a huge shake. A thrombosis.'

'Please,' said Jenkins, 'my own heart is listening. Don't give it notions.'

'So we did,' said Mac. 'There's no roof access from this flat right now; that's what your friend Mr C wants to improve by this rehab. We had to get the ladder out the study window, up in what you call the new house part. We had to steady one end on the window ledge and drop the other onto the pitched roof of the house next door to that, across the yard below. Not to cross to that house but just to have someplace to stand and get our balance so we could turn and begin to scrabble up the slope of the roof over the study, and then cross to where it joins the valley gutter of the older house – Rudge House as you have it – at the chimney stack.'

'Not my favorite thing, heights,' said Jenkins, and closed his eyes. 'But what else was to be done?'

'So we get out there in the filthy fecking weather, and the wind wobbles the ladder like a vengeance. But we get up onto the roof all right and walk around a bit.

'We're up there, poking about the rear chimney stack, the one that leads down here. It's nothing out of the ordinary. They capped it with an ironstone chimney pot shaped like a castle in a big chess game. The leads seemed snug enough. A little cracking in the mortar around the chimney pot. We think maybe this is it. We chip the chimney pot off its mount and set it to, on the parapet. It's a great monstrous thing, and heavy. And then the rapping begins up top, too, coming from inside the house, coming out. But it sounds different when you're outside.'

Winnie wanted to ask that they move into the front room, looking out over the staid, empty forecourt of Rudge House, farther away from the kitchen and the pantry wall still making Morse code at them. But she merely said, 'Oh?'

'It sounded like a voice, is what he wants to say,' said Jenkins. His eyes were brimming. 'Some sound pushed through a throat, that's all, but what throat, or whose, or when, we could not tell.'

'He had his little fit, he did,' said Mac, pointing at Jenkins. 'He lost his brekkie and clawed at his clothes. I wanted to go get the priest and nuke that buggery wailer into kingdom come. But he wouldn't let me.'

'He's a moron,' said Jenkins, not unkindly, 'he's that most superstitious sort of fellow; only bothers to believe in God and the blessed saints because he likes to believe in the devil and his army of familiars. In actual fact, of any given Sunday he'd just as soon run down a man of the cloth and rob the widow of her mite. He has no scruples, don't you know, no faith, only dim fears, which he populates out of *The X-Files* and *The Twilight Zone*.'

Mac said, 'It's a case of house possession, isn't it? And Mister Colum Jenkins bawled like an infant at the sound of it.'

'What did it say?' Winnie only asked because the longer they talked, the more time passed since the nails retracted into the wall, and the easier it became to breathe.

'The consonants were vowels, the vowels were mud, the language was far away, possibly beastly,' said Jenkins.

'Like if you gave a dog electroshock and convinced him he could speak English,' said Mac, 'only he couldn't, of course.'

'Why did you weep?' said Winnie.

'Everyone's got a grief,' said Jenkins, 'mine is mine and none of your concern, but mine came up the chimney to remind me of itself.'

'You're as superstitious as he is, only you use a different grammar,' said Winnie. 'How long did it go on? How loud was it? When did it stop? What did you do then?'

Mac said, 'We couldn't knock up the compound – so many parts sand to so many parts cement – to mortar it into place. Not till the rain let up. So we headed back in. Then the ladder jumped – it just jumped, like a skipping rope – and tipped into the alley. I was already in the window and Jenkins following; he fell on top of me to avoid losing his balance into the alley. He had a seizure then. His pills.'

'Bad heart,' said Jenkins. 'Been so for a while, but frights make it worse.'

'You went a bit snoozers on me. Browned your boxers too, didn't you. Talk about stink.'

'And the ladder . . . ?' said Winnie quickly.

'Still in the alley. Never got to it yet.' Jenkins avoided Mac's eye.

'And the chimney pot is up there uncemented?'

'It's forty, fifty pounds of fired clay. Short of a gale-force wind, nothing's going to budge it. We'll right it soon enough.'

'Tell her about your dream,' said Mac. His head was back and tilted, his eyes hooded, his lips on one side drawn up into a mean pucker. 'When you were out cold. Go on, then.'

'You shut your mouth,' said Jenkins. 'It's none of her concern, nor yours. I'm sorry I spoke of it.'

'Go on, tell her, Jenky-jenks.'

Jenkins took a breath. Winnie saw him halting in his thoughts. 'Now you,' she said to Mac, 'you just hold on.' To be funny, addressing the pantry wall: 'You, I don't want to hear it.' She took Jenkins by the elbow. 'Come on, then. Have a seat. There's nothing here that we can't all walk away from. I'm going to make a cup of tea.'

'Oh, you don't know,' said Jenkins, 'we can walk all we want, but the good it does?'

'You stupid git. Tell her the dream or I will.'

'I told you to shut up,' said Winnie. 'Why don't you just go. Please? Grab a sandwich or something. We're going to have some tea.'

'Wouldn't scarper off, leaving my mate here, not with dead Mr C in the walls, no, darlin', no.'

She stopped talking to him then, made two cups of tea, and sat down near to Jenkins. 'This is all going to seem so ridiculous when we get to the bottom of it,' she said. 'Please. I don't care what you dreamed.'

'Tell her.'

'I don't hold by dreams,' said Jenkins, 'it's not my way. But this was such a dream. I was so deep in it, not drowning but – bewildered – no word for it really. Everything hung in strands of gray, but it wasn't rain and it wasn't fog, it wasn't thread, it wasn't smoke, nor yet was it the scarring of stone with a chisel, nor the ripped seams of old plush curtains, but it was like all that.'

The house held its breath.

'Tell the part about your daughter. It's good, this,' said Mac. He looked ready to down a pint of Guinness and settle back to hear an old geezer retell the story of the Trojan horse. 'Listen and you'll see.'

'I don't want to hear it,' said Winnie. 'I'm not going to listen. The past has nothing to do with us, it's only what we make of the present that counts, the both of you.'

'She's a whore, works the Strand,' muttered Mac appreciatively. 'You want to hear a dream that a dad can have about his daughter?'

'Piss off, I'll skewer you with my screwdriver, you,' said Jenkins, half rising, his face now gamboge.

'What's wanted is a fecking exorcism here before the devil in the pantry wall gets out to claim your soul. What he dreamed,' said Mac, 'was a nightmare. Someone got his daughter, some fiend. His daughter. She's gone missing for several months. Or else she's gone swanning off somewhere, no forwarding address for old Da here. She doesn't come home to wash her smalls in the family sink anymore.'

She got between them before Jenkins attacked him, and there was just a little tussle then. She walloped Mac on the side of the head with a box of Weetabix, to score a point more than to hurt him. Mac retired to the front hall, snorting with laughter. He made a noisy show of taking a leak in the bathroom without closing the door. She stood and settled her hand on Jenkins as his shoulders

heaved and he worked to regain some dignity. 'Let it go, the pair of you,' she said in a low voice, as if he were four years old, 'you're each as bad as the other.' She dragged out a handkerchief from her jacket pocket and handed it to him. 'I don't believe a word of it, anyway; you two are having too much fun beating each other up for me to pay attention.'

'Ah, but he's telling the truth about the girl, she's missing,' wheezed Jenkins. 'And it was a harsh dream. It was my daughter and it was not, in that indecisive, maddening way of dreams. She was talking to me, but she was clawed and chewed—'

'I don't want—'

'It gets worse. There was a fiend; she's lashed—'

'I *don't want*,' said Winnie firmly but picking her way as kindly as she could. 'I have enough dreams of my own, and this is none of my business. I'm paying it no attention at all. It's John's being missing that's getting to you. To me too. Take some deep breaths now. It's okay.'

She waited for Jenkins to regain composure. Mac wandered back into the kitchen with a saucy expression. 'Why does a whore stop having Sunday tea with her da?' said Mac. 'He slags her off one time too many for having a job she can do lying down? His dream is all guilt, nothing but. What has he said to her that gets up her nose? It's his fault for being a silly preachy bugger. He's always telling me to make something of myself too. As if I need to hear his mind about it.'

She took a deep breath and said, 'Look, fellows. This is your job and I don't care if you walk out or if you tear the wall down. I'm going to go to the police, and then I'm going to pack my bags and get out of here.'

She picked up her coat with as much dignity as she could and made her way down the stairs. Out the front door into the sentimental rain that colored the world in halftone shades, as in

Jenkins's dream. How useless her mind was in this situation; it only knew how to work in stories. She couldn't think what could retract those nails into the wall that didn't have a supernatural origin.

She knew what Wendy Pritzke would make of this material, that was the curse: Wendy was with her, working on her own story even as Winnie went sliding and slopping down the hill, trying to remember where she might have seen a police station in Hampstead.

. . . that girl. Maybe one of those slim-hipped boy-girls, downright gaunt. Wearing clothes too big for her, all hanging on her like medieval rags – that coarse-woven stuff like burlap. She'd be out on the pavement where she usually did business, stalking the stalker. A modern-day Robo-prostitute, not to be trifled with, ready to wreak revenge at last on the ghost of Jack the Ripper. On behalf of all the women who'd died at his knife.

And what of this notion of Jack the Ripper, his ghost, howling up the chimney stack, ready to emerge when the time was right, ready to do battle again? He had been called the Ripper because of his tactics with the knife, his talent at bloody vivisection. Could some *fille* Jenkins or someone like her – some modern-day prostitute with an appetite for vengeance – take the life of a ghost? And how could you take the life of someone dead?

And how had he died? Who had ripped the Ripper a hundred-some years ago? The pater-familias, or an intended victim getting the upper hand?

But this was nonsense, a distraction. She had to focus. Could she remember where the police station was? Down Rosslyn Hill, was it? And what would she say when she got there? How could she tell the officer at the desk about superstitious Mac and skeptical Jenkins, and the rapping sound, and the retracting nails? Would the Metropolitan Police come by and tear the place apart? What if they did, and John showed up, having been out on an extended work emergency, or even a tryst of some sort that he was hiding from Allegra Lowe as well as Winnie Rudge? The authorities would be onto him about his plans to put an illegal staircase and deck onto a protected building without the proper permission.

The police would just get on the phone and call John's office; why hadn't she done that? Because she was in the custom usually of staying out of his life, she knew, but it was time to break that old habit.

She stopped and bought a phone card, found his work number in her book, dialed. 'Adjusting Services,' said the voice that answered, a woman's efficient voice in that faintly curdled South African accent.

'John Comestor, please.'

'Who is calling, please?'

'Winifred Rudge.'

She was put on hold a minute. The rain battered at her back. 'Sorry,' said the voice, returning, 'he's not here.'

'This is his cousin. Is he out of town, do you know?'

'I don't know his movements. Frightfully sorry.'

'But has he been in this week? I've just arrived from the States and I'm hoping to see him while I'm here.'

'I don't work this department usually; I'm filling in today for Gillian, who's out sick.'

Gillian and John, an item? No. Gillian was married and sixty besides.

'Look, can you please ask around? I really need to know where he is.'

'I'm afraid I can't do that, miss. It's company policy not to reveal the schedules or destinations of our adjustors. I'm sure you can understand. There's little else I can help you with. I do apologize.'

'You can tell me if you've seen him at least. Please.'

'There are other lines going. Dreadfully sorry.' She rang off.

He was traveling on work; he'd been called away suddenly; why couldn't they just say?

Unless – and this was her fiction spasm happening again – the office staff there had been coached to respond to her with no information at all about him. Why would John do that to her?

Turning back from the phone, blinking into the rain, Winnie thought that if Colum Jenkins called John's office, maybe he'd get a different answer than Winnie had gotten. Maybe the temp would think, 'Not a woman, so not the cousin he's avoiding; I can answer differently.' It was worth a try. There was nothing else to do.

Except, as she passed it, to step into the overheated offices of Bromley Channing Estate Agents, just as the thought struck her, and stand there dripping on the sisal matting. The properties were posted between laminated sheets in the window, hanging chicly on fishing line. Photographs of facades and aren't-we-smart parlors with fresh flowers. Winnie was grateful that the alibi of middle age made all kinds of mild lies possible. 'I was thinking of buying and I saw your sign,' she said to the receptionist, 'on a building in Holly Bush Hill, a flat. Is it taken yet?'

'Oh, a flat,' said the receptionist, as if dealing with anything less than former mansions of Sting was not worth swiveling around in her chair to check on. 'Not many of those this time of year. Spring is when they start to come on the market.'

'What's your range?' said an agent, bobbing forward between desks.

'I saw a sign,' said Winnie. She gave the address.

'That's in the three-to-five file,' said the agent. He meant three to five hundred thousand pounds. A hot market again.

'Oh, yes,' said the receptionist, finding the specs. 'It happens we've got a broker over there at the moment. Aren't we lucky. Can you pop round?'

'I'm on foot,' said Winnie. 'I don't pop anywhere, but I trudge pretty efficiently. Have him wait.'

'Let me get him on the mobile. He'll have to let you in. Hold on. Hello there Kendall Amanda here are you at the Weatherall Walk first-floor one-and-a-half bedrooms? Right. You just stepping out or will you be there a bit?' She aimed her pinky toward her mouth, ready to kill time by destroying her nails, then cocked her chin up toward Winnie to say, 'You can get there in ten minutes, he'll still be there, your name is?'

Winnie paused and then said, 'Wendy. Wendy Pritzke.'

'She'll be right over, American lady. Miss Pritzke.' Amanda slammed the phone and withdrew a photocopied map of Hampstead Village from a drawer, but Winnie said, 'I know where it is, I've told you. I'll just head over there.'

'He's Kendall Waugh,' called Amanda after Winnie.

Waugh was an overweight estate agent with a belt made of rattlesnake skin. He huffed and panted as he led Winnie toward the back of the flat, where a man and a woman were muttering to themselves in disagreement. 'My clients are nearly through here but we have another place to see down on Honeybourne Road,' said Kendall Waugh. 'Let me just answer their questions, Miss Prizzy, and then I'll show you round quickly.'

'I can have a look myself,' she said. She was looking as she spoke. The layout of the flat for sale was identical to John's flat above and, she assumed, to Mrs Maddingly's flat below. Three small rooms in the older building, facing Weatherall Walk, two additional rooms snugly joined to the newer house behind. The flat had belonged to Mrs Maddingly several decades ago, but there was no sign of her whimsical disarray. The place was empty of furniture and sorely in need of sprucing up. The coping was dingy. But Winnie wasn't in the market for a flat, she was supposed to be hunting for some natural cause of the unnatural disasters occurring in John's flat upstairs.

She could see nothing of interest. The chimney stack rose from below and continued above, exactly as geometry and architecture would have it. In the large room it had once heated and lit, the chimney breast was boarded over. 'Could this fireplace be opened up and made to work?' she said to Kendall Waugh.

'I'll just finish here if I may have a moment, one moment,' he called, affecting patience, but unconvincingly. Winnie stood in the gloom, in a box of cold room, and heard the voices in the annex. In certain sorts of rain, when the clouds come down close as they were today, it was sometimes hard to keep the mind fixed to the current year.

She'd noticed the syndrome mostly on gray February days, back when she was living in the more expensive and so more thinly developed Boston suburbs. The wet tree trunks, the low sky the color of tarnished silver, the muted smoky green of yews and white pines and arborvitae, the retracting mounds of dirty snow, the skin of the world pulling in phlegmy puddles, the occasional stab of red in holly berries. In palette, at least, it was the same cold world of the Wampanoags, the Puritans, the colonists and revolutionaries, the Federalists and revivalists and Victorians and so on.

Similarly, in London, the wind bullied the windows in their casings as rattlingly as it must have done all through the past three hundred years and more. The gray skies drawn in over the mighty

and inattentive Atlantic were the very same gray, corrected for reduction of pollution from coal fires, of course, thanks to the Clean Air Act.

She roused herself back to whatever of the here and now she could still trust, or care about. She heard Kendall Waugh answering a question. 'That, I can tell you actually. We've got at the office a very fine pamphlet that talks about this street and actually mentions the structure. It was put up in the early nineteenth century, which makes it almost two hundred years old of course as you know, by a merchant named Rudge. Rudge House and all that. He was in imports, the tea trade.'

'He wasn't a merchant,' said Winnie, 'he wasn't in tea. He started in Cornwall tin mining and became an expert in beam supports. Excuse me, and not to change the subject, but have you been showing people through here all day today?'

Kendall Waugh blinked as if she'd blasphemed against the Queen Mother. 'There's quite a lot of interest in this property actually, I don't think it'll be on the market for long, everything is being snatched up, you won't see its like, its' – he glanced about the icy dusty cramped space – 'period flavor.' Only of course it sounded like *flavour* the way he said it.

She said, 'I'm very sorry but I have to ask. Have you seen or heard anything unusual in this flat while you've been here? Any poundings or noise? Anything out of the ordinary?' The prospective buyers looked sniffy, as if they suspected her of trying to scare them from making an offer. She gave up and closed the door as silently as she could on her way out.

Upstairs, Mac and Jenkins were pacing. 'Mr Jenkins. Please. Call John Comestor at work,' she said to them, slamming her satchel down on John's good eighteenth-century occasional table and the hell with it. 'Ask for him. I'm at my wit's end.'

He did as he was told. 'Put it on speakerphone,' she told him, and when he wouldn't, she leaned over him and pressed the button herself.

There was the snippy receptionist again.

'I'd like to speak to Mr Comestor, please. Mr Colum Jenkins calling.'

'I'm afraid Mr Comestor is away for a while. May I put you in touch with one of his partners?'

'Do you know when he'll be back, or can you tell me where he went?'

'I'm afraid I don't know the answer to either. If you call again when his regular secretary is in you'll be able to find out, I'm sure. She'll be back tomorrow.'

'Well,' said Winnie when Jenkins had rung off, 'you got more than I did. She wouldn't even admit to me that he was away. But if that's the line she's giving out, then at least the company knows he's gone somewhere, and that eliminates the likelihood of' – oh, but she couldn't say the overheated words *foul play*.

They walked back to the kitchen, where they found Mac looking wild-eyed. 'Christ,' said Jenkins.

'You're fecking right,' said Mac in a throttled voice. 'I just thought of this at last.' Among the crowbars and screwdrivers on the floor lay a butcher's knife and a piece of Ethiopian silver. 'I found it in the study, on the wall.' She knew the piece; John had bought it in a market in Lamu, on the Kenyan coast. It was an elaborate cross, not all that finely finished, but beautiful in proportion and design, which probably derived from Byzantine-Coptic models. John was scarcely religious, but he'd liked the rectilinear turnings of its basket weave patterns. 'A key as much as a cross,' John had said.

'I went up to the wall—' Mac was almost in seizures. 'The thing shuddered, buckled; I mean the whole wall convulsed; the boards shook and waved; they went like this—' He undulated

the air with his palms, waist to shoulder heights. 'I was holding the cross and praying—'

'And well might the house protest; you're in no state of grace to be anywhere near a cross,' said Jenkins irritably. 'Now you're only pathetic, Mac. Get off home. You don't even believe in Jesus, you fool; you might as well be holding a plastic statue of Princess Diana. Give over.'

'Ah but—' Mac said, and then said, 'you bloody turncoat, denying me what my own eyes saw while you moon over your sorry dreams: look at that and call me pathetic.' He pointed. It seemed that the upright boards of the pantry wall were beginning to sweat.

'Rain coming in,' said Jenkins, 'surely? We oughtn't have moved that chimney pot. The wood is swelling from moisture.'

'You're a bloody eejit. Look at it.'

About chest height, in the center of the paneled section, the old white paint was beginning to blister bluely, to fester in small pustules, making a rash. Something – an earlier application of paint, surely? – was showing through. It looked like a bruise, eggplant now, now yellow-blue. There was a gash forming, like the place a knife would drive if it were slicing the heart out of a body. As they watched, the gash bled a ragged ghost of a line twelve, fourteen inches long, perpendicular to the floor, as if following the line of a row of buttons on a vest. Other marks began to appear, some on either side, slowly dripping on diagonals toward one another.

'A tree? A key? A snowflake?' said Winnie. 'A diagram of the Underground?'

'Jaysus mercy,' said Mac, 'look what it is. It's a crucifix with a figure on it, struggling to get off. It's a cross with an X through it.'

'It's a bad problem with moisture in the walls is what it is,' said Winnie, 'and if there's an older wall of plaster behind those boards, it's all crumbled? Something like that?'

'We'll sort it out Monday,' said Jenkins. He seemed better now.

'Sort it out Monday?' said Winnie. 'I'm not averse to a little inconvenience during renovations, but really: the hall has begun to do involuntary . . . *hieroglyphics* at us? And *now's* the time you decide to clock off?'

Jenkins said, 'Things in their own time, miss. Now, don't get riled up any more than you need. Mac's a good boy but he's barmy. Mac, get your things and let's go.'

'We can't leave now,' said Mac. 'She's right: something's there. Have you no eyes?'

'I have my duties.' Jenkins was going stodgy on them all at once. 'Obligation before hallucination, that's my order of business. I'm off, and I suggest you come with me.'

'God is talking to you and you're scarpering?' Mac was incredulous.

'God can get my ear anytime he wants, including on the Tube. Are you coming or are you waiting for another installment?'

'He's obsessed,' said Mac bitterly, kicking at the silver cross; Winnie scurried after it and picked it up. 'Every Friday and Saturday night up and down the Strand, interviewing the workforce to see if they know where his daughter is. She's probably emigrated to Australia.'

'I'll thank you to mind your own affairs.' Jenkins burrowed into his coat and hunched himself into its raised collar. 'He's a good boy, miss, but I'd turf him out, were I you.'

'I'll just pack up here and be out in a flash,' said Mac. 'I'm keeping vigil for no ghost, not if you're leaving.'

Jenkins shrugged and nodded ambiguously, and left the kitchen without looking again at the wall. One only needed a mission, that was all, and Jenkins had his mission. It was how he got through: committing himself to something impossible.

She heard his feet tramp down the staircase, and the wind picked up.

The pantry stopped performing for them, but there was a thud overhead. The wind whistled almost with the sound of a pig's squeal, or a baby's, and it was underscored by a percussive roll – Winnie thought it might be thunder. They heard an interior wallop, something breaking through in this flat, and an exterior crash, as of smashing pottery. She knew what that outside noise was, and so did Mac.

They hurried to the front room and craned to peer out the window. Jenkins had been struck on the back of the head. The chimney pot was in shards around him.

Winnie said, 'What is it, what is it in London, the number for emergency, I can't remember,' and she ran to the phone. 'Mac,' she said crossly when he didn't answer; she turned so abruptly that as the phone came away the plastic housing of the tip of the jack split into plastic fragments. The dial tone dried up.

Mac had gone downstairs to tend Jenkins. She hoped he would pull him out of the forecourt anyway in case someone nosed a car in and tried to park on the sidewalk as Hampstead locals often did. Winnie descended one flight and thumped on the door of the flat, in case the estate agent was still in there collecting a deposit check, but as far as she could tell the flat was deserted again. She continued to the ground floor to find Mrs Maddingly huddled in the doorway, several cats snaking around her ankles, and Mr Kendall Waugh on his cell phone dialing for rescue services. At the edge of the forecourt the rain-cloaked figures of neighbors hovered. 'Lost *that* sale,' Kendall Waugh was murmuring while he was on hold with emergency. 'The whole place is collapsing, said the husband, and they fled. Hello? Yes, are you there?'

'It's a good thing the cats are house cats,' said Mrs Maddingly in a carrying tone, as if addressing Jenkins's prone form reprovingly. 'It might have been one of them took the blow.'

'He's alive, he's breathing,' said Mac, on his knees in the wet, 'but they always say not to move the body in case of snapped spine.'

'Heard that before, and this one's no rag doll,' Winnie muttered. She came forward. Jenkins had a look of peace on his face, but his nose and mouth tilted too near the gushing gutter. She took off her sweater and folded it into a damp mound and elevated his head an inch or so, hoping she wasn't misaligning vertebrae in the neck column. Then Mrs Maddingly in her house slippers was leaning over with a vinyl tablecloth. 'Will keep the water off him, don't you know,' she said, and so it proved to do. He rested, comatose, under the red-and-white checks until the relief crew arrived and carried him away on a stretcher, with Mac in attendance – she could see it once he was in the ambulance – weeping.

Kendall Waugh departed for the office. Mrs Maddingly repaired to her parlor for her pills. There was nothing for Winnie to do but go back inside and see whether the place was less creepy now that the workmen were gone. They had after all been on-site for most of the day, and their superstitions had been contagious. She'd felt claustrophobic. Now the blistered cross on the pantry wall looked more imprecise, less a message from the otherworld and more a problem of woodworm and rot. The room was silent.

Winnie made herself a fresh cup of tea and spread her sweater out on some towels to dry. She changed her stockings and lit a few candles and looked at John's CD collection. She selected a Shostakovich compilation that led off with the String Quartet no. 8. A bit unnerving when it came to the first iteration of the three staccato notes, the same notes played in succession like a fist hammering against a door. But then she laughed at her imagination, at last, and felt better, and entirely alone in the flat, for the first time. The problem of John's absence was still unresolved, but at least his office knew he was away. It seemed less worrisome now that she could be alone here with her own thoughts.

Then she remembered that there had been two noises, one of

them inside. All of the flat was open to visual inspection from the front hall except John's room. She hesitated at the doorway and then she went in.

The painting of Scrooge or Rudge, whoever, had fallen off its picture hook. It had landed at an angle, wedged between floor and wall, face out. To her ignorant eye the thing seemed undamaged. The figure looked strange from this viewpoint, as if lurching up toward her from the depths of a pool, swimming lightward out of a menacing void of icy depths and pursuing spirits.

She slid the painting under the bed, so that she would have to look neither at the image nor its inscription.

She sat down at the table in the front room and peered out the windows again. No sign of the accident. No sign of much of anything, really; John's front window had a protected view. The house to one side was built forward by nine or ten feet; its tie-beamed wall facing Weatherall Walk was hung with ivy, since no windows looked out in this direction. The house on the other side, across the passage, had several windows; one was a medallion sort, clearly set high in a stairwell, and another had been bricked up. For all the intimacy of near buildings, there was no way to glimpse neighborly comings and goings. One might have been sitting in a Manhattan apartment looking into an unusually capacious air shaft, albeit one ornamented with vines and architectural niceties. In the gray rain-light, the privacy was intensified. Welcome too.

> Rain on the rooftop
> Rain on the tree
> Rain on the green grass
> But not on me.

She opened up her laptop and sat there thinking about the day and, inevitably, about Wendy Pritzke.

The row of new buildings in Rowancroft Gardens, erected in 1888, was among the first in Hampstead to be designed with electrification in mind. A household illuminated with clean safe light! The wattage was low at first, probably, only a half-step up from the murkiness of oil lamps or the dreary seepage of gaslight behind amber glass panels.

In the new modern shadows, a daughter of the paterfamilias, or a maid, might go upstairs, thinking herself alone in the house as she steps from room to room. Thinking the butcher's apprentice had left the premises when shown to the door, not knowing that he had cannily released the safety latch when she wasn't looking, so he'd be able to get back inside. Her shadow now preceding her, now following her, as she goes up the stairs to the top landing, along the passage, to the back of the house where the new house linked knuckles with the old one around the chimney stack. Her electrified shadow being met by the shadow of the intruder, and merging with it, so that the two shadows became one, and she doesn't notice until he flips the light off behind her, and the two shadows merge into the full darkness of the room, and she hears his breathing.

She jumped and cursed at the sound of the doorbell – then thought: John, wanting not to frighten me, as I had wanted not to frighten him. She ran to the buzzer and said, 'Yes, yes?'

'Winifred, it's Allegra. May I come up, please.'

The tone of voice made it sound as if this were a rhetorical question. Allegra was there to prove she had the run of the

place. 'Oh, of course,' Winnie answered, and pressed the electric door release, but once she heard the street door close and the footsteps on the stairs, she couldn't help but add, to herself, 'if you must.'

Winnie left the front door open and retreated – not as far as the kitchen, but to the more neutral arena of the sitting room, where she picked up the paperback copy of *The Black Prince*, as if she'd been interrupted. She wanted to be sitting. Allegra came in with a gymnastic lightness, shucking off her Burberry and draping it on a coat stand in the hall before Winnie looked up again and said, 'You've picked bad weather to come calling.'

'Well, I tried to ring,' said Allegra, 'but the phone seems to be out. The machine doesn't pick up and I got worried.'

'Oh, yes,' said Winnie, 'we had a problem with the phone. I ripped the wiring out of the wall by mistake. I'll have to go down to Camden and get a replacement line. Is there still a Rumbelow's in Camden?'

'I wouldn't know,' said Allegra. 'It's beastly and I'm soaked through after a mere five-minute walk. I'll make a cup of tea, if I might.' Before Winnie could approve or forbid it, Allegra slid into the kitchen and flipped on the light. 'Oh, the mess of home repair,' she called; 'how can you stand it? I'd take myself out to a hotel.'

'I'm at home in mess,' said Winnie. 'It's my natural habitat.' She turned over the pages of the book without seeing them. 'I don't suppose you've heard from John?'

'Right you are,' called Allegra. 'Nor you?'

'No, and now the phone's gone out, so I won't, I guess,' said Winnie. As before, in the interest of finding out what had happened to John, she wanted some intimacy with Allegra, but she also wanted to preserve her distance. She threw the paperback down and followed Allegra at least as far as the door of the kitchen. Displaying her own familiarity of the terrain Allegra was complaining, 'The workers have shifted everything; the tea is not here, and all the spoons are filthy. Don't they ever wash up?'

'Tea's on the window ledge there.'

'Foul smell. That's what you were over talking about? What about that sound?' said Allegra. 'I became interested despite myself. I thought I should come round to see how things stood—'

'Things are as I said before,' said Winnie, shrugging, 'except the sound seems to have stopped, I'm afraid. The way an ache inevitably does when you finally get to the dentist with your bad tooth.'

Allegra filled the electric kettle. 'I really came round to see you, I suppose,' she admitted. 'I wondered how you were getting on here.'

'I'm not moving,' said Winnie, dreading an invitation to stay at Allegra's.

'Oh, it's your choice, of course. I only thought you seemed on edge a bit, and when I ran into Rasia McIntyre in the hall she said you'd been up there visiting for an hour or so.'

'Rasia was the one on edge. She was in a mood to confide. I couldn't get away.'

'Well, she asked me if you were all right, and I got to thinking I might have been more— I mean, if John should be in touch and I chat with him before you do, I'd like to say that I had come round to make sure.'

'Oh, I'm fine here,' said Winnie. 'If John calls you, tell him that I thank him for leaving me the house to myself for a change. I'm getting some good work done.' The notion that John might talk to Allegra before attempting to reach her. The very notion of it. 'I wouldn't be as kind to you in the same circumstances,' she added. 'That wind.'

'Oh, it is fierce, isn't it? My late-afternoon client from

Hampstead Garden Suburb called to cancel because trees are down and the power's been cut. You should see the traffic coming up the high street. A river of lights rising out of Belsize Park, and the wipers going mad. The rain's just too heavy for them to do much good.' She dunked her tea bag a couple of times and then let it sink to the bottom. 'Shall we sit in the front room? I'll dry off before it's time to get wet again.'

'Maybe it'll stop.'

'Not till tomorrow morning, if then, according to Radio Four.' Allegra executed a beautifully balanced maneuver, setting her teacup on the copy of *The Black Prince* while at the same time lifting and positioning an ankle, heronlike, under her rear end before she sat down. 'You're reading Iris Murdoch, or is that John?'

'It's his copy,' said Winnie. She didn't want to talk about John or who was reading what. She went over to her computer and thought about turning it off. All its little electronic brains stewing about Wendy Pritzke in London, Wendy deluding herself over sensational Jack the Ripper nonsense while trying to avoid the more serious issues ahead in Romania. If late-nineteenth-century electrification brought a new grade of shadows into the world, computers ushered in a new category of ambiguity and untetheredness. All the possible lies and revelations that their million internal monkeys might type! 'Did you know,' she said, 'there was some notion at one point that a cousin of Virginia Woolf's was the Ripper? Someone who had delusions, a manic-depressive maybe, or a schizoid. She with her fine-grade madness was related to a cousin who I guess killed himself. Two versions of the family malady.'

'Are you writing about Virginia Woolf now?'

'I'm thinking about writing about a woman interested in Jack the Ripper.'

'I see.' Polite distaste.

And Wendy Pritzke sets her hooker revenge story *in your house*, Allegra, *in your kitchen*. A butcher boy delivers his merchandise right where you do your gluey handprints. Winnie didn't say this aloud. Instead, getting up to turn off the computer, she said, 'You were going to tell me about your oddest experience doing those hand molds. Remember?'

'I do,' said Allegra. She laughed, but not prettily, not throatily. 'You don't really want to hear it.'

'Oh, sure I do.'

'It was so silly. People can be perverse, when you come right down to it.'

'In their idiosyncrasies they reveal themselves, if they're lucky enough to have any.'

'A couple of parents had a premature baby who died, that's all,' said Allegra, looking away. 'They were friends of a cousin of mine and I couldn't squirm out of it. I had to go to the morgue in the hospital and take the mold there.'

'Surely that's against the law?'

'People bend around laws when it comes to times like that. Who cares, really?'

'You should move to Massachusetts, the baby trade is very strong there. You'd have no end of work. What did it look like?'

After a while, Allegra said, 'Well, in the twentieth week the thumb can oppose the other fingers.'

'I see,' said Winnie. 'Handy. No pun intended,' she added.

'I should think not.'

'I went to school at Skidmore,' said Winnie. 'We got the Albany papers sometimes. Once I read a historical feature about a baby dying back in the early twenties. Some dark-haired teenager walked into a post office to mail a package going to an address just around the corner. Later the postmistress remembered the customer, but she'd disappeared. The package turned out to be a naked, lifeless girl child born three days earlier. She'd been smothered, and mailed with a five-dollar bill to help defray funeral expenses. No one could track down her mother so she was buried at the city's expense under a headstone calling the infant Parcella Post.'

'Winnie,' said Allegra, 'it takes an awful lot to put me off my appetite, but *really*.'

Was there something about Jack the Ripper and his prostitutes, something about the babies that came and didn't come? What was it? Later.

She reached toward the off switch, a little panel to be depressed into the side of the screen. As her hand hovered, the endless snow-falling screen saver suddenly froze. (Screen saver of 'The Dead,' she called it, after Joyce's last line.) Every corner, every centimeter of grid filled up with random figures,

For an instant she thought the image had mirrored the marks on the pantry wall. But it was gone too quickly to be sure. Like most clues. 'Oh, Christ,' she said.

The lights flickered and went out. 'What are you trying to store in that thing, you're draining the power out of all of Ham and High,' said Allegra drolly, getting up behind her. 'Not enough memory. You've power-surged North London.'

'I just got a start. It's nothing. You've seen computer paralysis before, I'm sure.'

The pounding began again. 'Oh, is that the noise?' said Allegra calmly. The room was furred gray, darkening as they spoke. 'Is that what you were complaining of? And well you should. Who could write stories while that row is thundering on?'

'But it's not in the kitchen,' said Winnie. 'Before, it was in the kitchen.' Despite herself she reached out and gripped Allegra's elbow. 'Now it's in the hall.'

'Calm down,' said Allegra. 'I know you're excitable; just relax.'

They went into the dark foyer. The thudding was out in the stairwell, something hitting the door to the flat. 'There's a back entrance, isn't there?' Allegra said conversationally.

'No, there isn't, how could there be? The back of the house rears up against the back of yours, as you yourself explained to me. This is the only way in.'

A voice, a human voice out there. 'Damn.'

'Mac?' said Winnie with relief, and went to the door. 'What are you up to now?' She turned the handle. The door was locked – from the outside. She twisted the knob.

'I'm driving nails,' said Mac from the other side of the door, 'but the light's just gone out and I've bashed my fecking thumb.'

'What are you nailing?'

'The door shut,' said Mac thickly. 'I'm locking it in there. I'm going for a priest or something.'

'Don't be a fool. Open this door,' said Winnie.

'Winnie, who is this? One of the builders?' said Allegra. 'What do you mean by this?'

'Ah, it's got a voice now: and it is the voice of Jenkins's daughter,' cried Mac. He sounded bereft and beyond. A few moments later Allegra and Winnie were at the open window looking down into the forecourt, shouting at him, calling for help, but the wind was rising and their voices were lost. As Mac streaked away, he flung his hammer into the bushes. He didn't look back.

Stave Three

From the Chimney Inside the Chimney

– that was the best Winnie could imagine it for herself, a succession of shafts within shafts, like nesting dolls – the sound unsettled the silence. A hammering precisely parroted the noise of Mac's labors, as if the space behind the chimney breast harbored some thrumming armature. The realization dawned on Winnie – and, she guessed, on Allegra – that they were indeed imprisoned in John Comestor's flat, and the chimney's unmusical thud began to recede, but slowly, a long train passing very far away, on a very still night.

'Phone?' said Allegra.

'Disconnected. You remember – you tried to call,' said Winnie.

'We'll climb out through a window. He may be coming back here – with his mates or something.'

'We'll keep an eye out the windows. We'd see him coming. Don't be hysterical.'

'It would seem to me this is a singularly apt time for hysteria.' Allegra raised an eyebrow, which in her circle probably passed for an expression of extreme nervous agitation, Winnie supposed.

They paced the apartment. The back two Victorian rooms were windowless, boxed in by the vacant flat rented to Japanese in the adjoining building. Some dingy skylights were pocked with pellets of gray rain. 'Could we climb up there?'

'Doubtful.'

The forward Georgian rooms – the older rooms – were not much better. The side windows gave out on a bleak yard of rubbish bins, the front ones on the recessed forecourt. There was no convenient drainspout to scrabble down. And they could scream all they wanted – feeling idiotic, they tried – but the storm was hitting its stride, and the winds barreled abroad with vigor and commotion. And the lights were out, and the gloom was rising in the room.

Winnie, hunting for candles in the kitchen, afraid to turn her back to the chimney stack but doing it anyway, thought: Allegra Lowe is almost the last person I'd like to be incarcerated with. John Comestor's 'friend.' How those imagined double quotes clenched around the word *friend*. They squeezed the real meaning out of the word and made it vulnerable to infection by irony.

Winnie commanded herself to speak levelly. 'Here's some dinner tapers anyway, and there'll be matches by the fireplace, no doubt.'

'Trust John to be equipped with beeswax tapers and no torch.'

'How extensive do you think this power outage is?'

'Impossible to tell with the clouds so low. I suspect the damage is only local, though that doesn't do us any good.'

'Or any harm, either.'

'I'm not at all superstitious. But I don't care for the thing in the chimney. I'm glad it's quietened down some.' And so it had.

'It doesn't like the fellows.'

'What's the name of that cretin?'

'Mac. Our poltergeist doesn't trust him, or either of them. Maybe for good reason.'

They settled themselves in the front room, near the most public window. If Mac should come back and start opening the door, they'd holler bloody murder again, and maybe this time some neighbor struggling home in the storm would hear their cries. 'What in the world do you think the thing is?' said Allegra.

'I have no idea,' said Winnie, looking away.

They sipped. Somewhere, probably down the hill at the Royal Free Hospital, Jenkins's lungs were going up and down, up and down. Somewhere farther out, in the City, perhaps his errant daughter was having a twinge, pausing in the downpour, regretting the distance from her father. 'John told me,' said Allegra, 'your side of the family has some pretense to descending from Ebenezer Scrooge?'

'Oh did he. What else did he tell you?'

'Don't be like that. I'm only trying to make the best of a tiresome turn of events.'

Winnie thought it better to talk about the Scrooge nonsense than about John Comestor. If she slipped and let herself think he was dead, in any way – half dead, part dead, gone as gone – she would rise up shrieking.

But how much to tell? 'It's this house,' she said. 'Rudge House. The Scrooge stories that got passed down the family may derive primarily from that accident of sound. Rudge, Scrooge, Scrooge, Rudge. There's a little something in the family letters about it, but most of the references, after the fact, are mocking.'

'So what kind of story is it, to be mocked or believed?'

She didn't want to say. 'The builder of this house was my great-great-great-grandfather. Five generations back. A man named Ozias Rudge. His dates are – oh, I don't remember exactly, 1770s into the mid-Victorian age. He was involved in tin mines in Cornwall. He worked for a large firm – the Mines Royal or something like that – as an expert in timber supports. Something of an architectural engineer, I suppose you'd say now. There was a mine collapse, and many deaths, and Rudge lost his nerve in a big way. He came to London, took rooms in Lincoln's Inn Fields, and set himself up in the building trade. But bad London air scared him. Fearing consumption, maybe suffering from lung ailments from his mining days, he built a country house for himself in Hampstead to take the airs from time to time. This house, at the crown of Holly Hill, of course. To which he repaired alone, a middle-aged man without a wife and family.'

'This sounds very little like Scrooge. But you have the

conviction of the natural storyteller. Do go on. I'm enjoying this hugely.'

Winnie doubted that, but went on anyway. 'Be patient. Ozias Rudge had designed supports for the adits and stopes of tin mines. He parried this expertise into designing structural reinforcement of old buildings, using iron beams. He must have been close to a pioneer in the field. His clients included governors and overseers of ancient institutions, churches, the older colleges, that sort of thing. Here, and in France. There was good money to be had in architectural renovation and preservation at that time, and Ozias Rudge raked it in.'

Allegra suppressed a yawn. This pleased Winnie somehow and she continued more happily. 'During one particular exercise in the early 1820s, Ozias Rudge was called to Normandy – to Mont-Saint-Michel – where the walls of some crypt had begun to buckle, threatening the stability of the buildings that leaned upon it. Rudge went and did his work, and while he was gone, a business associate in London made himself overly familiar with a woman that O.R. had been courting, on and off. Rudge, on returning to England, learned the truth, and dueled with his partner and killed him. Or so it's said.'

'A horrible tale. Our ancestors were so . . . sincere. This did not win the widow back, I take it.'

'No.' Winnie was disappointed that Allegra wasn't more shocked. 'But now I'm arriving at the confluence of stories. All of that is prologue. Old O.R. apparently became a curmudgeon worthy of the title Scrooge. He grew sullen and inward. He retired full-time to his country house. I mean here.'

'Yes, yes, I understand. Rudge House.'

'Maybe Ozias Rudge suffered remorse about the man he'd killed, or the miners who lost their lives in the mine collapse. Maybe he had weak nerves. Anyway, he became celebrated in Hampstead as a man who was pestered by ghosts. You can see a reference to him in the histories of Hampstead under 'ghost stories.' The tourist pamphlets don't make the Dickens association, though. That's our own private family theory.'

'How do you work out such an association?'

'As a twelve-year-old boy Charles Dickens came to stay in Hampstead. In 1824, I think. All recollections of the young Dickens suggest that he had a lively and receptive mind. It's said that when Ozias Rudge was about fifty, a garrulous single man, probably lonely, a nutcake, he met the young Dickens and told him – as he told everyone – about his being haunted. Hampstead wasn't a large village in those days, and Rudge would have been a figure of some importance. And Dickens was always impressed by people of importance, and spent some time, especially as a young person, trying to be impressive back. We guess he may have befriended O.R., and listened to his tales of woe.'

'Shockingly thin evidence.'

'In adult life, Dickens said that the memory of children was prodigious. It was a mistake to fancy children ever forgot anything – those are nearly his exact words. So if he heard some tale of nocturnal hauntings of a guilt-ridden scoundrel, mightn't he have remembered enough of it to turn it into *A Christmas Carol*, twenty years or so later? It's not a very big jump from Rudge to Scrooge.'

'I see,' said Allegra. 'I'm rather less convinced than I expected, frankly.'

'Well, there's the painting too.'

'The painting?'

Winnie studied Allegra to see if she was putting on ignorance. 'You know, the painting in John's bedroom.'

'I couldn't say I know anything about paintings in John's bedroom.'

Oh, the coyness of it. Winnie was on her feet and feeling her way, and back with the painting in a moment. 'Look at the back,'

she said, 'there's one bit of business. *NOT Scrooge but O.R.* Then look at the image and tell me if you think it's the Scrooge that Dickens imagined or a painting of a real nineteenth-century nutcase.' She glanced around for a place to hang it, and feeling feisty, she thudded into the kitchen and picked up a hammer again. She jerked at a nailhead in the pantry wall, pulling it out an inch. This time it stayed put, and on it she slung the painting of the frantic old gentleman. 'Now look at it and tell me what you think.'

'Is this a quiz show? I have no opinions about this painting, nor about whether Rudge was the model for Scrooge or not. Does it matter that much?'

'I'm not saying I believe it,' said Winnie crossly. 'I'm telling you what I've been told.'

'So did your grand-thingy ever mention the ghosts of Christmas Past, Present, and to Come?'

'Of course not. That was the sentimental invention of Dickens the storyteller. Like any writer, Dickens stole what he wanted from someone's real life and made off with it, and richly bastardized it and gussied it up. But who do you think this is? In the painting? Is it a portrait of someone unsound, or someone seriously haunted?'

'You're the astrologer – I yield to your professional opinion.'

'Don't patronize me,' she said, in a temper, 'don't condescend.' She was rising, she was putting aside the teacup, she was working hard not to throw it against the wall. 'Let's just put this ghost to bed, this wobble in the drains, this nonsense. Come on.'

'You mean?'

'Let's exhume it.'

There was an electric surge, but it wasn't a phantasmic event, it was the faintest tremor that occurs when the nature of a relationship shifts. Maybe Allegra didn't feel it – who could tell what she felt? Rather than compete with Allegra for the attention of John Comestor, Winnie would prefer to ally herself with Allegra against some third agent. 'Come on, it's the ladies against the pantry, and not for the first time in history, I'll bet.'

Before long Winnie and Allegra had amassed a dozen or so tapers in a circle on the kitchen floor and windowsill and counters. The feeling began to be one of a Girl Scout campfire, the recital of a ghost story without teeth sufficient enough to bite.

'All right, you,' said Winnie to *Not Scrooge but O.R.* 'Stand aside.' But now he looked, with his hand against the shadowy doorframe, as if he were blocking the way, keeping them from the shrieky diaphanous thing painted in the shadowy background behind him. Winnie removed the painting anyway.

'I like working with my hands.' Allegra picked up a crowbar.

'You make better mistakes with your hands than your head,' said Winnie. 'I mean one does. I mean I do.' She took a hammer and a tea towel. 'Okay, pantry, we're getting in touch with our inner demolition team.'

'What mistakes do you make with your head? I don't know what you mean,' said Allegra.

'It's all plot. Life is plot. Plot mistakes,' said Winnie. 'What happens, and why.' She ran the towel over the surface of the wood, easily erasing the slashed sign of the cross. 'In life you get at least the appearance of choice. In a book, even one I'm writing myself, the characters seem to have no choices. Only destiny. How it will work out.'

'We *have* no choice,' said Allegra. 'We can't choose for this to be drains, or to be the ghost of your cousin. It will be whatever it is.'

'We can choose to stop exploring the minute we want,' said Winnie, 'the minute it's too much for us. Poor Wendy can't—' She didn't go on. She just began to extract the nails from the vertical planking. This time the nails did not sink back into the wall.

★

Wendy and John in a room, high up over a dark city.

'What if it is the ghost of Jack the Ripper in that chimney stack?'

'What if it is?'

'What if someone lets it out without knowing it?'

'The curse of the mummy? The revenge threat on the tombstone of William Shakespeare?'

'What if it needs to take some time to gather its – memory – its intentionality – to remember what it had been before it died? The way a child takes so long, coming up from a nap, to wake up? Come back to itself? What if the wall opens and nothing much emerges, but an invisible something, hovering in midair: taking its time to grow and amass invisible bulk to it, remember its appetites? Like a bundle of cancer cells, taking time to metastasize into a parasitic colony?'

'You mean,' said John, 'what if it has remembered its calling, and it has fastened on you as a possible victim?'

'I don't mean that, exactly,' she said. 'Everything isn't about me.'

They looked down on the city at night. It might have been a huddle of medieval houses and pubs and sheds, given how the silted shadows obliterated any telltale indication of the modern age. They might have been in Hamelin, with the circuit of rats making a hangman's rope around the perimeters of the town.

'That's the nails, then,' said Allegra. 'Not hard to grip, for all that; I guess your worker friends managed that much for us.' The extracted nails, some of them tooled four-sided, lay in a pile like ancient and capable thorns.

'To the boards, then,' said Winnie. She took a hammer and used it to drive the screwdriver between the uprights. The paint was old and hard, and enough layers thick that the boards resisted separation, but as soon as Winnie had managed a small purchase Allegra joined with a chisel. The top of the first board came away from its backing with a sound like dry suction. A stir of dusty plaster breathed into the hollow made by the board pulling away from the wall.

'Not a sound. Nobody home,' said Allegra.

'Not yet,' said Winnie.

'Well, let's demolish the home before it gets back, and then maybe it'll go someplace else.'

'There's not always someplace else to go,' said Winnie.

'There's always someplace else to go,' said Wendy.

Then the first board was off, set down delicately on the floor. The wall behind it, bricks laid slapdashedly, cemented with a coarse mortar.

'Surely this can't be a chimney stack?' said Allegra.

'Why can't it be?'

'Look at the joining compound. Hardly smoothed over, and full of gaps. A chimney fire should have burned this house down long ago. Furthermore, no evidence of smoke on the back of this board.'

'So you be the detective for a change. Or the novelist. What do you think it means?'

'I don't know, but there's no chimney here.'

'Of course there is, be reasonable,' said Winnie. 'There are fireplaces on each of the floors below, and there's a chimney stack up top. Jenkins and Mac told me. How was the house heated and its smoke vented for two hundred years without a functioning respiratory system?'

'Well, I don't know. Let's keep going. Maybe we'll find something else.'

The second board was easier than the first, and the third easier still. Some boards had to be broken in half, and the upper and lower parts extracted with force, dislodging ceiling plaster, which was making ghosts of Allegra and Winnie, and dusting their eyes.

'None of these boards look like one another,' said Winnie, looking more closely. 'Different heights, widths, and thicknesses too – you didn't notice that from the pantry side; the wall seemed smooth.'

'Meaning there were gaps, and air passages.'

'Chimney flutes. The origin of the noise.'

'Which is even more gone than it seemed before.'

'All we need is the lights back on, and someone to jump through the door and say, 'Surprise, it's your birthday,' and balloons and cake and confetti.'

'Right. But what about the bricking of this chimney stack?'

The exposed wall was a crazy quilt of handiwork. The bricks were of uneven shapes, some laid in vertical patches suggestive of a lazy herringbone. 'The one thing that could be supposed,' said Allegra, running a hand over the surface ruminatively, 'is that this wall was put up hastily.'

Winnie saw she was right. The worker or workers hadn't stopped to trim excess filler with a trowel or make sure the line was true. Maybe the boards had been slapped up hastily, too, before the mortar was dry.

Winnie stooped down and looked at the boards again. 'If there was some sort of pattern appearing on the surface of the planks, maybe it was just moisture sponging out through nail holes punched in two hundred years ago. Just a freak natural phenomenon. Or who knows, maybe the workers were superstitious, and hammered in a design of nails to represent a cross.'

'Unlikely, though I suppose possible. But that is no reason for the nails to retract themselves showily into the wall when your men Jenkins and Mac were around to witness it.'

'I witnessed it too, Allegra, and my vision is twenty-twenty. Furthermore—' She didn't continue her sentence, which had threatened to be 'there's still no explanation why the same pattern would show up on my computer screen just before the power went out.' But one thing at a time.

'I feel fairly confident that there's no ghost of John Comestor back here,' said Allegra. 'Not even any interestingly dirty laundry.'

'No,' Winnie agreed, 'slapdash as it is, this wall has been up for a while.'

The rain. The wind around the house. Noise outside, interior stillness. Silence settling upon them, as if snow, doing the thing that snow does: erasing the margins, blunting the particularities, distorting the differences between near and far.

She had to look to see for sure; no, it wasn't snow. Just the silence that snow often implies.

If Jack the Ripper were abroad again, pale as a sheet of cellophane, would a sudden squall of snow fill in his outline, make him look like the ghosts in Saturday morning cartoons? White on white, the ghost in the snow, more visible yet still invisible.

'Damn John for his little renovations!' said Allegra suddenly, in the silence, as the darkness did nothing but deepen, by degrees almost as distinct one from its neighbor as seconds marked by a loud clock.

She looked at the bricks, and then put a hand against them. The bricks had no way of speaking to her, not like the boards oozing their blisters. Now that the boards were removed, she imagined that they had bled, that the nail holes had been small valves pumping blood. The liquor seeping in obscene drips along the warped surfaces of some long-dead tree. But there had been no blood, only paint blisters.

'If it is Jack the Ripper,' she said, 'maybe after all this time, he doesn't want to come out. He doesn't want to be exhumed. He doesn't want to be called back to the only service he knew, that of ripping the throats of prostitutes, that of murdering fertile women.'

He tore out the voices of his victims when he slit their throats; that much was documented fact. The harsher truth was that he also tore the voices out of their wombs: the life stories that their unborn children would never tell. The story of the future that only children can tell back to their parents.

He wanted no future for those women. Why would he want a future for himself, now? Killed himself, maybe by suicide, his bones plastered into a fake chimney stack—

'The chimney inside the chimney,' said Winnie, getting it. 'That's a fake chimney stack.'

'What do you mean?'

'There's no need for the bricks to be laid true, or for the mortar to be smooth. This is only a second skin of brick around the genuine chimney stack. That's why there's no smoke on the inside of the boards, that's why the house never burned down due to bad flues. This wall was put up hastily, to box up whatever is in there.'

'You may be right.' Allegra sounded surprised. She didn't get up to look closer. 'But we still don't know what's inside.'

Wendy would not release him upon the world; that was, perhaps, his only refuge. Perhaps he'd killed himself to keep from killing more women. Why undo his death?

But why wasn't he dead in there, then?

'I don't get it about ghosts,' said Winnie. 'We all die unsatisfied. We all leave unfinished business. Only the Virgin Mother, assumed into heaven, managed to book the flight she wanted. Everyone else goes on crisis standby. What makes some figures capable of becoming phantoms, and others not?'

'Maybe it has to do with how much we want to leave unfinished business,' said Allegra. 'Some days, if I'm annoyed enough, I'd like nothing better than to be struck down by a number forty-six bus on Rosslyn Hill and leave my heirs and assigns a mare's nest of unfinished business, just to punish them for being a trial to me while I was alive. Don't you want to open that wall, after all this?'

'I won't do it,' said Wendy. 'I won't.'

John said, 'You've come this far, and you won't?'

'No.' She wouldn't tell him her thesis about Jack the Ripper and his preference to stay in his own cask of amontillado. She didn't care to sound as if she were in any way sympathetic to a mass murderer. She revived in herself an air of business snap. 'It's better to leave the possibilities as possibilities, rather than dry them up in the hot air of scrutiny. Besides, John' – looking at her watch – 'haven't we a plane to catch?'

'We've hours yet.'

'I'm done with London. Let's go early and get a meal at Heathrow. It'll be better than whatever pig's hoofs they serve on Air Tarom.'

'Now you've got me pestered with curiosity. Let's just dislodge a few bricks and see.'

'I won't do it,' she said again, being in charge.

'I won't,' said Winnie. Allegra's expression was hidden in the gloom, but Winnie could almost hear the lifting of her eyebrows. 'I wouldn't open that wall of brick for all the tea in China.'

Allegra sighed and turned her head. The thunder fell in flatfooted paces on the Heath a half mile off. Lightning in London was not all that common, in Winnie's experience, and the flashes glazed the room with sudden blue. Slowly the thunder, rolling a few feet this way and that, shifted its timbre, and delivered itself of a second, hollower sound, which proved to be feet on the stairs.

'Oh, God,' said Allegra.

'It's the cavalry arriving,' whispered Winnie. 'It's John coming home at last.'

'It's not John. It's Mac come back.'

So it was, for he didn't bother to work the key in the lock. By the sound of it, he was setting to the door with another hammer, withdrawing the nails he had slammed in earlier. He was drunk and singing some rebel's song.

'Remove those nails and then go away.' Winnie got to her feet, thumping out to the door of the apartment, securing the chain. 'Open the door for us and then back off. I'm warning you.'

Mac was musical with drink. His songs were hymns of revenge, evoking the bloody king of heaven and the bloody kings of Boyne and the bloody bull of Maeve and the bloody guns of Provos.

'We've opened the cage, Mac,' shouted Winnie over his racket. 'We've got it open, we've let it out. You come in here and it'll get you.'

'I've fecking Christ on my shoulder and a fecking pecker in my Y-fronts, don't mess with me, you bloody cow.'

'Now here is someone I seriously intend to haunt,' said Allegra coldly, from behind Winnie, 'if he should manage to get in here and lay a hand on us.'

'We'll kill him first,' said Winnie. 'We will.'

'With what? A first edition of Trevelyan? A bootlegged tape of Callas in rehearsal, Milan, summer 1953? Maybe we could break a Waterford whiskey tumbler into pieces and slice his face off with the shards.'

'You're good, you should go on *Whose Line Is It Anyway?*' said Winnie. The wood of the door began to split.

'Though I'm generally not a churchgoer,' said Allegra, 'Jesus H-for-Himself Christ.'

They were backing up into the shadows of the kitchen.

'There's always the crowbar,' said Allegra.

Winnie grabbed it. A flush of something, almost glee. 'Let the monsters at each other, and we'll wait on the sidelines.' Hardly believing her own behavior, she notched one edge of the crowbar into a hole in the crumbling mortar and gave a good yank.

'Help me,' she said, and Allegra grabbed hold too.

Three bricks came out as easily as books sliding off a shelf.

Mac was a buffalo, shoulder ramming against the door.

'More,' said Winnie, and the purchase was easier this time. They had to leap back to keep their feet from being rained upon by falling bricks. A candle knocked over and went out.

'We could always brain Mac and tie him up and deface him with hot wax,' said Allegra.

'This is not the time for sex fantasies,' said Winnie. 'Heave. Ho.'

A third of the wall was down by the time the chain on the door gave way, and Mac lurched into the hall. He was drawn toward the light of the kitchen, hulking in the doorway, groggy with ale, swollen with fear and bravado.

'Got it,' said Winnie, and reached her hands into the revealed recess.

'Bloody what,' said Mac, belching.

'I could run for help,' suggested Allegra, 'but I wouldn't leave you.'

'It's an old horse blanket, nothing more,' said Winnie.

As she pulled it out, the lights came back on. Mac blinked and Allegra hit him over the head with a piece of glazed pottery from Tuscany. He didn't fall to the ground, just said, 'Ow, stop that,' and blinked again. 'What old scrap of nappy is that?'

In the electric light, the thing was a sad bit of potato sacking, a shapeless turn of cloth, almost indistinguishably black-gray-brown, with some uneven seams sewn in with coarse stitches.

'That's a hundred years old if it's a day,' said Allegra, 'but so what?'

'Whatever it is,' said Winnie, with relief, 'it isn't John.'

'Saints be praised,' said Mac. 'Jenkins lives.'

'You went to see him?' said Winnie.

'No, I just guess he lives. He was afraid it was John too.'

'Whatever was here,' said Winnie, 'is gone. This is just some old trashy cloth.' She dropped it on the floor. It was not running with lice, nor especially greasy or smoky. Just dusty, dry, and old; a worker's smock, maybe, hung on a nook in there and bricked up. Maybe by accident. Maybe it wasn't what had been intended for that cavity. Maybe the body put in there – for the space was deep enough for a human corpse – had been taken out earlier.

But the room was void of any spirit but those limited shades of Mac, Winnie, and Allegra. That meant, once again, that John Comestor was still missing, someplace else.

'We'll owe you fine ladies something as day laborers, for helping the job progress,' said Mac.

He pointed at the rubbled wall. Then he fell over and passed out. 'Shit, he's punctured the canvas, John'll kill me,' said Winnie, tugging the painting out from under Mac's chin before he vomited on it. There was no rip in the canvas, though. Old Scrooge/Rudge staggered away from his nightmare without regard to the indignity of being collapsed upon.

The genie uncorked was no genie, just an attractive illusion. The cryptic hammering was a loose board in a fake flue, the slashed cross on the computer courtesy of an emotional persistence of vision. The retracting nails no doubt just some other accident, as yet undiagnosed. The world shrugged itself smaller again, dying a little further.

How could you know anything for sure? The madmen and mystics of North London, hunting for significance, studied the pattern of browned oak leaves adhering to the wet pavements on Church Row. Unmask the world, rid it of theories and movements and dogmas, and what's left is something near to instinct, imagination's old curmudgeonly grandsire.

Probable-Possible, my black hen,
She lays eggs in the Relative When.
She doesn't lay eggs in the Positive Now
Because she's unable to Postulate How.

What stood between Winnie and the world was someone much like herself, though indistinct, and likely to remain so if Winnie couldn't see her better. But Wendy Pritzke, like most apparitions, dissolved into vagueness when more closely examined. So if, in middle age, Winnie had thought she might be due some more certain notion of how the world was arranged, she was disappointed. When she learned to take her own pulse she found she was registering Wendy Pritzke's instead.

Should Wendy jettison old-hat Jack the Ripper? Was the loss of a genuine ghost in Rudge House some sort of motion to dismiss the idea of an exhumed spirit of a fiend?

But the world couldn't map anything but itself, and sometimes not even that.

No one answered the phone at John's office. It was the weekend.

As quickly as they had united forces over a common perceived threat, Winnie and Allegra recoiled from each other, back to their natural state of antipathy and theatrical caution. Neither of them were inclined to press charges against Mac, since that might embroil Colum Jenkins in depositions, and who knew if he was either willing or up to such a thing: Winnie's phone inquiries to the Royal Free Hospital about the status of Jenkins's health had resulted in remarks neither clear nor useful. Though perhaps this was the institutional tone taken by anyone laboring under the auspices of the NHS. Winnie had no way of knowing.

Winnie got a fellow in to repair the damage to John's door, and restore the locks.

She sorted John's mail, pretending not to be looking for a letter addressed to her as she did it.

Gill, John's staffer, seemed to be on permanent sick leave or something. The several other office temps were ill-informed, rude, or lazy; they offered no clue as to John's whereabouts.

Winnie went round to Allegra's with a parcel of treats from Louis' Patisserie. She could see by the look on her face that Allegra was ashamed at having betrayed some fear. Allegra did not ask her in to sample the pastries. Am I offended? Winnie asked herself as she left, though the question inevitably contorted itself to mean: Would Wendy Pritzke be offended in an instance such as this? What does it say about her if she would? If she wouldn't?

At the height of the November storm every starkly improbable thing had seemed possible, especially with Winnie gripped in the early stages of realization that John was missing without explanation. Several days later, with Mac disappeared into the downscale depths of Kilburn High Road and Jenkins still in hospital, Winnie Rudge moved cautiously about the sunny, vacant flat, tidying up the detritus, restoring the place to a minimum level of comfort while she should care to stay, and began to concentrate, at last, on the reason she'd come to London. To tell the story of Wendy Pritzke. Well, to find it first, and then to tell it if it proved worth telling.

She ran into Britt over the racks of Cadburys at the Hampstead Food Hall.

'Still no word from John?' he asked brightly.

'Oh, is that so?' she answered, with a more fluting inquisitive upturn than his, and she shrugged as if to say, *Well, there's not much*

more I can add if he's chosen to keep it all secret from you. And how satisfying that was, turning away before he could invent the next move.

London had emerged, blinking, from the tempers and vapors of Hurricane Gretl, such as they'd been, and the bricks of damp Hampstead steamed as if with tropical aspirations. The pavements dried, the winds stilled for once, even on the Heath; the sun came out like a sissy on the playground once the bully's gone home for lunch. Unseasonable warmth. Some of the cafés dared to open their windows to the street again. Police did double-time ticketing, to make up for lost revenue during the storm days.

Mrs Maddingly on the front steps. 'He's gone missing, he has.'

'Who has?'

'Chutney.'

'Oh, dear' – with shameful brightness – 'well, he'll turn up, or there'll be others.'

'Of course there'll be others, but by then it'll be another me to feed them! And the other me could hardly be expected to recognize Chutney when he comes home from his tomcatting.'

'Stick with your pills, you'll pull through.'

'Pull through what?'

Winnie didn't answer.

'And *your* tomcat? Back yet?' asked Mrs Maddingly.

Wendy, Wendy. Winnie went back to particulars, doodling on the margin of a paper napkin at a coffee shop down in West End Lane. What did she know about Wendy? The name itself, she remembered, was an invention of J.M. Barrie's; the popularity of *Peter Pan* had launched the name into common usage. Wendy Darling followed the rude hero to Neverland. But once there, she settled, she nested. She brooded over the Lost Boys and demanded they be led back to London.

Did any of this feed into her secret mental picture of Wendy Pritzke? It might not, but she had to turn over the pieces to see if something glinted.

She walked the old haunts, thinking, waiting for a glimmer. One lunchtime she decided to take a look in the churchyard of Hampstead Parish Church and see if she could find the tombstone of the Llewelyn Davies family, the sons of which had been the Lost Boys who inspired J.M. Barrie to invent Peter Pan games, and then to write the stories down. Armed with a mimeographed map from the church vestibule, she went poking about the old section of the churchyard, noting without interest the grave of Ozias Rudge, its simple stone frugally engraved only with the names and dates: 1775–1851.

Laden with red berries, limbs of yew had been torn off by the storm, and been brought down atop the split covers of old tombs, giving the appearance of having cracked the lids.

Unable to follow the map, she wandered aimlessly, closed in from Hampstead traffic by the greened-brick walls. In the deepest part of the graveyard she came upon five sleeping bags laid out on boughs used as mattresses. Plastic sacks from a department store: *Argos: Brighter Shopping.* Discarded rubbish from packaged meals. A group of indigents dossing down there, though at noontime gone for the day. In the economic revival of Tony Blair's tenure, had the bums and street people to go more deeply underground?

A good woman of the church emerged from a side door and scowled helpfully at Winnie. 'I am useless at following this map, I can't make out any of the coordinates,' said Winnie.

'You're looking in the wrong place. This is the map of the graveyard extension across the road,' said the woman in an aggrieved tone.

'How stupid we Americans are, I more than most,' Winnie said, more snippily than was her custom. But across the road, all fell into place. The Llewelyn Davies family was almost in the corner. On the stone memorializing the father, she read, 'What is to come we know not but we know that what has been was good.' She looked down to find the details of Peter who, as she recalled, wasn't quite Peter Pan, but who could fail to be interested? His stone was a kind of postscript below his parents'. On the black granite slab she read:

Peter
Soldier M.C. & Publisher
whose ashes lie here
'Et in Arcadia Ego'

So many ways to be a lost boy.

Or Wendy, concentrate on her. A lost girl, at least lost to her author, so far.

And where the hell, by the way, was John?

She continued along Church Row. It wouldn't look like working to the IRS, but it was her professional tic. She wandered and watched, let things emerge and detach, seeing what stuck. She imagined Wendy peering down onto the countertops in the bright kitchens below street level. A plastic bottle of Fairy liquid soap, a blue and white bowl with bloated Cheerios in milk, a crust of bread for a teething child. The tired mother and the tiresome babe apparently having fled from the domestic scene, the room seemed more vacant, for the sunlight on milk beaded on the counter, than even John's apartment had.

It was a day, up and down Hampstead High Street, for the elderly to be out collecting with handheld green plastic drums. The old ones shook the coins in their cups like rattles. Ashamed at her gibe at the churchwoman, Winnie stopped and pushed a ten-quid note she could hardly spare into the slit on top. The cause was Amnesty International.

It was all of a piece, but what did it make?

She paused at a stall, thinking to buy flowers to cheer herself up. A handful of daffodils, some freesia flown in from the Continent or maybe Africa. The beefy clerk, shivering cheerily, said, 'Out of acetate, luv, newsprint'll do, I daresay.'

She lapped it up, the 'luv,' and smiled. It felt like the first smile since she'd arrived.

At home, the flowers looked rangier and more frost damaged than she'd noticed. They didn't enliven the place, just made it seem more funereal.

The newspaper was *The Times*, a health page. A photo on the top right leaped out at her. It looked like a small witch being burned at a stake. The headlines read 'Eyes at Risk from Fireworks,' and the story was about casualties expected on Bonfire Night – November fifth, coming up.

But the way the Guy Fawkes figure reared back! – the flames jumping out of brambles, the sparks caught on the photographic plate as dashes and hyphens against newsprint's grimy blackness. Winnie looked. Wendy looked. How hugely powerful the image, though why, to an American eye, Winnie couldn't say.

> Yesterday upon the stair
> I met a man who wasn't there.
> He wasn't there again today.
> I wish to hell he'd go away.

When she had managed to buy and successfully install a new phone cord, Winnie rang Rasia McIntyre.

'Oh, yes, you,' said Rasia. 'No, in fact, I admit: I have put my

ear to the chimney stack more than once a day, and never again heard that distant drumming, or was it like waves? – except that once I thought I heard a cat.'

Winnie laughed. 'Chutney is now bricked up inside some chimney on some other floor! Well, let him get himself out. I'm through with the ghostbusting business. I'm calling to make good on an offer of tea or something, if you can lose the kids someplace so we can talk.'

'The children are at their grandmother's in Balham, and I'm hideously busy,' said Rasia. 'Deadlines and all that. Couldn't possibly make it anytime in the next twenty minutes. How's half eleven? And let's just walk; I need the exercise.'

They met by the newsstand at the Hampstead Tube station. Rasia's neck was ringed with a cherry-red scarf. A heavy shoulder bag, maybe carrying a laptop, dragged down her shoulder. She had twenty-first-century-here-we-come written all over her.

'The client called; I've a bit of work to deliver in town on my way to pick up the children. It'll mean lugging this satchel, so a long healthy walk is out. Let's have our teas and chat, and then I'll skive off.'

They settled at the cramped tables of the Coffee Cup Café a few doors down from Waterstone's. The waitress, Italian, sulked at them for ordering tea without even toast. 'Did you bring it?' said Rasia.

Winnie pulled it out. In the low light of the café the thing looked even more moldery than it had at John's. But there was no odor, neither dung nor earth nor soil of any sort, which seemed odd. Only, if you put your nostrils right to it, a faint reek of applewood smoke or some such sweet fragrance, across a distance of how many years?

'Maybe a century of airing has expunged the barnyard smell; it certainly has a barnyard look,' said Rasia, 'and a very coarse weave.

Done by a handmade loom? It can't be very old or the threads surely would have rotted.'

'It must be at least as old as that brickwork,' said Winnie, 'and while I'm no expert, the faux chimney stack looked like it wasn't done yesterday.'

Rasia puckered her mouth, a kind of facial shrug. 'Doesn't do anything for me. You were expecting perhaps a holographic image from the Great Beyond? Help me, Obi-Wan Kenobi, help me?'

'I was expecting either the body of my missing cousin John, or—' But no, it was Wendy Pritzke who had been happily anticipating the corpse of Jack the Ripper.

Rasia lifted up the cloth. In her hands it looked bigger, like a horse blanket of some sort; it had seemed more like a worker's apron when Winnie held it. 'There's no sign that a hem of pearls has been ripped out, no secret lining holding the last will and testament of anyone rich and generous,' said Rasia, 'so as far as your storytelling needs go, I think you've been digging in barren soil here.'

'Oh, well.' Winnie folded it up. 'I didn't expect you suddenly to have a vision or anything. You're far too modern and capable for that.'

'Oh, my family has been mystical since ages. But I've been westernized and incapacitated. The only visions I have are my bad dreams. Of Quentin loving me, rejecting me, my being angry at him, my cheating on him, anything to get his attention, even in the afterlife.'

'Which you don't believe in.'

'Right. But one can't fall back on one's knee-jerk skepticism when one is trapped in a dream.'

'The suspension of disbelief . . . How do you by-step your own ambushing memories?'

'By waking up. Sometimes with a shiver, sometimes a shout,

sometimes a lump in my throat. Always to the mercy of the kids, who are better than pharmaceuticals at inducing calm, even when they're noisy and hateful. They say, Hey, it's me, it's my life, and Mummy, you have only a walk-on role, but you better do it right or you're sacked. And I have no recourse but to behave.'

'You sound like a bit player in your own life.' Which was, of course, how Winnie felt in hers, most of the time, only whoever was supposed to do the star turn was stuck in a dressing room somewhere. 'By-stepping memories of Quentin through raising his kids, that's a tall order.'

'I try to forget. I fail. I don't have any imagination, really; I can't think of another man, another life; I can't get that far. When I do have a moment – like now – I think of what I know and miss. Poor Quen, with his confused smile, his little habits. You know about habits: first they seem endearing gestures and then they become maddening tics and finally they settle at being what makes a person *there*. What made Quentin McIntyre *Quen* to me. I'd rather forget him, but as I say, I've a concrete mind better suited to solving software problems than imagining any life for myself other than the one in which I'm a widow. No imagination, my teachers used to say back in Kampala.'

'A real liability, that,' said Winnie.

'We used to play poltergeist baby with Tariq,' said Rasia after a while. 'I would grab Tariq by the ankles when he was lying on his back on our big bed. Quen would loom overhead like a thundercloud, saying, 'Oh, my sweet little baby, I think I'll give him a big kiss.' Then he'd lean down, aiming his lips at his forehead, and just before he'd make contact, I would drag the baby away, along the sheets, so that Quen was just kissing the air. Tariq squealed with glee. I think of it sometimes, especially with Fiona, who never knew—'

She caught her breath.

'I think of it sometimes now, and imagine that Quen is the poltergeist father, leaning down to kiss his baby, only none of us here can tell it's happening.'

'Oh, let's go,' said Winnie, 'let's go, let's get out of here.' They left the Italian waitress more tip than she deserved.

'Sorry about that,' said Rasia, 'you bring it out of me, why is that? I'll be good. Anyway, a change. I've had a great idea. Let's take this old bit of sacking into a place I know near Farringdon, a tearoom where a kind of dyspeptic clairvoyant named Ritzi reads tea leaves. Let's find out what old gypsy Ritzi can pick up. It'll amuse us. I'm sorry for blubbing all the time. We'll laugh.' She tugged Winnie up the hill toward the Hampstead Tube station.

'Your meeting?'

'Not far from there. I'll go on and deliver my goods and keep on and get the kids in Balham by half two. Do come, Ritzi is a twitch and then some. There's the lift alarm beeping – Two singles to Farringdon,' she said to the cage, thrusting a ten-pound note under the bars, 'hurry.'

They rattled through the dark, past the vertebrae of buried foundations, past unmarked tombs, nests of rats, conduits of wires, sewers and buried streams, the whole obscured process of the present chewing ruinously on the past.

'But you have no imagination,' said Winnie, 'how can you stomach the notion of a seer?'

'It's because I have no imagination that I enjoy it. Enjoy it, nothing more. And with Quentin so obnoxiously dead, and likely to remain so, this gives me the pretense of mystical communication. It's a fix, I admit it.'

'Were you dead,' said Wendy Pritzke, 'would you bother to be in touch with me through a medium?'

'As in, "You've got mail?"' said John. 'No, I doubt it. When I do manage to die, if there's any choice in the matter of the afterlife, I have every intention of traveling on, the farthest spot within my ability to reach.' He pointed out the window of the Tarom flight. They were high enough above the Alps to see early stars. 'All those immensities of distance, all the refigured lengths of the past and the present wrapped in transparent sleeves around us. Whatever Terra Infinita I can explore, I'm there, honey, not nosing about my old haunts.'

His chin against her cheek, a cousinly nuzzle: 'You're thinking about the ghosts of old victims of Jack the Ripper, trying to get home—'

'I most assuredly am not,' she said, 'everything is not fiction for me.'

The stars watched, no comment.

They turned left out of the Farringdon Station in Cowcross Street, whose rural name was belied by buildings of blood-colored brick in a kind of budget International style. Still, the street curved pleasingly to the right, as if cows might once have meandered that way. Looming in the sky several blocks to the east, an office block or a tower of council estates made the final statement about the urbanization of the neighborhood, in concrete graver than tombstones. Or was that the Barbican? The clairvoyant's rooms were past a Starbucks, at the top of one of the few remaining buildings that rose only two or three stories.

Ritzi, it turned out, was Moritz Ostertag, an attenuated balding man discreetly made up with powder, doused with lemon verbena cologne. He wore ratty carpet slippers, and around his neck he sported a scarf sewn over with tiny mirrors. 'Rasia,' he said, hardening the *a* to make it *Raay-seee-ya*. 'But you are takink care of your beautiful self! You are learnink to cope. You are haffink ze facial and ze massage, and, I am zinkink, you are beink ready to touch ze infinite.'

'I am having ze migraine and ze overdraft. Are you booked?'

'I am sensink you vill come. Naturally I turn avay everyvone.' The place was deserted, and deservedly so: it smelled of cat piss. Chutney, thought Winnie suddenly; where *did* that tomcat go? Ritzi Ostertag dipped and swayed around a couple of ferns, moisturizing with a mister. 'I am tendink ze vegetable kingdom. Zen I am haffink ze afternoon off and succumbink to electrolysis. Ze betrayink eyebrows, you know. I am haffink to prepare for a ball tonight. I'm goink as Clare Buoyant ze Clairvoyant.'

'I'm in a little bit of a hurry. I've got the kids to collect and, Ritzi, I've brought you fresh trade.'

'Not all zat fresh,' he said, eyeing Winnie from over half-lens glasses, but she was meant to be amused, and she didn't mind.

'She'll be a challenge. Come on, don't turf us out.'

He sighed, putting down the mister and beginning to fuss with a Russell Hobbs electrical kettle painted over with runic symbols. 'In ze mood for somevone new I am not beink. But Rasia, I luff you, zo I zay, as you like. You will be havink Lapsang souchong or it's out on ze street with you and your' – he looked Winnie up and down – 'bodyguard.'

'I prefer Earl Grey.'

'You heard me.' He lowered some musty purple velvet drapes that looked as if they'd been cut down from prewar theater hangings. The light turned sodden and cancerous. Winnie was reminded of the bed-curtains in the Scrooge/O.R. painting, and had to suppress a snort. Did Rasia take this bozo seriously? Ritzi lit a few small pyramids of incense and disappeared behind a door.

They heard him taking a piss. 'It's all zis fortune-tellink, ze tea my bladder is beink tired of,' he called out to them.

Winnie was beginning to realize that this charade was going to cost her money. But since Wendy Pritzke might take it into her head to do such a thing, the cost of the experience would be deductible as a research expense on this year's taxes. So Winnie kept her mental Palm Pilot open. She noted the smells, the light, the dust underneath the radiator. The confusion of images on the walls, Buddhist, Himalayan, druidic; not a bricolage, but a hodgepodge, like a decoration from the inside of a high school locker, vintage Reefer Era.

'Tea,' said Ritzi Ostertag, indicating chairs, pointing: Sit.

Winnie looked about. The place was done up as a genuine tearoom, she guessed, with several small tables covered with paisley shawls, crowded around with unmatched chairs. One corner was fitted out with bookcases and display shelves, stacked with packs of tarot cards and incense sticks. A glass-fronted bookcase, crammed with some old volumes and pamphlets, was guarded up top by a skull and jawbone, real or plastic, jutting its toothy smile. In another corner a computer screen's e-mail display had lapsed into a screen saver featuring flying monkeys out of MGM's Technicolor Oz. Used videos, for sale or rent, were propped up on a windowsill, including *The Sixth Sense, Ghost*, and *Blithe Spirit*, as well as, for paranormal reasons indecipherable to Winnie, *Gentlemen Prefer Blondes*.

Ritzi bustled about, but it was a quiet bustling, setting a mood. He took a hand-lettered sign that read READING IN PROGRESS: PLEASE WAIT and hung it on a hook on the door, then closed the door and latched it with a hook. He disappeared, and the music emanating from the back, a techno remix of Shirley Bassey's 'Goldfinger,' was replaced a moment or two later with something sounding more like Hildegard von Bingen, sorrowful monks droning in open fourths. Ritzi reappeared, balancing cups of tea on a tray while adjusting the dimmer switch adroitly with his bare elbow. A gypsy he was not, decidedly; it was apparent in the fussiness with which he prepared the tea. He was more likely a marginal scion of a wealthy German family, playing at supernatural games while dining off dividends. The accent, the more Winnie considered, was stagy too; probably he really spoke in that new Euro-English, fairly neutral, betraying little of its origins. 'In silence ve drink, ve are not talkink, I am not beink colored by your remarks,' he said. 'Of your silly reservations and your scoffinks your minds to be empty, pliss. Breathe in ze varmth of ze tea and zink of ze nuzzinkness of your life.'

Not hard to do, even for a skeptic. In fact, most days, hard to avoid doing.

Winnie suddenly, again, felt the absence of her cousin, and her worry for him. How she'd enjoy retelling this bit of nonsense to him, were he waiting in the wings to hear it. How far he seemed from her, wherever he was.

The room darkened still, as if Ritzi had summoned a light cloud cover over Cowcross Street. But nothing like Hurricane Gretl or its afterbirth. Just a pressing down against the light, a purring of silence. The tea did smell nice, to be sure. It also cloaked the smell of cat piss.

'Now ve finish our tea,' said Ritzi, eyes closed, drawing out his syllables, 'and ve wait, and zen' – he demonstrated – 've put our saucers upside down on our teacups, and ve turn ze cups over and zet zem down – so – cup reversed, leaves settled. Put your hands on ze cup made topsy-turvy. Leave behind your past and your future. On ve go, deeper into ze present.'

They did so. Silence. Ritzi murmured to Winnie, stage whisper, 'You, breathe.'

She had forgotten for a moment, and resumed breathing.

Upon her hands he placed his greasy palms. She observed his chewed cuticles, the soft wren-colored hairs on his upper fingers glistening in what she realized was candlelight. When had he lit candles? 'You come to laugh,' he said softly. 'It is no matter. In laughing some muscles relax but other muscles tighten. You must stop laughing, though, if you want to listen.' She hoped she wouldn't belch out a rich imperial guffaw.

'Yes,' she said submissively, as if to a traffic cop brandishing a ticket pad.

'You must listen to yourself when you are ready to listen. Do not listen to me. You are laughing but it is a thin laughter and no one joins in.'

The flying monkeys kept winging, left to right.

'And upon the tea leaves let us look. So.' He lifted his hands and then hers, and set them down – they felt dead, paralyzed – on either side of the saucer. He lifted the cup, a nice ironstone second with a chipped handle and a pattern of blue vines running their mathematically spaced leaves up to the gold-leaf rim. The residue of tea leaves had fallen in a crescent shape.

His voice sounded different. Not inspired, not possessed, just softer, with more hesitations. His stage-German accent had fallen away, she noticed. It made him slightly less preposterous.

'You are a woman in need.'

No surprise there. What woman wasn't?

'You make pictures of things, you arrange everything; you are like a governess, pushing the wardrobe here, there, rolling back the carpet, directing the sun to fall at this angle and not at that. A stager of effects.'

She tried to still her bucking doubt, for the sake of the money this would cost.

'You move from place to place. You are allowed to do so through luck or financial success. Or maybe you married well. But

I think you are, if married, not all that married. He is looking the other way. You arrange his face to turn on you; you require it. He will not look. You need the thing he will not give. You look elsewhere. You move this, you move that. You move a teacup from this table to that windowsill, to ease your heart. You move it back, studying how your heart will feel. Or maybe it is people you move. You paint people, perhaps, on canvas, on little bits of paper? You move them here and there to see how they look. To see how they make your heart feel. I think you are a painter, you paint people.'
He looked up briefly, but his expression was blank.

Well, he wasn't doing so bad. Maybe you could say writing stories, even composing dreadful fake horoscopes, was painting people. But this hardly constituted telling the future; it was more like telling the present, if you could give him the benefit of the doubt about any of it.

'Here there is a window, there we find a door. A lot of water, water in all its forms. Rain and snow, oceans and tears, dew in the morning, fog at night. But not the right water. You are barren, you are void. Why are you void? This is not what you should be. Despite your age. It's not too late.'

Rasia stirred, as if she guessed just how uncomfortable this might be making Winnie, though how could Rasia know? She couldn't.

He regarded the tea leaves, as if studying a specimen through a microscope. 'You are suspicious, yet you have so much to share,' he said. He sighed, disappointed in her. 'You are full of life, yet you stamp upon it. You are like a sea horse, pretty but rigid, and far smaller than you know. You are only a little person, so stop worrying. As if it matters to the world what you do. It only matters to you. But it does matter, in its small way.' He smiled at the tea leaves, as if seeing the profile of a friend there. 'Hello, small thing. Your name is Wendy.'

He looked up for the first time, confused. 'Is that a name I should read here?'

'Very close,' said Rasia, who did not know about Wendy Pritzke.

'Or your sister is named Wendy. Is there another man? I see a dark man approaching—'

And riches, and travel, and children and horses and paintings and lovers. 'We didn't come for this sort of thing,' said Winnie, alarmed at all that passed for accuracy, and the ache that her gullibility revealed to her. 'We came to see if you could tell us anything about this cloth.' She found the brown throw and pulled an edge up onto the table. He recoiled.

'This is nothing to do with you, this is wild nonsense!' he said. He flicked his fingers at it, shooing. But his hands fell on it reluctantly and he closed his eyes.

'Or is it stronger than you?' he said.

'What is it?' said Rasia.

'Hush, you, you interfere with the reception.'

A clock measured out a noon's worth of bells. On the faraway street a truck backed up. Cloud continents shifted, and behind the purple hangings, light strengthened, spent itself, and delivered the room back into séance gloom. Any minute now Ritzi would bring out a Ouiji board from the 1970s and they'd contact Elvis or Madame Blavatsky or Napoleon or James Merrill.

'Is it you with the windows, the doors, the tides of the womb, or is it someone more truly done wrong?' He looked at Winnie without benefit of misty second sight, just with the usual human severity. 'You do not seem the type to allow wrong done you.'

'Who ever allows it? Still, wrong is as strong as ever,' she said.

'This thing is a woman's garment.'

'Nonsense. No sleeves, no hem, no collar, no pleats? No bow or tuck or dart or filigree? It's a utilitarian wrap, a bit of sackcloth.'

'It is not a blanket for a baby—'

'I'd hate to be the baby who had to cuddle in that for a blankie—'

'—but it covered a woman's nakedness, before her life was done.'

Was she all wrong, was it not the ghost of Jack the Ripper but the spirit of one of his victims? That pretty Irish housemaid killed and her body stowed in the yawning architecture of a home under construction? But this was no woman's body, not even a black skirt and starched apron, nothing but a filthy rag . . .

'Come back here,' said Ritzi Ostertag sternly. Winnie jumped.

'Don't go hiding in someone else's mind,' he said.

'I've had enough of this,' said Winnie. 'You're telling us, what, that this is the blanket of some poor woman?'

'I'm telling you,' he said, 'it is no blanket. It is her shroud.'

The door came open, the hook-and-eye lock pulled from the jamb. A fellow stumbled in, blinking in the gloom. For an instant Winnie thought it might be Mac hunting them again, but it was a larger man, with a big loden coat and a staticky stand of fine hair. 'Jesus, you've gotten more secret than the catacombs, Herr Ostertag,' he said. American to the nines. 'Sorry about the lock. I was leaning on your door to leave you a message.'

'The sign, you're not welcome yet, out,' said Ritzi.

'Sorry. I won't bother you. I'll just finish this note and you can call me. Unless you can just sell me something while I'm here? I'm just looking for that book listed on your Web page. That monograph on *Les Fleurs des chroniques* of Bernard Gui, by, oh you know, who is it. Crowther. The one about the dead *clavelière* nun who came back from her grave to deliver the keys to her abbess—'

'It's not for sale.'

'You advertised it.'

'I'm busy, can't you see it, I have patrons.'

'Just tell me how much. I've got cash, I'll leave it right here on the table. Sneak right out without interrupting. Excuse me, ladies, but as long as I've already barged in—'

'I sold it yesterday.'

'No kidding. How much?'

'Forty-eight pounds.' Ritzi smirked. 'Now will you be leaving?'

'I'd have given you seventy,' said the newcomer. 'You're not much of a fortune-teller if you couldn't see that coming. You should have updated your entry? So I wouldn't have wasted my time? Sorry, ladies.'

'Zis mornink ze entry I am updating. You should haff rung first and saved yourself ze trip. Pliss, sir, vill you leave?' The accent was getting embarrassing. Winnie couldn't look up for fear she'd lose it.

The customer didn't seem to notice, or mind. 'You always have good stuff,' he said. 'I don't know what deposit libraries you steal from. I don't ask questions and mum's the word anyway.' He unfolded a piece of paper from a coat pocket. 'What about *Recherches sur les phénomènes du spiritualisme*, the 1923 edition out of Paris or even the first English edition, 1878?'

'I don't haff a catalog,' said Ritzi, 'in my brain. I haff to look and you'll haff to come back. Tomorrow.'

'May I browse? Is this your new stock over here? Any backroom stuff? Anything on the Londonian Society of Psychical Research of the last century? I mean, sorry, the nineteenth century? I keep forgetting we're twenty-first now. You can't teach old dogs new calendars.'

'Ze sign said closed,' said Ritzi, 'and now I am beink closed.

Everyvone, out. You, don't bring zat shroud back. It is for me too upsettink.'

'You didn't read my leaves,' said Rasia, getting up.

'I am beink knackered. Your friend is too obscure, her aura is wounded. My eyes are hurtink. And zat fabric! Who can be concentratink? Besides, with you, it's alvays *Quentin, my Quentin*. Too redundant. Brink me a new ghost, like zis lady, or go find another psychic.'

'What do I owe you?' said Winnie, glad to be sprung from this. But he wouldn't take a penny.

'Not if zat's involved,' he said, brisking his fingers at the chimney cloth. 'Vhatever's involved with zat is too much for me. I don't vant to get involved. Out now, pliss, I'm tired, my head aches. Am I puttink on a *performance* here?' He slammed the door on all three of his visitors, and they filed down the steep steps to Cowcross Street, newly bleached by the next spilled cargo of sunlight.

'Well,' said Rasia. 'Satisfied?'

Winnie could only laugh, but it was a fake laugh of sorts; she waved Rasia toward the Tube stop, saying, 'Next time let's smoke some peyote and try to contact some archangel or shaman or bodhisattva that way.' She didn't want to get back in the underground, not yet. Rasia threw air kisses and disappeared. Then Winnie realized the other customer was lurching along behind her, nearly beside her.

'Sorry about that,' he said. 'I aborted your session.'

'I didn't care for what I got, but what it was, I got for free, thanks to you,' she said. 'I guess I owe you.'

'The sign said closed and I didn't mean to trespass. Did I really break that lock? I don't think I did. Did I? I'm not exactly the Incredible Hulk.' He laughed at himself. 'The Unremarkable Hulk, more like.' He wasn't blubbery, but he was – Winnie considered the right word – portly. It was nice, for a moment anyway, to be sharing a sidewalk with a man who looked as if he could bounce the Ghost of Jack the Ripper into the gutter if it possessed the *cojones* to come sidling by.

A small rain hit them, on a search-and-drench mission; the other side of the street stayed dry and even sunny. 'Shoot, I dropped my Old Navy rain hat,' he said, riffling his sparse hair so it looked like a stand of baby beach grass. 'We'll have to go back.'

'*You'll* have to go back,' she said. 'We're not together.'

'He won't open the door to me. Please, it's my favorite hat. I'll buy you coffee afterward.'

'I'll do it on the condition you buy me no coffee and we go our own ways immediately after.'

'Deal.'

But Ritzi, seeing it was them, said, 'Go avay, vhat is zis, conspiracy? I don't vant to zee zat shroud again! I'll ring ze police and haff you arrested. I'm closed for business. I'm plucking.' He slammed the door.

'No hat,' she said.

'What shroud?' said the American man.

'It's still raining, would you like to borrow said shroud in lieu of your missing hat?'

'I'd rather coffee. Reconsider?'

A few doors down from Ritzi's they found a tiny lunch place. It was nearly deserted but for an ancient slope-stomached waitress who warbled 'You're too seraphic to go out in traffic' as she made her way from the back.

'A full cream tea. Two of them,' declared the beefy man.

'We do fresh sandwiches. Egg mayonnaise, prawn and avocado, minty lamb, cheese and pickle, chicken tikka. On your choice of sandwich bread, bap, ciabatta, or foccacina.'

'No cream teas in central London?'

'You poor ducks, we don't. Not since the Blitz. The cows ran away.'

'I didn't know anyone said "ducks" anymore.' He was charmed.

'Only to Americans. They like it and tip healthily.' She performed a moue for them, betrayed no surprise when they opted only for tea, and she hobbled away humming.

'Irv Hausserman,' he said.

'Opal Marley,' she replied.

'Delighted, et cetera. How's that guy as a psychic, by the way?'

'You should try him yourself and see.'

'Had I done so, he'd have said, "You will leave your hat behind, and I'll sell it back to you for forty-eight pounds plus VAT."'

She laughed. It was a relief to laugh about nothing much. 'What secrets were you there to see if he could sniff out?'

'None. I'm tedious and I have no secrets. I just wanted to buy something. He deals in out-of-print stuff, ephemera, most of it schlocky and awful, but good things with some historical interest come his way, too, so I look in whenever I'm in town. He's a shrewd bargainer. I bet he still has the pamphlet I want. I'll have to go back tomorrow and he'll say he spent the afternoon hunting up another copy for me. Then he'll charge me a hundred pounds for it, saying it's in better condition than the one he just sold. Can't blame him.'

He was from the University of Pittsburgh, history department, an associate professor, still pretenure because he'd come into the field late after a career as financial officer of several high-tech start-ups that skyrocketed and tanked one after the other, before he had the chance to bail. History a much more sober and safe environment.

'Your field?' she said.

'Western medievalism, English, Frankish, Norman, from the time of monks to the time of parliaments. Roughly. Kids take my courses wanting to do papers on *The Name of the Rose* and the

Brother Cadfael mysteries. When I point out that Brother Cadfael's worldview is decidedly post-Freudian, they think I'm defaming the dead of long ago. In the student guidebooks I get high marks because I give them high marks – grade inflation is contagious. But I can't sell my old-fashioned notion, my pre-postmodern notion of history. I still think history is really the study of how we change, even how human psychology changes. Not how universal and interchangeable we all are across the ages. And you?'

She dandled her spoon in the slurry-colored tea and considered the public relations campaign. She had no reason to mistrust him. So why had she started out with an alibi? Instinct? Neurosis? And it wasn't an alibi, it was a lie: call it what it was. A habit that was getting more and more entrenched. Why couldn't she shuck it off? A question she might have asked Ritzi Ostertag.

'Recovering from a broken marriage,' she said.

'Oh, that.'

'Not to worry.' She hastened to extemporize her way out of danger. 'Not broken in the traditional sense. Really, just frayed a little. He's having a rest cure at a ranch in Arizona and I'm on my own for two months. The damp of English winters is just exactly what he can't stand. It's Jack Sprat and his wife; he can breathe no mold and I find dry sunny heat stultifying and it makes me drink gin at ten A.M.'

'So the happy medium is . . .'

'Ritzi Ostertag,' she couldn't resist, 'a happy medium, or gay anyway.'

He blinked. She suspected he was willfully not following. She didn't blame him; she was being feeble. 'I was taking him this cloth I found,' she said, trying for honesty of some sort. 'For a lark, and because I'm bored.'

'Because you miss your husband.'

'I do.' She looked him in the eye in case he was getting ideas.

But he was looking fondly at her, fondly and without any predatory gleam of interest. 'Don't worry about me. I admire people who stick by their spouses.'

'Meaning you don't?'

'Meaning nothing of the sort. May I see the cloth?'

She drew it out. In this atmosphere it looked more brittle, filthy, more barnyard.

He looked at it closely, as if he could read a language in its warp and weft. Then he pushed it away. 'I don't know anything about cloth.'

'Some historian you are.'

'It looks old,' he said. He laughed. 'I'm a better historian when it comes to reading books than reading artifacts, I admit it.'

'What's your particular field?' she said. 'Your professional idée fixe?'

'Aspects of the supernatural in medieval thought. How Christian concepts of the supernatural derive in part from origins dating back to late antiquity. How the scribes and bishops encountered Roman and Teutonic myths and legends, and grafted them in a crafty local way upon Hebraic and early Christian theology and lore. How incompatible some of that lore was, how the Church used it anyway, that line of goods.'

'Why aren't you engaged in a history of, oh, cooking pots? Or the migration of nomadic populations? Of course your field is the occult. Naturally, supernatural. Everything is, these days. I'm feeling quite paranoid.'

'Nothing odd in the supernatural as a field of interest. Nor in our sharing the interest. We did meet in a clairvoyant's salon, after all.'

'But what do you believe of it?'

'You mean would I go to have my palm read, my I Ching thrown? My fate in the cards, the tea leaves? The crystal ball? Balderdash. Balderdash, idiocy, poppycock. Stuff and nonsense. You

want more? Codswallop. I hardly even believe in the Internet. I can't get my head around ley lines and crop circles and such.'

'Makes you good at your job, then. The appreciative skeptic. Publish much?'

'Too much, in the wrong journals.'

But she realized she didn't want to talk about publishing. 'I have to go.'

'You believe in some of it, or you wouldn't have been there,' he said to her. 'It's okay. People believe in different things. Some people believe in dreams and voices. I think dreams and voices are important, but primarily as a way your psyche has of getting your own attention, that's all.'

'Have you ever seen a ghost?'

'If I had, I'd have to be a believer, and you already know I'm not. Of course I haven't. But people in the Middle Ages thought they did, all the time.'

'Maybe their innocence allowed them to see what our eyes are clouded to.'

'More things in heaven and earth, et cetera. Have *you* ever seen a ghost?'

'I have to go,' she said again. 'Our meeting was an accident and I don't read significance into it. I'm not looking for a dalliance while my husband is recuperating with a pulmonary ailment in Scottsdale. Thanks for the coffee. I'll leave the tip.'

'You look as if you've seen a ghost,' he said. 'I didn't mean anything by the questions. Hell, I wouldn't know a ghost if it stopped and asked me for directions.'

The day was nice. She walked all the way back up the hill to Hampstead, thinking of anything except for the catalog of ghosts scrolling in her head. Medieval, Jack the Ripper, some Irish housemaid he might have killed, the ghost of Marley, the Spirits of Christmas Past, Present, and to Come.

The ghost of old Scrooge himself, bequeathed to the world by Dickens, and still haunting it.

The ghost of old Ozias Rudge, hovering about Rudge House? The Either/OR of it.

No, she was not thinking about ghosts, not at all. The day was bright now, clouds sent scudding southeast toward the lowlands, France, and beyond that the Alps, the Tyrol, the great Danubian plain. All this clutter, this nonsense, swept with the biggest broom, cobwebs torn from the sky. Exercise always made her mind cleverer. The sun a merciful tonic, the November brightness a bromide.

They landed in Bucureşt long after dark. The Alps behind them, physically and mentally, bunched and puckered in slow silken ripples of stone and snow. The airport was in a state of construction, or demolition, or both. Arriving passengers had to step over slabs of stone left higgledy-piggledy, had to avoid staggering into electrical wires that snaked out of unfinished walls.

John took her by the elbow – she was tired, the seats had been lumpy and the food poor – and as she began to fret, he rose to the occasion. He loved the obstacles of the third world, the wooden-handled seals thumping down into the passport, the self-importance of two-bit officials, the smell of open drains. The world seemed realer to him there.

'This place is total mayhem. Everything's in the most ghastly state,' he said gleefully. The driver was waiting with a lit cigarette in his mouth. He pulled out of his belt two other cigarettes, straightened them, and offered them around. He had a lovely gap between his teeth. His eyes for

that matter were broadly spaced, and even his
nostrils seemed an inch apart. And bovine in
temperament as well as physique. He drove as if
he'd only been behind a wheel for several hours,
which they later learned to be true; his brother had
been arrested, and so he'd got the keys and taught
himself to drive on the way to the airport. His
name was Costal Doroftei.

He took them to the best restaurant in town
and pushed them in the door, announcing that he
would wait outside while they ate. They were the
only diners in a large square Second Empire room
badly in need of refurbishing. Doroftei drifted back
in from the sidewalk almost immediately, realizing
he hadn't told them exactly where they were. The
Capşa Restaurant. He pulled out a chair and joined
their meal. John was thrilled, remembering
characters in Olivia Manning's *Balkan Trilogy*
eating there. Wendy decided that the fictional
characters had apparently consumed everything in
the country worth eating. The waiter, answering
their question about the best item on the menu,
lavishly described something that sounded like
Muscat Otonel, turkey and mushrooms in sweet
white wine, but just as in a cheap movie, he
concluded the description by admitting the chef
hadn't any left. All he could offer, really, was soup
made from cow's stomachs.

'We don't need to eat, we're full from airline
food,' said Wendy firmly.

Doroftei took them on a night tour of the
capital. It was lucky that the peace dividends

hadn't been paid yet in outposts as far as Bucharest, because the streets were almost empty of cars. This meant Doroftei could swerve and veer as he tried to master the controls, endangering only the few pedestrians unlucky enough to be scrambling home on this very cold night.

'You'll remember every scrap of this,' said John, delirious with joy as they nearly felled an elderly man pushing a wheelbarrow full of old clothes.

'That's precisely what I'm afraid of,' she said.

By the time Winnie had reached Hampstead, she was panting, and she had to stop at a café and get a cold drink. She made a note to herself of things yet to do before ducking more fully into the Jack the Ripper novel. She would go over to the Royal Free and check on Colum Jenkins; by now he must be up to visitors. She would tell him that Mac was dangerously wacky and that anyway he had disappeared and never returned. She'd try John's office again for the umpteenth time.

And then she'd have done what she could, and the hell with him. She'd clock on to her work, and begin to roam about Angel Alley, Thrawl Street, Brick Lane, with the ghost of Jack the Ripper in her mind. With luck her narrative mind would waken and seize what it could.

A few days in the big city were more than enough. An hour would have been more than enough, really: she was eager to get going. But they had to follow the schedule as given them.

At last, though, they were out, begun on their motoring trip, circling in, nearer and nearer. Gas

queues on the road. Some of the pollarded trees
whitewashed with lime, to shoulder height, like
lanes in rural France. Doroftei singing Christmas
carols to them, because the snow began to fall.
Heading toward Braşov. On the highway the snow
seemed as gray as the bread. Once off the road,
though, on rural stretches, it whitened: snow dense
and heavy on the ground, as if heaved in by winds
from the very heart of the Siberian steppes.

'On to Poiana Braşov. Is the plan,' said
Doroftei. 'Means Sunny Clearing. Weariness and
monotony to disappear. We rest and wait.'

'I don't want to wait,' said Wendy, 'why must
we?'

'Is the plan,' said Doroftei. 'Trust me.' He
smoked the way you would if you were hoping to
die of lung cancer by morning.

At the front door of Rudge House, the estate agent was just letting
another couple in. 'Oh, a neighbor,' he said, and hustled them
through the entranceway before Winnie had a chance to queer the
deal, intentionally or by accident.

'Oh, it's you again,' said Mrs Maddingly. 'Would you come in
here and look for Chutney?'

'I don't have an inkling of how to find a cat, I'm afraid,' said
Winnie.

'That's all right, he doesn't have an inkling of how to be found,
so you're made for each other,' said Mrs Maddingly. 'It would be a
kindness.'

'I do have work to do,' Winnie said, as if she did – well, she
did, if she'd get around to it – but she let herself be led into the old
woman's rooms, which if anything looked more disheveled and

captioned than before. WHERE ARE YOU, CHUTNEY? said one note. I MEAN IT, COME BACK, said another. THE DAMN PILLS said a third.

'Sit down,' said Mrs Maddingly.

'I'll stand,' said Winnie, after she noticed each chair had an instruction taped to its seat: SIT or HERE or DON'T FORGET TO REST ONCE IN A WHILE IT'S ONLY THURSDAY.

'What do you think?'

Mrs Maddingly looked perched on a notion, Winnie thought, like someone badly wanting a drink with an olive in it. Winnie tried to be patient. 'About the cat? I don't know. Have you any ideas?'

'Ideas I have plenty of, but ideas!' She waved her hand, as if perfectly aware how demented she was becoming. 'It's fur and claw I want, not ideas!'

'The other cats are around, I guess?'

'Around, I guess, yes, I'd say they were.'

Winnie neither saw nor heard anything of them, but the distinctive house smell was recently refreshed, even ripe.

'Did you look outside?'

'He's not an outside cat,' said Mrs Maddingly with sudden irritation. 'How many times have I to remind you?'

'Has he died, maybe, under a piece of furniture?'

'I wouldn't know. But what a shame if he has done.'

'All cats die. Do you want me to bend down and look?' Considering the poor housekeeping, she was somewhat afraid of what she'd find, but once embarked on a mission of charity it was hard to justify changing course.

'I know all cats die,' said Mrs Maddingly. 'I'm not a fool. But if it was his turn I wish he'd warned me. I'd have given him a message for Alan.'

'Oh, Alan?' The husband, that's right. 'What message?' Winnie was on her hands and knees, looking under a cherry sideboard. No cat. Several dropped bottles of pills, though. She left them there; they could be years old, and poisonous by now.

'I'm afraid if I go in hospital, matron will cut my hair,' said Mrs Maddingly.

'You won't go in the hospital. Why should you?'

'I'm an ailing old lady and it'll happen sooner than I think. But what if they cut my hair?' She began to cry. Jesus.

'You'd still look fine even if they did. Though they won't. They don't do things like that.'

'They might,' she said. 'And then I'd die of shame, probably, and go to heaven or – Brighton – or wherever Alan is, and he won't know me without my hair!'

'Please, they won't touch the hair.'

'You'll tell them?'

She gritted her teeth. 'Yes. Should I look in the other rooms?'

'If you like,' said Mrs Maddingly doubtfully, drawing her sweater the tighter about her shoulders, as if afraid Winnie was about to propose a full-body search.

Winnie began to push doors open and disturb stacked sections of cold air, in rooms where the windows weren't true in their frames or the heating was broken. Eddies of lavender-scented chill, in shadowed alcoves and heavily curtained rooms. She thought she saw the tip of a whisker, but really she couldn't see anything much. And not having met the other cats, anyway, how would she recognize Chutney when she saw him?

Winnie felt a certain sympathy for poor dead Alan, blearily trying to identify his shorn wife as she came through Processing with the streams of hundreds of thousands of other old geese.

'I don't suppose he'd come if I called?' said Winnie. 'Chutney? Kitty?'

'I address him all the time,' the old woman called from the front room. A cork came sucking out of the throat of a bottle.

Then Winnie saw him, a flash in a Victorian mirror in the gloom of the old gal's boudoir. Calling it a mirror was rash: it was a genuine looking-glass, for sure. The glass was beveled, frosted, and etched. In its smoky backward recitation of reality Winnie caught just the flip of a tail. An eye like a nugget of smoldering bronze. She saw a sliver of feline sneer without seeing anything as recognizable as a small, perfect mouth with its small darts for teeth. It was like the Cheshire Cat – the smile without the cat, the attribute without the subject. Free-floating disdain.

Then it was gone.

'Oh, sweetheart, come out,' said Winnie. 'What are you scared of? Your old mama out there is going bonkers with grief. Come on.' She raised her voice. 'You'll have some tinned fish or liver, something with a smell?'

'Not for me, thank you, I've had my elevenses.'

'I mean for the cat. Here, kitty kitty kitty.'

Mrs Maddingly didn't answer. Perhaps she'd forgotten what Winnie was doing. 'Oh, well, I suppose another little drop won't hurt, if you must,' she was saying to herself. The sound of sherry pouring gluggily.

'Here, kitty,' said Winnie.

She switched on a bedside lamp; the bulb, all ten watts of it, flickered. She angled the shade, a cone of cinnamon-colored cardboard, to try to get more light. Something twitched. A sliding heap of old-lady housedresses or nightgowns, their nylon surfaces whispering against one another. 'Come on, you cat; no sense scaring the poor thing out of her mind. God knows she's half there already.' Yeah, she and who else? Winnie thought to herself: Here you are being jittery about a housecat?

Fearing a slicing claw, Winnie picked up a walker that the old woman no doubt used to get out of bed. She touched the laundry with the leg of it. Then she reached and tugged at a hem. The top garment lifted up at an angle, caught on something unseen. With a crusty ripping sound, it came away. A clot of dried sherry or some other more intimate fluid, patching one garment against another? The far edge of the next garment rippled; the cat was backing up underneath.

She said a poem to stiffen her nerves.

> 'Pussycat, Pussycat, where have you been?
> I've been to London to visit the Queen.
> Pussycat, Pussycat, what did you there?
> I frightened a little mouse—'

She stifled a gag as she peeled back the top nightgown.

Two, then three cats came to light, blood matting their fur to the nightdress below. Each one had wounds about the head or neck. They'd been chewed at. And they'd been dead long enough to stiffen. The smell was atrocious.

'Oh, Christ.'

The nightgown twitched some more, and the living cat beneath it flexed and complained in a voice more alto than, in Winnie's experience, was customary for a cat. She held the walker in front of her, ready to poke its rubber-tipped feet into the animal's face should it attack her. Then she whisked away the garment. The cat was a burnt persimmon color, like ancient orange rind. It looked twice its size, hissing, its back a wicket of radiating spikes.

She tried to speak in a level voice, as if a cat could care whether she screamed or not. 'Easy, boy, what's gotten at your poor friends?' Chutney, if so it was, launched himself into the air. Despite herself Winnie raised the walker, in foolish terror; she batted the cat away. He fell back, wailing piteously or with venom, and spat. He drove his head into the neck of one of the cats, decking himself in its blood and gop, and before Winnie could see what had happened, the cat had disappeared. Just like that? She held the light up, breathing heavily. No – she wasn't that delusional, not yet – the cat had squeezed itself behind a jutting bit of wainscoting, and squirreled himself into the rubble of ancient lath and deteriorated plaster.

'Mrs Maddingly,' said Winnie. 'I think I found your other cats. And I hate to break the news to you but I think they're dead.'

'It's not them I'm worried about,' she answered. 'They're all safely accounted for. It's my darling. Have you laid eyes on him?'

'He's orange? I believe I have. We'd better get rid of the corpses.'

Mrs Maddingly shuffled in. She peered at them. 'Surely they're just sleeping?' she said. 'They do enjoy a nice long snooze, you know. Cats are like that. They sleep all day. I hear them up and cavorting at night, once I've gone to bed and turned the lamp down.'

'They're done cavorting, I'm afraid.'

'Well, they've been done cavorting for some time; they've been fixed for years, all of them,' said Mrs Maddingly. 'And a good thing too. Proper ladies they were. Look at them, all resting in peace.'

Mrs Maddingly braced herself with a sip of medicinal something and took herself off to the kitchen to locate a hand broom and a dustpan.

'I do find all that hard to believe,' said Allegra Lowe, when Winnie had taken herself in hand and called her to make further inquiry into news about John. 'Are you suggesting that Chutney killed his companions?'

'I have never heard of a cat killing another cat,' said Winnie. 'Have you?'

'It's vile, and I've a customer at the door,' said Allegra, as if Winnie was making it up, and rang off.

★

Winnie had moved the construction tools to one side and put John's kitchen as much back to rights as she could. When she went to the Royal Free Hospital to ask about Colum Jenkins, she was told he had been checked out by a family member several days earlier. The staff refused to divulge his home address. 'But he was all right?' Winnie said.

'He'd not have been released otherwise,' said the clerk.

'Well, hopeless cases, you know. Sending someone home to die. That sort of thing,' said Winnie apologetically, before wandering off.

Given the peculiarities of life in Rudge House, the slain cats, the increasing dottiness of Mrs Maddingly, it was beginning to seem entirely of a piece that Winnie's cousin was missing with no forwarding address. But what was there to do about it? Winnie made the place her own as best as she could. Reluctant to turn on her laptop, she set herself small exercises each day, trying to jump-start the story of Wendy Pritzke and her obsession with Jack the Ripper. Though as she headed in the Tube toward Aldgate one bitterly damp day, a tourist pamphlet advertising Jack the Ripper sites tucked in the inside pocket of her coat, it did occur to Winnie that Wendy Pritzke seemed to have left London.

Winnie didn't believe in writing as channeling, in any sense. She was a hack, a journeyman, a slogger. Yet usually she could prod a character into her consciousness by insulting it a bit, challenging it to respond. Not so on this trip. Like John Comestor, Wendy Pritzke appeared to have disappeared, just at the time that the thing, the shred, the shroud, had been exhumed, unhoused. Wendy was farther out already, in the hinterlands of Romania, for all she knew.

Still, work was work. Maybe some torrid bit of local color, some sleight-of-vision coincidence, would reveal Wendy Pritzke or her intentions, or the thing that threatened her, in what was left of Ripper London. Winnie felt increasingly dubious, but this was her work. She couldn't be doing nothing.

The Metropolitan Line train terminated at Aldgate. She was decanted into one end of a suburban shopping mall that seemed to burrow in the right direction, following the line of Whitechapel High Street above and heading toward Commercial Street. Winnie wasn't looking for much, not an exposé of Jack the Ripper, certainly not a real ghost, but a bit of charming overlap, the kind of thing that in someone else's hands might make an amusing *New Yorker* 'Talk of the Town' piece. Anything could be a germ. Anything could hot-wire a fever. Only when the fever took over was there a story.

But though she'd set her sights on Thrawl Street, because she loved the name, she began to lose heart once she emerged from the glassy fluorescence of the shopping mall into the gritted streets above. Commercial Street seemed largely Pakistani, as far as she could make out.

Thrawl Street, Angel Alley, Gunthorpe Street. Women turning to prostitution because of poverty, homelessness. All the dangers, all the huge lonelinesses, all the appurtenances of love with none of the affection. Martha Tabram mutilated, stabbed thirty-nine times after the 'cheap and quick knee trembler' her friend Pearly Poll reported to the police. All that tumbling of organs onto the ground, all that simple need for cash so that a woman could spend a night sleeping on a mattress out of the wind.

Sadly, Thrawl Street had nothing much to say to Winnie, or nothing of use. It seemed to have been subsumed into a housing estate of red brick and nicely slanting roofs. From doorways bloomed the ghosts of curry past, present, and yet to come. Midday, the place was largely deserted, and there was no kernel, no starter yeast. The whole district was airy and desolate.

Loneliness collapsed into her. She wandered by Indian takeaway and discount footware storefronts, feeling Jack the Ripper dissolving, the mystery of his indecency beyond either her power to call it up or to dismiss it. She gave up, feeling as if in abandoning the lookout for the ghost of Jack the Ripper, she was putting her dim Wendy Pritzke at greater risk. But Winnie knew nothing else to do. She went back to Hampstead.

That night she made herself a strong drink and set herself the mental task of remembering John's friend's name. When she woke up she had it: Britt Chalmers. Listed in the directory, hurrah. Chalmers, Girdlestone Walk, Highgate. She waited till a respectful 10 A.M. on a Saturday morning and woke him up.

'Oh, so sorry,' she said jollily. 'I always assume if people don't want to be awakened by the phone these days they turn the ringer off or pull the connection out. But there you are. While I've got you, Britt, I need to know where John Comestor is.'

'Who is this?' he said groggily.

'It's Winifred Rudge. We ran into each other some days ago at the Café Rouge. John still hasn't shown up and there's all sorts of funny business going on here.'

'Oh,' said Britt. 'Yes, I remember. Well, I'll be little help to you, I'm afraid. The man runs his affairs with the secrecy of MI5. I'm sure he's not half as full of derring-do as he'd like us to believe. He's probably planting a herbaceous border at some hideaway cottage in the Cotswolds. How long are you going to stay?'

'A while yet.' She felt stiff and faintly paranoid, for he was hiding something from her, she could tell it and not prove it. She continued. 'Quite a while, I guess. Or maybe not. I've got MI5 in my blood too, I suppose. We're cousins, after all.'

'Yes,' he said. 'Right. Well, then.' He rang off.

★

'Rice here.'

'Malcolm Rice. This is Winnie Rudge.'

'Yes. Oh, yes. You're still here, or have you gone away and come back already?'

'Still here. Look, I hate to seem a busybody, but I'm running out of ideas. It's closing in on two weeks and there's still no sign from John, no word, no phone call. Has he been in touch with you?'

There was a long pause. Winnie imagined the older man studying his cuticles, trying to remember his brief. 'Miss Rudge, do you think he's avoiding you?'

'I hardly think that, Malcolm.' She used his Christian name like an insult. 'What possible reason could he have for doing that?'

'Oh, far beyond me even to speculate. He just doesn't seem like the type of fellow to get in trouble of a serious nature. You haven't overlooked some note? You didn't scribble the dates in your diary wrong?'

'Should I go to the police? I don't want to get involved in raising suspicions about him at work.'

'It is not my business to say what you should do or not do, Miss Rudge. If you'll excuse me, I've guests in the lounge. There's nothing more to say. Don't bother to ring again; if I've anything to tell you, I'll take it upon myself to be in touch.'

I'm making a nuisance of myself, she thought. But what else can I do?

She rang Rasia. She got a child on the phone who with some prodding admitted his name. 'Tariq.'

'Tariq McIntyre,' said Winnie. 'May I speak to your mommy?'

'No,' said Tariq. He breathed asthmatically, waiting.

'Please?'

'She's not here. She's—' More breathing. 'Out.'

'Oh. Who's minding you?'

'Navida.'

'I see. Well, would you remember to tell her that I called?'

'Tell her what?'

'I mean, tell her I rang. Winnie. Can you remember? It's okay. I'm the one who came and we listened to the sounds in the closet? Your mom said sometimes she heard a cat there. Oh, you don't hear a cat anymore, do you?' She had a thought, of Chutney breaking through the shared wall, and coming into the McIntyre flat, and doing to the poor McIntyre baby what it might have done to Mrs Maddingly's cats. It was a stupid, silly thought, but it wouldn't go away. 'Is there a cat in your flat? Have you seen a cat? Don't go near it. Are you alone? Let me speak to Navida.'

'You can't.'

'Oh, it's important. Let me speak to Navida.'

'You can't. She can't.'

'Why not?'

'She's in the loo.'

'Oh. There's a baby, where is it?'

'With Mum.'

'Tariq. Tariq. Listen. Have you seen a cat in your flat?'

Tariq did a young person's version of the same sort of quiet rumination that Malcolm Rice had done. As if humoring her. 'Well . . .'

'Tariq, yes or no?'

'Sort of a cat.'

'Tariq, answer me. Yes or no.'

'I don't want to talk to you anymore,' he said. He rang off.

She walked around the block and knocked at the door. Navida and Tariq wouldn't let her in. Allegra Lowe came to the window and looked up from the kitchen, her hands all covered in plaster dust. With a huff of derision she disappeared and then a minute later opened the front door. 'It's you; are you becoming some sort of squatter around here?'

'Oh, I know you'll think I'm bonkers.' She spoke quickly because she knew that the words would certify her as a lunatic, and she couldn't help it. 'I'm worried that old Mrs Maddingly's cat has found a way to burrow through the walls and get into your side of the house. Have you heard anything? Any yowling?'

'There's only one thing yowling, and it isn't pretty.'

'Oh, stop, just *stop* it. You didn't see those cats laid out. Let me in, Allegra. Those kids are home alone up there.'

'Winnie, if you don't mind my being blunt, it's none of your concern.'

'It's absolutely of my concern and I do mind your being blunt.' She was ready to take offense at everything. 'Will you just let me pass? I'll be only a moment up there.'

But before they could come to a scuffle, Rasia came trodding along on the pavement, the baby in a Snugli and the computer weighing down her shoulder. 'Hello, a party,' she said. 'Just what I need after a long day.' But her face was clouded and the baby whimpering.

'Hardly a *party*,' said Allegra, and stomped away, slamming her inside door.

'I can't ask you in, I've left the little ones alone and this one needs a change of nappy. Another time?'

'Rasia, have you seen a cat in your apartment? An orange cat? Have you heard it mewing in the walls the way you did a week or two ago?'

'No cats,' said Rasia, 'and no time. Please, Winnie. I have to close this door.'

'Just tell me for sure. I'm not being silly.'

'I'm going to close the door now.'

There seemed no place else to turn. Winnie had folded the shroud into as regular a stack of cloth as she could, given its ragtag edges, and sprinkled it liberally with moth flakes. Then she'd tucked it in a plastic John Lewis bag and knotted the handles together. The parcel gave off no sinister reek of presence. It was just an old potato sack someone had hung on a nail, no matter what Ritzi Ostertag had said.

She sat at the kitchen table in the vacant flat, writing Wendy, Wendy, Wendy Pritzke, unable to find her.

Already through Ploişti, and Cimpina, and Sinaia, those pretty cities only a string of memories from Bucharest to Braşov. How quickly could memories be set in place, how firmly erased?

In each town that they stopped for the night, Wendy and John had requested separate rooms, as befits cousins, though they were stepcousins really, not blooded. After suffering separately the cold dribble that passed for a shower, they met in Wendy's room. She sat on the calcified mattress, which was made up with sheets and blanket in the usual manner, but also wrapped all round with a clean white sheet in which a central shape had been cut, so the blanket from beneath showed through as a lozenge of wool the color of horsehair.

She sipped her gray vodka and cut her lip on a chip in the glass.

'So we're here,' said John.

'We're here,' she answered, 'bleeding and all.'

'You're all here?'

'Meaning?'

'You're not chasing Jack the Ripper in your mind?'

'My job is to be here. We've left that fancy far behind. This is real.'

'Are you scared?'

'Only very scared, not very very scared.'

'It'll be more than all right. It's the beginning of everything good.'

'Don't say that.' She kicked off her shoes and lay back on the bed, not so much relaxing ostentatiously in front of him, but trying to work out the kinks in her lower spine from a day spent in the rackety car driven by Doroftei.

'I saved some bread from lunch, are you hungry?' he said.

'The bread is grayer than the vodka.'

'You have to keep up your strength.'

'More vodka, then, dear thing.'

He came to the edge of the bed and perched briefly on it, his rump making a pull in the sheet, a ripple of cotton. How could the Romanians get their linen so white when their flour was so ashen? She'd hardly eaten a thing but crackers since arriving.

She hoped he wouldn't stay on the bed, and he didn't, because Doroftei knocked on the door and he jumped up guiltily. Though there was nothing to be guilty about, nothing; there never had been.

'On to the holiday hour,' said Doroftei. He had rubbed something like motor oil in his hair, and his shirt was rakishly open to the second button. 'Such good time to enjoy, you tell everyone in U.S. and U.K., they all coming to Sunny Clearing, Poiana Braşov, and being happy.'

'Do we have to be happy tonight?' she said in a low voice, but John had been the one to hire the driver, through connections at his work; he couldn't allow Costal Doroftei to think them bored or uninterested for a moment.

'How many more nights have we?' John asked.

'Let's just go look and see.'

Once again she called John's office. She tried the main number this time.

'Who may I say is calling?' said the receptionist.

She mumbled, something sounding more like Wendy Pritzke than Winnie Rudge.

'I'm having a hard time catching that,' said the woman. 'With what firm, please?'

'Pritzke Enterprise,' said Winnie.

'I see. Just a minute, miss.' Winnie was put on hold. 'I'm sorry, Mr Comestor is out of the office indefinitely.'

'When will he be back?'

'I've no more information at present on Mr Comestor. Please try later.'

'When will he be back? I haven't got all day to keep ringing—'

She called Rasia.

'Look,' said Rasia, 'I know you're having a hard time of it. But I'm beyond frantic. You frightened Tariq rather badly, do you know that? I don't want you calling and scaring him, or Navida.'

'You should let me finish, Rasia. I know it sounds goofy, but that cat is on the loose somewhere in the building. This isn't my imagination. I saw those cats it killed.'

'Cats don't kill cats,' said Rasia. She sounded as if she thought Winnie had done it. 'Please don't ring me for a while. I have a new account and it's taking all my spare time.'

'Just one thing: promise me if the cat comes through the wall, you'll leave, you'll clear out.'

'Come through the wall like a ghost? Like your old Christmas Past? As they say on the American sitcoms, sweetheart: Get a grip.' She rang off.

All of London seemed in collusion to do one thing: Hang up the receiver on her. *brmmmmmmmmmmmm.*

'Oh, this is like Miami Beach or something.' The building was mostly concrete, like a convention center, though it had a spun sugar application of wooden eaves and painted fretwork, a nod to Bavarian chalets. The parking lot was largely empty, even on a Saturday night. Still, choking with laughter about seeing the Sunny Clearing at night, Wendy was not prepared for how lovely the walk was. Once out of the lot, they wound about on a snowy path over which freshly cut pine boughs had been spread. Their boots crushed the needles, and each step blossomed with resin scent, expressive of Christmas. The stars leered and leaned, brighter than any in London or Boston, almost pushpins, almost three-dimensional. John took her hand.

'A Christmas to remember,' he said.

'Nowhere near Christmas yet,' she said, legalistically.

'Yes, but as much like as to stand in for it.' He meant for the Christmas they would never share together. She nodded.

'Oh,' said Doroftei, 'this is sweet goodness; all that's missing is pussy.' He smiled unapologetically at Wendy, who felt as if she were supposed to nod and agree. But she was suddenly shy.

The walkway led over a wooden bridge. Small white lights were looped around the posts and struts of the bridge. The stream below was mostly snowed over, though there was a glassy jingle as of ice bits caught in a bottleneck.

She wanted to stand in the snow, on the pines, surrounded by lights, on a nine-foot bridge, under Romanian stars, all night long, and keep it as a memory. She didn't want to move forward to where she could hear a pulsing antiquated disco beat ready to drum the atmosphere into a pulp.

'As good as Christmas,' she allowed to John.

She was at a loss; how often did that happen? London usually felt full and redolent of the past, so saturated with atmosphere that one could sometimes hardly breathe – now it felt airless. Should she just go back to Boston, give up on the idea of a novel about Wendy Pritzke? Why not just bolt? Shrug off any remaining responsibility about home renovations in a property that didn't even belong to her, order a minicab, head for Heathrow, hit the bar for a glass of something with a lemon rind or a pickled onion in it.

Nothing called for her to come back to Boston, that was part of the problem. And the only thing really urging her to stay was the fey though ineffectual parasite that had seemed to infect Rudge House.

So she found herself, a few days later, back at the door of Ritzi Ostertag's place in Cowcross Street. A heavy tide of patchouli couldn't disguise a smell of roach spray. If an exorcism were needed, of any sort, Winnie deduced, either ectoplasm or vermin, Ritzi Ostertag probably wouldn't be up for the job.

Ritzi looked up from the cash register where he was writing out a receipt to a weeping young woman from the Caribbean. 'Four times a day rain or shine until ze full moon,' he said, handing her a paper sack. 'And zen ve'll see vhat ve'll zee.' He rolled his eyes at the sight of Winnie, but with a toss of his head he indicated: *Sit, ve vill talk.*

She tried to melt into the background, but the background was occupied by that American historian, Hausserman. She was surprised how quickly she remembered the name. He was leafing through an old dusty volume whose pages were deckled on side and bottom, and touched with gold on the top. 'Oh, you,' he said. 'If you've come to buy this early-nineteenth-century *Die Wunder-geschichten des Caesarius von Heisterbach*, you're out of luck. Dibs. But there's a duplicate *Fantômes et revenants au Moyen Age* by Lecouteux as a consolation prize.'

'I'm here to have my fortune told,' she said.

'Professional research or greedy for knowledge in a Faustian sense?'

'The silence of the confessional obtains, I believe. None of your beeswax, as we used to say in Simsbury, Connecticut.'

'I understand.' He nodded with a parody of British courtesy derived from Merchant Ivory films, and turned his attention back to the page.

'What are you looking for?' She didn't want to engage him, but she couldn't help herself.

He gave her a wink. 'Our dear Ostertag may be flighty but the boy does deliver the goods, I'll give him that.'

Ritzi came over. 'I can't be seeink you now,' he said to Winnie, 'I can't be givink myself over to ze spirit vorld.'

'I'll wait till you finish this sale. I can wait.'

'You're in hurry,' said Ritzi.

'No I'm not.'

'You are, you just are not yet knowink it.'

She let out a laugh that sounded too much like a high squeal. Then she shrugged. Irv Hausserman closed the book and he negotiated a price. A number of soft pale notes changed hands and Ritzi wrote up the exchange, and wrapped the book lovingly in a length of white muslin, and again in brown paper and string.

'What a pleasant surprise to run into you again,' said Irv. 'Opal, isn't it?' He nodded his good-byes, and left whistling, shunting the book lovingly from arm to arm. She hated to see him go, but she couldn't think of anything to say that would keep him.

'Now.' Ritzi Ostertag began the flourishes and flounces of his act. 'A new lock on ze door so zis time ve are not beink interrupted. I am knowink you vill return. Zat cloth has got you wrapped.' Or had he said 'rapt'? 'I believe I tell you you are not to be brinkink it back.'

'Yes, you told me not to.'

'But you disobey Ritzi and brink it.'

'Yes.'

'Good. I am vantink to look at it more closely.' He made hurrying motions, shaking his hands. She sat down and unwrapped the thing once again.

Though he seemed determined to keep up his accent this time, Ritzi Ostertag didn't attempt mood lighting or a medieval music soundtrack. He turned several desk lights on and sat down at a table like an Antwerp jeweler with an eyepiece studying an old diamond. 'Such strong – I don't know – associations I am gettink,' he said. 'It is strange. Bitter as radish is bitter.'

'Is it haunted?' said Winnie.

'A piece of cloth? How can a fragment of cloth be haunted?'

'How could a house be haunted, or a forest, or a person's dreams? I don't know. Is it?'

'Not my area of specialization. I haff no talent at zuch zinks.

But I can zense a great – somezink. Some *Schreck*.' He closed his eyes and rubbed his fingers very gently on the fabric. He was like a wine connoisseur proving his prowess over a mystery vintage. 'I can tell you very little about zis, but somezink about yourself comes through. I zink zis is about you, but I can't tell.'

'This cloth can't be about me. I merely helped find it.'

He took long, deep breaths. 'Oh, ze poor somezink. Vhatever it iz. You or it, or did I say last time it vas a she-thing? Yes, I zink it vas.'

'You think it was . . . ?'

'The shroud of a young voman.'

He opened his eyes. His hands had been roaming as if over a keyboard, and they stopped. He looked more closely, and held the cloth up. 'Damn zese bad eyes,' he said, 'gettink old is no fun. Vhat is zis?'

'I don't see anything,' she said.

'I can feel it. I zink I can see it. Yes, look, if you hold ze cloth so zat ze light falls against it like so – a pattern. Do you zee? A letter, perhaps, a numeral? Vhat is it?'

She could not see it at first, but then she thought she picked up a pattern of glazed threads with matted-down hairs, as distinct from the surround of coarser threads. She was hardly surprised. That same symbol, a cross with a zigzag slash through it. Four or five inches high, perhaps painted with wax, or a pigment whose color had long since faded, leaving only a residue of binder.

'What does it mean?' she said.

'Ask somevone else, not me,' he said, 'but it is feelink stronger to me zan ze rest.'

'What precisely do you mean?' she said.

'As a pepper soup is heartier zan a banana soup. Don't interrupt.' His hands moved slowly, reading like Braille, but stopped nowhere else, until, with eyes closed, his fingers roamed the cloth

to its hem, reached a few inches, and touched her fingertips. She sat there, frightened and angry.

'Vhat do you vant?' he asked her, more like a doctor than a priest.

'I am not getting through, anywhere,' she said. 'I am a writer whose character has left her; I don't even know where she went. If this is a block, it's a first time for me. I can't get her on the page, I can't see her in my lazy mind's eye before I go to sleep. I can't find my cousin, who has disappeared. I am afraid to admit that my cousin's house is mildly haunted by whoever it was who was wrapped in this cloth. I have a mad notion that one of my ancestors was the prototype for Charles Dickens's Ebenezer Scrooge, the one who suffered all those visitations by ghosts. I don't know if he was mad, or fanciful, or psychotic; I don't know if I am finding myself the same. Nothing is connected. Nothing makes sense. I am not getting through anywhere.'

Ritzi sighed. 'I don't know about writer's block. Ze only kind of writer's block I haff is in signink my name to bank checks vhen my bills come due. I can't make myself do it. But such blank valls, zere is so little to attach. Vhat haff you done to yourself?'

'So I've dyed my hair,' she admitted, 'only against a little gray.'

'No, not zat,' he said. 'Am I gettink you or am I gettink some whiff of ze shroud-phantom?'

'If you can get a whiff of anything over your industrial-strength patchouli, I'm surprised.'

'You hold me off, more zan you need,' he said. He opened his eyes and looked at her clinically. Once again the accent fell off. 'I may be a silly old bore but I'm not a fool, you know. I can tell you've had some doings with astrology somehow. I can tell that making fun of people is your professional strength and your living grave.'

'I asked for a reading of the future, not the present,' she said.

'You keep yearning to go east, but you're either going too far or you're not going far enough,' he said. 'You are not finding the right – destiny. Destination. It is not the Balkans. You're misled. Go nearer or go farther.'

'It was a character of mine who was going there. Not me.'

'Whoever this is,' he said, moving his hand back to the nearly invisible scar of marking on the edge of the cloth, 'wants to go back, but like you – cannot. It is a problem of getting through. She has lost the way to get through. She needs help. Who will be her helpmeet?'

After dropping thirty pounds into a brass scale held by a grinning Hanuman figure, Winnie made her way downstairs to Cowcross Street, thinking: What a bravura performance that was. He took what she gave off about herself – her intensely divided and lonely self – and made of it a story about a ghost who was equally indigent. He ought to go into fiction writing, why not? Maybe they should collaborate, and together they could find out what had happened to Wendy Pritzke.

But had she ever mentioned the Balkans to him? To Rasia? How did he know?

Irv Hausserman was waiting for her at the corner. 'Sorry,' he said, 'I know this seems like stalking, but by now my curiosity is piqued. Did Mr Ostertag tell you that you would run into me again in the near future, like half an hour or so?'

She wasn't happy to be waylaid, but it was better than seeing no one, since she seemed to have ostracized herself from every figment and figure she knew, in her mind and out of it. 'He said my ghost has a hard time getting home.'

'You have a ghost. A personal one? How leading edge of you. Is it lost?'

'It's all bunk, I know. Once upon a time I wrote faux

horoscopes and made a healthy living at it; anyone with a semblance of an imagination can do it. But there's just enough creepiness in the whole thing to make me very sad.' She told him about the finding of the cloth in her family home, and about the pattern daubed on the edge of the cloth.

'You're sure you saw that insignia on the pantry boards? On your computer screen?'

'Oh, once something happens, who can be sure of anything? I thought I did, but I am modern enough to mistrust my senses. Clearly I'm overwrought with worry over my cousin, and pretending not to be.'

'Why bother to pretend? Why not be overwrought?'

'I can see things that aren't there,' she said. 'I guard against that.'

'Like ghosts?'

'Like conspiracies. Like plots. Like narrative plots, I mean, but also like paranoia. I'm not superstitious but I am suspicious.'

'Give me an example.'

'Can't. I don't know you well enough; you might cut me off entirely. There, that's suspicion for you, see? And I—' She did not say, I like you, nor, worse, I need you, or someone.

'Oh, go ahead. There are only so many sentences you can stop in midstride before you yourself stop in midstride.'

She tried to smile wanly at that, but it was too true to ignore. 'All right. Let's leave aside all the business of a haunting. The ghost of Jack the Ripper, the ghost of Ebenezer Scrooge, the ghost of Ozias Rudge, the ghost of some poor murdered housemaid from the early nineteenth century.' He had heard none of this before; he bravely refrained from flinching. She rushed on. 'I'm a hack and I'm slightly haunted by my own professional skills – it's an occupational hazard. I accept that. I can't get through to my main character and so my novel is stalled. I accept that. I accept that I'm driving the neighbors crazy. Even the dotty old bat on the ground floor has begun to avoid me. Fair enough. But why do I get the feeling that my cousin's disappearance is a conspiracy against me?'

'So that's really what you're overwrought about.'

'Overwrought implies hysteria. I'm not overwrought, I'm just wrought. I feel as if his office is hiding something from me. The whole thing makes me feel paranoid, and then the world is all – oh – a shrill lemon color, a place without comforting shadows, or without clear lights. I can't think of the metaphor. Music has no charm to soothe this wild beast.'

'Sounds like depression to me.'

'Yes, doesn't it?'

'But could you be right? That there *is* a conspiracy?'

'You met me at a professional clairvoyant's,' she reminded him. 'Doesn't that suggest I'm a bit fringy? You're there buying your tools for academic research, I'm there getting a seer's evaluation of a horse blanket? Why shouldn't I be delusional too?'

They had walked out of Cowcross Street and meandered along, aimlessly heading deeper into the City. Finally, she repeated, 'I'll prove it to you, if you like,' as they paused on a street corner, unsure whether they were continuing together, but not ready to press on, nor to break off.

There was a phone box on the corner. 'I could call and be put off. You could see that. If you need proof.'

'Well, if you think it's a conspiracy against you,' he said, testing her, 'I could call. Let me. Shall I?'

'Why not? What is there to lose?'

What was there to lose?

He had coins and dropped them in. She told him the number by heart. The connection took a little while to make. She stood, struggling with all manner of perturbations.

Was there anything in the literature that ascertained for certain that Jack the Ripper was male? Could the Ripper have been a woman? Why would a woman kill other women? And if Jack the Ripper was a woman, could this shroud have been hers?

'Yes, I'll wait,' said Irv Hausserman. He leaned against the Plexiglas edge of what passed for a phone box – a boxless phone box, these days – obscuring the advertisements of hookers and lady companions and their phone numbers and special talents. The edge of Ripper territory, still served by prostitutes all these decades later.

She didn't want to appear too eager. She looked at a full-color advertisement of a dominatrix, a card about four by six, affixed to the glass with gum tack. The woman was laced into a corset of black leather. Her color was high and her eyes were hidden by a bar of black ink put in by the printer's studio. On either side of the photo her services were listed. Psychological Manipulation. Strict Discipline. Inescapable Bondage. Fetish Enhancement. Intense Torment Scenarios. She carried a riding crop like a cowgirl about to enter a bullpen. The typeface was Ye Olde Gothick.

What if this were Jenkins's daughter, her eyes hidden behind that privacy-protection device? What if Jenkins stopped to use this phone and saw her? Would he recognize her? Would he dare to call the number?

'So what's the deal?' she said belligerently, poking Hausserman in the shoulder.

'They said to hold the line,' he answered, 'they're putting me through.'

Stave Four

As Dante in the *Purgatorio*

hears the voice of his Beatrice before he sees her – by a good few lines, if Winnie remembered rightly – she heard the voice of John Comestor before she laid eyes on him. She didn't hear what he was saying, just his voice, his real living voice, around the iron pillar of a glossily overrestored late-Victorian pub off Fleet Street. She called out to him, 'John,' before she saw him.

The room full of lunching account execs – lunching on pints, that is – and he there, no fuller or realer than ever, banter to the bartender on his lips – then he was turning to Winnie. Apology and defense and, was it, a sort of mock inquisitiveness in his features. Cataloging these emotional stances helped her ignore things like the diverting color of his eyes, the killer-lover haircut, et cetera. 'Who could ever have guessed all *this*,' he said to her, and leaned forward. She was impatient with relief and anger, and so full of contradictions that her embrace in return felt like a kind of whiplash. She stiffened and yielded simultaneously.

'It's far too noisy here,' she said. 'Since when have pubs become so upmarket?'

'The rah-rah nineties. Have a quick bottoms-up and we'll find someplace else.'

'I don't know that I care to.' But she accepted a pint of Murphy's. They settled in the ambiguous light of frosted glass. 'Cheers,' she said, as if daring him to feel cheerful in the presence of her well-regulated fury.

Up to the challenge, he. 'Here's to us.'

'And,' she added, 'you have a lot of explaining to do.'

'Not as much as all that. If you give it a think.'

'I'll have a word with you. And the word is: why?'

A door opened in the wall; on a tray, out came jacket potatoes steaming and starchy, both moist and dry. A reek of Branston pickle. On an abandoned napkin that the busboy had overlooked lay an old hunk of cheese cracked like the glaze in an heirloom plate. She could harvest any moment and stuff her senses with nonsense, and that was what nonsense was: a kind of antimatter, a sexy sleight of hand that deflected attention from the urgent world.

'I am visiting London,' she said. 'Did you forget?'

'What a balls-up. I knew you'd been here. Thought you had left already. You were going on to Romania surely?'

'Maybe I was. But I haven't.' She relaxed her spine against the chair back. Her voice didn't tremble. 'We're talking so calmly. As if only about a missed bus or a lost library book. John, what happened? I was coming to London, you knew that. Where did you go? Why were you not there? Have you been at work? Why could Irv get through your secretarial defenses when I couldn't?'

'Irv?'

'And where are you staying? You're in town and you're not at home – where have you been? And all the commotion at your house?'

'Well, that; who could put up with the dust? I relocated, of course.'

'Do you know how worried I was? Do you know what I thought—' Her voice was rising. John paid and they left.

Resumed talking only after a good walk, heading toward the Embankment. The air was clammy, and an unsavory smell of sewage and mud lifted over the riverside traffic, cutting through even the heady edge of exhaust.

'Look, I know I was taking a risk,' he said, 'but I thought it might just help. I thought you might thank me in time. You might still.'

'Thank you for what? Scaring me out of my wits?'

'You'd no call to be scared.'

'Tell me where you have been.'

'I told you.' He shook his head with a brusque decisive movement. 'I had business in Denmark. It was last minute and I tried to ring. There was something wrong with your line. I couldn't get through. I knew you couldn't change your booking at the eleventh hour, or wouldn't, so it didn't much matter that your phone was wonky. I assumed you'd arrive, find my note, do your little local investigations for your book, and in three or four days be on to Romania—'

'What note?'

'I left you a note. You didn't see it?'

'There was nothing for me, no note, no you, only two crazy men doing God knows what to your kitchen, and the foolishness that followed on from that.'

'Well. No wonder, then. I don't know what happened to it. I stuck it under the door knocker, wedged it in between the appliance and the wood. Quite firmly. Your name on it, no one else's. Sorry about that.'

'*Sorry* about that?'

'Don't get huffy, Winnie. A change of plans compounded by a mishap.'

'John, would you stand still a moment so I can' – she looked around – 'wrench that pay phone box off its post and brain you with it? I'd be so grateful. Your house – Rudge House – is being haunted by something out of the chimney stack. You're back in town and back at work, avoiding my calls and staying somewhere else. You know I'm here. You're sidestepping the issues. Maybe you went away legitimately, but your workers said you'd been gone all week. Not just the night before. What are you hiding from me? Or *why* are you hiding from me?'

'I'm not hiding from you.'

'And where are you staying? With Allegra?'

He looked at her. 'Well, yes, as a matter of fact.'

She felt she had stumbled into yet another ring of Wonderland, as if rabbit hole after rabbit hole dropped her down farther and farther away from reality. 'Allegra lied to me when I asked her? Plain and simple, just like that?'

'I have only just come back to London the last day or so. Don't blame her. You know what this is about. Winnie, look at me. You know what this is about.'

'I don't know why you would lie to me.'

'It's a way of telling you the truth, Winnie, the truth you are so reluctant to hear. You know this.'

'The truth about Allegra? I've known that for years. You're welcome to her. If she'd lie for you, she's not worth you. And what do I care anyway?'

'Allegra Lowe has nothing to do with this. I'm talking about you and me and Romania, Winnie. I'm talking about the truth of that. I'd hoped to make an easier passage for you by absenting myself. I'd hoped to put myself out of the picture and let you do your London stay, probably irritated by my absence, but maybe compelled toward Romania to do what you had to do by yourself. By *yourself*. When I got back and called Allegra from Stansted, she said you were still here, and enmeshed in some—'

She could tell he was trying not to say *fiction*.

'– *puzzlement*,' he chose at last, 'having to do with the house renovation. And it seemed a sort of Romania all over again. Having started off on a campaign to let you work things out for yourself, I thought it only fair to continue.'

'Romania is a novel,' she said. 'What's happening at Rudge House is an apparition, a presence of some sort. And what you have done to me is a betrayal. Pure and simple. Save me from myself?

Who are you to save me from anyone? You are my cousin and my friend. You've behaved like neither.'

'Who is Irv?' he said.

'No one, an accident, a friendly nobody. Whose male voice apparently caused your secretary to relax her guard against female callers, and put you on the line.'

'American, I hear. Are you traveling with him?'

'John, he is a passerby – a nonentity. He did me a favor. He did me a favor. He prodded you out of the woodwork, and that's that. Meanwhile, I'm staying in your house, and the place is good and haunted, and you've made me crazy with your strategies—'

She continued. 'Certainly Allegra must have told you about the wild night of the storm, when we were nailed into your flat? That I found no note, that I had no way of knowing where you were?'

'She told me about the former. Bizarre, but no harm done, I trust. As to the note, she couldn't tell whether you were lying about not having seen a message from me.'

'You are deeply charmed by this notion of lying.'

'You are capable of lying to yourself.' Suddenly she heard something new in his voice, not venom, not anger, but regret so fiercely stated as to seem a type of anger. 'You are *entirely* capable of lying to yourself. As you no doubt know. Your professional training if nothing else. Are you sure you didn't see a note from me, and conveniently forget it?'

'I saw nothing but ghostly presence and human absence.' The tears of a teenager leaped stupidly to her middle-aged eyes, those aching eyes flanged with crow's-feet, her lashes thinned out by nocturnal rubbings. Straining to see whatever was real and reliable in this story of deceptions and revelations. The tears were comforting, though the mucus from her nose a mess. Still, she felt better after a moment or two. But then, he was holding her to keep her safe.

At last she said, 'Aren't you going to ask me about the ghost?'

'Some other ghost than you?'

'This time, yes.'

They went to a restaurant, but Winnie couldn't eat. She rearranged the translucent rounds of tomato on the plate and required cup after cup of tea, and then several visits to the cold toilets. The meal was recreational and neutral. A pas de deux composed entirely of side-steps. John drank a bottle of Riesling by himself. 'The afternoon off,' he said.

When the waitress had removed their plates and the debit card had been taken and returned, John said, 'I suppose I do want to know what you think is going on in the house.'

'Aren't you coming back to see for yourself?'

'I am not sure that's entirely sensible.'

'Oh, well, nothing about this is *sensible*.' She had intended to sound irate, but in fact there *was* nothing sensible about any of these events. And maybe admitting that and moving on was the only way through.

'Just tell me what you think.'

She did not start at the beginning, she did not tell a story. So often the details obscured the – the intention. She gave a précis, an abstract, as best she could.

'There is a paranormal presence in the house, and I believe it's been blocked up for decades, and your home handymen inadvertently woke it up. It was wrapped in a shawl or a shroud of some sort, age indeterminate, hanging on a nail against the Georgian chimney stack, though whether it was put there then or when the house was renovated in late-nineteenth-century Victorian times, I don't know.'

He didn't comment on this. He looked at her with a waiting expression. She felt obscure, difficult, like a computer screen that hadn't finished booting up properly, offering him nothing yet to work with. The Microsoft icon of the hourglass frozen in one place, no single grain of cybernetic sand sifting through to change a blessed thing. 'There's a part of my mind that thinks in story—'

'Do you have any other part?' he inquired, the first sign of affection today, albeit a patronizing one.

'Don't interrupt. Imagination could be partly intuition. It could be. And my imagination is caught on the idea of a Jack the Ripper figure – or figurine, since Ritzi Ostertag thinks the ghost is a female.'

'Ritzi who?'

'But I also wonder if this thing has been there longer, maybe as long ago as when our own Ozias Rudge built this house. Perhaps the story of haunting he is said to have told young Dickens was derived from some apparition he had, courtesy of this same poltergeist.'

'What is the dickens in the phrase "What the Dickens?"'

He was humoring her. She struggled to keep her voice level. 'Allegra will have told you all. The sounds in the chimney, the accident of the chimney pot braining poor Jenkins. None of this, I might add, would have taken on such an overtone of doom if I had known where you were, or even why you were absent. I half thought the malicious sprite was the ghost of you.'

'Winnie.' He held her hand briefly. 'It wasn't me. I'm right here.'

'I know that, I'm not a fool, don't condescend.' She snatched her hand away, triumphantly. Perhaps her recoiling was what he had intended, what he was intending through this whole campaign of absence he'd been waging. 'But I thought it was you. And I'm sure I was on edge.'

'Reading into things.'

'Not paranoid, if that's what you're getting at.'

'Of course not. But sensitive. Or sensitized. You get like that.'

'John,' she said, 'there is a ghost in your house. Are you coming to see it or not?'

'If you can show it to me,' he said, 'I'll see it.'

They left, and hailed a cab.

Then, for a small and agreeable respite, everything went back to normal, only, of course, normal did Winnie no good in this instance. Normal meant, on the one hand, that John was there, that they were together, that small practices and domestic policies were reinstated. He paid the cab, always, a longstanding agreement between them born of some forgotten misunderstanding dating back twenty years and now aged nicely into a joke of sorts. She did the key, saying, 'Ah, Rudge House, back where I belong, smack smack,' and patted the Georgian surround to the front door with affection. There was no sound from Mrs Maddingly's quarters, just a familiar reek of stewing celery. No prospective buyers were nosing about the flat on the next level. In fact, the house seemed empty, except for them. The ghost had disappeared into a vacuum.

John scowled at the supplies stockpiled on either side of his door, at the drop cloths laid out for wet boots, the ladders and unremoved detritus from the deconstruction of his kitchen pantry. 'You can hardly blame them,' said Winnie. 'Where did you get them anyway? Wasn't it a bit risky leaving your home to them for a whole week or so?'

'I'd tidied away anything of real value,' said John. 'Besides, thieves take cash or electronic appliances, usually. They don't riffle through your poetry bookcase looking for signed first editions of Larkin or Betjeman.' He nodded to the door knocker. 'See, there is where I left you a note – stuck under the edge of that thing.'

'Oh, well,' said Winnie, trying not to think he was lying. 'The door knocker in Dickens's version of Great-great-great-grandfather's story talked to him, remember, but this one kept silent.'

'Amazing, when the rest of the house wouldn't shut up.' John's tone was dry and even. She was determined, for as long as she could manage, not to take offense. It was sweetly relieving to have him home.

They entered the flat. Late-November light, already graying in the early afternoon, seeped through the rooms. Dust motes of plaster picked out the grain of the air. Winnie noticed she'd let grit build up on John's mahogany sideboard. Hell, the house is haunted, she thought; who am I to be cleaning up on his behalf? As John wandered into the kitchen Winnie trailed a finger along the surface, absentmindedly graphing the slashed cross pattern that had attended the more inexplicable of the recent events.

'Well, this is a fine mess,' said John from the kitchen.

'They've made a good beginning,' she said. She, defending Mac and Jenkins? Topsy-turvy everything.

'Yes, but a beginning of what?'

He poked about a while and then came back into the foyer. Alert, he saw the drawn mark in the dust. 'Messages from the resident apparition?' he said. She suffered an instant's temptation to play it that way, but shook her head.

'This is all?' he said. 'It seems like my place in a mess, no more, no less.'

'I know. Except that you're here, it feels silent as the tomb.'

'Empty as the tomb too. The tomb isn't supposed to be a carrying case for the spirit, is it? Just a storage unit for the body, while the body lasts.'

'The body is the transport vehicle for the spirit. I mean, if you think that way.'

'We're the bodies here, we're the spirits. I deduce no others, Winnie.'

'We're enough. Aren't we?'

During the evening the auditorium at Poiana Braşov grew cold. The columnar radiators stationed every forty feet knocked and hissed for all they were worth, but the effect was negligible. 'Look, the ice in our drink isn't melting, it's growing,' said John.

Though the room could have accommodated a national congress, no more than two dozen tables were in use. But the floor show was no less aerobic for that. A stout fellow singing Placido Domingo numbers in Romanian. A corps of busty mountain girls, with legs like professional cyclists, made it their business to kick and cavort behind him. A magician pulled a white dove out of a box. The dove hopped to the edge of a table covered in purple sequined cloth. It flapped its wings once and then fell over, apparently dead.

'Hypothermia got him,' said Wendy.

'How long do we have to stay?' muttered John. They sat with their knees close, for warmth.

'You have better entertainment in mind back at the room?' Wendy whispered back.

'Is good, is very good,' said Doroftei. 'Peoples come from every places to see, to laugh, to sing.' He grinned as if, anticipating their need for pleasure this very evening, he had spent a lifetime erecting the entire mountain range beyond, and training the performers from infancy.

'I've got some decent whiskey smuggled in my luggage,' said John. 'I was keeping it for a bribe, but maybe we need to bribe ourselves.'

'I'm all for that.'

They began to work their way into their outer garments, but Doroftei didn't take the hint, as the room was cold enough that most of the audience was already sitting in overcoats. Even the taffeta-bound fat lady singer who waltzed onstage sported a grim shawl the color of old iron, with matching hat perched jauntily over her left eyebrow.

Wendy was warmed, though, by the notion of a return to the hotel. So she could wait through the performance. She smiled at John. Nothing served a friendship so well as mutual discomfort.

'Well,' he said, 'look what's here.'

As they were leaving, he was organizing the mess on the landing. He had picked up the boot scraper hedgehog to fold the drop cloths back nearer the wall. And underneath the canvas, underneath the hedgehog, a letter on its back. Winnie saw it there, emerging; John couldn't have just sneaked it there to corroborate his story. He turned it over and winced, and handed it to her. *Winnie* it said.

'Do I have to read it now?' she asked.

'You have to read it sometime.'

'Where are you going? Back to work?'

'I can't stay here while you're here. And I certainly won't ask you to leave. Just let me know what you plan. You'll be able to reach me at the office.'

'You'll stay with Allegra, then?'

'No,' he said. 'Not now.'

'It means nothing to me.'

'It doesn't matter—'

'John, you're not listening. It means nothing to me. I don't care.'

'I don't believe you, but it doesn't matter if I did. I'll do what I want.' He was testy and severe, and paused at the head of the stairs to look back at her. 'I'm not easy with all this. Think what you like. The company retains a suite in a Swiss Cottage hotel for visiting luminaries and functionaries. I can use it for a while. I've done so in the past, when I was having the front rooms redone. That's where I'll be. You can have the phone number and we can meet for meals from time to time. The place is yours until you go. You *are* going on to Romania?'

'I think I am. But it's hard to think.'

'Take your time,' he said, turning around. He sounded so like another therapist, dismissing her, she imagined kicking him in the back of the head while she had him in such close range. She could see him sprawl against the corner, his teeth scraping the wallpaper as he fell, his lip split open, gushing, his forehead a sudden explosion of color.

'I can as easily go,' she said. 'I can find a B-and-B, or just – go. Just go. This is your house and frankly, my love, it's your mess.'

But he didn't hear her, or attend. As they descended to the main entrance hall, they saw now that Mrs Maddingly's door was ajar an inch or two. Perhaps it had been so earlier and they hadn't noticed.

'Mrs M?' said Winnie. She moved ahead of John.

'Do you think—?' he said, but followed. 'Someone is annotating the text of this room?'

'She talks to herself in notes. Her short-term memory bank is broken.'

'Bankrupt memories. What does she go on about?'

Closer up, the smell wasn't celery, was it, but a kind of char, as if wet were seeping into the chimneys from above, and depositing soot all the way down on the brick hearths of the ground floor.

'Mrs M?'

John began to read. 'THE PILLS ARE SPEAKING. What does that mean? REMEMBER TUESDAY. REMEMBER CHUTNEY. REMEMBER ALAN, HE'S YOUR HUSBAND. We're on a roll here, she's remembering fairly well I think. At least she's remembering to remind herself.' He approached the chimney. The mantel was fringed with gummed notes, each one featuring a single letter, quaveringly shaped. But the line of letters did not read as a word. Some of the letters were backward.

'Seven letters. It's a sort of Scrabble,' he said. 'Maybe she's trying to address the thing you say was haunting the fireplace.' He sounded as if he thought he was in a Noël Coward play; even the way he stood infuriated Winnie. One hand out at the mantelpiece. So proprietary.

'Mrs M, I'm coming through; don't be startled,' said Winnie in a loud voice, and went into the kitchen, pulling a string attached to an overhead light.

The charred smell wasn't damp smoke, but something in the oven, set at a low heat. 'Apparently she's as bad a chef as she is a housekeeper,' said Winnie in a stage whisper. 'I've always wanted to write a book for the culinarily impaired: *The Despair of Cooking*.' She rummaged for a pot holder and ended up using a tea towel folded over several times.

'Jesus, that's vile.' John wouldn't even come in the kitchen. She singsonged to give herself the nerve.

'Davy Davy Dumpling,
Put him in a pot.
Sugar him and butter him
And eat him while he's hot.'

She opened the door with the tips of her fingers. Her gag reflex kicked in and she tried to hold it in, but couldn't, and slopped all over the floor. She managed to close her eyes to keep from studying the splash of lunch to see if it had fallen in the jagged shapes of the slashed cross, but the imagined pattern of it was engrained in vermilion on the inside of her eyelids.

'Bloody hell,' said John, 'as if it didn't smell bad enough in here already.' But he came into the room and ran water, and dampened the tea towel to pass to her. 'Sit down, dear; you're more overwrought than I thought.'

'I'm not overwrought,' she said, when she could speak, when the ropes of liquefied lunch had been cleared from her sinuses. 'She's gone bonkers, not me. She's baking Chutney.'

'I think he's done,' said John, and turned the oven off.

They found Mrs Maddingly in the bedroom. She was dressed in a tartan overcoat and a hat, and she wore grimy lilac gloves. The coat had fallen open and beneath it she was naked and soiled. 'She may be dead,' said John into the phone, miraculously getting someone in emergency services instead of a recording. 'We don't know. We haven't approached her as close as that and we don't intend to. She's not family.'

Winnie felt as if she had had a part in Mrs Maddingly's demise. The feeling was old and powerful. It was one she had felt before. It was a feeling that Winnie could wear like a coat herself, and be naked and ugly underneath it.

She sat primly on an upholstered footstool in the parlor as they waited for the ambulance. She looked at the letters on the mantel.

G   BR   WA   Ƨ   A

And what could it mean?

G BR. *Great Britain?*

W A near the S: did that mean *was?*

Great Britain was . . . A? A? Avalon? Atlantis? Avaricious?

'Don't move off, now,' said John. 'Don't leave us.'

'How dare you say that when you just abandoned me? To all of it, to all this? *And* lied to me about it too? Don't talk to me, and don't mind me, I'm just upset.'

But she couldn't help it.

While the floor show had been lumbering on, the roads had become slick. The car Doroftei drove was old, its back fitted out with one long vinyl-covered seat. The car slithered and swerved down the mountainside, though it didn't frighten her, as both sides of the road were heaped with plowed snow, readying a soft landing in the event of an accident. Doroftei was driving slowly enough, safely, and no other traffic to worry about, really. So when the centrifugal force of the car urged her over, nearly into John's lap, she slid, laughing, as if at a carnival ride. Put there by the force of the weather of another country, another culture. She did not pull away. Her hand slid out of her glove, or did John slip it out himself, and their hands, in the dark, clasped with

something other than a handshake.

'Anchor you,' he said, a promise or a threat.

'Anchor me?' she said, a request or a protest.

Mrs Maddingly was bundled onto a stretcher. She was not dead yet, apparently.

'You want to do the cat thing or the hospital thing?' asked Winnie, now in control, at least as much as she ever was.

'Hospital,' he said. 'She's my neighbor. I suppose I ought.'

That left Winnie to dispose of the soft-fleshed cat.

She brought some newspapers from John's flat so she could soak up the remaining blood. She'd never been squeamish and she worked delicately, as if it made a difference to poor Chutney that her gestures were slow and patient. The brown goo sponged into the paper, overtaking a headline. *Wake up that hedgehog sleeping in your bonfire,* said Derwent May. *Protect animals on November 5, particularly hibernating hedgehogs.* The story warned about more Guy Fawkes Day disasters, and the proclivity of hedgehogs to nestle deeply into bonfire piles erected in advance and unattended for some time. The story ended as the blood seeped over the text: 'Last year the RSPCA even reported some youths throwing two hedgehogs into a bonfire at Biggleswade in Bedfordshire. Their bodies were discovered in the smouldering remains of the fire. Hedgehogs are not like phoenixes: they will not rise again with glittering prickles from the ashes.'

'Nor will you, Chutney,' said Winnie, 'or at least you better not.' She double-bagged the corpse, roasting pan and all, in some Sainsbury plastic bags and then dropped the whole mess into a white bin liner. She couldn't bring herself to leave *another* dead cat out for Camden Council rubbish removers to collect. So, praying that Chutney hadn't had some sort of collar with identifying tags, Winnie waited until dark and then walked over to West Heath, which local lore considered a cruising site for gay men. She found a dense growth of bushes, shoulder height. Hoping that there were no fellows hidden inside busy at getting jolly, she lobbed the remains of Chutney as far as she could, and walked soberly back to Rudge House, for all the world like a solicitor on her way back from the office in Golders Green.

'Be glad you're made of stone,' she said to the hedgehog outside John's door.

And now the place was empty, in a way it had never been: vacated of everything that had intention or motivation. The furniture seemed incoherently arranged. The prints of roses still lining one of John's baseboards did not look like roses with their echo of lilt and perfume, but only like old faded paint on old paper, encased in glass and wood. The painting of Ebenezer Scrooge/Ozias Rudge was mawkish, and it now seemed as if the old geezer was struggling to get away from being encased in a sentimental legend.

Winnie was gripped with a dull remorse. She had neglected the needs of old Mrs Maddingly. Winnie had not been responsible for her, of course, but presumably there'd been no issue of the Maddingly marriage. Who knew if the old lady or her dead spouse had had siblings, cousins, nieces, or nephews?

Next to the chair, on the telephone table, was today's *Independent*. John had dropped it there when they'd come in. Because the exposed pantry walls in the kitchen now made the whole flat seem as repugnant as an open sore, Winnie had no urge to move around in the apartment. She was not very religious, preferring to take her fantasy safely in the pages of books rather than in the uplifting superstitions of ideologues, but she couldn't help thinking suddenly that the house felt like the tomb of Jesus in the garden. What a nightmare for those women coming to mourn their friend and brother, the crucified rabbi, to see the tomb open and his body gone! One of the original horror stories. How did any of them survive without benefit of intensive modern psychotherapy?

Maybe they had themselves exorcised. Could you actually arrange an exorcism with the Church these days, especially if you were neither a believer nor a major donor?

She picked up the newspaper and gave herself a stern upbraiding: Look at the real, harsh, stupid world. A by-election contested. The Liberal Democrats in an internal snarl. A polio scare in Lithuania. Feng shui hits the East End at last. The revival of an early Buñuel film. She didn't care about any of this, but read it as if searching for the answers to secrets. She could find none.

The phone rang, startling her. Her paper fell, making a tent, as she reached for the receiver. She was sure it would be news of Mrs Maddingly. 'John,' she said.

'No, Irv,' he answered. 'That is Winnie Rudge, I take it?'

She had not given him her number. She had never told him her name. 'What are you calling me for?' Her tone was neutral; it might be Opal Marley's, it might not.

'You took off in something of a rush, as you may remember. You were so distraught you left behind your parcel. The cloth thing. So I'm calling about that, but also I'm calling to see how you are. You had me no small amount of worried, the way you reacted to the news that your cousin was in his office working.'

She took a moment to remember. 'That wasn't the kindest thing for me to do, I suppose.'

'Oh, kindness, it takes a while for a fellow to request kindness of someone. It comes, eventually, but kindness isn't what I'm looking for. I'm much more basic. I'm looking for information.'

'Namely?'

'Namely, are you all right?'

But she didn't deserve that much attention. 'Oh, I'm going

mad, you can see that as well as anyone. Of course I'm not all right. First I learn my only remaining friend of the heart has been avoiding me and lying about it, for reasons I still can't fathom. Then I come back to this place with him, hoping for a shred of normalcy, a return to the way things used to be – and what next? You want to know what next? The old bat downstairs has cooked her cat, the one that attacked and killed its siblings and companions. I don't know how she did it, but then she put on a coat and collapsed, a stroke or something, we don't know yet.' The *we* slipped out, she hadn't meant it. 'I mean I haven't heard from John since he left for the hospital with her. You're tying up the phone line.'

'He'll call later,' said Irv, unruffled. 'When am I going to see you again?'

'Why do you want to see me?'

'Do I have to have a reason?'

'Yes. No one wants to see me at all, much less without a reason.'

'Well, that's self-derision of a particularly high school variety. How's this for a reason: to return your shroud to you.'

'It's not mine. I suppose technically it's John's.'

'I'm not going to return it to him. I'll give it to you. Look, I know you're in Hampstead. I'll come up there. I don't mind.'

'Where are you? I don't even know where you're staying.'

'I've rented one of those sublets you find advertised at the back of the *New York Review of Books*. A flat in Maida Vale. But I'm not there, I'm at a phone booth. I'll grab a cab and come over. You sound as if you need not to be alone.'

'I don't know if I'm fit company. As you sweetly pointed out.'

'I don't want to come up to the house. Not that I'm spooked by your ghost story, I just don't want to meet your cousin yet. I'll be at the door of the Hampstead Tube station in forty-five minutes, say.'

She brushed her hair. She could do that much to make herself fit company. She left John a note. If he had rung while she was on the line with Irv Hausserman, he didn't ring back. She taped the note to John's front door with nine inches of adhesive tape. Then she headed out into the early evening, threading her way through rush hour at full gridlock, her calves lit rosy by brake lights.

They went to the King William IV and perched on unreasonable stools. The clamor of businesspeople having the first drink of the evening was comforting. Behind the bar hung a sign: IF YOU WANT A NIGHT OF PASSION, TALK TO THE BARTENDER. 'I don't believe I'm that desperate,' said Irv.

'I wonder if she was actually intending to eat that cat? You're very good to see me when I'm like this.'

'I don't know you any other way.'

'You don't know me at all.'

'Touché. You're right. But I know you better than I did this morning. I spent some time on the computer when I got back to my little bedsit. I checked Amazon-dot-com for Winifred Rudge and, while I was at it, Opal Marley. I found an Ophelia Marley, Ph.D. Any relation?'

'Oh, all that.' She was surprised how nervous she felt. 'Look, I'm sorry. I was rather mortified to be meeting compatriots in a gypsy's tea room. I should have owned up. It *is* Winnie Rudge. Promise. But how did you find out? And John's number?'

'I phoned Ostertag, badgered him to phone your friend Rasia, who didn't know any Opal Marley but who knew that someone named Winnie Rudge was in residence. And Rasia rang some neighbor of hers to get your cousin's phone number.'

So everyone in Hampstead knew that Winnie had been introducing herself as Opal Marley. That would surely help her public relations campaign. She waved her hand. 'Noms de plume, you get attached to them.'

'I suppose you might. Well, I clicked on the Amazon-dot-com message that said "Other books by Winifred Rudge" and I got a list of your publications. Kiddie lit, right? Fairly complete, I would warrant. But I saw that your last new book was published three years ago, and prior to that you'd been putting out at least two books a year for a decade or more. Why the hiatus? Do you have several other pen names? Or are you working on a new book?'

'You mean, am I inventing all this parapsychology stuff so I can hew out a chunk of narrative from my experience? That's not how it works. And anyway, why are you asking?'

'You seem bent on presenting yourself as a total flake, and you don't seem a total flake. Not really. You seem like someone having a hard month or two. Slightly cagey about your past. So what? I've had my share of hard months and I know. If you're working on a novel, maybe your senses get heightened and your reactions get more, oh, extreme. I don't know, I'm not a novelist. But also if you're working – well, that's a good sign. A person who can work is, in my limited experience, capable of a certain amount of happiness. And I hope that for you.'

'Why should you bother? Why should you care?'

'Vague low-grade busybody interest. Nothing more than that. *Are* you working?'

She didn't answer at first. He laughed and said, 'If you're seriously nuts, you'll imagine I'm an emissary of your publisher sent to nudge you along, a kind of amanuensis.'

She was greedy over the little bowl of dried wheat things, thinking. 'I intended to work,' she said at last. 'And my mind turns over various plot devices, it's true. But if you mean am I sitting daily and scribbling strings of jeweled thought in jeweled prose, the answer is no.'

'I see. Fair enough.'

She couldn't tell if he looked relieved or disappointed. But he went on. 'Well, then this next won't be of use to you as a novelist, but it's still interesting. It was just noon when you rushed off, leaving behind the parcel of cloth on the pavement. It was about one-thirty when I got home. Eight-thirty A.M. back on the East Coast. I e-mailed a colleague in the history department, knowing he'd be there; he always schedules himself to teach in the morning so he can start drinking at noon. Thinking about your shroud, I asked him to poke around in the indexes and find me a local authority on the fabric arts. Best he could do at short notice was the V and A. In all its huge depths I thought I'd get shunted into the sidetrack of some underling's voice mail, but then I got served up a steaming hot slice of luck. Turns out there's a Belgian expert visiting for a few weeks, on a grant. Very eager to appear the affable guest and be invited back. Agreed to see me and look at the cloth. I got a cup of lukewarm tea out of the exercise.'

'You went there? You showed him the shroud? What did he say?'

Irv patted the plastic bag holding the exhumed garment. 'Madame Professor Annelise Berchstein said there were many chemical tests, processes of examination by electron microscope, et cetera, that could be conducted, at some cost. She said that wool fibers exposed to light and air tended to rot in a matter of decades, but that in some circumstances, due to a combination of how they were treated and a history of sound storage, the rare cloth came to light that was quite a bit older.'

'Older than what? What are we talking about here?'

'She's an expert. She wouldn't go on record, of course. But she said to the naked eye there were anomalies in the knotting techniques – yes, with her trained eye she could detect knotted strings in the warp that neither you nor I can see – that suggest this fabric is old enough to be interesting and perhaps even valuable.'

'You wouldn't have let her off the hook without taking a rough guess. Stop stringing me along.'

'Old enough for her to have scribbled down a quote from Jean Lurçat, whoever he is, on the back of her business card.' He fumbled for it. So she had given him her business card with, presumably, her phone number and e-mail address. The professional businesswoman's *Come hither*. 'Here's what Lurçat said, in something called *Le travail dans la tapisserie au moyen âge*. 1947. "Well, it is a fabric, no more nor less than a fabric. But it is a coarse, vigorous, organic fabric; supple, certainly, but of a less yielding suppleness than silk or linen. It is heavy … it is heavy with matter and heavy with meaning. But it is more, it is heavy with intentions."'

'Very lovely. Right up your alley, I see. She comes prepared with quotes and sources.'

He emptied his pint and belched in a quiet but very American way, a way she was, just now, not displeased to witness. 'Here's her best guess. Her specialty is hemp or linen or anything of leaf fiber; she doesn't know as much about wool or how to authenticate its age or provenance. She says carbon dating of cloth, while rarely done, is possible. A lot of advances in microscopy made during that recent examination of the Shroud of Turin. Without a woven design or the application of paint it's hard to be certain, but she guessed maybe six, maybe seven hundred years old. And no doubt deteriorating at an exponential rate, now that you've exposed it to light and air. Look, the fibers are dancing off the thing like dandruff.' And so they were.

'I don't believe it for a moment,' she said. 'A six-hundred-year-old shroud? When is that? I can't count backward after one drink.'

'She thought sometime between 1300 and 1400. Possibly French or Flemish. She didn't want to give it back to me, in fact.'

'Did you show her the little mark in it, the little icon?'

'I did. She made nothing of it. Spilled blood, perhaps. She didn't see it as an identifying code of any sort.'

'Dr Annelise Berchstein.'

'She'd be delighted to consider the matter further, but unless it comes to her under the auspices of a professional collection like a museum, she's not able to spend much time at it gratis.'

'Did you tell her where it was found?'

'Not the part of town, no. But where it was stored, yes, hammered into a dark pocket against a flue. She ventured that the dryness, the airlessness, the protection from insects preserved it these past hundred years or so. But it's much older than the house, of course, so where it came from originally must also have been a protected space.'

She did not speak, she did not say what she knew, or guessed. They left the pub and walked to Waterstone's. Irv led her directly to the shelf of the Self-Help/Spirituality section and found *The Dark Side of the Zodiac*, the Partridge and Sons paperback edition. Ophelia Marley, Ph.D. He knew right where it was. He'd been checking up on her. He pointed out the print number – 33 – and said, 'You've been living off this for a while, I see.'

She was meant to be flattered that he was noticing her success, but all she could say was, 'Sales slowing down in a worrying fashion.'

'What does it say about me?' He flipped the book open.

'It's all bunk,' she said crossly. 'You're out to shame me. Close it.'

'This is bunk,' he said, 'but you believe in ghosts. You believe there's a seven-hundred-year-old ghost haunting Rudge House, which is only two hundred years old, by your reckoning.'

'You and your Annelise have given a birth date to this cloth, not to anything else.'

'Dr Berchstein to you,' he replied. 'This is England, after all.

We respect the formalities here.' He brushed her hand lightly to show he was making a joke, that he was near enough to her, now, to be able to tease her about a rival for his affections, a certain Madame Professor Fraülein Doktor Annelise Berchstein.

'He should be here with you,' he said, 'not me.' But she didn't answer.

There was a streetlight outside the hotel window, and as they stood there, the light flickered and went out. The instant it flickered, as if light in the godforsaken Balkans moved much more slowly than the speed of light – it moved at the speed of snow – their eyes met as they both were pausing in the first gesture of undress. She had dropped her coat on the floor and was bending to undo the clasp of a boot. She looked up at him like a washerwoman or a bending Degas dancer, from an odd position, seeing him towering at an unfamiliar angle – he was not of the build to tower, particularly. And he had let his coat slide from his shoulders and halfway down his arms, but there it stuck. A lick of light on his nose, on the snowy damp of his matted-down hair, and on his upper lip. She was in the frumpiest position imaginable, and about to stand up, when before she could, before their eyes could adjust to the ambient light outside, patterned by falling snow, he dropped to his knees, his coat a sodden carpet on which they clutched and fell.

Then the usual business, all willpower and honorable intention taken hostage by lips, fingers, tongues. He smelled of a lemony sort of turpentine,

not the sort of male smell she was used to. He was leaner than he seemed when dressed – she had never seen him naked before – and the sheets were like frost. She clung and pulled away and returned, making bearable the clammy cold sheets. He entered her – was there no other word for it than that? – how like an Old Testament possession by unclean spirits, it sounded, to be entered – and then, the cost of it too. But the act erased the last grasp she had of thinking, and she surrendered to the prehuman realm without language.

The truth: sayable or not, she fucked back as hard as she was fucked.

'Are you trying to spook me or something?'

'No – no.' She shook her head. 'Sorry. There's just . . .' Her voice trailed off.

'I've never believed in ghosts, but if anyone ever looked haunted, it's you.'

'Well, I'll tell you, some days,' she said, and she began to laugh, 'being haunted would seem a mighty relief. I mean, what better to take your mind off your own troubles than to be faced fair and square by a being so very aggrieved that it decides to hang on in the afterlife? Might help you remember how to count your blessings, if you needed reminding on how to do it.'

'Will you autograph this book if I buy it?'

'Will you buy it if I promise it's nothing but hokum?'

'Only then. If I thought you actually believed it I'd be polite and scram as soon as I could.'

They wandered out of the bookstore and, without a word of negotiation about it, began to look at menus posted outside restaurants. Settled on the Café des Artistes, and got a table hunched into the corner. 'White or red?' she said, studying the menu, unwilling to let him be too avuncular about this evening.

'Champagne doesn't come in red.'

'How can you study ghosts if you don't believe in them?' she said after the first sip, which she had taken in a hurry so he wouldn't propose a toast and turn this into a ceremony.

'The only way to study them is if you don't believe in them,' he said. 'Otherwise, it's not study, it's – ancestor worship – or a particular kind of prurience, maybe.'

'Go on.'

'It's not ghosts I study, really. I study what people believed about them. How, in age after age, the notion of the afterlife serves the living, helps them reclaim their own lives with some urgency. How the Church tolerated stories of ghostly apparitions and remonstrations of the dead, to further its work of salvation.'

'Salvation. Hah. A likely concept.'

'Well, the afterlife was all the poor had. Their real lives being nasty, brutish, and short, as Hobbes's catchphrase goes. Our notion that life can improve for individuals *within* their own lifetimes is a fairly modern one. Avoiding being damned was about all that you could hope for. That, and a potato for supper.'

'So where do ghosts come in?'

'They've always been around. You understand I mean' – he clinked his glass against hers, deviously working in a toast – 'the notion of ghosts, not ghosts themselves.'

'An eternal concept.'

'The ancestor worship of our cave-dweller forebears is related to a very peculiarly human function. Our ability to anticipate our own mortality by deducing from the deaths of our loved ones what death *means*. Ghosts, it seems to me, are evidence of human panic.'

'They're portrayed otherwise, though, aren't they? To me a

ghost doesn't have anything to do with the grief of those it left behind,' said Winnie. 'A ghost is evidence only of its own panic. A ghost is the foul sad excrement of a life. The code word is "unfinished business"—'

'What human soul have you ever known to die at a proper time, having finished all its business? Fulfilled all its human potential, exchanged all its sorrow for joy? I'm going for the lamb, by the way.'

'Risotto with pulled chicken and asparagus for me.'

The waiter took their order. 'Besides,' Irv continued, 'if a ghost is a figment of a life, some bit that has unfinished business, then the world should be overpopulated by ghosts. There should be no air left for the present moment to breathe.'

'Suppose it is true that all humans have the ability to cast ghosts when they die. In your period of expertise, what did the Church make of the fact that ghosts aren't universal?'

'You pick up on one of my favorite threads. It's always seemed to me unfair – these rolls are warm and Parmesany, try one – that so often it seems to be the well-connected dead who get to be ghosts. In medieval times, this usually means saints. Those dead ones rich in virtue. Saints could be counted on to be recognized, thanks to some characteristic tic or totem. But increasingly scholars are seeing that the apparition of the dead to the living was often a hallmark of a fucked-up funeral transaction.'

'Transaction?'

'After all, a proper burial was the sorry best that the living could offer the dead as a passkey to the afterlife. This was true for the Vikings and for the Egyptians and the Romans too of course. But what happened when a son was lost at sea, or a suicide couldn't be buried in hallowed ground? Ghost tales coalesce around these sorts who provided worry and dread to the living.'

'Then what did the ghosts say to the living?'

'They asked help of the living, so that the souls of the ghosts could be at better rest. But I think we can take the abundance of tales of this variety as being an inclination of the living to say to the dead: *Leave us alone.* We want to go on. Our small community is blemished by your stupid botched death. Because what, really, is the job of the dead? It's *not* to hang around, but to disappear – to clear the air for the living. As Jean-Claude Schmitt said – oh, apologies for the references, I'm an unrepentant lecturer – the goal of Christian memorial masses and the celebration of All Saints' Day, et cetera, was to separate the dead from the living, to keep the dead in their place. Once the living had discharged their duties to their dead relatives and companions, they could go back to living a full life.'

'And that's it, then: the goal of a ghost—'

'To find someone who has the authority to dismiss it into full death. Leaving the dismissee the permission to live a full life without guilt or undue grief.'

'The quick and the dead.' She mused. 'It is, I suppose, part of what Dickens was saying. But in *A Christmas Carol*, Scrooge could have no effect on the sufferings of his poor partner, Marley. He could only save himself.'

'Theme and variation. Nonetheless, the effect of Scrooge's being haunted was that he dismissed his own fears and became a hugely fun guy again, a regular party animal.'

Scrooge in the painting, his haunted, Bergmanesque inward torment? Hardly a party animal. 'He's my forebear, more or less. If not actual, then literary, in a way.'

'You said something of the sort once before. I'm aquiver with professional curiosity. Pass your glass.'

The lamb smelled glorious, all garlic and rosemary. The light of the candle flickered on the silver and the bleached linen. The murmur of Japanese tourists at the next table, their high exotic voices, made Winnie begin to be glad for the champagne. 'So you don't think the house is haunted.'

'Your house? The flat where you found the cloth? No, of course not,' he said. 'I'm a crusty old pedant. And if I saw your trademark slashed cross appear in the condensation of this window here, before my very eyes, I'd begin to murmur about statistical models regarding coincidences.'

'And what if I said I saw such a cross and you didn't?'

'I'd believe with all my might that you said you saw it.'

'Would you believe that I did see it?'

'I don't know. Experience so far in my life suggests not. But I'm not a novelist, and maybe it's given to novelists to see things that associate professors can't.'

'You are being tolerant of a high-strung person in some degree of middle-class distress,' she said. 'And after I gave you a false identity too. You're not after me in any way, are you?'

'You mean sexually? I'm not young enough and brash enough to answer you directly in any case. But a man is still allowed to care about a woman, is that not so? And vice versa? Without either of us knowing if we are in a prelude to friendship or romance, or if we're just having an interlude of camaraderie due to the accident of having met each other at a fortune-teller's? That's the definition of being not haunted, by the way: being able to live in the moment without having either to lust for the future or to dread it.'

'It's only fair to say,' she ventured, 'that I'm not available, for many reasons, to engage in romance.'

'Maybe eventually that'll break my heart. So far, I think: Oh, well, what do you know? For that matter, what do I know? I'm enjoying the lamb. What exactly is a noisette, do you know?'

'But you have said nothing about your status. I mean married or gay or what?'

'Every unmarried man of a certain age is presumed to be gay

these days. Lots of married men too for that matter. I wouldn't so much mind the presumption of it if a gay man would ask me out on a date, but since I don't register on their meters as of particular merit I just blunder my way through parties, hunting for the nearest kid or grandparent or household pet to befriend.' He speared three julienned carrots on his fork and held them up and waggled them at her. 'I'm a widower, so if anyone has a reason to believe in ghosts, it's me. And I don't.'

'Oh. Oh, dear. I am very sorry.'

'It was long ago,' he said, 'and not as long as all that, either.'

'I was married too.' She was unsure of her reasons for saying this.

'I see,' he said, but did not press for more information. Of course, she had already invented for his behalf a husband in Scottsdale. No wonder he didn't seem surprised.

She looked at him, as close as she could, trying not to list the observations for a writer's apprehension of this moment:

His head turned down as if reading auguries in the roasted fennel and garlic mashed potatoes.

His hair neither sandy with youth nor silver with age, just hair, just fair hair.

The blush in his rough-scraped cheeks probably due not so much to the Veuve Clicquot as to the discomfort of talking about himself.

Probably she could do no more than have dinner with this man, tonight, but she could do that.

'Irv,' she said, and she put her hand lightly on his.

The jolt of the touch kicked them both back, taking them unawares, and he smiled and blinked and said, 'There there, no need to fuss over me. I'm a big boy. So tell me a little more of your family ghost story. The grandpappy Rudge piece. What's the oldest proof you have that your great-great-et cetera grandfather was the

model for Ebenezer Scrooge? Don't tell me' – he held up his fork – 'it isn't a journal or a letter he wrote, but the written record of someone else.'

'Well, I hate for you to be right so soon. But you are. As far as we can trace the source of the family gossip about it, the oldest mention is made in a letter from Ozias Rudge's son Edward to Edward's niece Dorothea.'

'What does Edward say? Do you remember?'

'Oh, I don't recall verbatim, but I've seen the pages in question many times. John probably has them in photocopy, or did. The originals are in Boston. Anyway, through several family recollections, we deduce that late in life, Ozias came to know the immortal work of Christmas joy by Dickens. Then he, old Ozias Rudge, recalled the occasion of his being haunted by a specter. O.R., as we affectionately call him, had terrified the neighborhood children of Hampstead with his ghost story, and O.R. assumed that the boy Dickens must have been one of the Hampstead urchins to stand slack-jawed at the narration. Dickens, at age twelve, did live in Hampstead briefly, at just the time of the supposed hauntings.'

'You know a lot about what happened, what, a hundred fifty years ago?'

'I researched it all once when I thought I could make a book of it. Don't interrupt. Dickens had an obsession with his childhood. He loved recalling its griefs and reliving its brief but intense pleasures. You see that in how Ebenezer Scrooge is haunted at first. The Ghost of Christmas Past takes Scrooge to see himself as a boy. Do you remember? The lonely young Ebenezer was reading by a fire in a huge deserted house. To the window beyond the chair there came Ali Baba and, oh, Robinson Crusoe, I think, and creatures from fairy tales. The figures of the boy's reading and imaginative life were still there embedded in the mind of crabby old

Scrooge. You could hazard the guess that the same is true of all of us – especially Dickens. In his later life the imaginary figures of childhood still obtained, emotionally I mean. Including the memory, maybe, of an old man made miserable from sleepless nights of being haunted.'

'Well, then the most scary ghosts of *A Christmas Carol* are really the figures of Scrooge himself. The past child Scrooge, the embittered current one, the future dead Scrooge. If you press me for a psychological reading about it, I'd say there's your ticket. Folks are more haunted by themselves than anything else.'

'Very slick. And who can argue with that, except, perhaps, a real ghost.' She was enjoying this. 'But of course there's no way of saying anything assured about the roots of *A Christmas Carol.*'

'How much of O.R.'s recollection had to do with Christmas past, present, or to come?'

'None at all, except that the hauntings, which happened on successive nights, occurred during the winter solstice. Rudge didn't mention any Christmas overtones to it, but then, as we know, back then Christmas wasn't celebrated with the hoopla and hysteria that it has come to be – thanks in part to Dickens himself.'

'So what were the hauntings about, then?'

All this scrutiny of a hoary old family legend, and the night darkening above London. Above London's cystic blur of electric lights, its frizz of cosmopolitan energy leaching ever deeper into the stratosphere, but the night darkened nonetheless, a gathering heaviness, year by year. 'Why are you so intent to know?'

'Is my interest unseemly? Sorry. This is a busman's holiday for me. I derive some of my notions by examining the distance between the supernatural event and the telling of it. In the Middle Ages, we see few firsthand accounts about the experience of being haunted. Far more often, a prelate transcribes a story of haunting as told to

him. This lends a kind of journalistic objectivity to the narrative, broadens its credibility – after all, if it weren't true, the good cleric wouldn't have taken his holy time to record it for posterity. I find it charming, really, that you have no scrap of evidence of this story from Ozias Rudge's own hand. It quite follows the norm. And supports my humble thesis.'

'Glad to oblige. I guess. Anyway, Ozias Rudge was apparently vague about it. One of the other relatives, later a convert to the Clapham Sect, remembered it like this: Ozias Rudge – as verbatim as I can manage – Ozias Rudge was visited by a wraith whose language he could not understand, and for fear of his sanity he closed his ears against all entreaty and determined to live a blameless life for others, in the hope of certain pardon for his sins when it was his turn to cross. You see, there's nothing said about who the wraith was or what it wanted. If anything.'

'The dead ask a lot of favors.'

'The exceptional dead. As you point out.'

'As I point out. But most of the dead are mute. And most of the living know how to grieve without inventing phantasms or going psychotic.'

'I have no evidence that O.R. went psychotic. I only know this: after the supposed visitations by a ghost, he never went abroad again. He found someone else to marry, someone younger and more fertile than the old widow, and at the age of fifty he began to beget Edward and Harriet and Marianne and Jane.'

'I'd love to see Edward's letter sometime. Though of course in the written word the reality of the situation has no choice but to calcify and become less thrilling.'

'How well I know that.'

'Have you opened the letter from your cousin John? To see what excuse he gave for standing you up?'

She had been led there without seeing it coming. She flinched.

'That's none of your business at all.'

'Oh, please, how you rush to take offense!' He threw up his hands good-naturedly. 'I only point it out so that . . .'

'So that what?'

'Oh, well,' he said, 'never mind, then. We're having a nice night.'

She decided to let it go. He was right. It was a nice night.

Champagne was replaced by wine, and wine by snifters of cognac, and by the time they yielded their table, there were no other diners hulking about the cold doorway. As Winnie and Irv steered their way lopsidedly up Hampstead High Street, Winnie wondered where, in ten minutes, she wanted to find herself. Irv was a solid mailbox of a man, a throwback. He wore a tie, for Christ's sake, and some sort of aftershave you could buy by the quart at CVS. He looked as if he'd be at home in a fifties homburg chatting with Edward R. Murrow. And John – though John not in the running of course – but John so opposite, so lightly penned in and at the same time so fierce, so defined. It was an exercise she didn't want to be engaging in. She gave up when, bumping into Irv and giggling, they met up with a crowd of people emerging from the doors of the Tube station and sallying across the street. One of them was Rasia McIntyre, who had been doing some partying of her own.

'Where are the kids?' said Winnie, forsaking hellos.

'Oh, you,' said Rasia, 'out on the town, I see?' She smiled with a colluding earnestness at Irv.

'Where are the kids?' said Winnie.

'Don't panic; why the panic?' Irv put his hand on Winnie's shoulder, neither an embrace nor a squeeze, but a gesture of caution. She shrugged him off.

Rasia was too giddy herself to take offense 'They're at my mother's in Balham. I was at a girls' night out – a friend getting

married. We knew there'd be wine, so I dropped the kiddos in front of the telly.'

Winnie sagged a bit. She could sense in Irv's bearing a certain misgiving rising through him. And well he might have misgivings. She was grateful, oddly, for bumping into Rasia. It put things back where they belonged. Winnie about to entertain notions of romance? It wasn't to be.

Rasia put both her hands out. 'Hello, I'm Rasia McIntyre,' she said. 'I remember you from crashing through Ritzi's door. You rang me for Winnie's number.' Winnie thought: Go ahead, Rasia, take him if you want him; I was a fool, for an evening, to imagine I was deserving of a surprise. And Rasia was all charm, letting her brown shawl slip off her head to show her beautiful crimped black hair. Her eyes were made sensual by kohl or a Revlon approximation. A blue and gold sari enveloping her ample bosom slipped back along her *cioccolata* arms to reveal a stenciled pattern of dots, an organized rash. Irv Hausserman was a study in American composure, that little-known quality so often eclipsed by the spectacle of bumpkiny American forwardness. He even said 'How do you do?' as if he were at a gentlemen's club.

'Your hands,' said Winnie, because she felt awkward. She was thrashing about in the deep water, forgetting again how adults proceeded in situations like this. 'What happened to your hands?'

'Oh, a wedding custom. Nothing much. The night before, the ladies of the wedding party and the family get together with the bride and ornament her palms with henna.' Rasia threw back her head, an apparition of louche sexiness. 'It's called a *mehndi* ceremony. Traditional singing. Lots of good good food. The *mehndi* is henna; you can't see it in this sodium glare, but it's really dark red. Nowadays we ditch the kids and have a drink and do our own hands too, not just our palms – we get carried away sometimes. Then we tell horror stories about wedding nights.'

'Like?' said Irv, betraying his professional interest in stories.

Rasia began to laugh. 'The drunken bridegroom with a herniated umbilical cord that the wife mistakes for a cock and mounts. The bridegroom with a donkey's penis. Everyone laughs and the bride gets scared, or pretends to. These days chances are she isn't unfamiliar with her boyfriend's cock, but we're all too polite to presume, and we play the part nicely.' She rotated her hands, as if displaying rings and baubles, and turned her palms up to the light. Winnie caught her right wrist and drew it nearer.

'You – you've borrowed that – the slashed cross,' she said.

Rasia snatched her hand back. 'You leave me alone,' she said. 'I'm trying to be ordinary with you, but it's just a no-go, isn't it?' She tucked her hands back into her shawl and looked at Irving Hausserman, as if to see if he shared Winnie's obsessions.

'I saw it. Did you put it there on purpose? I saw those dots. Just like the pattern I showed you on the cloth.'

'Leave me alone. I'll thank you for that.' Rasia cloaked her clouded face with her shawl and moved back, turned to slip into a newsagent's for a newspaper or a carton of milk for the morning.

'I am not making it up,' said Winnie. 'Did you see it? Did you see, Irv?'

'It was too fast for me to see, and I don't know what I'm looking for.'

She scowled at him. Was he avoiding corroborating what was plainly there, for the sake of gentility, or was he dim?

'Leave me here, I'll go on alone,' she said.

'I'll see you home.'

'It's not necessary and, more to the point, I want to be alone.'

'I'll see you home,' he said again, and did.

She did not ask him in, of course; nor would he have come, most likely. There was a light on in the top floor of Rudge House. But John wasn't there, just another note, this one affixed with a

magnet to the door of the small fridge that crouched on a countertop. '*Bonne nuit*,' it said, 'I'll call tomorrow.'

When he came by the next day, with two paper cups of coffee and a *Sunday Times*, Winnie had already finished with her shower and was packing her bags.

'You needn't do that,' he said. 'You still have research to do, I suppose?'

'There is nothing to write about,' she said. 'It was a good effort, but I've taken it as far as it could go. I kept trying to find Jack the Ripper in the tale, but my protagonist would keep leaning toward Romania. There's no point. Maybe another year.'

At the word *Romania* John sighed and tossed his coffee, undrunk, down the sink. 'Are you just never going to let it go?' he said. 'Are you just going to give up and rotate there endlessly, in the maelstrom? In the toilet? With everyone throwing you lifelines to drag you back, and you won't reach out and grab on? It's just tedious is what it is. If there were no other reason, Winnie, for me to have vacated the premises, being royally bored by your persistent self-loathing would have sufficed.'

'What, you had a bad night with Allegra?' said Winnie as coldly as she could.

'Don't change the subject.'

She didn't have to. A knock on the door served that purpose. John looked at her. 'I'm not expecting anyone,' she said.

He strode over and flung open the door, revealing Colum Jenkins, the very same, though thinner and grayer, his face sagged with new lines. Behind him, a young woman in a fat coat made of blue synthetic fur, standing on lollipop-stick legs sheathed in red spandex.

'So it's you,' said Jenkins. 'I thought the lady might still be here alone, and I brought my daughter for propriety's sake.'

This the daughter that Mac had blabbered about? The whore? Despite the clothes she looked sensible and somewhat urgent. About thirty, maybe. Good skin, unflinching eyes, and nice crisp gestures as she followed her father into the flat. She didn't look like a hooker, but like someone acting in an Almodóvar film. If she were a dominatrix by night, she appeared a physical therapist by seemly daylight. 'It's not the propriety of it,' she said to Winnie and John. 'He shouldn't be doing any heavy lifting, and that yob Mac has disappeared back to North Dublin, as far as we can tell.'

'I can't finish the job, sir,' said Jenkins to John. 'No doubt your guest has told you about the accident. I had a concussion followed the next day by heart failure. Whether one brought on the other or if the heart failure was just waiting to happen, they can't say, but at least I was in the surgery when it happened and they could attend to me at once. But I've had to slow myself down. And I'll find you some alternate builders to come round if you require.'

'What *has* been going on here?' said John. 'I've heard all sorts of stories.'

'Oh, I daresay it was coming on.' Jenkins was vague in his expression. How we move toward the margins of our own lives, inch by inch, Winnie thought; we concede our own centrality. 'I certainly wasn't feeling myself the days leading up to it. Look at how little we got done. I won't trouble you with a bill for the hours spent, sir, just for the materials in the hall, which your next contractor can use.'

'What happened to you?' Winnie was pleased to hear the calm in her own voice. 'Can you say?'

'I had a spell, that was all.' Jenkins didn't look at her. 'It could've been the end of me, I suppose, but it wasn't. It turns out my Kat was always keeping closer tabs on me than I could manage to keep on her. She showed her old da up in that department, I should say.'

'Enough,' said Kat Jenkins fiercely, to Winnie. 'We're not here to be interviewed.'

'How I'll manage the bills without this sort of work,' said Jenkins, 'a mystery.'

'Da,' said Kat, 'this your wrench? This your hammer? Let's collect these things and not bother these people.'

'But I suppose we'll manage,' said Jenkins.

'We'll manage,' said Kat. The face of Jenkins *père* showed a contradiction: some relief at being reunited with his daughter, and some worry about just how she intended to raise funds to help him pay the outgoings.

'There was all that noise in the chimney stack,' said Winnie. 'Tell him. Tell John.'

'I'm not – I'm not,' said Jenkins, shaking his head, 'I'm not certain of what was going on with me. Early warning signs of a systemic arrest, they say in the clinic. I should have paid more attention. Anyway, it was all quite dreamlike, wasn't it? I shouldn't wonder if there was a minute little gas leak or the like, making us fanciful.'

'There was no gas leak,' said Winnie.

'Stow it,' said Kat belligerently. 'Leave it be.' She held up a crowbar as if ready to use it on Winnie. 'This your crowbar, Da?'

''Tis.'

Winnie had no choice but to let them pack. She watched Jenkins gingerly make his way out the door. John carried the toolbox down the stairs for him, and Kat turned at the top of the stairs to look at Winnie.

'I don't know what that Mac said to you,' she said, 'but it's a load of bollocks. Whatever he said means sod-all, and anyway it's none of your affair.'

'I never would,' said Winnie, *use your life in a fiction*, but that the thought could occur to her made her hesitate. Kat closed the door and was gone. With her, at last, dissolved the final remnant of the notion of a prostitute murdered and bricked up in the chimney stack of Rudge House, or of Jack the Ripper himself disappeared there. Kat Jenkins was too competent and real for fictional trappings to adhere to her. The Jack the Ripper exploration was proving a dead end.

But something had happened, no matter what Jenkins had said. No matter how Rasia had turned on her. Something was blurting into her life, even if all corroborating testimony was failing. She was alone in her conviction of a haunting.

One by one the supporting staff was falling by the wayside. But they were following the lead set by her cousin. John Comestor had abdicated first, the very day she arrived.

Bucharest to Ploeşti to Sinaia to Braşov. From there, Costal Doroftei would take them on, he said, through the Transylvanian Alps, on toward Sighişoara. But there was snow farther on, more in the northwest than here; they were in the grip of a storm front up there and the party of travelers would have to wait. Doroftei delivered the news in the lobby of the hotel, where, in morning light that had the filmy transparency of gin, Wendy sat dressed in her coat, surrounded by her luggage. 'We can't wait,' she said. 'I don't believe this. We haven't come this far to wait.'

'There is no choice in mountain region. You move through mountains only when they say: Move.'

'I can't wait,' she said, starting to panic. 'I've come this far!'

'No, dear lady, I am thorouffly in mindfulness of your situation. You are needful of distraction and Doroftei will make you and Mr Pritzke to do wonderful trip. Here in Braşov we are not far from Bran, and so we go to wonderful castle. Everyone at home you tell, you never see such wonderful thing.'

Wendy could not catch her breath to say that John was not her husband, he was not Mr Pritzke. What had they done? Last night, what had they done?

'He won't want to be making tour!' she said. Constructing sentences in erratic syntax was contagious. John, awakening in her bed, had fled down the hall to his own room. That he had left her room rather than she his made it feel that the dalliance had been at her invitation, but is that how it really had been?

Doroftei explained, 'Then we leave him reading gentlemen's papers, or smoking his pipe in lounge. Come, the car is all heat and ready.' She allowed herself to be dragged off by Doroftei, more for distraction than anything else.

The castle at Bran, it turned out, was none other than the home of Vlad the Impaler – the original Count Dracula. At the sloping approach to the castle huddled a sort of Ye Olde Transylvanian Village, unpeopled and dull. Little else but chickens squawking in the dusting of snow, looking for frozen grubs or Lord knew what. The steep stairs leading up to the front door were huge stone slabs, lacking railings or balustrades. Very Hollywood, early talkies; very convincing. But once inside the castle, Wendy could catch no whiff of vampirism, could impugn no castle corridor or winding staircase with the drama of that old hackneyed tale. The place was beautifully plastered and entirely whitewashed, and if it were tricked out in tapestries of flowers and unicorns, it might serve handily as the setting of half a dozen European fairy tales.

There were no other visitors, due to the snow or to the rude good sense of the locals. Wendy didn't even know why the place bothered to open its gates to the public. The only person in residence seemed to be the babka-faced auntie selling tickets, who sat in a tiny booth listening to an early Beastie Boys tape on a cassette recorder as she knitted an ugly olive drab sweater three feet high and five feet across, useful only to a troll.

It was good, though, to lose Doroftei, to be alone. She wandered about, seeing the white lightlessness in the sky, a low screen rolling down and cloaking the view beyond the valley.

Back at the car, she said suddenly, 'Could we not just go on? Right now? Leave John at the hotel, and just try? It's midday, certainly they'll have cleared the road to Sighişoara by now?'

'We never could do that, I would not speak to myself again for weeks!' said Doroftei. 'Leave the gentleman behind? For why you do that?'

'I am the one arranging this trip,' she said, in as steely a voice as she could.

'It is not you the one arranging the snow, I think,' said Doroftei.

'I insist. I may insist, and I do.'

Even as she spoke, however, the snow began again.

The road back to Braşov was treacherous now, and scary, but for so many reasons other than ice and snow.

'So,' said John, breathing a bit heavily due to the climb back up the stairs.

'There is news about Mrs Maddingly?'

'Little news. She is in stable condition and resting comfortably but in and out of consciousness, mostly out. No diagnosis when I left. I don't suppose you know if she has any relatives?'

'John, she's your neighbor, not mine.'

'Understood. But you seem to have made yourself familiar with her while I've been away.'

'I don't know what that's supposed to mean, John. It sounds more disapproving even than your usual. But to answer your question, as far as I know she's alone in the world. Her husband died long ago.'

'If she dies, someone will have to see to her affairs. I wonder if Camden Council takes care of such things?'

'Completely beyond me. I took care of the cat, that was my job.'

'What was that business with the cat, anyway?'

'You didn't ask her?'

'She didn't know anyone else was in the ambulance with her. She was too busy carrying on a conversation with herself to talk to me. But you must have an idea.'

Winnie did have an idea, but it was old, and tired, and stupid, like most of her ideas these days. 'I know what Wendy would have said. It was the ghost of Jack the Ripper that your workers uncorked from your pantry wall. It floated free-form through the house and dislodged the chimney pot that nearly took out old Jenkins. It found a footing in Chutney and began to stretch its claws – to stretch Chutney's claws, I mean – and Chutney became a lethal house pet, murdering its companions. Then, who knows, Mrs M passed her own sell-by date, and the idea of the dead cats sent her over the edge. How she caught Chutney and why she cooked him I don't know, but in the best of times she wasn't all there. Remember that phrase, whose is it, about a place: there isn't any there there? Is it Gertrude Stein? Doesn't matter. Of Mrs M, there wasn't much there there even in her better days.'

'Wendy?' said John.

'Wendy,' she said impatiently, 'Wendy Pritzke.'

'Oh oh oh oh,' he said. 'Oh.'

'But she would have been wrong, of course, because the ghost that came out wasn't Jack the Ripper, it wasn't a man. Unless Jack the Ripper was a woman, a possibility that's never been disproven. According to Ritzi Ostertag—'

'Ritzi Ostertag?'

'The medium. The seer. I told you. Didn't I? The fortune-teller. He said the cloth hanging behind your pantry wall was the shroud of a woman, and Irv Hausserman—'

'Irv Hausserman. That's right. You've been consulting a bevy of experts.'

'Don't be a bastard. I'm only answering the question you asked. Irv as I may have mentioned is a historian, and someone at the V and A said the shroud was much older than that. Possibly real solid Middle Ages.'

'So,' said John. 'To sum up. You come to town and I leave, and you handily avoid facing the facts of why I have done so—'

'I have avoided no facts, John. I have been rather busy with affairs stemming from your absence as you can tell—'

'And I see the note I left you is there on the desk' – he pointed at it – 'unopened and unread. As I say, you avoid the reality and instead find a medieval ghost to exhume out of this very non-medieval home. You are not writing just now, you say. But you are stalking through a plot constructed out of unverifiable bits and pieces and stupid – I will say it – stupid hypotheses by fringe characters posing as experts in parapsychology and medieval history? Why are you embellishing a sad and real story with nonsense out of some juvenile campfire ghost story? Is it to keep from acknowledging that the real story is *done*, Winnie? And that there's no life on the other side of it for you – and frankly no relief for me either – until you acknowledge it? You're madder than Mrs Maddingly, and that takes some doing.'

'John, I saw what I saw.'

'You will see anything but what is in front of your face.' He picked up the envelope. 'Read this in front of me. Now. Read it before I go. And I'm not coming back until you're gone out of here.'

'I'll leave now. I'll just finish packing and be gone in ten minutes—'

'*Read it.*' He looked as if he would strangle her. She turned her head away from him, hating to see his face. But he would not move and she could not, so finally she gave a whimper and tore open the damned thing.

'Read it aloud.'

'I will not.'

'You do or I'll take it from you and read it to you myself. I want to know you have heard the words it says. Winnie. Please. For your sake. For mine. *Please.*'

She shrugged, held it out to him but still didn't turn to look at his face. He cursed her under his breath and opened the folded page.

'Dated October thirtieth,' he said. 'And before I start I should say I resent your shirking this responsibility. Classic, though. You despise certain kinds of privilege in others but you take every kind of liberty for yourself that suits you. The letter.'

'"Dear Winnie. I'm not the writer you are so as you know I take pen to hand unwillingly. But I have had no luck in reaching you by phone and the post is unreliable at best. I have been trying to get your attention and you deftly sidestep everything with your gaze focused on some internal middle distance. In fairness I usually put it down to artistic temperament but enough is enough. So with reluctance I am writing you this note for you to find on your arrival in London. I am not going to be here while you are here. I am not able to stay in the same place with you. I have to go abroad for work, somewhat unexpectedly. I could postpone it but why. I think it better I should go. I assume you will use my flat overnight or even for several nights while you make adjustments to your plans. You'll find workers on the premises by the way; that's accidental, but since I think and hope it unlikely you'll stay it'll be a chance for some work to be done while I'm gone."'

'New paragraph. "The thing Winnie is this: I can no longer waltz around the regret about what happened in Romania as if it hadn't happened. I had thought a little time would put a helpful distance on things, would allow us to forgive and find a new footing for our long friendship. We can choose either to die of shame and sorrow or we can recover. I have no intention of dying but I fear you have no intention of recovering. And I am not the person I was before we went to Romania. I miss that fellow sometimes, that aging undergraduate, who into his early forties could still smile with a certain amount of foolish innocence. And I certainly miss you, in every way. (Every way but one, as you will

237

have trouble hearing, but I need to say it so that you face it: I do not miss you as a lover.) But I have access to nothing of you, just a simulacrum, is that the word? – a gluey-eyed manikin. Not Winifred Rudge, my cousin and dear friend, but some sort of Winnie-the-Scrooge, stuck in your sorrows and unable to reform yourself the way your famous great-great-great-grandfather could and did."

'New paragraph. Last one. "So this is what I cannot say to you in person, because you will not listen, you leave the room, you get a sudden inspiration and dive into a notebook or flee to a library to do some research or have a sudden appetite for a nap. *You must put Romania behind you.* It is over. There is nothing you can do about it. You are not responsible and *more to the point*" (this part, Winnie, I underlined for emphasis) "*no more am I.* I only hope that my writing this and my leaving you alone here until next time will finally register with you. I truly can't imagine what else I can do to get your attention. Your loving friend. J."'

He handed her the envelope and the letter. 'That's it. Now did you hear it?'

The notebook that was to have been the Wendy Pritzke story, these weeks later, was still full of empty white pages. Something in Winnie couldn't make the simple gestures anymore: the shrug, the middle finger, the wink, the wince, the kiss, the genuflection. She was trying as hard as she could to unriddle herself, wasn't she? What more could she do?

'You've no right to intrude,' she said at last. 'You gave up that right. And there is no longer such a thing as reform, not the way old Ozias Rudge managed it, nor Ebenezer Scrooge. Things don't really get better in life. Do you remember the text? Dickens Hallmarked it up. In the book, Tiny Tim didn't die. But in Victorian England, he would have *died.*'

'I know,' said John. 'And I know people die. And people leave. And people change. But so must you.'

'If you're right, if I'm stalled, it's not because of a weakness in the fabric of my soul. I don't believe in the soul, anyway, and I hardly believe in character anymore. If I'm stuck in one place, it's because some little wooden sphere in a precise place on my personal double-helix model of DNA doesn't allow me to obey the instructional poem. Do you remember it?'

'I don't know what you're on about.'

She imagined wagging her finger at him as she recited:

> 'When in danger, when in doubt,
> Run in circles, scream and shout.

'But that's not what I do, John. I don't scream and shout. My personal inheritance of genetic code says: When in doubt, freeze.'

'DNA as fate is just as much a cop-out as Freudianism. Or as astrology.'

'Touché, my dear.'

He wiped his eyes on the back of his palms. 'If you could work over your own life as you so willingly work out your fictions.'

'Do you think I have had my soul cauterized on purpose?'

'You are too busy working on some fiction in your head that says you and I are to blame for what happened. We're not. There's no – no contingency – in it, it's just accident and coincidence at work. That you refuse to move forward is to lend—'

But she couldn't listen to this anymore. She dropped the letter on the floor and stood looking at John with her hand open, flapping, exaggerating with cruelty the gesture of dismissal, and then she raked her hair behind her ears with two fingers. She picked up her leather catchall and her computer case and left the larger suitcase where it stood.

'It's your house,' she said, 'handle your ghosts on your own.'

'A deal.' Spoken to her back as she headed down the stairs. 'If you grapple with yours.'

She took a tiny airless room near the British Museum, and couldn't sleep for the traffic noise. What a pig's breakfast she was making of things – the ghosts of Christmas Past and Present and Yet to Come vying for attention with the ghost of Jack the Ripper, or Jacqueline the Ripstress, or some parlor maid behind a wall.

She went to Ritzi Ostertag's, but his place seemed closed for business, some bottles of unclaimed milk going sour at his door. She tacked a note to his door anyway, saying: *RITZI: Please give my whereabouts to Irving Hausserman if he should request it*, and below that she scrawled the hotel phone number and address.

She made a call to Boston. She did not want to speak to anyone from her former life. She called Adrian Moscou instead. She got him. She told him where her key was hidden and what the security code was for the alarm system. (She didn't tell him the alarm had malfunctioned recently, and hoped that if he was arrested and jailed for trespassing the other detainees would be pleasant to him.) She explained where the photocopied pages of Edward Rudge's letters were kept, and asked for them to be sent by air express to London.

'And what do I get out of it?' said Adrian.

'If I get a story out of it,' she said, 'I'll dedicate it to you and your boyfriend.'

'That's thin beer. How about a dinner date, the three of us, when you get back?'

'You have no business liking me, you don't even know me. No one who knows me likes me anymore. Just save the receipt and I'll reimburse you.'

'You better. Forever Families is milking us dry. We're going to be welfare dads.'

She wandered around Whitechapel, trying to get back into the Jack the Ripper story that Wendy Pritzke was supposed to be writing. It was too far away. She felt like Ritzi Ostertag on a bad day, unable to get a reading on anything.

He showed up a day or two later, with a bunch of treats from the food hall at Harrods. They lunched on a bench in Green Park, huddled under an umbrella that kept tipping over. 'Smart of you to leave that note for me at Ostertag's,' he said. 'I kept calling your cousin but only got the answering machine.'

'I suspect he's steering clear of the place until the renovation is done.'

'Or until he sees you've come in during the day and removed the rest of your luggage. How are you managing?'

'I replenished the basic toiletries at Boots, and did some emergency clothes shopping at John Lewis. What are your plans?'

'I'm not here much longer,' he said. 'I've a return ticket for a week from Thursday. The semester's coming to an end. There are department meetings I need to sit in on, to make sure I don't get elected chair of the history department in my absence.'

'Has it been valuable for you? The research? Sounds as if you've been more successful than I.'

'I hate the new British Library, but I'm an antediluvian. Yes, it's been okay. I've been concentrating on manuscripts about charivaris.'

'Charivaris being what?'

'Not sure of the etymology – I think it's uncertain – but it refers to the raucous noise – the *OED* says "rough music" – made by banging pots and drums and household implements on the occasion of an unpopular marriage. The earliest literary reference is contained in a fourteenth-century manuscript, *Le Roman de Fauvel*, in which—'

'You can spare me the bibliographic citations.'

He looked hurt, but only for a moment. 'I thought you had a lively curiosity about such things.'

'I do, my dear,' she said, 'but I have my own rough music in my head. Charivari is as good a term for what ails me as anything else. But go on; I was being rude.'

'To prove that I can go on, I shall. Not for nothing have I been wearing out the seat of my pants at the British Library.' He flicked an olive pit into the shrubbery. 'The charivari in Fauvel is gorgeously specific. I care less about the allegorical characters of Fauvel and his new bride, Vainglory, than I do about the charivari designed to disrupt their wedding night. It's a kind of Feast of Fools carried out in the bedchamber. Youths dressed in clerical habits or old bits of sacking, youths dressed as girls, youths showing their bare bums, or masked as wild men of the forest. They tear the place up like a rock band in a hotel room, breaking windows and smashing doors and the like. They tease and they torment and jeer. They tickle the private parts of the wife, to distract her from her husband's attentions; they scare poor Fauvel with a funeral procession. It's just grand.' He sighed with gusto. 'Even grander that it doesn't work. Fauvel has his way with his wife despite the charivari. In Fauvel, see, marriage wins. Sex is more sexy than death.'

She said, 'We are all too fascinated with this stuff.'

'And why shouldn't we be?' he said. 'Look, but I didn't come to talk to you about my research. I came to see how you are.'

She shook her head. 'By now you should know that I never tell people how I am. I'm too good a liar.'

'You're too bad a liar, you mean. I can see for myself, plain as day. For one thing, the clothes you bought on Oxford Street are all black. But I have another bit of gossip as well. Have you been to see your so-called Mrs M in the hospital?'

'No. Surely you haven't been?'

'Are you kidding?' he said. 'After you told me about it that night at dinner, I went out of a simple need for you to be impressed with my charity. But after the first time, I went again. And I'm going back this afternoon.' He patted the canvas satchel on the bench beside him. 'With this.'

'What? You're bringing her a picnic hamper? Just because the hospital cuisine isn't up to snuff?'

'No. Underneath the food. A tape recorder.'

'What for?'

'Come,' he said. 'You'll see.'

They made their way gingerly along the sidewalk, the paving stones plastered with wet leaves. Winnie said, 'I can't imagine why you're doing this. Why you went to see her.'

'Can't you really?' He looked at her almost fondly. 'Want to take a guess?'

'Oh, that?' She felt horrible, ancient, an exhumed mummy herself. The waistband on her panties was unraveling, and she had a charley horse in her left calf. Also a lump in her throat. 'I told you I'm not free for a sentimental attachment.'

'What a lovely old-fashioned way to put it. And anyway, that makes you all the more novel to be with. Just in case.'

She felt cold and superior. 'You're following me about because I'm the only citizen of this modern world, at least of your acquaintance, to claim any truck with ghosts. You're examining me like a specimen. Maybe you'll have some flash of inspiration about how the medieval mind worked. Or are you intending to trot out a sidebar to some newspaper piece, or work me into the preface of your book, to give it commercial appeal? *Hauntings in the Twenty-First Century?*'

'You know, you are occasionally paranoid to the point of being delusional yourself. Would you like me to find you a room here at the Royal Free Hospital, as long as we're on the premises, so you can take a rest cure?

'Not,' he added, holding open the door for her, 'that your commercial instincts are off, at all. Mostly I do modest little essays in professional journals no one reads except professionals. Would that I had your grasp of what sold.'

They rode a lift to the seventh floor: Health Services for Elderly People. Outside the elevator doors, Winnie paused and put her hand out to stay Irv, for a moment, as she readied herself to see Mrs Maddingly. The throbbing of heat and ventilation systems, the hush of elevators rushing in their shafts, it all made a ringing in the air, as if the building had tinnitus.

They passed through the doors in the Berry ward, one of four arms reaching out from the heart of the building. The linoleum floor was the color of white coffee; the air smelled, inevitably, of overboiled brussels sprouts. There was a quiet buzz of competence in the nurses' station overlooking a central ward with multiple beds, all filled, none with anyone familiar.

Mrs Maddingly had been put in a double room made to serve as a triple. At the right doorway, Winnie made herself appraise the room's view first: nice bit of Heath, more trees than open land visible, terraced housing creeping on several sides. Buildings the color of tooth decay.

A radio from another room was broadcasting a jug band's rendition of 'The Holly and the Ivy.' Winnie gritted her teeth and went in.

Mrs M lay like a drying sheaf of something, in sheets too clean and good for her. Two other old hens, one on either side, chattering to each other. 'Are you here to quiet the duck down? She does go on,' said one, to Winnie and Irv.

'She needs a tonic,' opined the other. 'Or a jab.'

'Not my way to whinge, but I never heard such chatter, not before that one; she'd talk the skin off a Cumberland sausage.'

'Any decent child would remove the poor old thing and take her home.'

The second woman turned to look at the first. 'Then what are we doing here?'

'We haven't got children,' said the first, 'at least, not decent enough.' This caused them both to cackle and then lie still, thinking things over.

'Very sorry,' said Irv. 'We're just friends, looking in.'

Mrs Maddingly's eyes were open and Winnie was relieved to see there was life enough in them. But the old woman did not seem to notice her guests. Her voice went on in a singsong, at a varying volume, first high, then low. There were phrases Winnie could catch, *the stairs . . . I never use vinegar for that, dear . . . the blackout curtains in sad need of repair . . .* But there were other chortled phrases, syllables backed up against one another. 'Is she choking?' said Winnie. 'Mrs M, are you all right?'

'She's not choking,' said Irv Hausserman, setting up the tape recorder.

'We ought to have brought her some flowers, some candies or something.'

'*We'd* not have said no to jellied sweets,' said one of the roommates.

'Nor flowers,' said the other.

'But don't mind us. Just get her to belt up, will you? The bother of it!'

'I'll call the sister,' said Winnie. 'I think she's choking on her own spittle.'

'She's not choking,' said Irv again, pressing Play.

'Talk about reliving your childhood. She's wandering, then, back to before the days she had language.'

'She's reliving someone else's childhood,' said Irv. 'Sorry, that was a line I couldn't resist. I don't know what she's doing. But she's speaking, I believe, in medieval French, or something like it.'

Winnie said nothing.

'Let's just get some of it down,' said Irv. 'Sit tight, honey.' Winnie didn't know if he was addressing Mrs Maddingly or her, but she didn't feel she could move in any case. Mrs Maddingly's utterances did have a roll to them, and a quality more guttural than nasal, to Winnie's ear. Who knew what medieval French even sounded like? Winnie had not thrived in French class at Miss Porter's, and she could not manage an Inspector Clouseau accent even when drunk. But she supposed Irv must know enough French grammar and vocabulary to make such an assessment.

'Well, what is she saying?'

'It's far beyond me,' he whispered. 'Shh. Let's get a few minutes of it. I sat and listened last time. Incredible. She seems to do a kind of loop. Let's get a complete recital of it and we'll talk then.'

They sat while the tape ran, nearly the whole side. The other old women lapsed into their own hazes, reviving at the hope of lunch, but it was only a sister bearing pills on a tray.

'Got it, then, or most of it,' said Irv at last, and flipped the machine off. 'Now. Shall we find the matron and get an update on Mrs M's condition?'

'But what is she saying?' said Winnie. Her knees were locked, her gut clenched. 'If you could tell it was French – I couldn't even hear that, much less medieval French – what was she saying?'

'I don't know,' said Irv, 'or not much. The accent is way beyond me. But it's the simplest words that stay the same – I heard *knife*, and *water*, and, I think, *fire*.'

'What's happening to her?'

'It sounds like some kind of personality split, like a – what do you call it – schizophrenic episode, brought on maybe by a stroke? I don't know. I'm not a doctor. I think Mrs M was talking to herself in English and answering herself in French.'

'She's from, oh, someplace like Manchester.'

'I'm telling you what it sounded like to me. She was this way the other day – she keeps on all night, apparently, even in her sleep, if she does sleep. Listen – you'll hear it—'

'What am I listening for?'

'I think she's given a name to the other half of her. She addresses herself.'

'The dark side of Mrs Maddingly. Unbelievable. What's it called?'

'Listen: it crops up over and over, in the English phrases—'

'What am I listening for?'

'Jersey,' said Irv in a low whisper.

Mrs M bucked a little, as if perhaps she'd heard him say it. Her head moved from side to side. Winnie strained. The syllables slipped out, a kind of Jersey. Jervsey? Jarvis? One edge of Mrs M's mouth was pulled taut and the sound was indistinct. 'I don't know. Jersey as in the island? Maybe she had holidays there as a child and picked up some patois. Do they speak French in Jersey?'

'Beats me.'

'If you're not going to take her home, do us the pleasure of gluing her teeth together,' said desiccated woman number one.

'Or have her tongue removed?' said the other hopefully. 'By a procedure?'

'We need our sleep.'

'It's worse than *Spitting Image*, this prattle.'

The introduction of Mrs Maddingly into their room had given them something wonderful to resent. They laughed and laughed as Irv and Winnie crept out. Winnie hung back while Irv made an attempt at getting an update on Mrs Maddingly's prognosis. The staff was reluctant to give specifics, since Irv wasn't a relative, but they let it be known that they didn't expect her to be released anytime soon.

Once outside, Winnie felt no urgency to spend more time with Irv. The sense of people being on display, a freak show – not just poor Mrs Maddingly, but herself as well – had begun to sting. 'What are you going to do with that tape?' she said.

'See whether I can find someone in town to have a listen and do a spot translation. If I have to go to Oxford or Cambridge, I will. There'll be medievalists willing to have a go at deciphering this.'

'I think you are the crazy one. How could Mrs Maddingly be speaking medieval French? Are you proposing, in some Chomskyesque fashion, that we hold the grammar and syntax of ancient languages in our brain-boxes, passed down like Jung's theory of the collective unconscious? That some aneurysm or the like has turned Mrs Maddingly into a latter-day medieval scholar?'

'I don't know what I'm suggesting. Maybe once she went to a lecture with her husband and sat there knitting while some old coot read a medieval text. And though she didn't know it, her brain was turned on like a tape recorder, like this tape recorder. And the mental tape has been accidentally retrieved and she can't turn it off. How do I know?'

'This is so wildly crazy. You might as well say she was possessed.'

'I haven't said that. I'd opt for my theory first. I don't believe in possession.'

'Are you leading me on? To see whether I believe she's possessed?'

'You don't need to trust me about much. But you can risk trusting that I'm not such a dog as that.'

'I don't know what I trust,' she said. 'Go to your expert and leave me the hell alone.'

The voyeurism of it. She walked down the hill, angry enough to pass the entrance to the Northern Line at Belsize Park, and keep going, past Primrose Hill, right into Camden, where she pretended to look at racks of colored T-shirts. Thinking; trying to think, anyway.

There was something. Jersey. Jervsey.

Then she remembered the letters on Post-it notes stuck to Mrs Maddingly's mantel.

G	BR	WA	ε	A

What if she'd misread the *B*? What if it were an *E* that, in rounded scrawl, had looked *B*-ish?

G	ER	WA	S	A

And if the *W* was either a sloppy *V*, or pronounced as a *V*? The way Ritzi *V*'d his *W*'s? And the letters crowded to make a word? A name?

G	ER	VA	S	A

Jersey? Jervsey?
Gervasa?

For the first time in her life she doubted – well, what? Not her sanity, for she could not remember ever feeling more alert than walking back into the hotel in Braşov, and seeing John there. So her grasp on reality was not in doubt. It was just that she had not, since childhood, ever felt like a child.

All the attention she paid to childish

things! . . . the Pooh bear (Disney version) on her desk at home. The vague opinions spelled out by the arrangement of the stars in the sky. The scraps of verse, hoarded like prophecies – all these distractions had not made her carefree, just busy. Mentally cluttered.

    I like this book, said the King of Hearts.
It makes me laugh, the way it starts.
I like it also, said his mother.
So they sat down and read it to each other.

Sure, she had managed a career, building a reputation out of limited talents. She had taken her father in until he died, despite the cost to her marriage. She'd done quarterly taxes, collected for the American Heart Fund, et cetera. She had honored and loved her husband, and she had rarely found it hard to obey him, either. Up until now, when he was unpardonably missing from this most significant campaign of their marriage, and she had become demented – drunk maybe – and fallen into bed with the one fellow she had ever really wanted, and never imagined she'd be able to get.

    So what was she now, walking into the hotel, shaking the snow off her shoulders? No more than a teenager, trembling, more full of lust than she'd ever conceived possible. The old mocking truisms held. She was naked underneath her respectable wool coat and matching blue serge suit and bra and panties and hose. Her middle-aged body was reamed out with shock and desire. She had reverted to a being with breasts that felt things, didn't just provide a nice slope for the display of better necklaces. She could feel the blood flushing her buttocks. With a briefcase full of notarized files up in her room, extra money for bribery stitched into the padded shoulders of her pinstriped suit coat, she was nothing if not a woman of today: competent to the point of being a maniac about it. And here she stood, on the hotel lobby's terrazzo floor strewn with sawdust, the room circling because she was dizzy with hunger for John, again. She could not be sure who she was, a married woman or a teenager in love for the first time.

He should be here, she thought of Emil. Damn him! And John looked up from his club chair and smiled. Not, she saw, a smile of complicity, or passion, or even embarrassment, but perhaps a smile of worry.

'What, what is it?' she said, wondering if Emil had called.

'Oh, the snow, that's all; we're stuck here for some time, I think,' he said.

'We needn't see each other, if it seems I've taken advantage of the situation.' She felt like an Audrey Hepburn character. It was standing here in this retro lobby, which had not been redone to evoke an older, more sober time, but was the genuine article, seedy and tired, gently decadent. 'Perhaps I misunderstood – I am afraid that I moved too near.'

'It was not what I expected,' he said, 'last night
I mean. But that's not what I'm talking about.'

'What?'

'It's quite a serious storm, they say. Sighişoara
is right in its path, and there have been power
outages. It might be several days more before we
can get through.'

He meant – she thought – that they would
be locked in this hotel together, as snow hemmed
them in, imprisoned them, kept them from
completing their mission. Not like Omar Sharif and
Julie Christie, marooned in a fairy-tale dacha, but
here in a hotel that smelled of diesel fuel, with
little of interest to eat, nothing to read, the task
ahead postponed indefinitely, and only their illicit
and accidental romance to occupy them.

She said to him,

'Davy Dumpling,
Boil him in a pot,
Sugar him and butter him,
And eat him while he's hot.'

He answered, 'Davy's hot.'

So they went upstairs to bed, though not out
of passion this time, but out of regret and a certain
variety of terror. And this time, because perversity
is perverse, the sexual undertow was more
unfathomable – in the meaning of the word that
connotes not just the hidden distance of depths but
their secret nature as well.

Halfway back to lower Bloomsbury, she decided it was time to go. Go for good. She got off the Northern Line at Camden and crossed to the other side of the platform to head back to Hampstead. She could never regain her sense of moral decorum, but at least, with effort, she could act as if she had. That would have to do. And surely the first thing, or anyway the best thing, that she could think of to do was to evacuate herself out of John's digs. Get the last piece of luggage, get out, get out, and then worry about the next step later.

She didn't want to run into him, so she waited until dusk, when his presence would be marked by the switching on of lamps. When she noted no such illumination, she let herself in and went upstairs.

In just a day or two he had managed to get another contractor, though they had not shown up that day or she'd have seen them leave. The pantry wall was now down entirely, and the brick fire wall beyond had been scrubbed with an iron brush. The bricks looked perky, very period, as if baked to order by Martha Stewart. A few sawn bits of timber, the beginning structure of a staircase that would wrap about the bricks and head illegally to the roof. She wished it all well. A house gives up its ghosts every time some window is punched out, some molding is removed, some faded wallpaper is stripped or painted over.

She gave thought to placing a well-aimed kick at the sorrowing face of Scrooge/Rudge. Deal with it, she told him. Either stay in your house or get out of it. Just move over the threshold. How long can you stand there threatened by the bed-curtains?

Only, of course, maybe they weren't bed-curtains threatening him, but the shroud of the Jervsey creature.

Either way, get out, old man. Remove yourself to Brazil or the Punjab or the Antipodes. There isn't enough room in this place for the both of us to be haunted.

She threw open her suitcase and pulled things from the closet. Things she had left there in between visits. Her state of mind was becoming grim. As long as she was going to be here alone, she might as well steep herself in it. Looking for some music to wallow by, she found a CD of *Die Winterreise* and immediately began to hanker after its harrowing sonorities.

She folded her clothes with unusual slowness, unwilling, she guessed, to leave very quickly – why? To listen to the music? She even pressed the straps of her bra together and inverted one cup inside the other, for maximum efficiency. The fourth song came up in its sequence: 'Erstarrung.' She checked the libretto to make sure she was remembering the translation correctly. 'Numbness.' How strange that numbness should be given such an aggressive setting, the piano thrumming percussively rather than with languorous legatos. As if Schubert's idea of the nature of numbness were best characterized not by paralysis but by obsessive motion and iteration, ceaseless noise and distraction.

She heard:

> *'Ich such im Schnee vergebens*
> *Nach ihrer Tritte Spur,*
> *Wo sie an meinem Arme*
> *Durchstrich dei grüne Flur.*
> *Ich will den Boden küssen,*
> *Durchdringen Eis und Schnee*
> *Mit meinen heißen Tränen,*
> *Bis ich die Erde seh.'*

And then she found the text of, whose was it, Wilhelm Müller's poem, and sat on the edge of the bed, one leg over a knee and kicking in a bored way, and read:

> Vainly I search in the snow
> for the footprint she left
> when arm in arm with me she
> passed along the green meadow.
> I want to kiss the ground,
> pierce ice and snow
> with my hot tears
> until I see the soil beneath.

But the wanting, she thought, the wanting was an active thing, not a numbness. It was the world that was numb with cold and snow, not the singer. The singer was fiercely alive in a dead environment.

She heard the key in the lock and the door open, and sat up straight, determined to be neither frightened nor hostile. 'John?' said a voice.

'He's not here,' said Winnie.

'Oh.' Allegra paused at the door of the small room, holding something to her breast. A book? 'But you are. I thought you'd gone.'

'Nearly. As you can see.'

'Well.' Allegra seemed to be trying to decide what to do. Winnie did not get up. 'I suppose,' said Allegra, 'I can put to you what I was about to put to John, with some irritation.'

'Put what to me?'

Allegra lowered her arm. Not books, but two tiles. She held them out. 'I am clearing up the old work, ready to begin building the frames, and there are two extra plates on my drying rack in the kitchen.'

Winnie squinted at one. 'So?' she said, and then looked at the other. 'Oh,' she said in a different voice.

'Winnie. Have you been in my flat without my permission?

Have you found a key that John had tucked away somewhere? Have you been letting yourself in?'

'I don't know about these. Your guess is as good as mine.'

'This is your symbol.' Allegra pointed to the slashed cross that had been scraped and dug into the medium with a sharp implement. The motions had been swift and imprecise, and the hard edges were rucked back from the furrow.

'It's not my symbol, I don't have a "symbol." Leave me alone.'

'And then these aren't your big hands?' said Allegra, pointing to the other tablet.

'I don't know whose hands they are and I don't care.'

'They're yours. You are trying to intimidate me with tactics borrowed from some campy American movie.'

'I don't go around making impressions of my hands in wet cement like some starlet outside Grauman's Chinese Theatre. Give me a break, Allegra.'

'Put your hands in there and let me see that the prints aren't yours, then.'

'I'll do no such thing. Look, I didn't ask you in.'

'This is the last straw,' said Allegra. Her voice went up, to compete with Dietrich Fischer-Dieskau, who'd moved on to another meditation on loss. 'I did fourteen impressions over the past week, what with the holidays coming, and when I go to finish them with glaze and framing I find sixteen tiles. I won't have it. These are not child's hands! Put your hands in here, Winnie, and show me they're not yours.'

Ruminatively Winnie took the tile and then shattered it against the wall, which left a chalky scrape and flung plaster crumbs on the bedspread. 'Rather friable, your work. Must be a lot of repeat business from clumsy kids running to show their grandparents your handiwork.'

'John is right.'

'John is right about what?'

'You really are mad.'

'I am not mad. I'm not even annoyed. Maybe you did these in your sleep. Ever think of that?'

'Right. I'm leaving now. Shall I let John know you've moved out? Since I take it you're being incommunicado again?'

Winnie stood up and went to her suitcase, and laboriously heaved it up. 'I could use some help getting this down the stairs, if you're that eager to see me go.'

Allegra set down the remaining tile on the edge of the bookcase. 'Now hang fire, Winnie. I'm saying things I oughtn't because I'm upset about this. Let me take it back. I know things are hard. I shouldn't have accused you.'

'Let me just go,' said Winnie, with some degree of exhaustion.

'I'll help you,' said Allegra. 'Allow me that much, as apology.' Winnie tried not to suppose that Allegra offered so she could report to John that with her own eyes she had seen Winnie actually pack up and leave.

'All right,' she said.

By the time they were on the ground floor, huffing with the effort of hauling the luggage, some of Winnie's irritation had dissipated. 'I'm sorry about breaking your tile,' said Winnie. 'I just really, really resent being accused of madness if I have nothing productive to show for it, okay?'

Allegra looked poised for flight, but ventured, 'You could have had the tile if you hadn't broken it.'

Winnie laughed. 'If I go mad, I'm going to keep very careful notes so I can write a self-help book from the other side and make a million bucks. You know, if you weren't so edgy, I'd tell you even more to make you mistrust me. There's another twist, this time involving weird Mrs Maddingly.'

'Well, finding those tiles was upsetting,' said Allegra. 'What would you have thought? Having your home broken into is not delightful.'

'I'm sure you're right.'

They were at the corner where Allegra would turn to head up Rowancroft Gardens, and Winnie set course for the Tube station. 'Well, you might as well tell me,' said Allegra.

'So that you have more dirt on me to laugh about with John? Not in this lifetime.'

'Oh, come on,' said Allegra. 'I don't laugh about you with John. John and I aren't even seeing each other anymore, actually.'

Winnie looked at Allegra over the top of her glasses. A ploy of some sort? But to what end? 'That's not what I get from John.'

'John would say what he wanted to get what he needed, wouldn't he?' said Allegra. 'I mean, I love the bloke, but he *is* a bloke.'

'What does he need, though? From me?'

'He needs you – oh, why should I say? What business is it of mine?'

'It has to be someone's business,' said Winnie, starting to tear up. 'Something has to be someone's business, or where are we all?'

'All right,' said Allegra crossly. 'But I'm not standing here gossiping in the cold. Nor am I inviting you back to my house. Too awkward.'

'Because John still has a key.'

'He does,' she said defiantly, 'and he's welcome to use it when he likes. Come on. Have you been to Zinc's? It's on the site of the old White Horse Pub down Flask Walk. It's a really trendy little place, so overpriced even for Hampstead that it won't last long. We can get a drink in the bar. There's a jazz trio most evenings and they don't play too loudly.'

They had to wait for a table, but when one came free they dove upon it, poking away other after-work party animals. In a few moments they had settled with two tall glasses of Pimms. The jazz trio turned out to be a pianist accompanying a blonde chanteuse in a classic black cocktail sheath. 'A far cry from Schubert,' murmured Winnie.

'Or maybe not all that far,' she added, when the singer segued into 'I Get Along Without You Very Well.'

They sipped and didn't talk for a while.

'I do wonder,' said Winnie, when enough time seemed to have passed, 'what reason John gave you for his mounting this disappearing act for my benefit.'

'Winifred. I do heartily object to getting involved.'

'Another round,' said Winnie to the waiter. When two more Pimms arrived, she continued, 'John's likely to have said *something* to you.'

Allegra remarked, 'John is more circumspect than you might give him credit for being. He is, after all, English.'

'Really.' Winnie tried not to be too sincere. 'It might help. It might help me, I mean, to know what he's doing, and why.' She felt downright naked and disgusting.

' "It all depends on you," ' sang the cocktail waitress, fingering her pearls and biting them in well-practiced syncopation between notes.

'Oh, John,' said Allegra, shrugging, yielding, Winnie could see it.

'If he has a key, it might after all have been our own John who made those handprints, and left you a mark.'

'He'd never.' Defensively.

'But he'd say of me that I might?'

'He wouldn't know what to say of you. That's the truth.'

'But what does he say of me?' Winnie leaned forward. 'Come on now. I'm about to go. I've got my last suitcase packed and I've been forced out. What's to lose now? Tell me.'

She saw Allegra hesitating again. The damn reserve of the English! Winnie pressed her. 'What does he say about Romania?'

'You really do have me pegged wrongly, Winnie. I know he went there with you and that things went bad. Don't ask me to reveal his secrets. You might as well tell *me* what happened there.'

But that was what Winnie couldn't do.

Aspects of a novelty. The long white walls of snow built up on either side of the road. The romance going through a hundred permutations, as, daily, they were kept from moving on. Doroftei bringing pine branches into her room, and the haunting smell of Christmas hanging about. Real beeswax candles when the power went out. Soon they had to huddle not for sex but for warmth.

An apple left on a bedside table froze overnight – nothing but mealy pulp in the morning.

'It's not as if I mind now. I might have once,' said Allegra, 'but not now. I have my own fellow. Look, you who need everything spelled out, look.' She went pawing through her purse as the chanteuse began another torch song, this one a hymn to hopelessness, another rough music. The accompaniment was organized around a three-note motif, obsessively reiterated, the last note always falling, missing the mark. A breath rising but always falling.

'Not a day goes by,
Not a single day
But you're somewhere a part of my life
And it looks like you'll stay.'

'This isn't worth it,' said Allegra, the drink blurring her speech and blunting her fingers. She fumbled at the catch of the wallet. 'I mean this regretting music, sung over a man.' She was trying to make a point about Winnie and John. 'Can you imagine? All these torch songs are about obsessive-compulsive nymphos or something. Here, look.'

She had located a snapshot in her wallet. She tossed it, derisively, on the table toward Winnie. 'There he is, my new beau. A few months now.'

Winnie looked. In the dark she could hardly see it. 'Very nice. Very handsome.'

'Maybe you know him. Malcolm Rice?'

'Old guy? Not John's investment adviser? What do you know. And whatever does John think of that?'

'Oh, you know John.'

'No, not anymore. That's the problem, isn't it?' She took a huge swallow. 'Look, maybe I better just go.'

'Come on, stay till the end of the set anyway. Don't you want more of these sad songs? In a perverse way they make you feel better. I miss John too, you know. In my fashion.'

> 'As the days go by,
> I keep thinking, "When will it end?
> Where's the day I'll have started forgetting?"
> But I just go on
> Thinking and sweating
> And cursing and crying
> And turning and reaching
> And waking and dying . . .'

It was Winnie's turn to fumble through her purse, looking for a ten-pound note.

'You called Malcolm the first night you arrived, didn't you?' said Allegra. 'I was at Malcolm's that night, though John was off in Latvia, I think.'

'Denmark. Or so he told me. Did John know about you two already?'

'Of course. He introduced us.'

'For the purposes of romance?'

'Oh, well. As you know. Romance arises when least expected.'

As you know. Winnie was so eager to leave now she tore at the Velcro fastening her purse and a sheaf of business cards, credit cards, and other slips of paper spilled out, some on the floor. 'Sorry,' said Winnie. 'At least here's the money. I can't stay, Allegra, though it was nice of you to ask me out. Sorry. I really am leaving, I'm leaving entirely. Leaving London, leaving John, leaving. Just going. Sorry. Sorry.'

Allegra had leaned down to pick up what had fluttered to the floor. 'Twenty quid,' said Allegra, sitting up. 'Ooh, I'm light-headed. Thank you, Pimms. And here, some old underground passes by the look of it, and a photo. You have a new man too?' The photo was facing Winnie and she snatched for it, but Allegra already had rotated it and picked it up.

'Oh,' said Allegra, 'oh, what a sweetheart!'

'Give it to me, give it to me, give it to me.'

'Yes, of course. I'm sorry. Of course. But he's so darling! How old is he?'

Her hands closed on the snapshot, the only one. It felt rimmed over with hoarfrost. The singer concluded her song as Winnie stood.

'So there's hell to pay
And until I die

I'll die day after day after day after day after day after
    day after day
Till the days go by.'

Winnie couldn't speak. Pine boughs choked her esophagus.

'Winnie, I'm sorry. Lord, I'm sorry. Look, let me get you a minicab anyway.'

The baby's face in a three-quarter shot, showing his scrappy hair, his poky little nose, his serious eyes, his tentative toothless smile.

'Not a day goes by
Not a single day
But you're somewhere a part of my life
And it looks like you'll stay.'

The heat was off for the next two days. Wendy slept in her good wool coat, a pair of leggings pulled over her head down to her ears, her hair tucked up into the waistband, the legs tied together in a topknot. It could have made such droll comedy. So much for romance, anyway; the electric naked skin of John was no longer available. Even huddling together with all their clothes mounded on top of the bed it was just too cold to be intimate.

Ice had brought the phone lines down, and there was no way to contact Emil. She did her best not to think about it.

On the morning of the third day power was restored and the hotel furnace began to cough and kick. Pipes had frozen all over the building. Laborers came wandering through the rooms without knocking to look for water damage in the plaster and to trace the source of the trouble. By now it seemed John and Wendy were married to each other, and they would never leave Braşov. To avoid being surprised by hotel employees, they spent the third day of the snow emergency in the hotel lobby, in full outside gear, reading paperback copies of Georgette Heyer and Jeffrey Archer, the only books in English they could find in the rack.

But on the fourth day Costal Doroftei showed up, having located gasoline somewhere, and having learned that the roads were cleared again at least as far as Rupuea. He was full of beans and declared that it was time to set out, and they would take a hearty meal wrapped in newspapers to protect against hunger. They managed to wheedle two handfuls of potato chips from the aggrieved kitchen staff. The lone bottle of water froze before they were an hour on the road.

But they were on the road again, that was the important thing, skimming treacherously along the valley floors and hillsides, making their way slowly north and west without incident, through Feldiorara into tiny Măierus. Except for a few carriages mounded to twice their height with hay, obviously dispatched for the emergency feeding of snow-locked livestock, there was nothing but the occasional emergency vehicle on the road. This was not so surprising, for the road seemed unsure of itself, at times less a plowed passage than a curve in snowdrifts carved by the wind.

They found a café in Măierus that gave hot

dense coffee, sweet as melted pecan pie; Wendy chewed the grounds for nourishment. She hadn't realized how hungry she'd been. At the hotel she'd had little appetite, so she had paid scant attention when the food ran thin, and the bread plates were empty in the morning.

Măierus on to Rupuea, its little clutch of houses with roofs made blunt, prettified, by thirty inches of snow. On again to Vânători, where they had a car accident. They left Doroftei to scream at the driver of the other vehicle, and Wendy and John took what shelter they could in the frozen hulk of a church with an unlocked front door.

By late in the day they reached Sighişoara at last, on the north slopes of the Transylvanian Alps. It was a picturesque town, perhaps more so for the blandishments of the blizzard. Gated buildings and Romanesque towers, streets that ran beneath stone arches. 'Oh,' said Doroftei, rising to the occasion, 'Sighişoara she is our city having most beauty. She is full of the bright unknowns, she is thorouffly populate. Very very well known to her peoples who live here.'

They stopped and asked for directions. Doroftei fell into a long and muttered conversation with a police officer. Then Doroftei shrugged and spat and nodded, and when he turned back to his passengers he said, 'He is not wanting me to show you Asylum, so he is not telling me where she is. I say him we go back to Braşov, but I lie. With police you must always lie with very clean teeth showing. I ask another peoples.'

He did. Their destination was not far, but the car could not manage the streets anymore; in the older part of the city, the lanes were too mounded with snow. The travelers abandoned the car and Wendy most of her parcels. She brought only her purse and documents, and she made John carry a plastic string bag with cold stuffed animals inside.

The Asylum, as Doroftei called it, listed like a sandcastle, the stonework of its ground floor flaring at the base. The walls of the upper two levels had been painted some fierce orange color that, in the decades since its last repair, had faded to a warm and milky coral, not unlike a Venetian palazzo.

The gate was open. Unshoveled stone steps rose a full flight to a pair of double doors. Doroftei kicked and thrashed his way up, saying, 'You wait, you wait here for governor to permit you entry,' but they didn't wait. Not after all this time. Wendy pushed into the huge icy foyer, and stood under several dark oil paintings of saints levitating on sunny afternoons. They were hung so high that the paintings themselves seemed to be levitating into the gloom.

No light cast from the wall sconces. Power still off here.

An adult was wailing upstairs in a back room.

'Jesus,' said Wendy, 'Asylum is the right word. Not a moment too soon!'

John gripped her hand. Doroftei had disappeared down a hallway, opening doors, calling. He was hustled back into the lobby by an old man with a broom, yelling at him and threatening him. Doroftei raised his voice and his fist, and struck the old man. 'Stop, you bastard,' said John ineffectually, but before more could be done, a couple of young women, hardly more than girls, appeared in the gloom at a railing overhead. One of them called down, English lightened with an old-fashioned rural Irish accent, 'And are ye Americans, then, come all this way, the loves?'

'We're here,' said Wendy. Craning upward, pushing past John and Doroftei, mounting four steps, one hand on the rail, the other hand clutching the small photo, her heart in her throat, glad to hear English spoken again, and by women no less. 'We've come, the snow kept us, we're later than we said. Where are the babies?'

'Oh, Mother of God, I couldn't begin to tell ye's what they do for a mortuary in this black pit of a place,' said the one who had spoken earlier. 'Ask your translator to find out from old Ion, who ye have standing right there before ye.'

'Kathleen,' said the other in a moment, 'they've not heard the news.'

'Oh, Jaysus,' said Kathleen, running down the steps, turning corners, her face appearing again and again over the diagonal of the rail, getting closer, larger, as the words fell on them like stones, 'ye haven't come all this way for your baby, then, without knowing? Oh, Jaysus have mercy.' She was crying, clearly not for the first time but all over again, in a way that might never stop. 'They've all died, the whole lot that stopped here the week last. The eight of them died of exposure in the nursery when their nanny died and let the fire go out.'

Kathleen paused seven or eight steps up, unwilling to come near the small photo that Wendy held out.

Winnie bought a Zone 1–2 travelcard, but she didn't use it. She just needed a place to dump her big suitcase. It was too heavy to carry. She regretted the sweat and bother to the law enforcement officials who would need to have it sniffed for Semtex. And she regretted running out on poor Allegra. But really there was no choice.

She stood at a corner. For a minute it didn't even seem like London, but some city of the dead. Everyone rushing, everyone stalled in the traffic of NW3. She could not bear to go into a shop, nor back to John's, nor forward – to Romania? To Boston? The pain that had broken behind her breastplate made of her interior a hollow sack. Turn as she would, in her plans, in her schemings, there seemed little hope of relief.

Unable to settle on a destination, she wandered up and down the slopes of Hampstead. She paused outside Keats's house in Downshire Hill and murmured, 'The world is too much with us, late and soon,' before remembering the line was Wordsworth's. She pushed on. She passed the church building in which the Beatles were said to have recorded *Abbey Road*, and singsonged 'in my ears and in my eyes,' but was 'Penny Lane' from *Abbey Road*? She wasn't doing very well. She passed the Victorian pile said to belong to Boy George and kept her mouth shut.

How gray the world seemed, how savage and hollow, with winter coming on, with Christmas jangling its tinsel bones and jeering its carols. Eventually however the gluttony let up and even

Hampstead shops closed their doors to the purchasing public. She didn't want to drink anymore, nor to see people trying hard to be cheery. But the cold was coming on, and since she also didn't want to ride the Tube like an indigent person she found herself walking through one of the few doors that stayed open all night, the emergency clinic at the Royal Free Hospital.

She wandered upstairs, pretending she was a nurse reporting late for her shift. The hall lights were partly dimmed. Coded pings occasionally echoed down the halls.

With effort and zeal Mrs Maddingly's roommates were snoring. Between them, Mrs Maddingly looked at Winnie out of frightened eyes, as a hostage will stare from above its gagged mouth. But her mouth was free; her lips rotated and worried over soundless syllables.

Winnie sat close and pitched her voice low so as not to wake the roommates. 'There isn't any need of this. Don't abuse an old lady. Gervasa. I'm talking to you. I don't know who or what you are but I'm making contact. Gervasa – is that how it's said? If you want a hostage, take me. Leave Mrs Maddingly alone. You with the slashed cross – is that sign the denial of Christian solace? – or defiance of it? – well, I'm an atheist, you wouldn't find better quarters than I. I have no need of my life. I don't know what you do but make your move. I'm on offer.'

She leaned forward and gripped both of Mrs Maddingly's hands. The old woman held on, hung on. The grasp was stronger than an old woman's should be. She said something in that dead language; Winnie couldn't get it. 'Don't talk,' said Winnie, 'just come aboard.'

Once as a girl Winnie had fallen backward off a swing. She had been pumping very hard, and out of a suicidal glee at flight she had simply let go. Her back had hit the ground first and knocked the breath out of her. The slam of her skull rattled her brains. At first she'd thought she was dead. Still she actually managed to roll over on her side and then get up, not breathing, and she had begun to wander toward some grown-up at the edge of the playground. She didn't know what she would do when she got there, as she was trying to draw breath to scream and couldn't. She merely wanted to indicate to the grown-up, to mime if need be, 'I just want to let you know that I realize I'm about to die, and there's nothing anyone can do about it' – when at last the first knife-thrust of breath cut through again, reviving her sense both of destiny and of incipient disaster lurking somewhere further out, waiting for her.

The memory of that accident – like a foretaste of Sighişoara – came back now, with her hands trembling. She shuddered, not able to tell if she was being drilled in the sinuses or drained of blood. Perhaps, like Alice after the tea cake, she was suddenly grown larger than the rest of the world could accommodate. It was a physical rather than a mental sensation, but to the extent she could observe herself, she was merely leaning forward in an intrusive position, grabbing onto Mrs Maddingly's hands, and quivering.

Then she slumped into a chair and began to lose consciousness. The last thing she heard was Mrs Maddingly's voice, somewhat tentative but very much her own, saying, 'And if I find they've cut my hair, I'll write a disapproving letter to *The Times* and carry it down there myself. Bring me a mirror.'

'Yes, I know her,' said a voice.

'Winnie Rudge. There'll be a purse, surely, have you looked? Yes, I see. Oh, yes, well that's her married name. Winifred Pritzke née Rudge, then. Though I don't know that she's still married. Certainly separated and likely divorced. Can it be of much importance? I should very much like to speak to the clinician on duty if you don't mind.'

She tried to stir, if only to give her middle initial. *W.*
'Is she sleeping? Have you put her on medication already?'

'Is it too early to ask for a diagnosis?'
   Just ask for solid identification.

Gervasa.

Winifred Wendy Rudge. She'd dropped the Pritzke after the divorce.

Gervasa. Gervasa.
   She couldn't be two people. She struggled to open her eyes. They opened and didn't open. Everything was mothy, felted with dusty static. Ragged, feathery, unraveling. A sense of lumpen shapes indistinctly drawn, like cows seen across a field in early morning mist, or huge stones. Everything the color of the wren's plain breast.

Gervasa. Talking.

Talking to me?

'Just a minute now, missus; you'll feel better.'
   Why could she see nothing but bevels of brown and cinnamon, insinuating almost anything but conclusively stating nothing?

Something for the pain in the gut. Please.

The needle slipped in, making a small welcome point of now. Pain is a great aid to certain tasks of concentration and a deterrent to others. The needle withdrew, and as it did something more like

Winnie sat up in her skin, feeling the hospital sheets first and then seeing them.

'I'll stay with her. No, I'll ring if there's a change. Of course. Just tell me where's the gents?'

The Gervasa migraine began to dissolve, to sponge away into the dry surrounds of Winnie's life.

Wendy dissolved. So did her fictions of Jack the Ripper, her fiction of herself with John. Gone. Gone, as she stood on the stairs, suddenly straight and with shoulders thrown back, as if at this last possible second, good behavior, positive attitude, correct posture even, could cause the Irish girls to relent, to wipe away their tears and say, 'All dead but one, we mean, one little one who's been waiting for his mam: let us look at the picture and see if luck is with ye!'

John talked her into abandoning her demands to visit the city's mortuary. Instead, the Pritzke-Comestor party took poor distraught Annie Ní Fhailin with them as they made the trip back to Braşov and, a day later, to Bucareşt. Thirty miles out of the capital, no snow had fallen at all. Above the trunks of the pollarded trees on either side of the road, a thin cloud of yellow leaves still clung to their stems, waving Doroftei's brother's car by.

In his sudden and precisely calibrated distance, John Comestor became the soul of kindness, as she tried later to say, and he was in no way responsible for the collapse of her marriage. But they both knew, in months and years to come, that there could never be any way of assessing whether this was true.

Winnie did not so much float on tides of Halcion or Ativan as imitate the movement of tides themselves. Adrift from herself, she saw her clumsy maneuvers in a cool and pallid light. Her tentative fictions of Wendy Pritzke, even with the introduction of a standard-issue villain like Jack the Ripper, had not proven robust enough to obliterate the sorrier truth about Romania.

As a character, Wendy Pritzke had been judged and found wanting. Her punishment, then and now, was to be trapped in an old story with an inevitable ending. The baby who flew away before she could get there was still outside the barred window. But she could knock all she wanted and never get his attention.

Winnie went down on the playground in slow motion, the breath leaving by molecules, the blow to the head not so much a slap as a blanket of pain, applied with slowly mounting pressure. This time she blacked out.

Gervasa. A shadow, a manikin. Dissolved, evaporated, eclipsed by time and happenstance. A virus cloaked in the biochemical matter of a host.

'I do think there's some flicker in the eyes. Look.'

Desperately she wanted to bleat the lines of a heroine from the days of the silent film, to see her words in a balloon over her head: 'Wh – wh – where *am* I?'

Then she could open her eyes and be Dorothy at the door of the house, looking out on Technicolor Oz, or Alice at the bottom of the rabbit hole, still holding the marmalade jar she'd clutched for security from some shelf she'd dropped past. Or any one of a hundred intrepid kids for whom a mere shift in universe was not necessarily the onset of schizophrenic illusion. How she wanted to

put away adult things and go back to seeing through a looking-glass, darkly. Not merely her tragedy, not merely the tragedy of the baby – Vasile, his name had been, he was to have been Vasile Pritzke, and she didn't even know where his frozen body had been laid. No, she wanted to be buffeted away from the disgruntlement that disguises itself as wisdom.

But she opened her eyes. She was in the Royal Free Hospital, she remembered. And she was not alone. John Comestor was out there, and Gervasa, whoever that was, was within. Winnie was now without anything worthwhile as an adult life, but she had a rich inner life – someone else's. Who was Gervasa?

'Can you hear me?' said John. 'At last! Allegra rang me that night to say you had moved your things out of Rudge House, and I went back there the next morning to shower and get some things. While I was there, Irv Hausserman rang. He told me he'd been round to your hotel and they said you weren't answering the phone or the door. I got on to the police stations and then the hospitals and the description fit – they found you in Mrs M's room. What is it? Can you hear me?'

Her tongue felt like sludge. She prodded herself to learn the shape of her teeth. So many of them, so rounded and smooth and anonymous, without any little pressure points to claim identity within her mouth. Like polished stones at the sea. 'Mrumph,' she said. Another few syllables, working things out, and then: 'Shit.'

'I bet,' he said, pleased at a word he could recognize. 'I just bet.'

She garbled a few words more, and then tried harder, and then managed to push words, like cabbage through a grater, falling on the table without the shape of cabbage leaves but still, redolently, cabbage: 'Maddingly. After.' (Garble.) 'Together.' (Garble.) 'Menace,' she said, or had she meant to say 'medicine,' or 'nemesis'?

'That's more like it,' said John. 'I can't tell you how relieved I am. Are you alert enough to answer me? Can you nod or shake your head for yes or no?'

She bobbed and bucked and made reply, though she felt at a certain disadvantage, as if her body were both trying to comply and trying to obfuscate that same reply. *Down, girl,* she said to Gervasa. *Get a grip.*

That's just the point, said Gervasa. *I have.* But this seemed to Wendy like her own voice, being tart, taking on a new persona, not like the voice of the airy thing hanging inside her like a cloak on a hook. Talk about having your personal space violated. But the Gervasa thing had been invited, so it wasn't a violation. Just an inconvenience, or an opportunity.

John seemed satisfied. 'All right, then. Let me know. Do you want me to ring Emil?'

It was of no significance to Gervasa, so she let Winnie take this one. Without effort or misunderstanding Winnie was able to shake her head vigorously. *No.* Though her voice, when she tried to rally it, came out sounding absurd, certainly not linguistic in any sense.

'No Emil,' said John. 'Well, not yet anyway. Is there anyone else I should be in touch with?'

Gervasa, understanding, but cautious, unwilling to commit an opinion.

Winnie shook her head.

Who are you? she said to Gervasa. Can you say it?

But Gervasa was something to wait for, perhaps not to understand through language. Or not yet anyway.

'Irv,' Winnie managed to growl.

'Irv Hausserman? You want me to get him?'

Again, Gervasa was unconcerned, and Winnie nodded her assent.

'I'll ring him. He was here earlier, you know, sitting by your side. We've been taking turns. You've been here more than a week.'

Nonsense. It was not even a full night.

'M,' said Winnie, 'M. M. M.'

'Hungry?'

'M. *M.*'

John lifted his shoulders tentatively, and his eyebrows, and ventured, 'Music? You want music? You were listening to *Die Winterreise*, according to Allegra; shall I bring it over?'

She neatly brought forth bundles of expletives, hoarse and pinched, uncharacteristic and extremely effective. John recoiled. It felt rather nice to see him recoil. She went on for several minutes, telling him something most urgently, or asking it. He just shook his head in very very small motions, as if not wanting her to notice that he couldn't understand a word.

'Bitch!' she finally managed.

'Oh,' he said, 'you mean Mrs Maddingly. It was a stroke and she's in rehab. Only a mild one and what language she's lost she seems to have regained. Is that it?'

It was, except Winnie pressed her hands on her hair and mimed cutting it. John was unable to decipher her question, and she let it go. She smiled at him, to thank him for the patient attention, and only after he didn't smile back did she realize she was chattering away again in a burble of watery syllables, and his look was one of panic or grief.

Stop, Gervasa, she said, and Gervasa stopped.

He left. She slept. What Gervasa did she didn't know or care to find out.

When next she came to – the same day? The next day? – Irv Hausserman was in her room. He had a huge bunch of papery daffodils, looking well past their sell-by date, and he'd stuck them in a vase without any water. On the edge of the bed was the tape recorder.

'Now it's for you,' he said calmly, when she was more fully awake.

She said something that even to her sounded faintly like *bonjour*, but maybe that was wishful thinking. 'Hi,' she managed, faintly.

'Are you in there?' he said.

'Sometimes,' she said, and corrected, 'all the time.'

'Who are you?'

English asks that question the same way, whether the audience be singular or plural. Winnie heard it easily but found it hard to answer. She finally managed to say, 'Us,' and hoped that would do.

He didn't seem alarmed. But he didn't believe in possession. He was the staunchest skeptic she knew. 'Will you mind if I get your voice on tape?' he asked.

The voice he was referring to had a strong opinion, but Winnie didn't know what it was. When she could get a word in edgewise, she squeaked, 'Go ahead.'

He inserted a tape and pressed Record.

'What do you want to tell me?' he asked. 'Can you say how you are?'

That was two questions, the fool, and Gervasa had some things to say and Winnie others, so they struggled and interrupted each other for a few moments, until Gervasa in a fit of pique cried out in a loud voice, and Irv's eyebrows went up but he managed not to flinch, and in the backwash of silence Winnie muttered, 'What had Mrs M said, what? Tell me.'

'On my tape of her?' said Irv. He smiled for the first time. He seemed pleased to hear that Winnie had that much memory, however faulty her ability to steer a conversation had become.

Winnie nodded. Gervasa was sulking somewhere. Good riddance.

'I don't want to plant ideas,' he said.

'Tell me, fuckhead,' she answered.

She'd gotten his attention; he laughed. 'Oh, Winnie! Well, you're the boss.'

Not anymore, muttered Gervasa, but as a teenager will mutter, from a sidelines, ineffectually.

'I won't diagnose nor will I hypothesize,' he said. 'There are a great many gaps in understanding. But it's not a nice story such as I've been able to piece together. Are you sure you're up for it?'

Of course he didn't know that the Gervasa germ had migrated. But too bad. What was left of Winnie was curious enough to want to know. She nodded as if to say: *Hurry up and tell me.*

'Mrs Maddingly seems to have been speaking in the first person. Not in her own first person, you understand, but speaking as someone else.'

Yes, yes, that much was abundantly clear. Fire code was going to require that the place be cleared if Winnie got any more stuffed with identity. She tried to make a motion with her fingers, *roll on, speed it up*. But her finger got confused, and in a moment she realized her thumb had been resting comfortably in her mouth. She pulled it out, horrified, and tried to pay attention.

'The other voice, the French one, gave a narrative of sorts, broken by poor pronunciation and archaic or half-said words. And Mrs M interrupted constantly in her own voice. I'm not sure that the non-Mrs M speaker was all that – coherent.' His struggle for the word was admirable. He was clearly trying to keep from saying *bright*. On Gervasa's behalf Winnie took offense.

'A certain Gervase, perhaps of Normandy.'

'Gervasa,' said Winnie, easily enough, and hiked her boobs to make the point.

'Gervasa?' said Irv. 'I don't think there's a feminine variant.'

'Fuck yourself.'

'I'll take that under advisement,' said Irv. 'Whatever else has happened, your inhibitions as to language have been admirably loosened. Not quite Tourette's syndrome. More like Tourette's Lite. Shall I go on?'

She nodded, chagrined but eager.

'Gervase. Gervasa I mean. Of Normandy, let's say, or somewhere in northern France. She mentioned the Abbot of Saint-Evroult and the diocesan kingdom, if you will, of Lisieux, and I think Cluny came into it somewhere too.'

Winnie sat up more strictly, trying to pay the hardest attention she could; she wasn't sure if Gervasa was sitting up, too, seeing whether Irv would get it right.

'There was something about a fire, and a lost baby.'

Winnie slumped. She didn't want this story. There was no fire, there was not even any ghostly possession, just the same old nightmare reinventing itself in new garb at every turn.

'No fire,' she said, but then Gervasa said *Fire!* and it seemed as if Winnie's skin began to shrink and pucker. She clutched herself.

'Shall I stop?' said Irv, looking at some monitor.

'Not yet,' she managed, before Gervasa broke in excitedly. Irv waited with politeness, and though Winnie waved her hands he didn't catch her message: *Speak over the rabble, will you, while I'm awake.* Only when Gervasa's recitation faltered again did Irv say, 'There was an indictment by some tribunal, probably a clerical magistrate of some sort, against – uh, let's call the narrator Gervasa then. As you like. Something like an excommunication, we'd guess.'

We? Meaning exactly you and who else? thought Winnie with a shred of jealousy, but then managed to say to herself, Who am I to be sniffy about plurals? Who are we?

'Anyway, Gervasa was implicated. I can't figure it out,' said Irv. 'According to the story that Mrs Maddingly told, the G character was – well, I should add this is rather horrible – was burned alive.'

'When?'

'Gervasa doesn't give dates. I was hoping that you, the practicing novelist, might have some idea. Just for the sake of narrative satisfaction, mind you.'

Winnie didn't know if she was being asked to channel the deposition of a ghost or to write fiction on the spot. She winced. Gervasa thought no clear answer in her mind, only spewed forth useless syllables.

Maybe useless. They were being caught, anyway, on the tape.

A huge scowling cresty-haired sister came whisking in. 'The monitors signaled spiking levels; severe rest is required,' said the matron. Winnie wasn't sure that was the most legitimate use of the word *severe*, but she didn't care. Severe rest was what she needed, already. She was asleep before Irv Hausserman could be given the bum's rush by Sister Teutonia.

The doctors came and gabbled in med-speak. They made less sense than the noisy objections of Gervasa, who seemed to take umbrage at their examinations. But though Winnie could sense her mind seizing up on her from time to time, the tenancy of a Gervasa de Normandie within her apparently wasn't detectable by the doctors. Winnie's muscles and willpower remained her own, as far as she could tell. Gervasa was quiescent, did not flinch or flare up. Even the use of the muscles of the mouth to vocalize Gervasa's chortles and chirps seemed somehow voluntary, a shared effort. Winnie could claim not to be hijacked, but a partner.

Winnie wasn't able to glean what the doctors were diagnosing, if anything, but though they came regularly, they left just as regularly.

Winnie was beginning to think of Gervasa as her inner ghoul, half tomcat, half tomboy.

★

It seemed a little less hard to pay attention every additional time she was awake, except that it was hard to tell the time.

It was laughable, even slightly mortifying, to imagine being possessed by something so improbable, so foreign – a thirteenth-century peasant martyred at the stake? Puh-*lease*. But then perhaps not as surprising as all that. Every sane soul, thinking 'Curiouser and curiouser!' as she observes her own life, secretes a sort of chitinous shell around her own vulnerable keep. One presumably builds up resistance against more garden-variety infections and viruses. Over the deaths of her own parents, for instance, Winnie had not languished longer than propriety required. Sure, she had run through the usual catalog of residual effects – fond memories, resentments, unanswerable puzzlements – but a haunting by either of the Rudges, those gentle, slow-release Acts of God? It would be like being haunted by air or light – only a genius could manage even to notice such a thing.

For a ghost to take hold, perhaps it had to rely on the strategies of surprise or disguise, of nonsense even. A ghost had to be devious to slip past the phagocytes of the psyche that repel the more obvious invaders.

Winnie was awake, and talking to herself. She asked Gervasa questions in English, out loud, and Gervasa answered in what sounded like toddler patois. The tenant within managed to lapse into a sociable silence when John Comestor and Allegra Lowe came by, with a bouquet of lilies and hothouse snapdragons wrapped in a crinkly acetate. Winnie was beginning to realize that if she didn't open her mouth to speak any English, she could sometimes prevent Gervasa from yakking for attention.

John and Allegra, hmmm, thought Winnie. Suppose that

Allegra was only lying when she said she'd taken up with Malcolm Rice? But that was too tedious a path to follow. So what? What difference did it make even if she were? Gervasa was half the story now, and Gervasa didn't know John and Allegra from Adam and Eve.

'I had a devil of a time getting DHL to release this packet to me,' said John, brandishing an overnight mail parcel. 'I had to get the doctor to write that you were in seclusion for your health before the delivery service would let it out of their hands. Shall I open it?'

She wanted the heft and stress of a pull tab to jerk, cardboard to rip, but when she saw that it was several photocopied pages, she remembered her request of that fellow in Brookline.

There was a brief note. It began, 'Dear Winnie – The fourth grade is having a W. Rudge Read-a-thon in honor of a visit we hope you'll make to us—' She put the note aside.

She couldn't read the photocopied text aloud for fear of Gervasa's interruption. She handed the thing to John and motioned to him: Read.

He recognized it at once. 'This old stuff? Are you sure?'

She nodded. It had been a long time since she had looked at any of it.

'All of it?'

She managed to squeak, 'Start,' while Gervasa was having a think about something else.

John shrugged. 'As you wish.'

'Haverhill, Kent, August twelfth, '71.
'To my Dear Niece Dorothea from your Uncle.
'I endeavour to keep my promise to you today and pick up my pen to correct your mistaken notions of my father and your grandfather, the late Ozias Rudge. Since the death last year of Mr Dickens I have heard little but nonsense spoken about our good and decent forebear. To the silliness spoken at Miss Bairnfeather's table

on Saturday last I take the most extreme objection.

*   'There can be no doubt as you so engagingly related that your grandfather claimed nothing less than a ghostly visitation. His memories of such were often recounted in contradictory renditions depending on whether there were ladies present clergy et cet.'*

John said, 'Rather a failure as a prose stylist, our many-times-great-grandfather. Dry stuff. You could have a relapse.' She made a motion: Go on. She thought, Better get what I can while Gervasa is quiescent.

He ran his finger along the paper, squinting at the long flattened loops of the handwriting.

'Being sensitive and suggestible as the gentler sex must to their sorrow be, by rights you ought to be spared the details that surround the stories of your grandfather. But I am gravely discomforted by hearing you sport with your family's history and gabble such a confloption as turns your dear grandfather into a rustic fool.'

'What a lead-up,' said Allegra, who had been pretending not to listen.

'Well, here comes the good cheese. Here's Ozias's son lecturing poor Dorothea. As they say, the next voice you hear is Edward Rudge's.

'Quote.

'Ozias Rudge claimed to have engaged the young Master Dickens with a tale of hauntings said to have taken place in Rudge House, in the very darkest days of December, nearly fifty years ago – '24 I think it was, or '25. Having overseen a mining enterprise until a pit collapse cost a grievous loss of life, your grandfather fell into

low spirits. Past the springtime of his life, he repaired to Hampstead to take the healthful airs. His new work supplied him with connexions on the Continent and it was long supposed by his widow your grandmother Cornelia that he turned his gaze abroad to escape sad memories of the disaster at the mine.

'As you have persistently neglected your study of the affairs of nations I doubt you remember that across the Channel, the Bourbon monarchy had been briefly restored to the throne of France. In 1821 or thereabouts, the revenue accorded the Church by the state was increased above previous allotments. So the Church embarked upon renovations of their crumbling masterpieces of idolatry from which we English can happily count ourselves safely removed.

'Rudge and his associates undertook to advise Bishops and Chevaliers of the Church in their campaigns of preservation, and to supervise projects in Paris and in the outlying regions. It was in the curiosity of Mont-Saint-Michel off the coast of Normandy that the firm of Rudge and Blackwood discovered a small piece of statuary in some tomb or oubliette. A statue of the infant Christ held lovingly by his mother, not without a certain charm despite being sentimental and common. Your grandfather wondered if perhaps the thing had been hidden during one of the periodic attacks on the famous Mont in previous decades, or perhaps it had been there hundreds of years. It was impossible to tell. But your grandfather took a blanket from the cell in which it was found and smuggled the piece out from under the eyes of wolfish prelates, and back to London. I do not know what has become of the artifact but your objectionable narrative about a duel and a murder and an unfaithful woman was shrill and sensational. I should like you to know there is no truth to it at all. Furthermore it is an insult to your sainted grandmother, and she would be very aggrieved indeed to learn about your indiscreet remarks.'

At this John looked up and said, 'As far as I know, that's the sole mention in family records of a duel and a murder. So of course the later members of the family assumed Dorothea must have been telling the truth. But I read on.

> '*The dreams or visions that your grandfather had occurred a year or two after. He had built the house in Hampstead which you bind so fondly in memory's garland. Ozias Rudge was not a young man but, as yet unmarried, perhaps he was disposed to brooding. One year around the time of the solstice, he took ill and spent several days and nights in his bedroom. He claimed to be visited by a spirit from the afterlife, making some sort of a plea. The visions took several forms, and in his final years your grandfather would not always distinguish his original rendition of the tale from the famous Ghosts of Christmas that our Mister Dickens is said to have memorialized from Grandfather's memories.*
>
> '*My mother has confirmed what I say with firm conviction. The visiting spirits were said to keen and lament with all manner of distresses. Poor Grandfather! Whatever the ghost was asking, Ozias could not decipher. What remained to Ozias Rudge was this: to step forward into the unblemished life of a married man, to beget and raise his children, to turn his back upon melancholic fancies.*
>
> '*When my father died, I retired my own sentimental attachment to his stories of haunts and missions. On behalf of my mother, I boarded up all nonsense in which the future might take some interest. In the end, perhaps Charles Dickens made a happier man of Scrooge than my father could ever make of himself. Perhaps Dickens did Ozias a favor in revising and glorifying his own sad memories. Choleric or not, my father loved a good story. This is a regrettable characteristic that I was alarmed to see at Miss Bairnfeather's you seem to have inherited.*'

John turned the page over. 'There may have been more or perhaps this was posted without a signature. But the family legend begins with this document, and all corroborating gossip derives from it.'

Gervasa, bottled up too long, began to burble. Winnie couldn't help it.

'Oh, dear,' said Allegra, turning a shade of pale worthy of the Ghost of Christmas Yet to Come. 'I see what you mean. Oh, John.' She held his hand. He could not suppress a tear, but said huskily to Winnie, 'Do you want me to leave this letter here so you can look at it?'

Winnie nodded, not knowing whether Gervasa was approving or recoiling. Whatever she meant, she was saying it in a loud voice. Technically a scream. Nurse came through with a hypo. John and Allegra left. Winnie, tossed back in the sheets with Gervasa nearer than a lover could ever get, struggled to hold on to a few words:

. . . a blanket from the cell . . .

. . . I boarded up all nonsense in which the future might take some interest . . .

Only, Winnie couldn't tell if it was herself thinking this, or Gervasa beginning to think in English.

As far as she could tell, her next thoughts occurred in her dreams. Were they dreams of Gervasa de Normandie or dreams of Winifred Wendy Rudge Pritzke? There was little in them to get a fistful of, not much more than a notion of Ozias Rudge staggering from a room, bewitched by terrors too insubstantial to name. A shape loomed and lagged behind him. A man with a habit of brooding, surviving his trials by telling them as stories to young Dickens.

Her sense of herself shifted in its sleeve of sleep, collected itself. These days you are no more nor less than Madame Scrooge. Pestered by the same apparition that pestered your ancestor. Did Rudge take Gervasa unto his breast? If so, what did she ask of him there? Why – and how – did he relinquish her again?

Had the painter caught, not Rudge and Scrooge, really, not that coalescence of ancestral and literary figures, but Rudge and de Normandie, two spirits staggering to the door in one corruptible form?

And who was the painter of that picture? Maybe Edward Rudge himself, despite what he had written to his chattery niece. After all, he too may have inherited that choleric and fanciful temperament, and needed to expel the humors somehow.

When I wake up, I must compare the handwriting in Edward's letter with the scrawl on the back of the painting. But most likely I won't remember any of this.

Stepping nearer the threshold, struggling with the effort of walking for two. Every step a weight of the present against both the past and the future. In her dream, her feet hurt and she had to pee.

When she awoke, Irv Hausserman was bustling around again, this time with a swatch of ripe holly and pretty red berries he'd swiped with his penknife from the garden of some mansion block. Winnie almost chortled with pleasure. He had a man with him, looking familiar if shrunken and furtive. Quite out of place.

'Ah,' said Winnie. 'Curstace.' She was trying to say Christmas.

'Curses to you, too, and how do you do,' said Irv. 'It's about time. You're sleeping more, and more deeply, than before, and this after they've aborted your sleeping tablets. Great nuisance; I've had to delay my return home. Now here's Ritzi Ostertag. Do you remember him?'

Gervasa didn't. Winnie did. She shook her head and nodded, but in that order, hoping the result would be clear. '*Ach, mein Gott,*' said Ritzi, in panic, or a send-up of panic meant to make her laugh. But she was beyond such distinctions.

Irv blustered on. 'And how are we feeling today?'

We, a lovely joke, a lovely lovely joke. They both laughed.

'I thought,' said Irv, 'that I'd give you the latest we'd deduced from your remarks, and then maybe Ritzi could read your palms or your tea leaves or something. Anything for a diversion. Are you up for that?'

Gervasa didn't know what it meant, so Winnie shrugged. She'd rather have aromatherapy but that didn't seem to be on offer.

'Well, then,' he said. He placed the tape recorder on the bed and extracted from it a cassette. He held it up. 'This is my tape of you the other day. You've provided me with a very interesting document, my dear. Some would say that only a novelist could have managed it. You corroborate and extend what little sense I could make out of what Mrs M had said. Now let the record show that I post no claims of belief or disbelief, I'll be right up-front with you about that.' As he talked he was unwrapping the cellophane off a new ninety-minute cassette tape and snapping it into the machine, but he didn't start it recording yet, as she was being silent, and Gervasa cautious, scrutinizing, and mistrusting.

Did we sign a release, allowing ourselves to be recorded? thought Winnie. But then Gervasa made no growl of mutual irritation; how could she, the technology being unfathomable to her? And Winnie was beyond caring about herself. So she let it go.

'There's much that can't be made out,' said Irv. 'But exhibiting a suspension of disbelief that is nearly beyond me – I'll tell you that this tape makes it seem as if you occasionally speak, like Mrs M, with the voice of someone who died many hundreds of years ago.'

'Tell it as a story,' she said, and then Gervasa began to gargle, and Irv fumbled at the controls to record it. When Gervasa had dried up, though – Winnie had the sense that Gervasa wanted to hear the interpretation too – Irv stopped the machine and started over.

'All right, a story. You seem to be using a voice some of whose language suggests medieval northern France. Thirteenth, fourteenth century. Professor Ambrose Clements, a pleasantly tolerant senior lecturer who holds a post in modern and medieval languages at King's College, Cambridge, was intrigued enough to give a listen and float some hypotheses. The syntax, such as he can hear, is very simple, devoid of some of the more elegant forms of subjunctive you begin to find in early Renaissance courtly or ecclesiastic prose. He said Anglo-Norman was spoken by the aristocracy through about 1300, though there seems to be an element of Picard in it. But it's a mess, a pottage; he heard only a limited vocabulary of decodable words embedded within a dense mass of archaic or nonsense syllables. So what passes for a story is hard to say convincingly. Even so, there may be an outline of something. Professor Clements says that if you're attempting the language of a peasant rather than a nobleman or a clergyman, you're succeeding. The references are all very sketchy, the narrator has little sense of history or chronology, and the nouns are all common words familiar to a peasant mentality: farming and harvest, donkey, knife, fire, knave, mother, saint, that sort of thing.'

Winnie closed her eyes. Ritzi, bless him, said, 'Hausserman, she *vants ze story.*'

'I'm getting there. Don't rush me. All right. Assuming a Gervasa – and even Professor Clements isn't sure why it isn't Gervase – assuming a Gervasa, she's a young woman in trouble. In northern France, Normandy probably, in, oh, the thirteenth century. Gervasa seems illiterate. She seems not to know much about the world beyond Normandy, and the hubs of Paris and Würzburg. She's Catholic down to her dirty fingernails.'

Slyly Winnie inspected her nails. Bitten, perhaps, but hardly dirty.

'So Gervasa, if we get it right, is in trouble with the Church. Maybe she's been caught in adultery. Maybe she's carrying the child of some nobleman who doesn't want bastards growing up to claim the family pile or the title. Maybe she killed someone. Who knows. We can't tell or maybe she doesn't even know. But here's the drama, Winnie. You ready? The prelates and curias and the local rabble round her up, and tie her to a stake, and thrust burning ricks of hay at her to make her confess and repent.'

Ritzi Ostertag shuddered, possessed of his own tremors.

'So they're trying to get her to confess, and they promise a Christian burial if she does, and promise to deny her one if she doesn't. And she confesses, and repents her unnamed crime, but conditionally, because she makes a bargain – this is what she keeps talking about – she says, "The baby," over and over again.'

Winnie thought, *Well, big fucking surprise, that.*

'Seems,' said Irv, 'near as Professor Clements can make out, as if Gervasa has tried to make some bargain. They're going to kill her anyway, but she's asked that in return for her repentance, they slice open her belly – this is the knife part that keeps coming up – and save her baby from roasting within her. Sorry, my dear, sorry.' He angled forward to take her hand. 'I didn't want to tell you but you did ask.'

'She vants to know,' said Ritzi, of Winnie, not of Gervasa, studying her face, 'Hausserman, she vants to know if ze baby vas saved or not?'

'Who wants to know?' said Irv Hausserman.

'Vinnie,' said Ritzi Ostertag.

'Gervasa wants to know too,' said Irv. 'That's what it comes down to. She doesn't know. According to your narrative, she passed from this life and was interred in some charnel house reserved for undecided cases. A Christian burial meant a lot, as I well know from my own studies, and to deny one to a believer was possibly a responsibility a local curate wouldn't care to take. So there were halfway houses, so to speak, for the bodies of souls who died in extremis, without benefit of the blessing of the Church but without absolute condemnation either.'

Winnie thought, Hence the statue of the Virgin and Child. Some poor priest or nun knew whose corpse it was, or some old story about it, and left it a totem for comfort. What a correct totem. You didn't have to be Catholic to know what images of the Madonna and Child must mean to people with sorry, hurried lives, ringed round with so much everyday death.

'And that's the it of it,' said Irv.

Gervasa began to cry, because whatever huge blank pieces of the story were missing, or wrong, there was enough right about it, enough there, to make corroboration possible.

'Oh, no,' said Ritzi, and came forward. He took Winnie's hand, rather roughly, and turned over its palm. He ran a finger along a life line and said, 'Look, lots of branches here. A fertile vomb. A family line zat doesn't die out. Don't cry. Pliss.' It was all a load of bunk, unconvincingly said, and Winnie loved him for it, but she couldn't stop Gervasa using her eyes to cry.

'Please,' said Irv. He sat on the bed, rocking Winnie in his arms. 'You're going through too much, you don't have to do this. You don't have to have her story in you, you know. You don't have to.'

It wasn't a matter of choice now. Gervasa wouldn't be quiet until an older nurse came in with the morning pill in a paper cuplet and saw the raw eyes. 'Oh, you're stirring her up?' said the nurse. 'Mustn't do that, chaps.' She gave a sniffy look at Ritzi, and turned a separate variety of disapproval toward Irv. 'I'll call the supervisor and see if we can double the dose this morning. Can I ask you gentlemen to go wander off and have a cup of tea in the caff while I clean up our friend? She's made a mess of herself by the smell of it.'

Oh, the shame, she had.

So, too, she had when she fell off the swing, she remembered now.

While the nurse cleaned her, Winnie wept with very slow tears that had time to flatten on her face and evaporate.

'Hang on, I'll be back in a moment or two,' said the nurse, 'you rest up some.'

When the nurse had left, Winnie turned on her side and pulled her knees up to her womb. The tape recorder began to fall on the floor and she grabbed it. More to silence Gervasa than anything else, Winnie pushed the button to expel the new tape and she inserted the prior one, the one Professor Clements had heard. She rewound it for a few moments and then pressed Play.

She heard the voice of Gervasa in her voice. It was eerie. Too clipped and precious to stomach, the voice of Gervasa declaimed away urgently in some archaic dialect of French. It sounded, even to Winnie, as if she were making it up, doing some undergraduate exercise in dramatic improv. Were those words her voice? *Où est la bibliothèque?* was really about all she knew, besides *Oooh la la!* and the French verse of Lennon and McCartney's 'Michelle.'

Then the tape ran out, or seemed to, and Winnie was reaching her hand to press Stop when she heard Irv's voice, recorded. He said, 'So that's it. Impressive, isn't it?'

Irv Hausserman must have accidentally pressed Record instead of Stop after the airing of Winnie's rantings as Gervasa.

Another voice, an older, smugly polished one. 'That's twice now, but I'll want to hear it one more time. I pick up a little more each go-round.'

'You're holding by your initial outline of the story?'

'The narrator is consistent in the details, few as they are.'

'Well, she's a novelist by trade. She ought to be. What do you make of it, really?'

'Dr Hausserman. I'm a linguist, not a psychologist. But I propose either that Ms Rudge has hidden from you a deeply | refined study of Romance languages, more thorough than my own life's work has been, or that she has had exposure to French at some early stage in her life and is experiencing some wild sort of total recall without knowing it. Has she vacationed on the coast of Normandy? It's hardly possible I suppose that some old peasant type might have committed to memory some dialectic screed, a patch of local lore, passed on through the generations. And then babbled to a young, impressionable Miss Rudge. Following which, a trauma of some sort is making whole chunks of garbled French regurgitate. No, I am persuading myself not. I don't know that such a thing is at all possible. But I can't otherwise diagnose the event. You need someone trained in fields other than my own. I do wonder, however, the nature of your interest.'

'I can't help but be fascinated, Professor Clements. I'm fond of the subject – I mean the woman speaking, of course – which is how I come by the tape. But also, inevitably, what a case study for whatever discipline obtains! Leaving aside parapsychology, which I must—'

'As must we all.'

'The notion of a delusion so systemic that it can corrupt the language templates – I'm not sure what if anything has been written on this before. A sort of organized glossolalia.'

'Well, Miss Rudge has a highly active imagination. As you've indicated. I leave the diagnosis and therapy to my betters. I'm eager to hear some of this recording once more before my afternoon tutorial requires my attention. I hate to admit it's giving me notions about medieval grammar that I hadn't entertained. If we might?'

'Of course. Is there a diagnostician you might recommend in the field of—' Here the tape went silent.

The bastard. Talking about her over her head, behind her back. She knocked the tape recorder on the floor as she sat up suddenly. The hatch flew open and the tape sprang out. She kicked it under the bed, then, thinking better of it, got down on her hands and knees and reclaimed it. She stuffed it in her pocketbook, which mercifully had not been confiscated by the hospital staff. With shaking hands she clawed open the clasp. There were her keys, her wallet, her passport, her makeup, the essentials. She rammed the cassette in and stood up. Her clothes had been laundered and folded. She dressed herself as best she could, finding herself weak in the limbs, and, looking this way and that down the corridor, made for the elevators.

Once there, she found Gervasa unwilling to press the button. Shakily she took the stairs instead, hoping not to meet Irv and Ritzi on their way back from the cafeteria.

She'd grab a cab and go to John's. But though a London taxi stopped at her frantic wave, and she wrenched the door open, Gervasa wouldn't let her enter. There was a great balking in her spine, a terror in the temples and jaw. She brayed in impenetrable coarse syllables, and the driver said, 'Not in my vehicle, luv,' and drove away. So she walked up the hill, carefully crossing at the zebra stripes, training her eyes on the paving stones, trying to keep her voice down.

She rang Mrs Maddingly's bell. No answer. Mrs Maddingly was probably still recuperating in some dingy room at the hospital Winnie had just left. She rang John's bell and then, though she had trouble working the key, she let herself in. John wasn't there but the new staircase was. She mounted it and found herself on top of Rudge House, looking out over sunny London in – what was it now? Early December? How long had she slept? Look, Gervasa, she said, with some small sense of pride despite the general horror of everything. Look what we've done with the world.

Oh oh oh, said Gervasa, and this time in English. But how could Winnie tell the difference? She supposed that Gervasa merely seemed – closer.

'No,' said Winnie, 'I'm not hearing voices, please.'

Oh, tell it me, said Gervasa.

'I have nothing to tell you, I just want you to look, and despise it or love it, as you will.'

Gervasa made no promise.

'What crime did you commit, that they put you to death for it?'

Gervasa didn't understand or didn't care to answer. 'Was it murder, that you could not be buried in a Christian plot? Who did you kill? Why? You murderer, still at your task! When you were Chutney, you killed his companions. When you were Mrs Maddingly you turned and killed Chutney. Who will you kill now that you are me?'

A cat needs to eat, and that cat was locked up. It could find no food on its own. The old woman gave it no food. It had to eat.

'Cats don't eat each other. They don't.'

Gervasa did not reply. Cats kill mice and birds, everyone knew. And Chutney, Gervasa seemed to imply, had been slightly more than a cat when it went on the hunt.

'And then you killed Chutney when you were Mrs Maddingly. How come?'

A woman needs to eat, and that woman was locked up. She could find no other food.

'Roasting a cat?'

Again, no reply. Perhaps Gervasa had caused Mrs Maddingly to kill the cat, but Mrs Maddingly on her own was wacky enough to choose an appropriate recipe.

'Did you kill someone over food? To keep yourself and your baby from starving? Who will you kill now that you are me? Are you determined to slay every living creature in this house? Is Mrs

Maddingly going to die? Is John safe? Is Allegra, over the party wall? Did you go into Allegra's house and mark your hand in her plaster of Paris? In whose body did you dress? Is Allegra safe? Is Rasia?'

Rasia and the children. Winnie was thoroughly confused; what if the Gervasa in her made an attack on the children? Out of some mad fit of revenge? She loped across the flat roof to see if she could jump across to the roof of the abutting building, but as Mac and Jenkins had seen before her, there was no access to a window or door from the roof area.

'I won't let you do it. I won't let you attack Rasia or her children, I won't,' said Winnie. 'I don't care what vendetta you are conducting. I'll get to them before you do.'

Gervasa began to chortle and protest in her own language, and Winnie grabbed the chance to duck out, as if, vain thought, she could outrun Gervasa. She took the stairs at a gallop, pounding her heels till they sang with pain. Gervasa's odd words could hardly keep up; Winnie pictured them streaming up behind her as if printed on streamers, drawn by Edward Gorey to accompany one of his hellish visions.

> Life is distracting and uncertain,
> She said, and went to draw the curtain.

She passed the estate agent, what's-his-name, in the hall, showing a fair English rose of a girl into the vacant flat. Gervasa shrieked at them both, and the estate agent put his big shoulder up in the doorway to try to shield the client from the sight. 'She's training for the All-Europe marathon, they shriek like barbarians, part of the program,' he said as the door slammed behind him.

Winnie was out on the street, her pocketbook flapping against her side, which was beginning to hurt. What if during all those sleepy hours at the Royal Free, Gervasa had woken up, like Dr Jekyll and Lady Hyde, and had gone murderously back to Rudge House and its Rowancroft Gardens neighbor?

She rang the bell. One of the children answered through the intercom. 'Darling, it's Auntie Allegra from the garden flat,' said Winnie, breathing hard, in her best English accent. 'Do buzz me in, I need to borrow a spoon.'

'Uh,' said the child doubtfully, but did as he was told.

She heaved and panted, using her arms like a gorilla's natural grappling hooks, hauling herself up the staircase. The door was open a crack and a flimsy chain was on it. Gervasa and Winnie felt they had the strength of two people; the chain gave way as if it were made of cheap plastic.

'Mummy,' cried the boy. He tossed his play telephone on the floor and backed away. From her receiving blanket in front of the television the baby looked up and gurgled.

'Get out,' said Winnie, as sweetly as she could.

'Who is it?' called Rasia from the other room, her voice strong and fearful. She came in with a skillet in her hand, dropping bits of frying onion. The air was redolent with turmeric and crushed coriander and sizzling ghee.

The boy had grabbed the baby and retreated by the time Rasia was able to take it all in. 'What are you doing here?'

'Get out, get out before I kill you all, get out. Get out.'

'You get out, you bitch.' Rasia went at her with the skillet. 'Bloody hell. This is my house and you're not invited.'

Winnie fell to one knee and deflected the skillet with her forearm, which sounded as if it shattered. She grabbed what she could in defense – the plastic portable phone – and held it out entreatingly. 'Rasia, listen: for your safety and your kids: get out, leave the house! Get out.' Gervasa took over, arguing one side or another of the case, Winnie couldn't tell.

'Navida, ring 999, tell them to come at once.'

The skillet slid out of Rasia's hands and hit the wall, spattering it with grease. Winnie grabbed it, to show she didn't want to hurt anyone, and hurtled it out the window, removing it from the field of operations. 'Please leave,' said Winnie, 'I don't want to hurt anyone. Please.' She was weeping. But part of her wanted to kill Rasia and her son so she could get to the baby and hold it, just once.

Then the girl was there, the oldest child, with a revolver in her hand, and the boy and the baby huddled behind. 'Get out of our house,' said the girl coldly. The revolver was probably as plastic as the telephone, but something in Winnie was stopped, mercifully, and she turned and left the house, moving more slowly now so as to catch her breath. She could hear Rasia crumpled on the floor of the living room, weeping.

She went to Waterloo Station and bought a one-way ticket to France via the Eurostar. 'No luggage to check?' asked the attendant.

'None,' said Winnie. 'I'll shop in Paris for a new wardrobe.'

Stave Five

For the Time Being

there was little to do but lean against the wall and breathe in, breathe out, as if breath were a rare enough commodity to bother cherishing. The train was scheduled to leave at 15:23. It had been hard for Winnie to get Gervasa to Waterloo, down into the catacombs of the Tube, but Winnie had taken the upper hand as best she could, and people, she saw, gave her the widest possible berth. Appearing to be talking to yourself clears the way, she observed. And yelling does it more efficiently still.

She thought to look at the ticket. The twelfth of December. How had the time passed? She'd come to London more than a month ago. Two weeks or so spent in wrestling the reduced spirit of Gervasa out into the open. Was it true that Gervasa had resisted coming? Once upon a time Winnie had guessed some dim ghost of Jack the Ripper, reluctant to kill again. The falling chimney pot, all that stage business. Off. Way off.

Something didn't sit right with Winnie, and as the well-dressed travelers began to assemble themselves in the departure lounge of the Eurostar, off to do holiday shopping or have a dirty weekend in Paris, Winnie caught sight of what it was. According to Irv Hausserman, the ghosts of the past were usually of some renown, at least to the scribes who snatched their tales out of the air. What were the miracles of saints but the rough music of the good and the blessed still rousing folks up to betterment? And old sinners and reprobates had to be high-born in order to be remembered. But who cared for a dead pregnant peasant woman from six, seven hundred years ago? Someone who had left no mark, probably left no issue, surely disturbed history in no memorable way?

Winnie didn't like the class system of the ghostly world. No more than she liked these living rich rich people who smelled like attar of heirloom roses as they went swanning by. Why should that fop with the cell phone be the one to have so much obvious disposable income, and not the man who slept under the yew trees in the graveyard at Hampstead Parish Church? Why should this dead one leave a ghostly residue and not that? It seemed so capricious.

But it is not something I asked for, said Gervasa, as travelers who had cleared customs looked up over their *Independent*s and *Guardian*s and cafés au lait and then looked down again, too quickly.

Winnie hadn't realized she had been speaking aloud. She tried to lower her voice. 'What do you mean?' she tried to whisper.

It isn't something I asked for. She was speaking to Winnie out loud, in that muscle-bound Anglo-Norman, but though the sound was foreign, the meaning was coming through in something approximating English. That's the modern European Community for you, thought Winnie.

'You didn't ask to be a – a spirit?'

To last beyond my death? Who would ask that? I didn't believe in the Purgatory promised by the abbots. My punishment is to have been proven wrong.

'What did you do?' said Winnie. What a story she could write and sell to the *National Enquirer* about this: Thirteenth-Century Ghost Tells All.

It was the third year of the famine. For the sake of a morsel I did what I ought not to have done. They accused me, and set me up to burn like a martyr. To make me repent.

'What did you do? Did you murder for food?'

I will not say it.

An even more novel notion: Thirteenth-Century Ghost Refuses to Talk. 'And they killed you for it.'

I had a small life, but it was only half the life I had. The other half quickened within me. The first I was willing to lose to save the second. My bargaining failed me somehow. I am caught, for reasons I don't know, in between life and death. In this state I cannot learn whether my child lived or died. Such knowledge is too far. But I am caught, a dead leaf that will not detach and fall. I am in between the shadow world and the lighted one. I cannot die enough to follow the child into the dark garden to find its history. Nor can I live enough in the bright garden to remember its vanities and pleasures.

This doesn't sound like a peasant voice, observed Winnie, but maybe filtered through her own language skills . . . 'Why should you be privileged enough to be caught between?'

That you consider it a privilege . . .

And why do you presume to know how many of us, or how few, are caught? It is a tally I cannot make. But while I was fully alive, revenants attended every family I ever knew.

'Were you the ghost who haunted my forebear, Ozias Rudge?'

I do not know the things you know. I don't know souls by names, nor remember what happens, except I know that I am grateful when I am safe, and spend my best time as close to being dead as I can manage.

The announcer called them to the train. Winnie saw people hang back to see where she would place herself. The seats were reserved, but there were plenty of unoccupied places and the other travelers were wary. Well, fuck them all. She tried to hold her head up and walked shakily by, accepting the hand of an attendant into the car.

The train went in an unhurried pace through bemuraled, grimy Brixton, graffiti sprayed in Day-Glo paint on red and yellow Victorian brick. Then the beginning of the rust, as Forster called it in *Howards End*, the suburban Edwardian villas that metastasized all over southern England. Dulwich, Sydenham Hill. Into a tunnel. Gervasa flinched within Winnie at the dark and the noise. Out again, past the industrial lots and hangars of Tonbridge, giving way quickly and mercifully to orchards, fields with standing water in tractor ruts. Reflections of the fresh growth of newly planted winter crops. The strange cone-roofed grain houses, their tips tilted. Oast houses, was that the term?

The day grew wetter, brighter, as sunset neared. There ought to be a word for a kind of first direct daylight that occurs only before evening, when the angling sun finally manages by lowering itself to slip in under the clouds that have ceilinged the day. A dusky sunrise is what it was, thought Winnie.

As the land began to peter out, the train picked up speed. The land mounded to the east in a green henge. Then concrete retaining walls, grids, screens, wires. In.

Gervasa didn't like the Chunnel. 'Only a few moments, don't panic,' said Winnie. 'As if dark and silence are a problem for you.' But perhaps it was the speed, the hopeless onrush. Gervasa began to babble more noisily and Winnie needed to talk herself in order to keep the Francophone syllables from offending any of the French passengers. She went hunting for a mint to suck on, hoping to shut Gervasa up, and found the toy phone. She must have stuffed it in there. She pulled it out and pretended to punch some numbers, and held it up to her ear.

'Don't worry,' she said, 'please. There is nothing to this.'

None of this is going to help.

'What help can you possibly need? What can I do?'

Gervasa was silent for a moment.

'What? Don't make me beg. I invited you here, remember? I've already proven my hospitality. Just tell me.'

Exchange places with me.

It was Winnie's turn to be silent.

I have no further death possible without you. And you are not living your life. You know it. You don't want your life. You've turned your back on it.

'I haven't.'

You who do no good could yet do good. What are you now? A thief, a parasite. You steal the meat of other people's lives and lie about it in words on a page. You turn your eyes away from your own life. You live in a sequence of punishments, in sacrifices and penances.

'Not me, you've the wrong gal. I don't believe in all that Church stuff.'

Tell me, if you want your life at all, why you bothered to exhume what was left of mine?

'I,' she began. 'I.' But it was hard to finish any sentence that started with *I*.

'Listen.' She held the phone so hard, so close to her face, that the casing began to crack and the plastic to sweat in her palm. 'Something happened to me. I didn't expect it and I didn't ask for it. But it happened, a tragedy, an awful dreadful thing.'

What?

But Winnie no more wanted to tell Gervasa this than Gervasa wanted to reveal what sin or crime she had committed. And died for. More or less died, that is.

What?

'It doesn't matter what. Just this. When I came to – when I came back to myself – I wasn't myself anymore. I was a living plant that had been cut down at the ground level – flower, fruit, and stem. I thought I should die. I wanted to. But I didn't die. I just became redundant in my own life. I lost weight, I let my hair go back to its tired natural color. I was living the semblance of my old life, with all my books, my friends, my same old history behind me, but I wasn't myself.'

So if you're not yourself, let me be you.

Winnie pushed on. 'My husband divorced me and I thought I deserved it. My doctors said the word *hedonophobia* – I who drank the best scotch, who flew business class when my air miles allowed it. But it was true. For several years I couldn't listen to music, not because it made me sad but because it didn't make me feel anything. And I couldn't work. I tried to write. This whole trip to England was meant to jostle me to face what I had not faced. To face the facts with John, to try to move out of this half-life I inhabit. But it hasn't worked.'

Someone a seat or two ahead, an American, turned and said bluntly to Winnie, 'You can't even get any reception for that thing in here so you might as well hang up.'

'This is a conference call, you fat prick,' said Winnie, and turned her head toward the window. She could see her reflection in the dark glass, a puzzled face swimming in black water.

If you give me your life, then I can use it. When you die I will go with you. With a guide I can make it, into knowledge or oblivion, either is acceptable. I can ride your corpse into the death I couldn't manage for myself.

'Is that what you asked of my great-great-great-grandfather?'

I have asked it before was all Gervasa would say.

Of whom? Of Ozias Rudge? Had he resisted, gone on to have something of a real life? Of Chutney? Of Mrs Maddingly? Maybe they killed – Chutney slaying the other cats, Mrs M roasting poor Chutney – as a kind of kicking action, trying to evacuate the murderous Gervasa virus.

If I give myself over to her, I'll be the reborn Jack the Ripper, she thought. But at least I'd be somebody.

'What would happen to me? Is this like a sublease? Do I go hang in a closet somewhere?'

How different would that be?

'Don't be withering. Without me you're nothing.'

If Gervasa had a witty reply to that, she kept it to herself.

Then the train was through the Chunnel, zipping faster and faster, on flatter, cleaner land, with grayer grass. The first building that came into view was unquestionably French, a brick farmhouse with an oriel window. Odd how the look was unmistakably foreign, yet as the crow flies so close . . .

Alighting at the terminus, Gare du Nord, Winnie had the feeling of floating, like a ghost, down the rail platform. There was no longer a customs officer to approve the passports. Whoever could know she was in another country now?

A cold rain was spitting, making the shuttered stone buildings more blurred, more soft-focus. She ducked into a fancy enough restaurant only a block or two from the station and, too tired to sink the bucket into the memory well for high school French, in as polite and apologetic a voice as she could manage, said in English, 'Please, a table, for one; just me, alone?'

The maître d' stared at her with consummate Parisian disdain. Then he shrugged wide-eyed, as if she'd just spoken in Choctaw and he passed beyond her, to a sullen French businessman who'd come in the door behind her. The maître d' pointed him toward a table for one, just a few feet away. The fellow sat down, slung his silk tie over his shoulder, and began to pick apart the bread and feed himself with both hands.

Winnie approached the maître d' and grabbed his shoulder, and Gervasa said, out loud, in her own tongue, something like, 'You smelly old pompous shithole, give me a table before I slice off your nuts, or you'll be speaking in neither French *nor* English, but in baby squeals.'

It was a lovely table. The waiters hovered fawningly. A small vase of fresh flowers was located promptly and set down in the candlelight. Winnie held the plastic phone in her left hand. With her right she sipped soup and polished off a carafe of wine.

Then she rented a room for the night, and two days later the hotel staff broke the door down, thinking she was dead. She had slept for so long that her bowels were stone and her bladder had leaked in the bed. She paid extra for the trouble she'd caused,

apologizing all the while, and then rented a car and bought a map, and ventured out onto the Autoroute Périphérique, heading south a bit for the A6 toward Orly. And then (she'd written it in large letters so she could study it while driving),

the *A10 toward Chartres*
the *A11 toward Le Mans*
the *A81 toward Rennes*

and onto some smaller *D* roads. But as the land grew flatter and emptier – and from the motorways, the countryside in France was always broader and emptier than she remembered – the night drew in, with swiftness and force, and Winnie didn't want to drive on without knowing where she would sleep.

She found a motor court on the outskirts of Le Mans, where the concierge welcomed her in polite and flawless English, and in polite and flawless English, the preteen boy offered to park her car, and the Moroccan maid coming back from a janitor's closet with a damp mop and a bucket said 'Pardon me, please' in flawless English. And very polite. So it was only in Paris, apparently, near the train station that brought visitors from England, that the French behaved as if they'd never come across the English language before.

She sat in a room the color of stewed celery. She didn't lie down for fear of sleeping for two days again and drawing attention to herself. Her eyes closed once or twice. Her imagination cast upon the backs of her eyelids the flickering semblance of images. Harsh or furtive faces, seen in glimpses. A streambed glistening in early spring runoff, the stream channeled by boulders into sleek silvery bolts of water. A hulk of a building, a church perhaps, in the sunrise, with an open door. 'Is that a church?' said Winnie. 'Is this my imagination?' When Gervasa answered her: *What if it is?* – the answer seemed to be about the whole condition of being haunted.

A man's face, seen leaning forward, looking loving. Not a face that Winnie could find attractive, but one that Gervasa might. A handle of a nose, a rucked-up lip, sweet belaboring eyes.

A pair of cows knee-deep in snow.

A pennant, or skirt, or something, tied to a limb of a tree and held aloft, in scorn or play, Winnie couldn't tell.

The play of flame along a bundle of kindling.

None of this seemed related, nor was it clear. She had to name it with words, even – cows in snow, flame along kindling – to bring the loose sense of things into something identifiable.

But her mind worked like this when she was writing. She recognized that, at least. Gervasa's memories? Or was it just Winnie filling in as she could? Hard to tell.

She felt herself beginning to nod off. What time was it? When she looked at the bedside clock, at first she thought it said *00:00, 00:00.* But that was a figment; she blinked and the clock remarked *03:00.*

She put her things together. She left all of her cash except for a few francs for the Moroccan maid. There was no one behind the counter, so Winnie scribbled a note in English – 'Charge my card; thanks, WR' – and got on the road again. Would her accountant be required to pay that bill if it turned out she had gone schizoid on this trip? If she let Gervasa have more of the view, and Winnie retired to a dark back corner of her own body? Or, in the event things went wrong, would her estate have to honor the debt if it was posted after the moment of her death?

She had gassed up the car before stopping and had no trouble finding the road back toward Rennes, and peeling off at last around Vitré toward Fougères. She coursed through what looked like the county seat, taking no care in the minute traffic circles, since no one else was on the road at this hour. If Gervasa was taking in any of this, she made no comment. Well, even if she were using Winnie's eyes, how could she recognize such things – not just the automobiles and streetlights, more or less universal around the world and certainly familiar to Winnie, but also the small details that make this place superficially, or subtly, different from Paris, from England, from Massachusetts?

Fougères must be prosperous. Lights left burning the night through. Green neon crosses, denoting pharmacies. And everywhere, colored Christmas lights, that ubiquitous necklacing of the world to guard against solstice panic.

'Gervasa,' said Winnie – driving alone was proving the least self-conscious way to converse with the phantom – 'Gervasa, what about that mark?'

The mark?

'The Christian cross, through which strokes are drawn. It showed up here, and there; on the boards, on the computer . . . in Allegra's plaster of Paris.'

A kind of prohibition. Laid upon me. It says, to anyone who sees my dying body or my corpse, do not pray for the repose of this soul.

'Oh.' And Winnie didn't dare ask if it referred to the child who might or might not have died with her. And what about the Madonna and child statue laid in the tomb? 'How can all this be, and I not quaking with born-again faith? I don't believe in Christian charms anymore. They obliterated the sacraments of my own senses, so I left all that years ago.'

Gervasa did not reply. The notion of choice seemed beyond her.

The sky was lengthening and the black terrain taking on definition as, behind them to the east, dawn light seeped through damp clouds. The car sped on a track of wet pavement, between fields, past isolated houses of brown stone. On the road toward Saint-Malo but not that far, passing signs announcing Saint-Brice-en-Coglès.

What did happen to you?

Past a stand of poplars, past an abandoned car with its blinkers flashing.

'It all came to a crash, my whole life. It wasn't just poor Vasile being dead. We were going to call him Basil, you know, an odd name for an American boy, but it means king, or prince. Basil Pritzke. It wasn't just that he died, while John and I, in panic and surprise, had fallen into love at last, briefly, and into bed with each other too. It wasn't that. This is now. You can survive adultery now. You can recover, you can go on. Since I don't believe in God anymore, I can't believe in punishment. Just the banality of coincidence, just fate, that John and I should be screwing ourselves warm while Basil was succumbing to hypothermia. If the snowfall hadn't come, we'd have arrived four days earlier; he was still alive then. Awful as that was, I could have survived all that.'

Into Antraín and through it in a whisker, and a few cars on the road now, and a little spotted fawn looking up from some bracken, and flashing away. Turning north, the sun now in real evidence. It was what, nearly seven o'clock? Winnie shifted the visor on the passenger's side to block the glare.

'It was losing Emil on top of losing Basil,' she said. 'He didn't leave me because of my infidelity. Which after all hadn't been my first. Nor because of the last-minute death of our baby. He left me because I couldn't find my way back to being myself. I got lost. For the same reason, John is leaving me too.'

Here the sign: D976, Mont-Saint-Michel – Pontorson.

'John knew that though I did love him, in some ways I had been using him to stand in for Emil. The State Department having said that Emil couldn't safely travel in the former Eastern Europe. But I wanted Emil to risk it. I wanted him there. This was our child, and he was letting John go in his stead.'

So why not deed it to me, since your life is worth nothing?

Gervasa was not being ironic, not Dr Laura or Dr Ruth or Dr

Oprah. She meant it. When you lose all, there is nothing to relish. The sun comes up as it does right now, streaking the land with buttery blandishments, gray-blue shadows; a few birds wheel high in the sky, suggesting the nearness of the sea. Every hour past present and to come emerges out of this very moment, here on this road barreling toward a headland: every last sensation of life has accelerated toward this day and is derived from it, somehow. But birds can wheel all they want; all they do is define the emptiness of the sky. The whole planet spreads out from this Renault Elf, corrupt and formidable and regenerative, wrinkling into Himalayas and Alps and Andes, rocking with Atlantics and Pacifics, pocked with Aleutians and Azores and Falklands and Cyclades, sectored into time zones, blanketed with weather, gripped in space, lost in admiration of itself, and none of it has the power to charm anymore. Not the smallest swallow on that ledge, pecking a crumb. She'd as soon kill it as look at it. The magic world, the world of childhood, was dead.

'There was so much promised us, as kids,' she murmured at last. 'It was all lies and adults should be shot. There was a poem – you won't know it. Grandma used to rock me to sleep with it.

'How many miles to Babylon?
Three score miles and ten, sir.
Can I get there by candlelight?
Yes, and back again, sir.

'Poetry is all charms and promises. The impossible journey made possible. In poetry maybe you can get to the holy city and back again, even before it's time to sleep. But it's not really true. You can't get anywhere but to the slow understanding of how, every day, you die, until there's nothing left to die and you are dead.'

Then change with me. All you do with your life is lie.

Winnie could think of no argument against this. By trying to lie about who she was, she had been bounced by Forever Families out of the informational meeting.

The land, looking north, began to seem hurrying, rushing to meet the sea that must be just beyond. The terrain dipped and rose. On either side of the road, the last several miles of approach were sentineled by big tatty Alpenhuis hotels and souvenir shacks, though the local stone was still the color of golden pears, and the poplars shook their branches in the strengthening wind. Then, at last, looking like a Byzantine monastery from this distance, only brown, the color of dung and wet bark, Mont-Saint-Michel.

Gervasa had paid no attention to the charms of Normandy. She had made no mew of pleasure at being on home territory. Now she began to be more alert, as if she could sense the age of this holy site. Perhaps it was not so much place as time in which a creature could sense being at home.

And how much of Mont-Saint-Michel was as it had been in 1350? At least some of it, no doubt.

From a distance, an island joined by a causeway, Mont-Saint-Michel looked more remote and spectacular than Notre Dame, or the Agia Sophia, or St Peter's. Perfect, tiny, spectacular, like a child's sand castle writ large, all one color in this light. Winnie parked. Hers was the first car in the visitors' lot. She walked the sands up to the gate. She, who knew herself incapable of anything approaching religious feeling, was relieved to see that the entire rock wasn't peopled by mendicants, clerics, and pilgrims, but shored up and buttressed by the needs and pleasures of commerce.

A center street wound and zigzagged up the hill. Houses, some dating from the late Middle Ages, were crammed on every inch, one rooftop craning over the other to see out, toward the mainland or the sea. And the ground floors of every building featured plate glass and open windows and outdoor shelving. The houses were gutted

in the service of floor space for shops, crêperies. Selling plastic junk, holy nothings. Winnie stopped and bought a guidebook in English at a shop just being opened by a sweet-faced red-haired boy about ten, who smoked a Gitane and spoke polite and perfect English.

'I shouldn't be offended,' said Winnie. 'If I don't believe in the Church, or any of this, why not make a buck off the site? The Church surely sold indulgences here. This is a different kind of indulgence, I guess.' Still, she was glad she was so early, and didn't have to dodge crowds rocking from one stall to the other.

She took her time. The incline was steep. She stopped halfway up, to catch her breath, by a graveyard decorated with flowers and Christmas trees. In the spirit of the season, some sort of fake snow had been trained to adhere to the branches of real trees. But the air had a kind of winter warmth to it, and the snow looked idiotic.

She read a bit in the guidebook, to postpone restarting her climb. Mont-Saint-Michel, she saw, was originally called Mont-Tombe, from the Low Latin word *tomba*, meaning both mound and tomb. Well, they got that right, she thought. How many ghosts does this place have? Is this as good a place as any, in this foreign and unwelcoming world, to give myself over?

She rose. From this height she could see other tourists arriving. The parking lot was beginning to look busy. Visitors were making a slow progress up the hill, but she was ahead of them, and at this hour she was still alone except for the residents going about their work of opening for business. She drew a deep breath. 'Are you happy?' she said to Gervasa.

Gervasa didn't answer. Winnie assumed the concept was beyond her, and maybe, really, the expectation of personal happiness was one of the especial sadnesses that democracy had ushered in.

On she went. A Wednesday morning in mid-December, a bit ahead of the tourist traffic that no doubt would flood the place come the solstice and Christmastide. Winnie paid forty francs to get into the chapel and mounted dozens of more steps to look at a room the color of toast. If Gervasa were religious, she might have thrilled to be back in a sanctified zone again, but she made no comment. Biding her time.

Then up yet more steps, arriving at last at a lofty enclosed garden, where the light was welcomed in a fresher way. A cloister aerie, with an actual lawn, almost as high as one could get if one was not about to scale the buttresses or the leaded roofs of the chapel.

No one else was here.

Roses, red and white, rustled in a small wind. Silver king in the garden, boxwood in good trim, and the grass in its rectilinear inset richly, improbably green. A space as close as you might ever get, Winnie guessed, to featuring all landscape pleasures at once: the wind buffeted in, but lightly; the sun stroked the stone and pooled on one corner of the grass. You were safe in a fisthold of the strongest stone, yet you could move to the three arches that looked out over the sand and sea, feel the pleasure of height. You were higher than the birds, whose wings flashing with sunlight made a dancing punctuation of the view of the rooftops below.

The village fell so steeply beneath that Winnie might have been in a helicopter over it.

And still, there was nothing to love, no way to wrench anything from this. There was language to talk about it, sure, but that wasn't the same as love.

Will you do it? Will you exchange places with me? Give me your life?

'If my life means little to me, it can hardly mean more to you,' she said. 'Not that I mind if you have it. But what you need isn't my life, since you can't find in it what you want. What you need—'

She looked around to see how it might be done.

'I could just leap through this glass. Then, think how in

between things you would be: in between the earth and the sky, the water and the wind. Neither in Babylon nor home again. I could just die, and if I die' – she started to laugh, for when had this hoary old line ever been said as a charitable offer? – 'if I die, I take you with me.'

An old priest pattered in with a breviary. He looked up at Winnie and heard her speaking. He probably thought she was saying her Matins. He bent down over his prayerbook again.

'Why not?' said Winnie to herself and Gervasa both.

Why not?

Winnie went up to the glass and felt it with her hands. It was impossible to tell if it was Plexiglas or standard window glass. Could she get far enough back to make a real running start at it? No half efforts now.

She moved around the perimeter of the garden. If it was to be done, it should be done quickly, before the place grew more crowded. The elderly priest was keeping to his side of the cloister, turning up and down the walk so as not to interrupt her conversation. But, she saw, he was talking into a cell phone. He pocketed it as she came nearer to calculate the distance and speed it might take to break the barrier.

'My apologies,' he said. English with a lovely soft accent. 'Moments for prayer, even here, are never as many as one would like.'

She didn't answer. She felt Gervasa stiffen.

'Do you suffer visions?' he asked.

Don't answer.

'I don't believe in visions.'

He smiled, lifting a red satin ribbon with care and replacing it when the page was turned. 'Neither did Saint Paul until he was halfway to Damascus.'

Get away.

'What a beautiful antique French you speak,' he said, but still in English, as if knowing French could not be her first language.

I accept your offer. Do it now.

'What offer is this?' said the priest. 'Would you like to sit down on this bench and speak to me?'

Winnie turned her head this way and that. The sky looked cold and ready beyond the glass. Gervasa wanted to spit. The priest said, apropos nothing, 'At Christmastide, so our dear ancestors believed, the souls of the dead are freed from their torment. They can visit the living.'

'You have no call to talk to me about such things,' said Winnie.

'Christmas is coming,' said the priest. 'I mean no more than that. You are the woman with the spirit in her, I think. I only mean to remark on that.'

'How do you know about me?'

He shrugged and put out his old leathery fingertips on her wrist. 'Stay a while longer,' he said. As he spoke, a uniformed security officer, some sort of gendarme, came through the doorway, politely standing back until the priest had removed his hand. When he did, Winnie made an effort to wrench free and begin her long approach to a flight worthy of angels, and a fall the same. Before she could take three steps the guard brought her down onto the greensward as gently and perhaps religiously as he could, which wasn't very.

He rolled over her to keep her prostrate while a backup officer was summoned. She lay under the weight of his strong form. With respect to France's great tradition of civility his face was turned from hers so, she thought, to protect her dignity. Her eyes blinked without tears at the clouds over the cloister garden. They shriveled and tore their edges, making a sound in the sky too terrible to be heard. A pale blue tinted with ocher showed through.

Gervasa lay in shock within her, a frightened bird in its casing.

Winnie imagined Gervasa entertaining the temptation to take her body hostage – with a final effort of will to make Winnie do what she'd promised, and deliver her incubus into a fuller death. But that, indeed, would be murder, a virus infecting a host to death, and would Gervasa's restless soul find any grade of rest through such an exercise of power?

With a pendulum motion of pain in her upper respiratory tract she realized that she had not been breathing, and now she was. The gendarme's tackle had knocked her breath out. With breath came shame, regret, and the mortal and immortal childhood fear of having soiled her panties, a fear that with a little exploratory wriggling proved to be unfounded.

The old priest continued on his cell phone and then snapped it shut. He motioned the gendarme to crawl off Winnie. The security person was young and blushing from the contact, Winnie saw. Don't mind me, I'm an old sow next to you, she thought, but corrected herself. Well, good. Mind me a little, as you clearly have. I'm not so old that I can't make you uncomfortable.

This thought made her cheerful, at least for a moment. She sat up.

With Winnie's breath returned, taken in frosty gulps – it was cold up here, now that she'd stopped climbing – the claw-tongued opinions of Gervasa began to publish themselves aloud again. The speech was no longer coherent. Winnie could not understand the language. It was as if a few of the connections had been knocked loose. The priest attempted to kneel by Winnie, perhaps to pray for an evacuation of an unclean spirit, an exorcism even, but Winnie was glad to see that arthritis gripped his knees too firmly. He had to stand up as he flipped pages in his breviary.

'They'll be here within the hour,' he said then, in English.

'Who?' Winnie squeezed out the single English word while Gervasa, in her ranting at the priest, at Winnie, had paused to gather steam.

'Your companions. Your family.'

She didn't know who he meant. She thought: I am going to look up and see Ozias Rudge himself in his greatcoat and pince-nez, stepping down from the haunted omnibus to collect me and take me home. But only another gendarme arrived, an older, stockier one, who when summoned had not had the younger partner's vigor at sprinting up steps. Between them they lifted Winnie to her feet and in a modified frog-march escorted her from the garden. The priest followed, watching where he put his brogans.

'Where are we going?'

'Down.'

For the first part of the descent, the parade was difficult. The halest of tourists had already achieved the chapel, ponying up forty francs to gawk at its Gothic solemnity. 'La Merveille,' said the priest, as if sensing Winnie's discomfiture through Gervasa's braying commentary. 'Built in the 1200s, four centuries after the first chapel was consecrated here. A Benedictine glory.'

Winnie managed to say, 'You live here?'

'I make an extended visitation for purposes of prayer and devotion. Less a reward than a penance, sometimes,' he said, rolling his eyes at the families in sweats and running shoes, noisily pawing through postcards and memorabilia at the shop in the chapel's antechamber. Gervasa's protests were causing heads to turn. Several visitors, yielding to the mood of the place, blessed themselves ostentatiously as they passed. Perhaps to have mercy on Winnie, the priest led the party past a sign that said *INTERDIT* and through an oaken door on massive iron hinges.

'We take the private passage, and wait until your family arrives.'

They had entered a stone corridor lit with high, arrow-slit windows, and passed along to the top of a staircase with splintery wooden rails. They descended into the bowels of the building, or

into the stone of the Mount itself. The way was lit by timid light-bulbs at unhelpful distances apart.

Then Gervasa fell silent, so utterly that for an instant Winnie wondered if she had escaped, or fled. Winnie had the feeling of a gong struck some moments ago, a quiver, a disturbance in the air. It was Rudge/Scrooge on the doorsill, eyes inward, hand to his brow, leaving a room and not seeing where he was headed next. 'What is in there?' she said, stopping in her tracks, nodding her head at a door set in a crude archway.

The priest shrugged and put the question to the gendarmes, who growled in response. He then interpreted. 'A stairway to some crypts. Nothing of note.'

'Let me see.'

'You have no right to ask.' But he didn't sound offended, and after a grudging negotiation with the escorts and a glance at his wristwatch, he pushed open the door.

Another set of steps, cleanly swept, at the foot of which had been erected a makeshift table, an old door set on sawhorses. A table lamp worked off a long rope of extension cords looping toward some electric socket in the dark distance. Above a huge cup of coffee bloomed the face of an old nun. Hunks of bread floated in the coffee and crumbs stuck to her airy mustache. She was dressed in the traditional garb and looked pearly skinned, as if she'd been born an infant nun and raised down there like a mushroom in the caves. Her skin was blued by the light of the screen of a Powerbook, working on a battery pack, and a few tomes with rotting leather spines lay open on top of one another.

More negotiation. The priest reported, 'She is Soeur Godelieve Bernaert of Louvain, Belgium. She is the Hound of Hell. Ask her what you will.'

'May I pass?'

Winnie expected an objection, but there was none. The sister leveled herself to her feet and fortified herself with a dripping hunk of bread. Then, rasping like an asthmatic, she collected a commercial-strength flashlight from a shelf and led the priest, the guards, Winnie and Gervasa down a sloping corridor in which occasional random steps were cut. She moved slowly, shining the light backward for their safety; she seemed to know this passage like a mole. She showed no fear of taking a wrong step.

At the end of the corridor were four or five archways. Soeur Godelieve spoke in a monotone, as if for several decades she'd given tours every hour on the hour.

'An . . . ossuary?' said the priest, reducing the speech to a phrase. 'Is that the word?'

Winnie put her hand out. An old iron beam wedged into the floor was leaning outward, like the trunk of a riverside tree. It supported another beam, more thinly hammered, that ran five feet each way along the ceiling, holding it up.

'Maybe my ancestor did this.'

'If you have an ancestor who is a Benedictine monk, we would rather not know it,' said the priest,

Winnie said, 'May I?' The priest, the nun, the gendarmes, Gervasa: no one objected. She ducked her head through the second of the five archways, feeling her way in all the varieties of dark.

'We are very close.'

They were very close.

Before the nun could bring the light around to a helpful angle, Winnie had found the far wall, five feet in – just deep enough to have room to rotate a shrouded corpse stiff with rigor mortis. She ran her hands up and down the dry stones. She felt the ruts and edges of carven marks before the light arrived, but then it did. She saw rude crosses carved in the wall, done, she imagined, with hasty chisel strokes, by monks or artisans or servants eager to make their retreat from what once must have been a malodorous tomb.

The light splashed as much shadow as anything else, and in the arrangement of shadows could the architecture of the crypt be understood. A dozen or so separate walled-up chambers, like closed bread ovens. On either side of the doors were the lopsided crosses. An inventory system, no doubt, to help Brother Cryptmaster know when a chamber was full.

She sank to her haunches, feeling more than seeing. Feeling was the only sense that made sense, here.

It was, she imagined, Gervasa's hands within hers that found the cross with the slash through it, next to an opening near the floor that, yes, just might appear a bit more tidily bricked in than its neighbors. As if the shroud and the statue had been removed and the wall repaired 150 or 170 years ago. Certainly more recently than seven hundred years ago.

'Here we are. This is it. The slashed cross. A poor woman who died without the benefit of the final sacrament. As good as cursed.'

The priest translated. The nun sighed in mild irritation.

'No,' said Soeur Godelieve, through the labyrinth of translation. 'Someone cared enough for the deceased to lay the body here, after all. This is not hallowed ground, we think, but this entire place is holy. The earth is sacred here. No one is cursed.'

'She was a peasant, burned to death. She was buried with a child inside her womb, nearly ready to be born,' explained Winnie.

'No, she wasn't,' said Soeur Godelieve. She trained her flashlight to other walled-up apertures. 'Look here. Look here.' A few more crosses. 'Noblewomen dying in childbirth and their infants not surviving them – look.' The light centered on a small cross next to a larger one and slightly superimposed upon it. The cross-piece of the baby one bisected the upright of the larger one. 'Mother and child. Mother and child. Very common. That's how they marked it, so that the prayers for the remembrance of the souls of the dead could be said.'

'But this body is not with them. It is apart,' said Winnie. 'The cross with the slash through it.'

'But you are wrong. Very wrong. It is not a slash. Look, foolish child.' The priest did not flinch at translating the remonstrating adjective. 'No one would bury a body in a crypt and say, "Don't remember me, don't pray for me." A waste of effort. If she was not to be prayed for, she'd have been dumped in a bog, a pauper's grave somewhere. This is not a slash. It's not a prohibitive mark. Look. It's a sprig of holly. It's a bit of life marking this grave. If she was pregnant, the baby lived. That's what the sign says. In this chamber, anyway, of women and infants dead in childbirth.'

Winnie's voice trembled. 'Some time ago a statue was found in there. A Virgin and Child. It was removed and taken to England.'

'Bring it back,' said the nun, as if Winnie were talking yesterday.

'I can't do everything.'

'Hmmmmph.'

The priest said, 'It will take me a long time to climb all those stairs back up. Your family is waiting. Let us go.'

'If someone thought to lay a corpse with a holy statue of the Madonna and Child,' said Soeur Godelieve, with a gleam of historiographic conviction, 'it was an act of charity, to comfort the corpse. The statue was put in there for consolation. Christ is the child of every mother,' she concluded smugly.

'Someone loved that dead woman,' said the priest. 'Come.'

The Gervasa virus sat within Winnie with a different heft now. If it were a meal, it would be curdling, but the ghost was not a meal to be digested, nor a tumor to be excised. The effects on Winnie were peculiar. Her palms were damp and her temples pulsed, and the wood grain on the arms of the chair in which she sat seemed alert enough to raise its ridges and bite her forearms. The news had been good, had it not? Proof, of a sort, the only proof possible, that

Gervasa had been buried without her baby. The twitching limbs of the medieval Church had managed to honor her plea bargain. But why was there no sense of elation? Gervasa was pooled in a sack of silence. Maybe she was dying in there, finishing her dying, now, at last.

'*Who* is coming?' asked Winnie, to change the subject, though no one was speaking.

'Your family.' The priest shrugged as if to say, Family, who can even recognize the concept anymore?

Winnie looked at the priest and thought of her own father. She rarely thought of him. But there was a cat in her childhood, some selfish bag of bones named Fluffy or such, who died as cats are prone to do, without giving proper notice. The cat had received as much of a Catholic burial as was permitted cats, but Winnie had nonetheless been hard to console. Her dad had taken her up on his lap and spooled out platitudes about God and the afterlife. God and God's plan. 'But Daddy,' she'd wailed, taking no comfort, 'what would God want with a dead cat?'

Her father, her mother, all the people standing in a line back to Ozias Rudge and further; that crowd so long obliterated from her thoughts by the death of Vasile and the departure of Emil. She imagined her forebears coming for her. Would they accept the Gervasa infection? They'll think I've gone lesbian, she thought with a small pleasure at the notion, just before she fell asleep in the chair.

The priest sat with her, praying the Prayers for the Dead, or so she imagined.

The 'family' turned out to mean John Comestor. He'd arrived and checked in with the police the day before. The Mont-Saint-Michel security force had located him having croissants and coffee in some overpriced atmosphere-laden café. The priest and the gendarmes eyed him distastefully, as if suspecting him incapable of keeping

Winnie from doing harm to herself. Many more words were suppressed than exchanged. The priest gave Winnie a blessing before they left. She shuddered and said, 'You're sweet, but don't. It's an affront.' With the pernicious myopia of the devout he didn't seem to mind her tart tongue.

The younger gendarme winked at her. Bloody cheek, she thought, and caught herself reverting to Brit-speak, in this instance fake as all get-out, and knew it was a way of her sidestepping the assault of the wink. The redeeming, enlivening assault of it.

John arranged with the gendarmerie to have his own rental car returned. Then he wheedled the keys of the Renault Elf from Winnie and settled her in the passenger seat, going so far as to fasten her seat belt for her, as if she were five years old. Gervasa was turned, deep in, not sleeping, but batting at something, making fists against Winnie's intestines.

After a while Winnie said, 'How did you know where I was?'

John laughed. A nice laugh, obviously full of relief, perhaps that Winnie could speak in her own voice, at least a little. 'If you can believe it, Ritzi Ostertag read some tea leaves. He decided to be firm about it. The auguries predicted some old place in Normandy, probably someplace high enough to leap from. And your friend Irv, a nice enough fellow, thought the antiquity of Mont-Saint-Michel would probably appeal to the storyteller in you. What with old Ozias's connection to it, et cetera. It wasn't all that hard to work out. He sent his love – and apologies, he made clear. I am to be sure to tell you.'

The car went on, the world flashed by, unspooling off its invisible pins.

She continued, 'But why? Why did you bother? Any of you?'

'Not just for you. In case you're thinking of feeling sentimental. I came on behalf of Mrs Maddingly too. She is failing fast. They've cut her hair, you see, and she's afraid her husband won't recognize her when she arrives. She wants a traveling companion. She said she'll take Gervasa with her when she goes, and save you the bother.'

Winnie had no way of knowing if this was John pandering to the loony in her or if he believed that such a transaction was possible. Maybe belief came in more than two varieties anyway, yes or no. The mucous membranes in her sinuses became swollen with moisture. 'But,' said Winnie, 'I don't know if I can live anymore.'

'It's sad,' agreed John, patting her hand like the brother he most nearly was, passing her a disagreeable handkerchief badly in need of laundering. 'It's all so very sad, but I'm afraid, you moron, you're going to have to try.'

They didn't speak for an hour. The scenery of Normandy scrolled past in translucent slices, a pressed landscape of moss green undergrowth and spinneys of larch, of stone corbels and persimmon-colored tiles, and petrol stations in their antiseptic state of readiness for business.

In the Chunnel streaking back to London, a moan unfolded out of Winnie's mouth. For the first time she did not know if it was Gervasa's voice or her own. John held her hand cautiously until she withdrew it.

Then a cab through fiendish traffic, across the muscled river slatted with reflections: Christmastime in modern London, dusk. Winnie insisted that John sit in the rear-facing jump seats. She sprawled, recumbent, unable to care about looking ungainly. She thought she might be dying herself, and was curiously objective about it. For once she felt some relief from the itch that could be satisfied only by inserting a pen between her thumb and fingers and working it against ruled paper. How little is left when you die, even if you have scribbled and typed through the decades. Of old Ozias Rudge nothing in his own hand, only secondhand, hand-me-down stories of his life. Did his memories live, were they sacramentalized by Dickens, were they stolen by him and desecrated? It didn't matter.

'A and E?' said the cabbie. Meaning *Accident and emergency?*
'Main entrance,' John said. 'We'll take our chances.'

John more or less kept her on her feet, at least as far as the elevator. There, as they were rising to the seventh floor, her system revolted against the affront to gravity. Her stomach lurched, and she sank to her knees. Very calm, the going out.
'Easy does it,' said John in an inaccurate John Wayne accent, hauling her up by force of will alone.
Breath stood still in Winnie's lungs, resting, then walked again.
Mrs Maddingly in no worse state than Winnie, by the look of things. She was tucked into her hospital linens so well that the sheet hadn't lost its pleats. Her eyes were alert. Ritzi Ostertag was sitting beside her, knitting. At the sight of her visitors Mrs Maddingly took pains to ready herself. She required Ritzi to apply the lipstick to her, achieving a lopsided effect more whoopsy-daisy than anything else. 'Oh, my,' said Mrs Maddingly at Winnie, 'she's in a sadder way than some, in't she.' An older accent, from a childhood long paved over, was clawing through.
'She came to say good-bye,' said John.
'Who's leaving who, is what the gossips want to know.'
The two old biddies on either side of Mrs Maddingly were deep into their pudding and paid no attention.
'Come aboard, then, as you're asked.' Mrs Maddingly patted the sheet below her belly, remembering where a lap would occur if she were ever to sit up again to have one.

How to release Gervasa to her? An act of will? – but Winnie had no willpower any longer.

Ritzi took a vanilla-scented candle from his pocket. It was a freebie, a promo, the name of a candle supplier etched in gold on one side. He turned the advertisement to the wall and lit the wick. By candlelight, yes, and back again.

Where's Jack the Ripper when you really need him? The life in her wanting to leave so badly, needing so much help. Needing a Dr Kevorkian to midwife it.

The nurse came running in at the noise of her knocking over the side table. 'She filled up on bubbly at lunch, she banged her head,' said John. Nice. From this position on the floor, her legs drawn up, Winnie couldn't see the nurse, nor Mrs Maddingly. Just the burnish of overwaxed linoleum and a paper cup that had rolled under the bed.

'Are you mad, bringing her up here? That one wants rescue. I'm ringing the lads downstairs for a gurney.' The nurse disappeared, giving every indication of relishing her brisk professional panic.

John held her hand. 'Are you going to do it?' he said to her.

'I do believe we're ready.' Mrs Maddingly's voice came from over the side of the bed. 'Give you a piece of advice, dear. Dye your hair. That color. You look a proper cow, you do.'

'No advice,' said Winnie, having the nerve to speak, and breath to push it out.

Mrs Maddingly's hand fell to the side of the bed. Its palm opened up and its fingers moved, as if to beckon. And that was that.

Now this is this, or seems to be.

When you're haunted by any variety of effective nonsense, like love or guilt or poetry or memory, which are anyway at their bitter root the same thing – the primary symptom is paralysis. You just can't move.

Then, all too rarely, the virus is vanquished, the contagion concluded, the spell is broken, the cold front snaps in prismatic splinters. Bright moment, that, and bright moment, next, and so on and so forth. What returns is a sense of the present tense as being not only available, but valid.

So, some time later, Winnie boards a plane at Logan Airport in Boston. She is with Mary Lenahan Fogarty. They are on their way to Cambodia to collect the new baby. Malachy Fogarty is staying home so that one parent will be prepared in the right time zone to nurse the baby during the day until the other parent survives jet lag.

It is an amazing journey. Phnom Penh is twelve thousand miles from Boston. It is more Babylon than Babylon itself. Can I get there by candlelight? It is stretching a metaphor beyond acceptability to think like this, but Winnie has changed and not changed, and she thinks the way she likes.

They streak west. She sinks into a bleary haze due to the excitement. It occurs to her that, long as days can seem, this day is unnaturally long. Hour after hour they fly, over the Mississippi, over the Great Plains, over the Rocky Mountains. Then over the coastal vineyards, and out over the endless unchartable blue fields of the Pacific. Still it is light. And on again, and yet on, till Hawaii is just a shadow on the map beneath them, and Japan blooms ahead around the circumference of the earth. And still it is light. The sun is the biggest metaphor. The sun is the first candle. She can get there by its light.

It is new and old as Babylon. She hasn't been able to picture it in advance. The steamy streets, the shabby genteel French provincial buildings, the wicker barber chairs at dusty curbsides. The Malay script across the doors of shops, a kind of ribbon candy folding out a message she can't read. If there is one place in the world an orphan child can't freeze to death, it is on the banks of the Mekong or the Ton Lap Rivers.

It is the rush hour. An ageless Khmer woman is riding sidesaddle on a moped behind her husband or brother. She holds the man's waist with her left hand. Her right hand is elevated above her head. At first it looks like a queenly salute, but as Mary Lenahan Fogarty's chauffeured car draws abreast of the moped, Winnie sees that the woman's right hand is cradling a glass bottle filled no doubt with a sucrose solution. Holding it above the height of her heart. The IV drip tube sways in the jostle of traffic and slips into the starched sleeve of the woman's blouse. Look, Mary, Winnie wants to say, but Mary has eyes only for the terrified child clinging to her shoulder.

At night, jet-lagged, Winnie hardly sleeps; she just hangs in slow motion, easing into the rest of her life. Her body is still urging itself along at 550 miles an hour, the ghostly law of inertia invoking itself – a body in motion remains in motion until some force acts against it.

The trip back is harder, of course. The baby is dosed with Benadryl to keep him soft and drowsy, but the week away, across a dozen time zones – as far away as you can get in the world before you begin to come back, despite yourself – well, time has taken its toll. Mary nods in sleep. Winnie watches the baby. His eyes are such ink black holes, it is hard to see the pupils within the irises. It is hard to know whether he can even see her.

Were Mary cognizant enough to pose a question just now, she might ask: So, Winnie, what gives? Is this a trial run so you can go solo next year? Or are you here just to observe? Or are you really here at all, in any way that matters?

But Mary needs her sleep.

She sat in a room somewhere. At her elbow, a notebook. A cup of tea steamed against the air. It clouded the window, letting only pallid sunlight through. What was out that window? She couldn't begin to imagine. If she leaned forward and cleared the glass with her hand, would she see him coming? At last? Him with his heart in his hands? She wondered.

For a moment she considered how she might have concluded the book that she would not write. In a ghost story worthy of its name, someone would have had to die. But who?

The page stayed blank. She made no mark.

By the time the lights of eastern Massachusetts grow recognizable, marking out early rush hour along the Mass Pike, Route 128, the JFK Expressway, Winnie is more or less awake and focusing. Who will be gathering down there? Adrian and Geoff, who have decided to do foster parenting in Massachusetts rather than an international adoption? Will they be leading a Forever Families support group to cheer Mary and the baby on their arrival? Malachy of course, breezy and ruddy with the shock of delight. Winnie will slip down the jetway on the sidelines, an escort, unnoticed, and that is as it should be. Will anyone else be waiting? Has enough time gone by? Will he be there? It matters and it doesn't matter.

The 767 overshoots to the south to make the approach from the Atlantic side. The ocean is opaque. Attractively, Boston springs up like a film snip from the opening credits of a network news program, black silhouette of city skyline interrupted by a million windows. The city lights sparkle with human sentiment. The sky behind, higher up, bleeding the last of the sunset, is bright with disillusion.

Acknowledgments

I would like to acknowledge these writers and publishers for permission to quote from the following works:

From *Ghosts in the Middle Ages: The Living and the Dead in Medieval Society*, by Jean-Claude Schmitt, translated by Teresa Lavender Fagan, copyright © 1998 by The University of Chicago Press, Chicago and London.

'The King of Hearts' from *Laughing Time: Collected Nonsense* by William Jay Smith, copyright © 1990 by William Jay Smith. Reprinted with permission of Farrar, Straus & Giroux.

From *One Fish, Two Fish, Red Fish, Blue Fish* by Dr Seuss®, & copyright © by Dr Seuss Enterprises, L. P. 1960, renewed 1988. Used by permission of Random House Children's Books, a division of Random House, Inc.

'Not a Day Goes By' by Stephen Sondheim, copyright © 1981 by Rilting Music. Inc. All rights administered by WB Music Corp. All rights reserved. Used by permission.

From *The Black Prince* by Iris Murdoch, copyright © 1973 by Iris Murdoch. Used by permission of Viking Penguin, a division of Penguin Putnam Inc.

The poem 'Probable-Possible, My Black Hen' is from *The Space Child's Mother Goose* by Frederick Winsor. Reprinted with permission from Purple House Press, Texas.

ACKNOWLEDGEMENTS

Lines from 'The Eleventh Episode,' copyright © 1972 by Edward Gorey, are reprinted by permission of Donadio & Olson, Inc.

Assistance of many varieties was offered me in the writing of *Lost*. I would like to thank the following:

Harriet Barlow, Sheila Kinney, and Ben Strader of Blue Mountain Center, New York, for the persistence of their welcome;

Karen Latuchie and Betty Levin for early readings of the manuscript;

Anthony and Jane Bicknell, Putney, for letting me riffle through their library as I researched urban domestic construction in London in the nineteenth century;

Professor Bill Burgwinkle, King's College, Cambridge, for his expertise in medieval and early modern Romance languages;

Kathy Francis, textile conservator at the Isabella Stewart Gardner Museum, Boston, for advice on fabric and how it ages;

Fiona North of Clapham, England, for sharing some but not all of the particulars of her business in plaster-casting the hands of children;

Jill Paton Walsh and John Rowe Townsend, Cambridge, England, for answering any number of questions about matters of Britain;

Jean-Claude Schmitt, whose book *Ghosts in the Middle Ages: The Living and the Dead in Medieval Society* (The University of Chicago Press) was an invaluable research tool;

Ann, Sid, and Heather Seamans for their hospitality in Hampstead, London;

Ellen Gutman Chenaux of The Birchwood Inn, Lenox, Massachusetts, for being the chatelaine of an ideal place to read and work.

And, not least,

William Reiss of John Hawkins and Associates, New York;

Judith Regan and Cassie Jones of ReganBooks, New York;

Jen Suitor of the HarperCollins publicity department;

. . . and Andy Newman, of Concord, Massachusetts, for making my travel arrangements in Paris and Normandy and for providing a home to which to return.